The Lighthouse Secret

Carmel Harrington is from Co. Wexford, where she lives with her husband, her children, and their rescue dog, George Bailey. An international bestseller, her warm and emotional storytelling has captured the hearts of readers worldwide.

Carmel's novels have been shortlisted for Irish Book Awards, and her debut, *Beyond Grace's Rainbow*, won several awards, including Kindle Book of the Year. Her most recent novel, *The Girl from Donegal*, was an instant *Irish Times* bestseller.

To keep in touch with Carmel, follow her on social media or visit her website:

Twitter | Facebook | Instagram @HappyMrsH
www.carmelharrington.com

Also by Carmel Harrington

Carmel Harrington

The
Lighthouse
Secret

HarperCollins*Publishers*

HarperCollins*Publishers* Ltd
1 London Bridge Street,
London SE1 9GF
www.harpercollins.co.uk

HarperCollins*Publishers*
Macken House,
39/40 Mayor Street Upper,
Dublin 1
D01 C9W8

First published by HarperCollins*Publishers* 2024
2

A catalogue record for this book is available from the British Library

ISBN: 978-0-00-852863-8

Set in 11/14 Sabon LT Std by HarperCollins*Publishers* India

Printed and bound in the UK using 100% Renewable Electricity by
CPI Group (UK) Ltd

For Evelyn Harrington
My mother-in-law and dear friend

PROLOGUE

Friday, 25 May 1951

Ballycotton, Cork

Four women stood shoulder to shoulder at the harbour. They looked out to the statuesque black lighthouse which rose proudly on Ballycotton Island, a few miles across the bay. The skies overhead darkened once more, and a rush of wind whipped across their faces. It moved the youngest one's long brown hair, revealing a bloodied gash above her cheek. Next to her stood her mother, the oldest of the group, but with the same oval face and denim-blue eyes as her daughter. With a shaking maternal hand, the elder woman pressed a handkerchief against the younger's wound, red blood staining the white cotton.

Third in line, a woman with a headscarf tied tight under her chin winced as she held her bruised abdomen. 'Whist,' she called out to three children who played a few feet behind them. 'The handover is happening.'

The only sound to fill the air was their laboured breathing and the lap of the waves breaking against the sands of the bay below.

'There it is,' the last woman said, with lips stained with ruby-red lipstick, pursed tight. The dark clouds parted to reveal the lighthouse beacon as it flickered across the Irish Sea towards them.

The young woman with brown hair began counting to ten softly, marking the beats between each flash of light, as she'd done hundreds of times throughout her childhood. Her blue eyes glistened with threatened tears, a long sigh lost among the cries of the gulls.

Stuffing her handkerchief into her coat pocket, her eyes never leaving the distant lighthouse, her mother finally spoke: 'If anyone finds out, we'll hang for what we've done. Make a solemn vow, here and now, that we will never speak of what happened yesterday. Not to each other, nor to another living soul.'

Silence hung between them as the women watched the horizon until the relief boat appeared. The sound of a seagull's caw echoed around them.

'I never thought I'd have a marriage with so many secrets and lies,' the woman with the ruby-red lips said, her voice quivering.

'We had no choice,' the elder woman replied, as she placed her hand in front of her. 'What's done is done. Now, let's swear our silence and put a smile on our faces. The principal keeper is coming home.'

PART ONE

Don't forget that maybe you are the lighthouse in someone's storm

Unknown

ONE

Mollie

Saturday, 8 July 2023

Camden, Maine

Mollie paused at Hogg Cove, doubling over to catch her breath. She looked through the green-leaved trees which bent so low they almost kissed the water's edge. An early-morning jog on the Beauchamp Point trail shouldn't be this taxing. But her body wasn't her own anymore, was it?

Her phone buzzed in her pocket with a text message from her husband, Nolan.

Nolan: *I'm guessing you are with Albie. I hope you are okay. I'm sorry about . . . well, I'm sorry about everything.*

4

Mollie pushed her phone back into her Lycra running shorts pocket, her stomach constricting in guilt. She loved her husband. That was never in question. But it was too painful to think about him right now. He knew her well though, guessing that she'd come here. She was nothing but predictable. She always ran back to her childhood home, to her dad, when she was in trouble.

She carried on, moving from a slow jog to a run. Mollie wanted to push herself, feel the burn in every muscle until her mind stopped turning, only focusing on the mud track she was on. She hadn't run for months on the advice of her doctor, but there was nothing to stop her now and she was desperate to embrace it.

A red-tailed hawk cried out as it patrolled the skies overhead, but Mollie didn't stop to look up; she continued pounding the path, her head low. Early morning sunlight peeped through the green canopy of tall trees. Juniper and wildflowers lined the trail, and a rich jewelled green moss plaited itself amongst the tangle of tree roots. Once Mollie reached Vesper Hill Chapel, she turned and began the descent.

Mollie walked the last hundred yards, allowing her body to cool down. She breathed in and out deeply and, for a moment, thought she might spit up the glass of lemon water she'd had when she awoke. And then she was back on Calderwood Lane, making her way home. She knew it was strange that at thirty-five years old, she still called it that. Because home should be with her husband in Portland, not here in Camden where she had grown up. Immediately, her mind began throwing questions she refused to acknowledge. *Damn it.* Mollie began jogging again, pushing herself forward once more and burying the questions deep inside of her.

'Mollie!'

She looked up, startled when she heard her name called out. Her father, Albie, was staring at her, his brow furrowed in worry. 'Sorry, I was miles away,' she responded.

'The speed you came up the driveway, I thought you would take the front gate off its hinges,' her dad said, leading the way into the house and kitchen. 'Sit down, catch your breath, and I'll get you a cold drink.'

Mollie looked around the cosy kitchen, a throwback to another era. It had changed very little over the decades since her grandparents had first moved in and decorated it in the late 1950s. Or since her father and Mollie had moved back in, once her parents divorced. It had always felt like home, in a way that the townhouse she shared with Nolan never had.

She watched her dad take a glass from the open shelf, rinse it quickly, and then fill it with iced water from the large double-sided fridge.

'Drink it slowly. Anyone would think you have the devil on your tail.' Her dad narrowed his eyes as he watched his daughter.

'Nah. Just your neighbours. I didn't stop to say hello when I ran past them earlier. Fair warning.'

'Hah! They'll be over within the hour, I've no doubt. To see the celeb.' Her dad winked.

'Don't tease. You know I hate all that nonsense.'

'Goes with the territory, Mollie. You're a household name, whether you intended to be one or not. You are one of the voices that wakes up Maine every morning. That's a big deal for most around here.'

Mollie held back a sigh. 'I'm only the sidekick. The real celeb is Donnie. The clue is in the show name, *Breakfast with Donnie*.'

And Mollie wasn't being coy. Her co-host was a national treasure, had been the lead anchor for over forty years. Mollie just felt lucky to have a seat beside him every day.

'As far as I'm concerned, you're the shining star. And last time I checked, the show garnered at least a hundred thousand views every day. That's a lot of people watching not just Donnie, but you too,' her dad said firmly, signalling the debate was over.

Mollie and her dad swapped smiles. He was her biggest supporter and she loved him for it.

'Pancakes?'

'No thanks. But a green tea would be nice.' Mollie was carrying an extra ten pounds that the TV screens did not forgive. She knew she shouldn't care, that she should say to hell with it and flaunt her curves. But the truth was, she *did*. And she planned on getting rid of her flabby tummy and double chin over the next two weeks while she was on vacation. Her dad shrugged in defeat. Mollie was thankful that he simply put the kettle on to do as she asked.

Once the tea was made, he beckoned her to join him at the window seat in the dining room. It had always been her favourite spot in the house. They could see the ocean from all the rooms at the front of the cottage, but here, it was extra special. With the large glass window framing the view, Mollie always felt she was looking at a painting that shifted beautifully alongside the changing tides and seasons.

'You enjoying summer break?' Mollie asked. Her father was a professor at the University of New England. Mollie had arrived at her dad's house late the evening before and gone straight to bed. They had a lot to catch up on, as she'd not seen him for several weeks.

'I'm enjoying myself. Been shore-fishing most days out of Penobscot Bay. Gets me out of the house, what with Mom away.'

Her nana was in Ireland on vacation, and even though Mollie had only been at home for less than twenty-four hours, the house felt quiet without her here.

The sun bounced off her dad's dark wavy hair. He was unshaven, but that wasn't unusual while he was off campus. His skin was tanned, making his light blue eyes pop, and he looked relaxed, younger than his sixty years. Most people couldn't believe that he was old enough to be her father. Thankfully, he was proud to admit he was. Unlike Lindsay, Mollie's mother, who decided to freeze time on her fiftieth birthday almost ten years ago and had long since instructed Mollie to stop calling her mom.

'You look good, Dad,' Mollie said.

'Must be in the genes! I get that from your nana,' he replied. 'By the way, have you seen your mother recently?'

Her parents had been divorced since she was a teenager, but in the main got on quite well. 'We had a very nice afternoon at the spa in Portland last month, where she of course pretended we were sisters.'

'I can't wait till she's a grandmother. I plan to train your children to call her *Granny* loudly at every possible moment.' Her dad cackled with laughter at his own joke, then stopped when he noticed his daughter wasn't joining in. 'Sorry. I'm an oaf. I should know better.'

Heat flamed Mollie's face and her stomach twisted in a new knot. It wasn't her father's fault. Her family knew nothing of the battle she'd been through for the past year as she'd tried to conceive. Mollie had never found the right time to share that IVF was her and Nolan's only hope of becoming pregnant.

The glossy brochures never told you that infertility was such an isolating condition.

'Gonna be a hot one today,' Mollie said through gritted teeth, changing the subject. 'Might go for a swim later.'

'Good idea. I'll join you.' Her dad reached over to squeeze her hand, a further gesture of apology. He knew the subject of children was a no-go area for Mollie. She managed a weak smile of reassurance. It seemed to do the trick, because he continued, 'I need to talk to you about something. I'm going to Ireland!' he said, taking her by surprise. 'Tomorrow. I know it's last minute, but I only decided yesterday when your nana called. She had a nasty cough that I didn't like the sound of. I never wanted her to go to Ireland on her own, but you know what she's like.'

'Stubborn as a mule,' Mollie said, smiling as she thought of Nana Beth, whom she adored. 'She can take care of herself though. As she tells us constantly, she's fit as a fiddle.'

'A fiddle that forgets she's almost ninety years old!' her dad said, throwing his eyes upwards.

Mollie saw an array of conflicting emotions run across her father's face. While she had a loving relationship with her nana, mother and son often clashed. Her nana could be distant and difficult one moment, and then as if a cloud lifted, she'd bring sunshine to all their lives.

'Where is she now?'

'Still in Wexford. She's been visiting friends there, and is staying in a small hotel in Dunbrody. Close enough to Hook Lighthouse, where she was stationed for a number of years as a child. I think this trip is a bit of a pilgrimage for her. She's revisiting all her old haunts. Ballycotton is next on the agenda. She's booked herself into a cottage close by to Aunt Jane's.'

'Have you told her you're going?' Mollie asked, feeling a stab of jealousy at the thought of her father heading off across the Atlantic.

'Yes. And I expected a list of reasons why I shouldn't join her, but she seemed pleased to hear it. I'm looking forward to the trip. I've not been to Ireland for nearly five years now. Too long. I know you've just arrived, but you can stay here as long as you like while I'm gone. You have your own key.'

'Thanks, Dad,' Mollie said gratefully. The truth was, she wasn't ready to go back to Portland yet. Even a good sleep had not stopped her mind from reeling with a confused jumble of thoughts about Nolan and their relationship.

'Is Nolan joining you here later?' her dad asked gently, as if reading her mind.

Mollie knew the question was coming. It was a fair one. She made a concerted effort to keep her voice even. 'Not today.'

When she'd turned on her phone this morning, there had been several voice messages and a string of texts from him. It had never been Mollie's intention to hurt him. Goodness, she knew he was in enough pain as it was, without her adding to it. But she couldn't cope with Nolan's feelings on top of her own. She was drowning right before him, but he couldn't see that. Or perhaps *wouldn't*.

'Dad, how would you feel about having company on your trip to Ireland?' Mollie asked impulsively. 'I'm on vacation for two weeks. And I need to think . . . about stuff. I can't do that here.' Mollie's voice wobbled as she continued, 'Is that okay?'

Her dad's answer was to whoop out loud, a broad grin on his face. 'Well, the best place to think about *stuff*, whatever that may be, is in Ireland. Wait till your nana hears. She'll be so excited! I bet it will be just the medicine she needs to beat that cough she has.'

Mollie felt like whooping herself too. Her dad had unknowingly given her a chance to escape her life for a few weeks. With a quick kiss of thanks to her dad, she excused herself to call Nolan from the hall. He answered on the second ring.

'Are you okay?' Nolan asked in a rush, the sound of a drill droning in the background. She heard a door close, and then the background noise quietened.

Mollie could picture him, probably in his hard hat, on-site somewhere. Nolan was a General Contractor with a successful company that bought and resold homes once he'd given them a makeover. And this familiar image

11

of her husband made her throat constrict, as a rush of emotion overcame her.

'I'm fine. I'm more worried about you,' Mollie said. Her voice trembled, and she felt guilt stab her, knowing that he'd been going through his own hell too.

The phone went silent and Mollie imagined that, like her, Nolan was thinking about their meeting at the doctor's surgery for their embryo transfer appointment two days ago. Where they were informed that there were no viable embryos.

Finally Nolan broke the silence, his voice bringing her back to him. 'I've had better days. Was I right? Are you in Camden?'

'Yes. And I'm so sorry to have run away. But I can't talk. I don't want to hurt you any more than I already have. I love you. But I feel like I'm teetering on the edge of an abyss.'

'I wish you'd let me make sure you don't fall anywhere,' Nolan begged. Was he crying? She thought she heard tears in his voice. He'd brush them aside, trying to be strong. He was a good man, and he deserved better. But she didn't have it in her to put him first right now.

'Dad is going to Ireland to be with Nana. I've decided to go with him.'

Another silence as he digested this bombshell. There was resignation in his voice as he asked, 'How long will you be gone?'

'I have two weeks' vacation from work, so probably that,' Mollie answered, grateful for Nolan's graceful acceptance of her last-minute decision to travel overseas.

Another intake of breath. A hammer drill started, loud, and Nolan shouted to a colleague, 'Can you stop that for a minute? I can't hear myself think.' Then he gave a sigh and said, softer, gentler, 'I'm worried about you, Mol.'

'I know. And I you.' Last night, all Mollie could think about was the look on her husband's face when they'd been delivered the knockout blow by Dr Laslo. Tears began to fall, and she couldn't stop them. And there was no doubt that Nolan was crying now, too. She wished she had it in her to go to him. 'I'm so sorry,' she repeated.

'You don't need to apologize.' Nolan's voice dropped to a whisper. 'I hope you find some peace in Ireland. I'll be here waiting for you, when you get back.'

There was nothing else to say, so they both hung up.

Mollie made her way back to her window seat, and looked out to the Atlantic Ocean.

She felt her dad's eyes watching her closely, 'You two okay?'

She shook her head sadly.

'Want to talk about it?'

Another shake.

'When you do, I'm here. But what I *can* do is this.' He put his mug down on the table, then did the same for Mollie. He pulled her towards him and wrapped his two arms around her. And he held her, strong arms resolute, as she tried to resist. Until she didn't want to fight anymore, and she sank into him.

'Oh, Daddy . . .' she whispered. She'd not called him that for a long time. But in this moment, she felt like a child again in the safe harbour of her father's arms.

'I know you are a grown woman, but will you indulge me this morning? Let your daddy make you breakfast like I used to when you were little. Whatever diet you're on can wait till tomorrow.'

Mollie's stomach betrayed her by grumbling at the thought of her dad's famous stack of golden pancakes with maple syrup dripping down their side. 'With a scoop of vanilla ice-cream?'

'Sacrilegious to serve with anything else!' he declared, then he moved back to the kitchen, gathering flour and eggs from the pantry.

While he busied himself with breakfast, Mollie reached into her purse to retrieve a sizeable stack of mail that one of the TV runners had given her yesterday before she left the studio. While most of her fans corresponded through comments on social media posts, some still preferred snail mail. Mollie began opening them, one by one. Half a dozen were from fans asking her which hair salon she favoured, presumably because her hair had been having quite a few good days recently. This was balanced out by a lengthy critique from a Pamela in Idaho, who told Mollie that the length of her hair aged her. There were seven pretty notecards, all sharing stories of solidarity, condemning the recent fat-shaming photograph of Mollie published in one of the glossy tabloids. Mollie had in fact been blissfully unaware of the picture herself, until right now. Thanks to a quick Google search, it took her mere seconds to find the unflattering shot taken of her in profile now doing the rounds. The wind had flattened her dress against her rounding tummy and

14

online debates about whether she was fat or pregnant were flamed further.

Cursing under her breath, she put her phone down. She should have known better than to look at it. Next in the pile was a cute card from a kid sharing her ambition to be like Mollie one day. *Don't wish that, kiddo,* Mollie thought, tears suddenly springing to her eyes. She blinked them away, refusing to give in to weakness.

She took a sip of her green tea, then picked up the final envelope, long and white, the standard office stationery kind. The first thing she noticed in surprise, was the Irish postmark. It had the studio address typed, by what looked like an old-fashioned typewriter. She didn't see much of that anymore. Mollie braced herself. Typed envelopes usually meant typed manifestos inside. The kind written by a sender who had a lot to say.

She was surprised to see a single folded A4 page inside. But her blood ran cold when she read the sentence typed in the centre of the page in large bold font. She blinked, then re-read it out loud, not quite believing the words in front of her.

Family secrets never stay buried.

TWO

Beth

Thursday, 5 April, 1951

Ballycotton, Cork

Beth stormed through the small cottage's bright yellow front door, waving a poster above her head. 'The circus is coming to Ballycotton,' she screamed to her mother, Kathleen, who was elbow-deep in sudsy water at the kitchen sink.

'Slow down, Beth, you're making me dizzy!' her mammy reprimanded, but a hint of a smile hovered on her lips. Mammy scrubbed at the collar of one of her father's shirts one last time on a washboard, then moved it to the mangle to remove excess water.

'I'm too excited to go any slower than this very speed! Nothing exciting ever happens in Ballycotton, but next

16

month there'll be elephants, tigers, clowns, and maybe a flying trapeze!' Beth was breathless at the mere thought of anyone throwing themselves through the air.

'Do you know, you look about ten years old again,' her mammy said, smiling at her eldest daughter. 'It's nice to see you happy. You've had a face like a wet weekend for weeks, moping about without your Ted.'

'Have I? Well, consider me bathed in glorious sunshine from now on,' Beth replied, waltzing around the large oak kitchen table, pulling her mammy by the waist to take her with her. 'Wait until I tell John and Katie when they get home from school.' Beth adored her ten-year-old brother and eleven-year-old sister, and knew they would be as excited as she was with the news.

'Don't tell them until they've done their chores and homework.' Her mammy dried her hands on a tea towel as she disentangled herself from Beth. 'You were supposed to help me with the laundry this morning. Just because you've finished school, doesn't mean you get to run around the village like you've no care in the world. You have chores around the house. And responsibilities in the community.'

Beth rolled her eyes. Her mother's sole purpose these days was to teach her daughter how to be a good keeper's wife, ready for the inevitable moment that she followed in the family tradition. 'I heard on the radio that Aer Lingus have started doing night flights to London from Dublin. They are called Starflights. Doesn't that sound wonderful? I want to apply for a position as an air hostess with them.' Beth held her breath as her mother took in this statement. She waited for the inevitable rebuttal and Kathleen didn't disappoint her.

'Last month it was the Ford factory you wanted to work in. The month before that, Roches department store in the city. And you know full well what your father said to each of those notions. Your job is here, supporting me. And preparing yourself for when you need to run your own house.'

Beth opened her mouth to protest but was cut off by one of her mother's looks, which left her under no illusion that further discussion was not allowed. Kathleen reached for the poster from her daughter's hands and smoothed out the wrinkles so she could read the details.

Fosset's Circus Cavalcade and Menagerie.

13-25 May 1951,

For Two Weeks Only, Every evening from 6 p.m.

'Your father, and I daresay the other keepers, would like the chance to see the circus,' her mammy said, then walked over to the black diary that sat on the dresser to check Patrick's rota.

Patrick Kenefick, Beth's father, was the principal keeper at Ballycotton Lighthouse. He had followed in the footsteps of his own father and grandfather before him. He worked alongside Peter Craig, Lee Higgins and Beth's boyfriend Ted Braddy, who were the assistant keepers. The four men worked three-week block shifts on the island, which sat a short fifteen-minute boat ride away from the village. Her father's week off finished the following morning, and he was due to leave at 11 a.m. for the changeover, hence Kathleen laundering his shirts.

Beth felt Lady Luck had dealt them all a happy reprieve, if she was honest. While she loved her father, he had a habit of dampening enthusiasm. Since he'd been promoted to his current position, he had become a strict authoritarian and frowned upon public displays of excitement, stating that such things were not becoming for the family of a principal lighthouse keeper.

'We have a standing in the community. People look up to us,' Patrick was fond of stating to his family if he felt they were stepping out of line. As well as his normal watch-keeping duties, he was now responsible for the discipline of the junior keepers at his station, and Beth sometimes thought that he treated his family like employees.

The Keneficks had lived in Ballycotton for three years now. Before that they had been stationed in lighthouses in Hook, Fastnet, Clare Island and Black Rock. And while each location offered something unique, so far, Ballycotton was their favourite. The small coastal community had welcomed them with open arms.

And thank goodness the Ballycotton keepers' families no longer had to live on the island. Fifty years ago, she would have been stuck on the rock, getting a boat to school in the village every day. She shuddered at the thought of the isolation and monotony of what that life would have been like back then, with only goats and birds for company.

Kathleen snapped the diary shut, then said with a sigh, 'Your father will return on the twenty-fifth. We'll have to see how he feels on the day. He's often only fit for bed after three weeks on the rock,' her mammy remarked. 'But your Ted will be off on the eleventh, so you can go together. That will be nice for you.'

At her mother's words, her boyfriend's face came to her mind and she felt an ache, because it had been two weeks now since she'd seen him. How Ted could bear living on a lighthouse with only two others for company, she could not understand. He had been an assistant keeper for two years, the youngest of the Ballycotton keepers, at only twenty years old. But he came with the best of pedigrees, part of a renowned dynasty – the Braddy family, with several generations of keepers on his mother and father's side.

Beth remembered the day he arrived in Ballycotton like it was yesterday. She had clutched her best friend Joanne Craig's hand as they watched him walk up Main Street in his keeper's uniform. The brass buttons on his jacket glinted in the sunlight.

'He looks like Gary Cooper,' Joanne had gushed.

And she had a point. Ted's blond hair was brushed back, held in place by Brylcreem, and his blue eyes sparkled as he took in the villagers who had lined the street to watch his arrival. When he passed the girls, he'd winked at them, making them giggle. It wasn't long before he held the title of most eligible bachelor in the village. He was considered a catch, and Beth knew that he could have his pick of many of the girls in the area. But a little over a year ago, she had felt his eyes on her, seeking her out when the relief boat docked from the island. Beth knew what it meant. Ted had chosen her, just as she'd chosen him.

Last summer, shortly after Beth's seventeenth birthday, Ted escorted her to her very first dance at the Cliff Palace dance hall.

'Can you feel that?' Beth had asked breathlessly, giving her long brown hair a swish from side to side, as she'd seen Rita Hayworth do in the movie *Gilda*.

'Feel what?' Ted asked, watching her closely.

'The air. It's filled with every person's hopes and dreams here. All looking for adventure and excitement and—'

'And maybe love too?' Ted had interjected. Then he grabbed her hand and pulled her towards the dance floor, the underskirt of her navy-blue dress swishing against her legs. Ted proved himself to be more than a match for Beth's energy, and together they jived, waltzed and fox-trotted for hours.

When the band began to play the last song of the night, 'You're Nobody till Somebody Loves You', Ted had leaned down and whispered into Beth's ear, 'You could never be a nobody.'

His words had made her feel alive, and a shiver of excitement coursed through her body. She could feel herself standing on the brink of womanhood, and she could not wait to experience it all.

Since that night, each time Ted returned from the island, they had become regulars at the dance hall and had been to the movies in Cork city several times. Beth's parents encouraged the match. They both wanted nothing more for their daughter than to marry a keeper, thus continuing the family tradition for another generation. While this was annoying, there were advantages to her relationship with Ted. She had freedom she'd never been allowed before.

Beth also knew that this new-found freedom was irksome for her best friend Joanne, who was a year younger than her. Joanne was still in school and would have to wait until she was eighteen before her parents, Ellen and Peter Craig, allowed her to join Beth and Ted at the dance hall.

'Quit your daydreaming and hang the laundry out on the line,' her mammy instructed, pulling Beth out of her reverie and handing her a wicker basket of washed shirts. 'There's great drying out there today.'

The sun shone, the fifth day in a row they had been treated to gloriously hot weather. A heatwave was predicted for the summer, and Beth couldn't wait for Joanne's school holidays to start so that they could spend lazy days together at the beach, showing off the new swimsuit her mother had bought her in Roches store.

Once her father's shirts were dancing in the gentle breeze, Beth made her way back inside, pausing at the back door, when she heard her father's voice mentioning her name.

'Beth could do a lot worse than young Braddy.'

'Agreed. I like him. And he's from a good family . . .' Kathleen answered, but her voice sounded less sure than Patrick's.

'A good keeper's family, you should say,' her dad corrected. What would he have said if a man came calling for Beth, who wasn't a keeper, Beth wondered. But before she could ponder this any further, her father continued in a lower voice, 'Ted has asked for my permission to propose on Beth's eighteenth birthday at the end of May. I've said yes.'

Her mother gasped at the exact moment Beth clasped her hand over her mouth to contain her reaction.

'And you did not think to ask me my opinion before you gave your blessing?' her mammy's voice was clipped with irritation.

Nor mine! Beth thought, as a flash of anger rushed over her too.

'And why would I do that?' Her dad's voice had an edge to it now. He did not like to be questioned. Kathleen had once said he was too used to being the boss at the lighthouse, and that certainly had a ring of truth about it.

'It's just . . . she's too young.' Contrition now laced her mammy's words, making Beth want to scream. Why must her mother always bow to her father's will? Surely her father couldn't dispute the fact that Beth was young and had so much she wanted to do before she was married.

'You were eighteen when we wed,' her dad replied, but his voice was now tender. 'And I've given you a good life, I hope? I only wish for the same happiness we've had in our life together, for Beth.'

'You've given me a wonderful life,' Kathleen replied. 'I've always been proud to be a keeper's wife.'

And Beth felt a rush of affection for her father, as memories of her life as a keeper's daughter came to mind. His face set in concentration, as he dismantled and reassembled the paraffin-vapour burner. And his patience over the years, as he taught various supernumerary assistant keepers how to operate the fog signal, how to use ropes for rigging and tie knots, how to communicate with other lighthouses and ships. He commanded respect from his peers because he was a fair man, and always kept a good watch. She knew that while she at times disagreed with him, he always had her best interests at heart.

The sound of her father's chair scraping back along the flagstone floor sent Beth scurrying along the side of the house, in case he came out and caught her red-handed listening in.

With a racing heart, Beth leaned against the gable wall for support. Why must Ted go and change things? She was happy with the way things were.

There was no doubt that she cared for Ted. She loved him. And when he took her in his arms and held her, when he kissed her gently, she forgot everything but how he made her feel. But outside that loving hold, she also knew that she did not want the same life her mother had endured. Moving every four years to a new lighthouse, spending half of her time on her own, raising children, and keeping a home while her husband kept watch.

Did she even want to have a baby? Helping to care for her younger siblings was a lot of work, and theirs wasn't even a large family. If she married Ted, children would be expected to follow immediately. Would she ever see what the world looked like outside of Ireland's shores? Not if she married a keeper. Her life would be watching the waves and the ships that sailed upon them, as they moved to other worlds without her.

Beth held a hand over her mouth to hold back the scream that she desperately wanted to release to the sea air.

She had no more than seven weeks to work out what her heart truly desired. As soon as she turned eighteen, Ted would propose.

And she had no clue what her answer should be.

THREE

Kathleen

Sunday, 8 April, 1951

Ballycotton, Cork

Patrick had returned to the island two days ago. Now, Kathleen stood beside Ellen and Beth at the end of the pier, ready to talk to Patrick, Peter and Ted. Every Sunday afternoon the keepers' families would congregate together to communicate with their men on the island, who watched them through a telescope. Their only means to communicate was via semaphore flags – a second language for keepers and their families, used for generations. The alphabet signalling system was based on the waving of the handheld flags in a particular pattern to compose messages. There was a relief boat too, which travelled to the island once a fortnight with mail and provisions, and to transport the keepers on and off the island. But other than that, the keepers might as well have been on the other side of the world, as opposed to the other side of the bay.

Kathleen held two white cotton flags, ready to begin signalling as soon as the men arrived in eyesight. She glanced over her shoulder to her young children, Katie and John, who were playing tag with Ellen and Peter's youngest, Ger. He was the same age as John, and they were as close as brothers, never apart from each other.

It felt like only yesterday that Beth and Joanne would have been playing chase too. Now though, Beth would take her turn after Kathleen and Ellen to send her own message to the keepers – to Ted. Beth had always been so impatient to grow up, and Kathleen had thought she was ready to let her eldest daughter fly the nest. But as she watched her younger children's flushed, happy faces, Kathleen wasn't so sure that was the case now.

Kathleen caught a look on Joanne's face as she watched Beth from a distance. She looked annoyed with Beth. 'Is Joanne all right? She appears a little unhappy,' Kathleen remarked to Ellen.

'Sixteen is a tough age. She's desperate to fall in love, like your Beth,' Ellen said, watching her daughter. She called over to her, 'What are you doing over there on your own, Joanne? You can help me with my message to your father.'

Joanne walked over to join her mother.

'Ted has been gone for two weeks, but it feels like forever,' Beth said dreamily as she looked towards the black tower of Ballycotton Lighthouse.

'Ah that's young love for you,' Ellen said, smiling at Beth. 'I always feel that time moves slowly for the first two weeks, then speeds up double time to make up for that in the last week of their rota.'

Kathleen nodded her agreement as she watched the horizon for signs of the keepers. But in truth, she didn't feel the same way. Over the past year, she'd found herself not missing her husband as she once had. It had become a case of out of sight, out of mind. Was it the same for him, she wondered? Because an aloofness had crept into their marriage that had never been there before.

Kathleen looked down to check her watch with a frown, 'It's not like your father to be late,' she murmured to Beth.

'No, it isn't,' Beth agreed, straining her eyes to catch sight of the men.

At almost three o'clock, the edge of the cliff was still empty. You could usually set your watch by the keepers. They were methodical, which was one of the requirements of their job.

Ellen yawned loudly, then apologized, 'I was up at the Doyles' house in Garryvoe until the wee hours. Didn't get much sleep.'

'Did Maureen have the baby?' Kathleen asked, raising her eyebrows in surprise when Ellen nodded. 'That's early. I thought she was only seven months pregnant.'

Ellen passed a look to Kathleen – faint amusement laced between a knowing glance. 'That's right. Baby came early. For fourteen hours Maureen laboured. God help the poor woman. In the end, I had to get Tommy to go call the doctor. He was white as a sheet, worried for his wife. That's newlyweds for you! Anyhow, between the doctor and I, we got there in the end. A healthy baby boy.'

'Ah, God bless him,' Kathleen said, smiling with warmth. 'I'll call up there tomorrow with a casserole. We're lucky to have you in our village. But I daresay an early night is warranted, Ellen.'

'I won't need rocking tonight, that's for sure. But it's me who is lucky. Watching new life enter the world is a privilege.'

Kathleen noticed her daughter shudder at the mention of babies. She'd have to have a conversation with her soon, about marriage and what that entailed.

'Someone is coming. Look!' Ellen said, pointing to the island as a figure made its way along the rocks' edge.

'Only one keeper by the looks of it,' Joanne replied. 'That's odd. It's your Ted, I think.' She nudged Beth in the ribs. 'Dad and Patrick must be busy or running late.'

Sure enough, it was Ted's slender frame that came into view. He held up his flags as Ellen pulled out her notebook and pencil. Kathleen called out the semaphore letters signalled by Ted, and Ellen wrote them down. Once complete, she then read out the message softly, 'S.E.N.D. D.O.C.T.O.R.'

Kathleen saw the colour drain from Ellen's face as the message sank in. Panic began to bubble up inside her too. *What if something had happened to Patrick?*

'What should we do?' Beth asked, her eyes widening in panic.

Kathleen took control of the situation, turning to the girls standing beside her. 'Beth, I need you to go to Byrne's; tell him to get the relief boat ready for an emergency run to the island. Then go to Lee's cottage and tell him he might be needed back on the island. Joanne, you are to go get Dr Whitaker and tell him he's needed here immediately. Go! What are you waiting for?' She pushed the girls on their way, while she and Ellen responded to Ted, reassuring him that they had received his message. Ted disappeared from view as Beth and Joanne sprinted up the hill from the pier to do as they were bidden. Twenty minutes later, the doctor was sailing towards the lighthouse. News travelled fast in the small village and a crowd soon gathered on the pier to join the Kenefick and Craig families as they waited for news. Beth and Joanne anxiously comforted their younger siblings, while their mothers stood silently, their shawls wrapped tightly around their shoulders.

Within the hour, the silhouette of the relief boat came back into view. A hushed silence fell over the group gathered on the pier until the boat had docked, this time with one extra passenger. For a moment, Kathleen froze. It was only when she felt Beth's hand reach for hers that she came to her senses. She craned her neck to see who was in the relief boat, her body sagging with relief when she saw that it wasn't Patrick. Then immediately she tensed, the realization dawning on her of what this would mean for Ellen.

'Peter!' Ellen cried out, running towards the boat without stopping to think, her shawl falling to the ground behind her. Kathleen picked it up for her, then, with the children, she ran on behind her.

Two neighbours helped carry the stretcher with an unresponsive Peter to the Craigs' cottage.

Eventually, Dr Whitaker explained that Peter's illness was severe rheumatic fever. 'There's nothing further I can do for him,' he said, as Kathleen held Ellen's hand in her cramped living room. 'I'm sorry. All we can do now is pray.' The final damning statement sent Ellen tumbling to the floor, her face now as ashen as her husband's.

Kathleen had been witness to many breathing their last breath over the years; her grandparents, and several of the parishioners who had died in their village. But this was different. This was a dear family friend, and neighbour, a constant in her life as familiar to her as her own family. And such a kind man. Quiet and unassuming, but solid.

Seeing her friend fall asunder, and praying for a miracle, Kathleen sent for Father McEvoy, who she knew would give comfort to the Craig family. He led the gathered family and friends in a decade of the Rosary, all of them praying to spare Peter, but as the night wore on, Kathleen sensed that prayers were not going to save him now.

Before dawn broke the following morning, Peter succumbed to his fever and died.

The Craig children clung to Ellen as the cottage swelled with disbelief and sorrow. But as the family crumpled with grief, Kathleen knew she had to remain strong. If it were the other way around, Ellen would do the same for her. That was the way with keepers' wives. *With friends.* Kathleen walked to the windows and opened them all to allow the spirit of Peter to leave the house. Then she gave her son, John, orders to cycle to the local funeral director. Beth, too, was delegated a task, and was sent to organize a telegram to the Commissioners of Irish Lights to let them know of Peter's passing.

Finally, with a heavy heart, Kathleen sat down to write a letter to Patrick. The relief boat would take it to the island for one more unscheduled visit later that day, accompanied by Lee, pulled from his shore leave, ready to take Peter's place. The man did so without complaint. It was something of a comfort to Kathleen, as she watched the village surround the family, that in times of need, the entire community of Ballycotton all moved together, united. Not only was Peter a respected keeper, held in high esteem by the villagers, but Ellen had also assisted in every birth in the parish since they arrived in Ballycotton two years ago. The Craig family were liked by all.

Two days later, after the funeral service, an oak casket was lowered into a new grave. It was time to say one last goodbye to Peter Craig. As neighbours shook Ellen's hand, offering their sympathy, Kathleen and Beth stood close by, ready to catch their friends if they needed them.

'Dad should be here. He was Peter's friend. It's not right,' Beth complained angrily, her face scrunched in annoyance at their situation.

Kathleen sighed, because her thoughts had been with Patrick, Lee and young Ted too. Managing the light out on the rock, waiting for news on their colleague. It must have been such a devastating shock to hear of his death. And not to be able to attend the funeral was cruel. She turned to Beth and spoke quietly, 'It's the keeper's life. You cannot allow personal distractions to take you from your post when on duty. Not for baptisms or funerals. When your father returns from this shift, he'll pay his respects. We'll have a mass said for Peter's soul . . .'

Kathleen broke mid-sentence as a tall, stocky man pushed his way towards Ellen, shoving Joanne's younger sibling, Ger, out of the way. Kathleen didn't like how he looked Ellen and Joanne up and down, his eyes pausing on their curves. He pulled Joanne in for a rough hug, before turning his attention to Ellen, who grimaced as he held her close.

'Who is that?' Beth whispered in shock to her mother.

Kathleen tutted as the man held on to Ellen longer than was necessary or decent. 'He's Peter's older brother Benny. He's got a farm a few miles outside the village. They weren't close.'

Kathleen walked over and moved between Ellen and Benny. She offered the man her hand, 'My condolences on the loss of your brother.'

'Thank you. Such a sad time.' He fixed his dark eyes on her. 'Not to mention worrying for my sister-in-law. What with children, and they all about to be turfed out onto the streets.'

Ellen stumbled; she would have fallen had Kathleen not offered a steadying hand.

'But I don't want you to worry that pretty head of yours, Ellen. I'll not let that happen,' Benny continued, his face breaking into a smile that revealed two missing teeth.

Kathleen shivered; something about that man was deeply unsettling. 'If you excuse us. It's been a long day,' Kathleen said, taking a mute Ellen by the arm.

Her friend looked as though she'd aged ten years overnight, her face taut with worry.

'Don't pay any attention to what that man said. Nobody is going to turf you out of your home,' Kathleen soothed.

Ellen turned to her, her jaw clenched tight. 'Yes, they will, as well you know. Not today, but soon, they will ask us to leave. When a new keeper is appointed to take Peter's place, if he has a family, he will need our cottage and we'll have no choice but to go.'

There was nothing to say to this truth. With the children following on behind, the two women made their way out of the graveyard.

FOUR

Beth

Wednesday, 9 May 1951

Ballycotton, Cork

A month had passed since Peter's funeral, and Beth awoke at 6 a.m. with a start. Her night had been filled with dreams that made no sense. She had run down the ramp onto the pier, then into the sea, looking over her shoulder at a faceless predator. Who or what was chasing her, she did not know.

Beth felt restless and out of sorts, and she dressed quickly to go for a cycle to clear her head. Even her mother wasn't up yet, and pulling open the back door quietly, she was surprised to see the village clouded in mist. She pulled a cardigan from the back of the front door peg and set off.

35

Most of Ballycotton was still asleep, too. With the harbour behind her, Beth heard the sounds of the fishermen as they returned from their early-morning trawl, the only company at that hour. She passed the butcher's and the grocery store, flew by the church, and as she whizzed by the Cliff Palace dance hall, she relished the cold breeze rushing over her face. It had been a difficult month, and her heart ached for Jojo and the Craig family. This escape was a much-needed respite. What would happen if she just kept cycling, she thought as she left the village behind her and began her descent on the twisting roads out of Ballycotton towards Garryvoe.

But as she moved around a sharp bend, the mist in front of her shimmered and changed. Beth stopped pedalling at once, putting a hand to her brakes and pressing heavily on them. Out of the mist, a black horse with a long flowing mane and tail appeared. Beth sucked in her breath as her eyes moved from the horse's white fetlocks upwards.

And that was when she saw him.

The mist seemed to melt away as Beth took in the man in front of her. His hair was ebony-black, and longer than any local man's. It moved through the air, in the same way the horse's mane and tail did. He was roughly her age, she surmised, maybe a year or two older at most. She locked eyes with him. His eyes seared into Beth's own, and she felt herself flush from head to toe. And then, with the briefest nod of his head, his only acknowledgement that she existed, he turned his horse, and galloped back into the mist.

Beth's heart beat so fast that she held her hand to her chest to try to quieten it. She blinked twice. Had she just imagined that? She pushed her feet back onto the pedals and continued her ride, following him into the mist. Her curiosity was spiked, and she had to know who he was and where he'd come from.

About half a mile out of the village, she heard the rumble of wagons, followed by the shrieking neigh of a horse and the roar of something she'd only heard in the movies. Beth cycled faster until, on her right-hand side, in Doody Murphy's newly mowed field, she saw the brightly coloured tents and wagons, in jewelled tones of red-and-blue, scattered prettily in the large green field.

The circus.

Beth had forgotten all about it, with her worry and upset for the Craig family. Her heart raced with excitement as she took it in.

'A visit from a young lady as pretty as the morning dew,' a voice said, making Beth start. She swung to her right, and there he was there again, the long-haired stranger, standing at a distance, this time without his black horse. His voice was heavily accented, but she couldn't tell where he was from.

Smoothing her hair back behind her ears, Beth blushed.

'I had forgotten the circus was coming. This visit is a happy coincidence for me as I took an early-morning cycle.'

He bowed, then began moving back towards the tents, calling over his shoulder as he went, 'Come. I shall give you a tour before everyone awakes.'

Without hesitation, Beth leaned her bike against a tree on the side of the road, then ran after the man. She felt like she'd been waiting her whole life for something this exciting to happen in Ballycotton. Her eyes took in his every detail. He wore a green silk shirt, only half buttoned-up, tucked into a pair of tight blue jeans. Men in Ballycotton did not dress like this. She tried to imagine Ted open-shirted, but the thought almost made her giggle. She'd tell Ted all about this when she saw him next, whenever that might be. Since Peter's death, all three keepers had worked extra shifts while they awaited a new keeper to be appointed.

'What's your name?' she asked, then added, 'I'm Beth.'

He repeated her name softly, 'Beth. It suits you. You look like a Beth.' Then, with a pause, he added, 'I'm Christian Banvard.'

Was it a good or a bad thing to look like a Beth, she wondered. She'd never thought about her name before, but suddenly she wished she had a more exotic one, perhaps Marlene or Marilyn. Maybe she should start using her full name, Elizabeth.

As her thoughts tumbled through her mind, they passed an enclosure where horses, ponies, donkeys and goats stood in a huddle together.

'Do you ride?' Christian asked, pausing at the picket fence and petting a black horse that Beth presumed was the same one from earlier.

'No,' Beth admitted.

'Before I could walk, I was riding horses.'

Beth didn't like the dismissive way he'd said that, so she countered with her own boast, 'Before I could walk, I could swim and captain my own boat.'

Not strictly true, but Christian got the message, and a half-smile appeared on his face. Beth felt her stomach lurch. He was so handsome it almost hurt.

'Where are you from?' Beth asked.

'I was born in Nice, but it's been a long time since I lived there. My parents are French and are circus performers too. They manage the Wonder Horses and Ponies. Trick riding and equestrian stunts.'

'Is that what you do too?' Beth asked.

He shook his head, then said one word that practically made her swoon, 'No, I'm a trapeze artist. Along with my older sister Delphine.'

Beth felt breathless at the mention of the word trapeze. There was something about it, that felt so romantic; it was certainly the most daring of all the circus acts Beth had read about. Christian didn't linger by the enclosure long, instead moved on, taking long strides that made Beth run to keep up with him.

Next, he showed her two carriages that sat side by side. He placed his finger to his mouth, indicating to Beth that she should remain quiet. Black bars ran down the side of each pillar-box-red carriage, keeping whatever was inside caged. Beth's eyes widened and she moved closer on tiptoes. In the first carriage were two large lions, sleeping side by side, their long bodies stretched out. Each had a golden coat, one with a full luscious mane.

'Magnificent,' she whispered.

Christian nodded, satisfied by her reaction, then took her arm to lead her to the next carriage. His touch sent a shiver that ran from her arm up and down her body.

'The lion tamer's tricks will make you gasp with his daring. But I prefer Billy.' He nodded into the dark cage. Sitting at the back of the small carriage was a large brown bear. Its immense bulk took up over half of the cage. Awake, he glanced over to Beth and Christian with little interest.

'I've never seen anything like Billy . . . or the lions before.'

'Come to the big top,' Christian commanded, then led Beth to the other end of the field, where a large red tent stood proudly, bunting and flags waving from its front. Christian pulled open the red-and-white draped curtains that framed the entrance, and they walked inside the sizeable domed space.

Beth greedily took it all in. Around the perimeter of the tent were wooden benches, which stood empty now. Three rings, one large and two smaller, sat side by side. In the centre ring, a roped ladder hung from the draped ceiling.

Beth felt dizzy looking at the sheer height of the trapezes. On the ground below them were a couple of old mattresses Beth wasn't sure would break anyone's fall from that far up.

'Take a seat; you can watch me rehearse,' Christian said.

Then he ran to the rope ladder and climbed up in seconds to the waiting trapeze. Hanging on to a long rope, he swung himself to a seated position on the cream bar before beginning to move back and forth, gathering speed. He leaned backwards until he was hanging upside down off the trapeze by his knees, his two arms swinging on either side of him. Then, in a moment of daring that made Beth call out in surprise, his knees dropped, and he hung by the heels of his feet. Before Beth had a chance to breathe, Christian took a standing position on the trapeze, each foot placed on the corner of the cream bar. He jumped onto the rope, legs entwining it as he gracefully lowered himself to the sawdust floor.

Beth stood up and clapped, whooping out loud. 'That was the most incredible thing I've ever seen!'

Christian laughed as he took a bow. 'Wait until you see the live show. There are three of us on the trapeze and tightrope. Delphine, her husband Louis, and me. We somersault between the two trapezes, catching each other in the most dramatic ways. You won't be disappointed.'

'Death-defying acts,' Beth said in her best ringmaster voice, which made Christian smile. The first time he'd done so in her company. For a man who put his life at risk every day, he appeared to be a serious one.

'I need to get home,' she announced, suddenly aware that if she didn't get back to the house, her mammy would send out a search party.

'Come back and see me again. I like early mornings, before everyone wakes up and the air is filled with chatter.' And then his eyes searched hers, and there were questions within them that made Beth blush again. She waved goodbye, and made her way back to collect her bike.

As she cycled home, Beth replayed the short time she had spent in the Frenchman's company over and over, committing every detail to memory. She couldn't wait to see Joanne and share the experience with her. And then she felt a stab of guilt. Poor Joanne wouldn't care about a flying trapeze or a tall, dark stranger. She'd just lost her dad. And more than that, Beth felt confused by her own reaction to Christian. Surely she shouldn't have felt

41

butterflies in her stomach when he touched her, when she had a boyfriend who she loved?

'What has you so happy at this ungodly hour?' her mammy asked from beside the Aga stove as Beth burst into the kitchen. 'You're like a Cheshire Cat with that smile.'

'The circus is here!' Beth told her, running over to the larder press and pulling honey and salt over to the table. She grabbed bowls for the porridge and milk from the fridge.

'I hope you weren't making a nuisance of yourself up there,' Kathleen said. 'They've a job to do, same as any of us.'

'A trapeze artist called Christian Banvard gave me a guided tour, and then he gave me a sneak preview of his act!' Beth said, unable to contain the secret. She had to tell someone.

'Wet the tea, then tell me all. Would be nice to have something else to think about for a few moments.' Kathleen lifted the wooden spoon to her mouth to taste the oats. 'Almost ready.'

Beth noticed how pale her mammy was. Her face drawn with grief and worry. So Beth shared her visit with her, leaving nothing out. Except for one thing, that was. She kept to herself how she'd felt when Christian touched her arm. That was her secret.

FIVE

Kathleen

Thursday, 10 May 1951

Ballycotton, Cork

Kathleen paced the kitchen floor. She clutched a telegram in her hand, received an hour before, and her jaw was clenched so tight, it hurt. She felt anxiety dance inside her. John and Katie were at school, a small mercy, so at least the cottage was quiet.

Her eyes fell on Beth, who was sitting at the kitchen table. Her eldest child could be flighty, her head in the clouds most of the day, but she had always seemed to understand Kathleen, knowing when she needed to be still. Beth was flicking through her copy of *Woman's Life*. The monthly magazine of fashion and beauty articles was her daughter's bible. She watched her carefully fold a page over, marking it. No doubt a dress or perfume that would be added to her never-ending wish list.

The kettle whistled on the Aga, a cue for Beth to jump up and pour hot water into the heavy silver teapot. Then Beth went outside, returning a few moments later with a couple of long red carrots and creamy-white parsnips. She began washing them in the sink in preparation for the stew planned for dinner that evening.

Beth had been a tremendous help to Kathleen since she left school the previous summer. The girl was bright: when the *Cork Examiner* published the secondary school students' results, Kathleen had burst with pride to see Beth's name with a star beside it – denoting she was an honours student. And now her education was complete, Kathleen was doing all she could to teach her the life skills she'd need to become a keeper's wife. The jury was out on whether an honours result would be given for that.

'Make double the stew, love,' Kathleen eventually said to her daughter over at the sink. 'Poor Ellen won't have any thought of cooking when I land this trouble on her door.'

Beth paused slicing carrots and onions. 'The telegram has bad news, so.' This was more of a statement than a question.

'It was expected news, but bad all the same. The new assistant keeper is to arrive at the end of the week. A man by the name of Seamus Mythen. I've not come across him before.'

'I suppose it's been a month,' Beth replied.

'As I said, not unexpected. We all knew that the Irish Lights would appoint a new permanent keeper sooner rather than later. And it's welcome news in many ways. Your father, Lee and Ted have all had to work extra shifts, but they can't go on like that,' Kathleen sighed as she looked down to the telegram again. 'Seamus will be bringing his new wife with him. A lady called Mary.'

Kathleen watched understanding fall onto her daughter's face as to why it mattered that Seamus was married.

'He'll need the Craig cottage,' Beth said, her voice little more than a whisper. 'He'll take over that spot as a married keeper rather than go into digs with Ted and Lee, the single keepers.'

Kathleen nodded.

'That's not fair,' Beth shouted, rage now exploding from her on behalf of the Craig family. 'They can't be turfed out, surely?'

Kathleen walked over and took the kitchen knife from Beth, placing it back on the kitchen counter. 'Unfortunately, yes, they can. Ellen doesn't get to keep the cottage. The Irish Lights have been fair. By the time the Mythens move in, she will have had six weeks since poor Peter died.' Kathleen blessed herself. 'According to this telegram, the Mythens will stay in the Bayview Hotel for a few days when they arrive.'

'Why did the telegram go to you and not to them?' Beth asked.

'I'm the principal keeper's wife. It's my job to welcome the new keeper and his family. The commissioners will have written to Ellen too, but I can't have her hear this from them. I want to be the one to relay the information, before a letter arrives. Once the stew is prepared, ready to go into her oven, we'll go next door.'

But no sooner had she uttered this than they heard a loud rap on the front door. Beth ran to open it and found Ellen standing there, two pink spots on her pale face, her eyes flashing with anger.

'You won't believe the audacity . . . I can't even speak . . . the barefaced cheek . . .' Ellen spluttered, falling inside.

Kathleen and Beth shared an alarmed look. How had Ellen heard about the new keeper already?

'Sit down. Take a deep breath. There's tea in the pot. Beth will get you a cup.'

'It's more than tea I need,' Ellen said.

'Sherry, so,' Kathleen replied, nodding at Beth to get a glass for her friend from the dresser.

Once Ellen had taken a couple of sips of the amber liquid, she had calmed down enough to speak. 'Peter's brother Benny called over. Demanded food. While I organized the tea, he started going through a pile of letters and bills that were on the kitchen table.'

'The cheek of him,' Beth said.

'He has no shame; when I called him out, he just smiled,' Ellen said bitterly. 'And he barked orders at me on how he wanted his tea.'

Kathleen thought that it was no wonder Benny had never managed to find a woman to court him. There was cruelty in him. She could see it simmering away underneath the surface.

'I gave him two slices of the soda bread I'd baked the day before, with butter and crab-apple jelly. He ate the bread so fast, spraying breadcrumbs and spitting as he did, it made me gag.' Ellen shuddered at the memory. 'Then he said to me, "Nice little baker you are. Peter was always boasting about your bread-making skills, not that I've ever been invited over to *sample your goods*." It was the way he said those last three words.'

Kathleen felt anger dance its way around her. She wished Patrick were here. He would have run the man out of the cottage so fast, there would have been sparks. 'What did he want?'

'He eyed the children and me like we were animals on his farm.' Ellen's hand shook so much that she had to place her glass down on the table. 'He told me that he was willing to marry me. To take on the children. He needed help on the farm, he said. And while Ger looked mollycoddled, he was sure he'd whip him into shape soon enough.'

'He did not!' Kathleen said, horror on her face.

Ellen wrung her hands as she continued her tale, her face pinched, taut with worry. 'He told me that we would have to wait six months to get married. But that the kids could leave school and work as farmhands immediately.'

'Ger is only ten years old, same as my John!' Kathleen said in shock.

'Exactly. But he only laughed. Telling me that his offer was the only one I'll get. That no one would take on a widow with mouths to feed. And that I'll be on my hands and knees begging for shelter soon enough. And then he quoted the bible, saying that it was his Christian duty to fulfil the duty of a husband to me, now that his dear brother was dead.'

Kathleen was rarely shocked by anyone. But this . . . she couldn't quite believe her ears. Benny Craig was a coarse man, with never a kind word to say to anyone. While Peter had been gentle and kind, his brother was the complete antithesis of that. But even so, to be so unsympathetic to Ellen's grief was unbelievably cruel.

'You can't marry him!' Beth shouted before Kathleen had a chance to speak.

'I most certainly cannot,' Ellen agreed. 'Patrick is not even cold in the ground. I need time to work out what we will do next. But all the time in the world would not be enough for me to ever agree to live with that ogre.'

Kathleen felt the telegram stashed in the pocket of her apron burn her, as if it were on fire. How could she add further distress to her friend in this state? But she knew that there could be no running away from it either. She inched her chair closer to her friend, then urged Ellen to take another sip of the sherry. 'I'm afraid I have further bad news to share. I've had word from the commissioners.' She took the telegram from her apron pocket and laid it on the table so Ellen could read it.

It was as if someone had stuck a pin in Ellen. As she read the news of the new keeper's appointment, she slumped in her chair, deflated and dejected.

'I've got one week?' Ellen whispered. And then tears came again, silently spilling from her eyes.

Beth stood up, the outrage Ellen had walked in with now filling her body. 'We won't let this happen. We will fight it. Won't we?' She turned to Kathleen at this.

'Mammy always has a solution for every problem. She'll know what to do.'

'I can't do anything about this.' Kathleen tapped the letter gently with her fingertip. 'We all know the rules of the keepers. But you can stay here until you find somewhere else to live. You won't be on the streets, I give you my word. The children can top and tail in their beds; you can have the parlour.'

Ellen smiled through her tears, then patted her hand. 'You are a good friend. And I thank you for that kind offer and everything you've done for me over the years. But I can't move in here. You know Patrick won't be allowed to agree to that. Even for his dear friend's family. The Commissioners of Lights' annual inspection is coming up soon, and I'm not sure they'd approve of two families sharing. It's not the done thing.'

They all took a moment to acknowledge that. When the commissioner came to inspect their homes, he left no cupboard unopened and no mantelpiece un-swiped for dust. Ellen and her family could not camp out at the Kenefick home, no matter how much Kathleen and Patrick might want it to happen.

Ellen stood up and smoothed down the wrinkles in her dress. She held her head high, 'I have some thinking to do. I've spent the past month looking for accommodation locally, but there isn't anything suitable. While I don't want to pull the children from Ballycotton, not on top of losing their dad, I may not have a choice.'

Kathleen stood up too and put her arm around her friend, thinking of all the times they'd been by each other's side. This was the second time that their families had been posted to the same lighthouse. Her eyes filled with tears at the thought of not having Ellen close by. 'I'm here to help. We will find a way together.'

'I'm grateful for your support, I'm sure it will all be okay,' Ellen said, but her voice was weary, without a trace of hope.

SIX

Mollie

Ballycotton, Cork

Mollie parked her rental car in front of Peony Cottage. Her grandmother had rented this Airbnb, located on the road from Garryvoe to Ballycotton.

'How pretty,' Mollie said, taking in the ash, hazel and birch trees which lined the driveway of the small whitewashed cottage with its golden thatched roof.

A tall, curvy woman with grey hair cut in a blunt bob and fringe opened the front door and walked out into the sunshine.

'There's Aunty Jane. I wasn't expecting to see her today,' her dad said to Mollie before they got out of the car to greet her. Aunt Jane was Nana Beth's youngest sister, but was actually closer in age to her dad, as there were eighteen years between the two women.

'Hello, you two! I called over to say hello to Beth. She's inside,' Aunt Jane said, looking over her shoulder towards the cottage. She embraced Mollie and her dad warmly. 'It's a lovely little cottage. I think you'll both be comfortable here. I'm in the middle of a renovation and the house is in a right state, otherwise you could have stayed with me. I'm sorry I couldn't put you all up as I normally would when you visit.'

'We understand. And the cottage looks charming. I bet those trees look pretty in the fall,' her dad replied.

'I daresay not as pretty as trees do in your fall in Camden. Now that's a sight I'd never get tired of seeing,' Aunt Jane said.

People travelled many miles to New England to see the incredible beauty of the leaves changing from jewelled-greens to ochre-yellows, russet-reds to tangerine-orange. And their home in Camden had a spectacular backdrop of tall white pine, sturdy oaks and gnarly sycamores.

Mollie and her dad followed Aunt Jane through the front door, which was painted a vibrant yellow to match the stunning baskets of peonies that hung on either side. It opened directly into a mid-sized room that served as a kitchen, dining room and sitting room.

'You made good time!' Nana Beth called out from a battered-looking green sofa as soon as they walked in. She held her arms open wide for Mollie, who ran towards her embrace. 'There's my girl.'

But as she embraced Beth, Mollie heard a rattle in her chest that sounded nasty. 'I don't like the sound of that,' she said, pulling back to scrutinize her grandmother's face. She'd always marvelled at how her nana never seemed to age. For a woman who was close to ninety, she looked twenty years younger.

'Damn cough won't give up. But I'll be fine,' Nana Beth replied, then prodded Mollie's stomach. 'You've put on a few pounds.'

This was met with cries of denial from her dad and aunt. But despite her weight being a touchy subject for Mollie, somehow, she didn't mind the comment from her nana, who always said it like it was.

'Ten pounds up. But I'm working on losing it again,' Mollie answered.

'Leave it where it is – you were too scrawny before,' Nana Beth stated. Then she turned to look up to a hovering Albie. 'Hello, Son.'

'Hello, Mother.' He smiled tentatively. 'Good to see you.'

'Are you dyeing that hair of yours? It looks darker,' Nana Beth said, narrowing her eyes to squint.

'I am not! It's all my own,' her dad replied, indignant. 'But it's a wonder it's not turned grey after that drive here. Mollie has clearly never heard of a brake. I swear she took every hairpin bend on two wheels.'

'Wimp!' Mollie said, as a smile broke onto her face. Already, here only five minutes, she felt stronger in mind and body.

'Do you need to see a doctor about that cough?' her dad asked, taking a seat on the other side of Beth on the sofa.

'All I need is a day of rest,' Nana Beth insisted. 'There

was no need for you to rush over here.' But she was made a liar of by a fit of coughing that wracked her small frame. Aunt Jane moved to the kitchen and fetched her a glass of water.

They waited until Beth's cough subsided, then her dad said, 'I decided to visit because I wanted to see you. I hope that's okay.'

Mollie's heart constricted as she watched the easy smile that usually resided on her father's face crumple into uncertainty as he waited for a response from Nana Beth.

But Nana Beth surprised them all by reaching over to clasp her son's hand. 'I'm glad you're here. Both of you.'

'And how are the family?' Mollie asked her aunt.

'All good. The grandchildren will be down for their summer holidays in August, assuming I ever finish the renovations!'

'I bet you have them spoilt rotten,' her dad said wistfully.

Mollie bit back a sigh, feeling the weight of her dad's disappointment. She crossed her fingers that Jane didn't start asking when she would have a baby of her own. She could retire if she had a dollar for every time Nolan and she had been asked that loaded question. At first, it would make Nolan grin and her squirm, but these last few years, she just couldn't bear it. It brought up too many questions that she didn't know the answer to.

And on cue, as if she'd planted the seed in her brain, Aunt Jane turned to Mollie: 'What about you, when are you—'

Nana Beth cleared her throat, interrupting her sister. 'Mollie, I fancy some air. Join me for a walk in the garden.'

Mollie jumped up and offered her arm to her grandmother, grateful to leave what was about to become a hot seat. As soon as they were out in the garden, away from earshot, Mollie whispered, 'Thank you.'

'Shut them down. Only way. When I married your grandfather, it felt like the only thing family and friends wanted to know was when were we going to have a baby. You know what I'd say to them when they'd ask me that goddamn awful question?'

'Go on, tell me.'

'I'd square back my shoulders, lift my chin high and say, "Let's make a deal. How about I'll have a baby when you learn to mind your own business,"' Nana Beth said, and the two women laughed together in appreciation of a great comeback line.

'Best response ever. I'm remembering that one.'

'Well, here's another gem – but I did get in trouble with your grandfather when I said this to his boss at a Christmas party one year. When he started questioning us, I turned to him and replied, "I'm sorry, I'm sure I misheard you ask me a question that's completely none of your beeswax." You can have that one too. Don't be shy about using it with Jane, or anyone else who bothers you while you're here!'

'Nana, you are incorrigible. And I love you for it.'

'I've been told that once or twice in my life.' She paused, looking into Mollie's eyes. 'Something tells me that you've a lot on your mind. There's sadness in your pretty eyes. I've a good pair of ears working quite well now, thanks to my new hearing aids, if you want to talk.'

Mollie squeezed her nana's hand, which rested on her arm.

'I think it must be hard being an only child. I bet you'd love a sister who could be your confidante.' Nana Beth closed her eyes for a moment as if in prayer. 'I didn't think I'd outlive my younger siblings, John and Katie. I miss them.' Her voice broke at this.

'I know you do,' Mollie said; her great-uncle and great-aunt had both died within the past couple of years.

'But I mustn't get maudlin. I have Jane still.' Beth smiled again, 'And as she's only a young wan, I won't outlive her; thanks be to God.'

They paused at the end of the garden, and Mollie was delighted to discover that it overlooked the ocean. They took a seat on a wooden bench that sat underneath a canopy of branches from a weeping willow tree.

Mollie felt her grandmother's body shiver, even though the afternoon sun was warm. She shrugged her sweater off and placed it gently around her nana's shoulders.

'Do you believe in God, Mollie?'

Mollie exhaled deeply. She hadn't been expecting such a philosophical question. 'That's a gear shift, Nana. Truthfully, I don't know.'

She waited for her Nana Beth to expand but when she remained quiet, Mollie said, 'Why do you ask? Are you having doubts about what you believe in?' Her grandmother, like all her family, had grown up in the Catholic Church. But Mollie and her dad were lapsed Catholics – at best – who didn't go to church anymore except on holidays.

Nana Beth shook her head, her face darkening with a frown. 'I have no doubts about my faith. But I do have fear.'

'Of what?' Mollie moved closer, clasping her grandmother's arm tightly.

'I've plenty to be afraid of. Mostly of meeting my maker when I die. And facing my sins,' she answered. A breeze rose from across the ocean and made the trees in the garden rustle. 'I sometimes think that the trees are whispering to each other.'

'What are they saying?' Mollie asked, a shiver running down her spine as she took in the pain that now pierced Nana's blue eyes that were now faded to grey.

'That they know my secrets and that the time is up. That someone has to pay for what we did,' Nana Beth said, her eyes locked on the swaying branches of a silver birch.

Mollie felt the hairs on the back of her neck rise to attention. She had so many questions, but before she could ask them, her grandmother held her hand up, warding them off, as another bout of coughing overcame her.

Mollie rubbed her grandmother's back, feeling helpless to do anything else.

'My chest . . . it hurts . . .' Nana Beth said, her lips suddenly turning blue, starkly contrasted against her alabaster skin.

Mollie screamed for help at the top of her lungs as her grandmother collapsed into her arms.

SEVEN

Kathleen

Friday, 11 May 1951

Ballycotton, Cork

The sound of the seagull's caw started Kathleen awake. She'd fallen asleep mid-afternoon in Patrick's chair at the hearth. That wasn't like her. Guilt made her jump up and grab the brush, sweeping the kitchen for the second time that day. The past month had taken its toll on her and she felt older than her thirty-seven years.

Watching her friend Ellen grieve her husband's death, and seeing the children lost with their hearts broken, would melt the coldest of hearts. Kathleen glanced at the calendar that hung on the back of the kitchen door. The children took turns marking a cross at the end of each day. Patrick had sent a letter to Kathleen via the relief

58

boat this morning. He would stay on the island for two more weeks, so that he could settle in the new keeper, Seamus Mythen. So that meant fourteen more crosses to go until Patrick returned. While Kathleen understood why her husband elected to stay at the lighthouse rather than take his scheduled shore leave, she had felt stung by his decision all the same. Kathleen had done her best to be a shoulder for Ellen to cry on, to remain strong as her friend tried to make sense of her loss. But at night, as Kathleen lay in her double bed on her own, she felt herself grow more and more angry with Patrick. Where was *her* support? She longed for strong arms to wrap themselves around her as she wept. This unbidden thought was followed quickly by a stab of guilt. She was a wicked woman to be so selfish, to think about her own needs, when Patrick must be exhausted from his extended stint on the island.

She asked herself the same question she'd considered several times over the recent month. When had she stopped missing Patrick's presence? When they first married, she'd spent every waking moment they were not together yearning for him. They had been stationed at five different lighthouses over the nineteen years they'd been married, and in three of these, she lived in a cottage adjacent to the lighthouse Patrick worked in. Close to her man. It had felt like they were working together toward a common goal. So when they'd been sent here to Ballycotton Island, she'd been devastated that she would only see him one week in every four.

Kathleen learned that it didn't take long for a new normal to fit. But at what price to her marriage?

These days, when Patrick returned from the island, he felt like a stranger to her. It took days for him to settle back home and once he did, they struggled to regain their closeness. By the time they found their new rhythm again, it was time for him to go back to the lighthouse. Once, after a second glass of sherry, Ellen had confessed to her that when Peter returned from the island, he couldn't keep his hands off her – an indiscreet omission mentioned with loose lips, but one that had cut Kathleen. How long had it been since Patrick was like that with her?

When Ted appeared on the island last month and signalled for a doctor to be called for, a dark thought had crossed her mind. If Patrick were dead, would she miss him? She had regretted the thought ever since. None more so than when Ellen collapsed into her arms when Peter died, her devastation piercing the air around them.

Kathleen swept the dirt into the dustpan and threw it in the fire, as though throwing away the thoughts she didn't want to linger, then she retook her seat, feeling another wave of fatigue overrun her.

She imagined Patrick sitting in the lighthouse tower whittling wood, his favoured pastime. Had he any thought or worry for the family of his fellow keeper, Peter? A man he'd worked with many times throughout his career? And one that he valued as a friend. At one point in their marriage, Kathleen would have known the answer to that automatically, but now she was unsure. Patrick felt like a stranger to her. Lately they never talked other than to discuss practicalities about the children or the household.

Her body trembled as she wrapped her arms around herself. At this moment, though, more than anything, she wished she could talk to Patrick. Ask him for his counsel in this matter with the Craigs.

On a whim, she jumped up, desperate to do something about the situation she found her marriage in. She had to speak to her husband. Make him understand that she needed him. Together, they could find a way back to each other, out of this lonely life they'd carved. She grabbed the semaphore flags from the press in the hall and made her way towards the pier. It wasn't Sunday afternoon, the traditional day for semaphores, but in the early days of his deployment, Kathleen had often sent impromptu messages to her husband. And back then, he seemed to be on her wavelength and would appear in the distance, his flags in hand too. Their messages had been filled with *I love you*s.

As Kathleen stood at the edge of the pier, the wind loosening hair from her low bun, she signalled H.E.L.L.O. P.A.T.R.I.C.K. and waited, holding her breath, for him to appear. *Please, Patrick, I need you*. Her eyes searched the upper outline of the island, where the keepers gathered whenever they needed to signal the mainland. Maybe Ted or Lee would look in this direction. They would see her and call for Patrick, and he'd run for his flags, back on the same wavelength again. She repeated her message five more times until her arms began to ache. And then, feeling foolish, she turned back towards the harbour.

To her surprise, she noted a well-dressed man wearing a cravat and a black trilby hat, leaning against the harbour wall, watching her closely.

'You are mighty graceful with those flags, ma'am,' he said as Kathleen neared him.

American. A tourist perhaps, Kathleen thought.

'Thank you.'

'Semaphore signalling, right?'

Kathleen nodded.

'Did you get an answer?'

Kathleen shook her head, dismayed that tears had sprung into her eyes. The stranger saw her distress and a flash of sympathy appeared in his dark brown eyes. She pulled herself together. A grown woman crying like a child, it wouldn't do.

'Are you holidaying in the area?' Kathleen asked, taking the conversation to safer ground.

He looked out over the Atlantic Ocean as he replied, 'My family were from Cork originally but moved to Texas many years ago. Before I was born. I'm vacationing in Ireland. But I felt a tad under the weather last week, so my doctor suggested a few weeks in the restorative sea air of Ballycotton.'

'The sea air here is renowned for its healing abilities. We have many visitors who come for health reasons, like yourself. I hope Ballycotton works its magic on you too, Mr . . . ?'

'Mr Davis. Charles Davis. And since my arrival yesterday, I am happy to say that I do feel revived. So I believe the hype about the sea air, I promise you! And may I ask your name?'

'I'm Mrs Kenefick. Kathleen Kenefick.'

'And who were you sending secret messages to on the island?' Charles asked, his voice full of mischief.

Kathleen blushed, answering quickly, 'My husband is the principal keeper at Ballycotton Lighthouse.'

'Lucky him. But silly him too, not answering a lovely lady like you.'

Kathleen's stomach flipped over, and she felt her blush move from her cheeks throughout her body. She looked around her guiltily, feeling disloyal for even having this conversation with a stranger. 'I must be on my way, Mr Davis. My children will be home from school shortly.'

He tipped his trilby to her and smiled gently. 'It was nice chatting to you. And I hope to see you again sometime.'

Kathleen took a closer look at him. His dark temples were scattered with silver strands, and fine lines weaved around his eyes and lip. He was somewhere in his fifties, she guessed. She smiled back warmly. 'Nice to meet you, Mr Davis.'

'It's Charles. Until the next time, Kathleen.'

She liked the way her name sounded in his soft American drawl. As Kathleen began the hilly ascent up the harbour walkway, she could feel his eyes on her back and a smile crept to her face.

EIGHT

Mary

Mary opened her small compact mirror and checked her appearance once more. In a few moments, they would arrive in Ballycotton, the village that would be her new home for at least the next three years.

'You look fine. Beautiful. Perfect, in fact,' Seamus said reassuringly.

'Jaypers! Keep your eyes in front of you!' Mary replied as the road twisted into another sharp bend. 'We're not in Dublin anymore. I don't think I've ever driven on such narrow roads.'

'Don't be fretting; everyone says that the Morris Minor is the safest car on the market. Hey, look over

64

there!' Seamus shouted excitedly, putting his foot on the brakes to slow down.

Mary looked in disbelief. Was that an elephant walking through the field beside them? 'Seamus! How exciting, the circus is in town!'

'Well, I'll be darned. It sure is. I hope we can go before I head to the lighthouse,' Seamus replied, laughing out loud.

'Oh, that would be wonderful. I hope there are horses. I love equestrian tricks,' Mary said, as she lightly touched her new husband's arm. She liked touching him, whenever she could. And thankfully, Seamus felt the same way.

They'd gotten married on her twenty-first birthday, two weeks and three days ago. She swallowed back a lump in her throat as she thought about her mother and prayed that she was looking down from heaven, happy with the life her daughter was now carving out for herself. It was far removed from the one Mary had grown up in, living in a tenement building in Sean McDermott Street in Dublin's north inner city.

I got out, Ma, just as you wanted me to.

When Mary had met Seamus, a mere six months ago, they'd fallen in love by the end of their first dance. It sounded so romantic when he told her about his job as an assistant keeper. Her man, in his handsome uniform, standing guard at the top of a tower, looking at the dark seas. She sensed that he was a good person – someone who gave back to the community. Who didn't take, take, take, as her father had always done.

Mary shook her head, banishing her father's image. Today would not be ruined by thinking about *him*.

65

They continued their drive into the village, passing quaint thatched cottages and whitewashed walls. They followed a sign announcing the Bayview Hotel. The Commissioners of Irish Lights had booked them a room for the next week until their cottage became vacant. They'd been informed that the family they were replacing were in the process of moving out. Mary and Seamus had both been sad to hear about the death of Peter Craig. From what they'd been told, he left a young family behind. Nevertheless, she could not wait to see their new home; she'd already bought a few bits and pieces for their kitchen that she hoped would brighten it up.

But her new home was forgotten as she took in the incredible view from the front of the hotel. Blue skies kissed an even bluer sea, and in the background a small rugged island jutted out of craggy rocks, with a striking black lighthouse standing tall on its top.

'It's like the Italian Riviera! Or at least, like the photographs I've seen of Italy,' Mary said with a sigh.

'We'll go there one day,' Seamus promised. Until she met her husband, she'd not been further than Skerries in north County Dublin. He had made her life so much more significant in less than one year together. She could not wait to see how their future unfolded.

He swung his car into a parking spot near the front of the hotel, then pulled the lever for the boot and jumped out to take two large suitcases out. The cottage came fully furnished, so they only needed clothes. A couple of boxes held some furnishings that Mary had bought.

'Come here, Mrs Mythen,' he called out to Mary as she joined him by his side.

Mary loved hearing Seamus call her that. She moved closer, and he pulled her in tight, kissing her passionately.

'What will people think?' Mary said self-consciously, looking around her. But Seamus only laughed. He never worried about anyone but her.

'Sure, we're the only sinners in the car park,' Seamus said. Mary heard a giggle, which disputed that fact, and she turned to spot two girls running up the driveway from the hotel.

Hanging her handbag over her arm, Mary followed her husband inside the hotel. He carried all their luggage with ease and, again, Mary felt a burst of pride that this man was her husband. While he wasn't tall – only an inch above her five-foot-four stature – he was broad-shouldered and muscular, which made him seem more significant than his actual height. People stopped and looked when he walked into a room. Much like she had done, the night he swaggered into the Crystal Ballroom, a cigarette dangling from his lower lip. Mary was there with her co-workers from the Birds Eye factory. She'd worked on several factory floors since she left school at thirteen, joining her mother wherever she worked. Until her mam died, when she was only eighteen that was. But while Mary had been courted by several men, she had never been in love. That night, to her surprise and delight, Seamus had made his way towards Mary and asked her to dance. By the second spin on the mahogany dance floor, she was smitten.

They spent every bit of his time off in each other's company. Thus began months of counting down the days, marking Xs on a calendar, until they could be together again. He'd proposed before their six-month anniversary, and they got married immediately. She explained to him that her parents were dead – so she had no need or want for a big wedding – just the two of them at a small church on Stephen's Green.

The whirlwind of their romance continued when Seamus told her they were to be stationed in Cork a few weeks after their wedding. He had worried that she might hate leaving Dublin and all she knew, but Mary had been elated. A chance to make a fresh start where nobody knew who she was. Or, more importantly, who her da was.

While Seamus signed the registrar in the Bayview, checking them into their room, Mary quickly took a tour of the public areas. Half a dozen people were seated in the restaurant, and they looked up at her with interest. She smiled at each of them. The last person in the room was a man dining on his own, but he held up his newspaper so that it almost covered his face. For the briefest moment over the print, their eyes locked, and Mary felt a sudden uneasiness as his eyes bore into hers.

When Seamus called out her name, she hurried towards her husband, but she couldn't shake the man's dark eyes from her mind. There was something about the way he had looked at her that unnerved her, as if he knew her somehow. But that was impossible. Mary had never been to Cork, never mind Ballycotton, in her entire life.

A friendly porter showed them to their front-facing double room, with a stunning sea view that made her heart leap with joy. As she threw herself on the bed, Seamus waved a card at her.

'Don't get comfortable. This was waiting for us at check-in. It's a note from the principal keeper's wife, a Mrs Kathleen Kenefick. We've been invited to her house for afternoon tea today. She lives next door to what will be our new home, so it will be a chance to get our bearings.'

Mary blanched at this. She wasn't prepared to meet anyone this soon. 'I thought we'd have a day to settle in before we had to face anyone.'

'So did I, my love. But we can't say no. It's the principal keeper's wife. When she calls, we have to accept. Either way, you need to get to know her. You'll be her neighbour, and you'll rely on each other when I'm away. That's the way it works for the wives.'

Mary walked over to a large mahogany dressing table and looked at herself in the mirror. She wore a cream cotton dress with pink roses printed onto a full skirt that swished as she moved. She had felt pretty this morning when she got dressed. Ready to take on the world. Or at least this small part of it. But now she doubted herself.

'Are the roses too frivolous? Should I change it into something else? What do keepers' wives wear?' Mary asked, pulling at her skirt as she looked at herself critically. She'd always been sure of herself working on the factory floor. But this . . . she felt like a fish out of water.

'Stop worrying. Mrs Kenefick will be charmed by you. Just be yourself.'

But the problem was, there was one thing that Mary knew for sure that she could never truly be – and that was *herself*.

NINE

Beth

Saturday, 12 May 1951

Ballycotton, Cork

Beth couldn't understand why she had to attend the meet-and-greet for the new keeper and his wife. She itched to return to Murphy's field to see the circus again. Or, more precisely, to see if she could catch sight of Christian. Ever since Beth had met him three days ago, he had filled her every waking thought. And if Ted's kind face jumped into her guilty conscience, she pushed it away, telling herself that it was merely excitement for the circus that had piqued her interest in Christian.

But there was a problem. Her mam insisted that her gallivanting with the circus performers was unseemly. Not unchaperoned, at least. Plus, there hadn't been a chance to escape. She would never complain about helping out the Craigs or being there for Joanne, but the days were marching on and the circus was only here for a few weeks.

Today, she had a plan that would help her see Christian while also putting a smile on Joanne's face. Beth took the floor sweeper, cleaned the front parlour, and then dusted the ornaments atop the mantelpiece. She'd placed a bunch of wildflowers picked from the small back garden into a vase that now sat in the centre of the coffee table.

'Give the good china a wipe; make sure it's clean,' her mammy shouted from the kitchen as she iced a coffee buttercream sponge. 'Then tidy yourself up! They'll be here soon enough. Let's show them our Sunday best.'

After finishing the chores, Beth washed her face and brushed her long brown hair, tying it back into a low ponytail. She'd been the dutiful daughter all morning. Now it was time to make one more attempt to gain Kathleen's permission to miss afternoon tea with the Mythens.

'That cake looks amazing,' Beth said, dipping her finger into the rich, velvety buttercream.

Her mammy swiped her hand away, then stood back to admire her handiwork. 'Yes, I think it will do nicely.'

'What do we know about the new keeper and his wife?' Beth asked. She had to bite her tongue to stop telling her mammy she'd spied them kissing in front of the hotel. While that was juicy gossip, she knew Mammy would disapprove of the public display of affection. Beth didn't want to get anyone in trouble, and there was something about the way the couple had looked at each other that made her heart swell. The woman looked so glamorous, with her full skirt and red lips. She didn't look much older than Beth was. Maybe they could be friends. Someone Beth could talk to about love and romance. Joanne used to be her confidante, but lately – and not just since her dad died – she'd become a reluctant listener when Beth wanted to discuss the ins and outs of her relationship with Ted.

'Other than their names, nothing. We'll find out all we need to know soon enough,' her mammy replied.

'I like your hair like that,' Beth said, starting stage two of her charm offensive. Her mammy had put her curlers in overnight, tying back her newly wavy hair with a blue ribbon. 'You look younger.'

'I know what you're up to, young lady. Flatter me up, and I'll let you scoot off to the circus. I didn't come down in the last shower.'

'What does that even mean, come down in the last shower?' Beth muttered crossly.

'It means don't take me for a fool; that's what.'

Beth cursed under her breath. She could never get anything past her mother. But then she took a second look at her. Yes, she had been buttering her up. But Mammy did look different. Was that lip-gloss she was wearing?

'You *do* look nice. And where were you this morning? You never said; you just disappeared for an hour.'

Her mammy turned her back to Beth, folding and then unfolding a tea towel. 'I was visiting Maureen Doyle. She's having a hard time with that new baby of hers. Nonstop grizzle. I brought her some gripe water that should sort the baby out.'

Beth threw her eyes up to the ceiling. Her mother was a bloody saint. Kathleen visited the sick, volunteered in the community, and chaired the Women's Association; she was never done.

'Seriously, why must I be here when they visit? They won't want to meet me. I'm just the boring daughter.'

'But, love, you might be in the same situation as this young couple one day. Arriving at a new station, meeting new keepers' wives and families. And I hope you'll get as warm a welcome as I intend to give to the Mythens today.'

Beth shuddered at the very thought. 'Is that it, Mammy? My life laid out in front of me. Marry a keeper like you did? Bake coffee cakes and visit the sick children in the parish? That's when I'm not pushing out babies every year.'

'You make life sound so enticing,' her mammy said with a shake of her head. She pulled Beth by her hands and led her to the parlour, directing her to the brown velvet sofa. 'Sit.'

Beth did as she was told, then braced herself for a lecture. But to her surprise, Mammy pulled her into her arms and simply held her. An embrace like she used to give Beth when she was a young girl. As her mammy gently stroked her hair, she felt herself lean into her warmth. It felt like home. And love. And safety.

'This is nice,' Beth said, her voice choking up with emotion.

'Will you remember something for me?' Mammy stared into Beth's eyes. 'Remember that you have choices.

You don't have to marry someone just because they ask you.'

Beth pulled back in disbelief, hardly believing her ears. She assumed her mother had no other ambition for her than to follow in her own footsteps. 'I thought you *wanted* me to marry Ted.'

'I want you to marry someone you love. Not someone your father or I choose. And do you love Ted?' her mammy asked softly.

Beth's heart began to speed up as her stomach flipped in time to its beat. This was an impossible question for her. She knew that she loved being in his company when she was with him. But was that love? And if so, why was she thinking about the tall, muscular Christian Banvard so much? Last night she dreamt that she was on the trapeze, swinging back and forth, and then she fell, hurtling to the ground until someone's strong hands grabbed her arms, catching her. She had opened her eyes before she could see if it was Christian or Ted who had rescued her. And then felt shame and confusion that she'd been dreaming about someone other than her boyfriend. What was wrong with her?

'Beth?' her mammy asked, bringing her back to their conversation.

'I don't know if I love Ted. I might, but . . . how can I know for sure?'

Her mammy smiled in understanding. 'When I met your father, he was all I could think about. From the moment I opened my eyes to my last thought before sleep. When we were not together, I fretted. And I counted down the days until I could see him again. He only had to look at me, and I felt giddy.'

Beth frowned. This description summed up how she felt too. But the problem was, it was Christian's face she thought of, not her boyfriend's.

'Does Ted make you giddy?'

'He did in the beginning, but recently I'm not so sure,' Beth admitted. How could she make her mother understand that something had changed inside her? Doubt clouded her emotions, making her want to pull away from Ted, rather than towards his arms.

'You must work out how you feel, love. Ted is head over heels for you. I can see that from a mile off. And he's a good man. A kind soul. There's a lot to be said for that. But don't trifle with his emotions. That would be cruel.'

Beth disentangled herself from her mother's arms and turned to face her. 'I would never want to hurt Ted. But . . . I wish he weren't a lighthouse keeper. I know you love your life, but I don't want it, Mammy. Not yet, anyhow. I want to travel. See the world. Live my life!'

Beth waited for her mother's outrage at such a declaration. But once again, she had underestimated her mother.

'Then that's what you must tell Ted. You are not ready for marriage, Beth – or, I suspect, this *life*, either. Nor are you a green girl who knows nothing about what it is to be married to a keeper. You've grown up on the rocks of Ireland. You've lived remotely, at lighthouses and, like now, on shore, close by to your father. I don't need to tell you that it takes a certain type of person to live this life of solitude and service.'

75

'Oh Mammy,' Beth half sobbed. She'd never loved her more.

Then her mother clasped Beth's hands tightly between her own. 'You didn't choose to be a keeper's daughter. Fate made you that. But you can choose whether you wish to be a keeper's wife.'

Beth felt a weight fall from her shoulders as her mammy gave her a way out that she thought didn't exist. 'I was sure you'd hate me if I didn't marry Ted.'

'I could never hate you. I love you – my eldest daughter. I made my decision when I was your age. But for me, it was an easy choice. I loved your father and would have followed him to the world's edge. Lighthouses are in my blood, and I'm not sure I could ever settle into any other life.'

'They're in mine too. And I do love this life. It's not that I don't want to be part of it. But not yet. Why can't I disappear for a few years, see the world, and then come back?'

'Where does that leave Ted? Do you expect him to leave with you? Or wait here for you to return? And who would you go travelling with? The world is still broken, love, recovering from war. You can't go running off willy-nilly. Not without planning and support.'

Beth shrugged. She had no answers, just a strong will to escape. Would Ted wait for her if she left Ireland for a few years? Or would he find a friendly local girl who would happily stand by his side? A sharp pain hit her at this thought. Maybe she cared more than she thought.

'You've got a few weeks to work out what you want, Beth. At least when it comes to your relationship with

76

Ted. I daresay that you're too young to make a decision that affects the rest of your life. But mark my word; a decision is coming your way. Your father has given Ted permission to ask you to marry him.'

While this wasn't news to Beth, her stomach plummeted at the thought. A tap at the front door ended their conversation. Her mammy let Ellen and Joanne in. Ellen wore a black dress, her widow's weeds, and Joanne wore a black skirt and white blouse, a black velvet ribbon tying her light brown hair back. Beth started; she still hadn't got used to seeing them in their mourning clothes.

'I made scones,' Ellen said, handing a tin to her mammy.

'Wonderful. Come on into the kitchen. Girls, don't make a mess in here,' Mammy instructed.

'We're not kids,' Beth said, rolling her eyes.

'No, I don't suppose you are anymore.'

'Speaking of kids, I was up with Maureen Doyle earlier. Her baby is an absolute angel, not a peep out of her the entire visit,' Ellen said.

Beth looked at her in surprise. 'Mammy was up there earlier too.'

'Oh, Maureen never mentioned it,' Ellen replied. 'We must have missed each other.'

'Sure, when you have a baby, you forget your name. Remember what that was like,' her mammy said quickly, then left, leaving the girls on their own.

Beth moved closer to her friend and whispered, 'We need to escape from here. Have some fun. When the lads get home from school, they will distract our mams. We can sneak off then.'

'To where?' Joanne asked.

'To Murphy's field! The circus is getting ready to open tomorrow. And you will not believe this – I've already met one of the performers. A trapeze artist called Christian. Joanne, wait until you see him. He's got muscles on his muscles!' Beth flexed her puny arms and posed, but Joanne didn't laugh. The furrow in her forehead deepened.

'I saw a lion and a bear. And Christian gave me a sneak preview of his trapeze act. Honestly, Jojo, it was so daring, I could hardly breathe as he threw himself through the air.'

Joanne didn't share Beth's enthusiasm, though. She looked Beth square in the eye. She pursed her lips into a tight line and narrowed her eyes.

Beth shuddered. In that moment, her friend had a distinct look of the principal of their school, which was not a compliment.

'You have no idea, do you? Beth Kenefick, living in her perfect little dream world. Without a single care . . .' Joanne said, her voice clipped.

The sting of these words pierced Beth. 'That's not fair. I have problems.' Beth bit her bottom lip nervously. 'Ted will propose on his next shore leave, and I haven't a clue what to say to him. My head is full of what-ifs and maybes. I don't know what to do.'

Joanne's eyes filled with tears and she shook her head, as if she couldn't believe what she was hearing. 'Really? That's your big problem? A handsome bachelor with a good job wants to marry you? Not only giving you love but also security and a home. You expect me to offer sympathy for that?'

Joanne stood up from the couch and moved to the other side of the parlour as if being near Beth offended her every sense.

Then to Beth's horror, a single tear made its way down Joanne's ashen face. Beth jumped up and ran to her friend's side, clasping Joanne's hand and squeezing it tight.

'What's wrong, Jojo? Tell me. You've been distant with me for ages. And I miss our chats. Have I done something to upset you? Tell me so I can say sorry,' Beth begged, her own eyes filling with tears too.

'It's just . . . I feel . . . I mean . . .' Joanne faltered for a moment, then finally continued, 'We're about to be homeless. And Mr and Mrs Mythen are about to arrive here for afternoon tea to rub salt into our open wounds. I had to watch Mam make scones for people who are playing a part in our eviction. It's too cruel.'

Beth felt her hackles rise at the injustice of it all, but sagged with relief that there was nothing else bothering Joanne. 'Mammy will help find you somewhere to live. There's still hope. You won't be homeless. I'm sure of it.'

'I know Kathleen is doing her best. But even she can't solve this problem. There are no properties available, none that we can afford, at least. Mam has walked Ballycotton up and down, enquired into every possible option. But it's no go. She spoke about moving to Cork city last night, where we are more likely to find cheap accommodation. And today, Maureen Doyle offered to put a word in with one of the managers over in the shoe polish factory in Glanmire.'

Beth's jaw literally dropped open. 'Glanmire. But that's the other side of Cork! I'd never see you. You can't leave Ballycotton!'

'We don't want to. Ger cried for hours at the thought of leaving school. I'm so close to graduation, and Mam insists that I have to finish. But maybe I should get a job too. And that way Ger might get a chance at completing his education.'

Beth listened in horror. 'I have a savings account in the Post Office, and have been putting in my birthday gift of half a crown from my grandparents for years. I'll withdraw it tomorrow and it's yours.'

Joanne smiled sadly. 'Thank you. You offering to do that is one of the reasons I don't want to leave Ballycotton. I would miss you so.' Joanne's shoulders slumped in defeat, then with her eyes downcast, she whispered, her voice laden with hopelessness, 'Why didn't Ted fall in love with me instead of you? You don't even want to marry him. That would have solved everything.'

Beth didn't know what to say. She felt foolish and selfish all at once. And at a loss what to do to make this better.

'If I've been short with you, I'm sorry. It's not you I'm cross with,' Joanne eventually said, filling the silence. 'It's the situation our family find ourselves in. But Beth, you must realize I don't have time for silly trips to the circus. I have to find a way to help Mam. She cries herself to sleep every night. And Ger is like a lost lamb, following her wherever she goes. He misses Dad.'

'And what about you?' Beth asked quietly.

Joanne wiped the tears from her face. 'I have to be strong. And make sure that whatever happens, we don't end up at Uncle Benny's. I don't like the way he looks at me, Beth. It feels like he's undressing me with his eyes. I'm scared.'

Beth was shocked into silence. But before she could collect her thoughts to answer Joanne, another knock on the front door rapped loudly down the hall.

'They're here,' Beth whispered. 'This conversation isn't over, I promise. I'm here, Joanne, and I'm not going anywhere. We'll get through this together. You'll see.'

Then they both stood up, ready to meet the Mythens.

TEN

Mary

Saturday, 12 May 1951

Ballycotton, Cork

The silence stretched taut through the small parlour. Mary sat on the edge of the velvet sofa, marvelling at Seamus, who lounged against the soft cushions, legs akimbo in front of him, as he answered questions about his keeper experience. Nothing ever bothered her husband.

'I was stationed at Bailey Lighthouse in Dublin for almost four years, and in all that time, I stayed locally in Howth village for my shore leave. But Lady Luck was on my side, sending me to the Crystal Ballroom six months ago. Cos it was there that I met Mary. The rest, as they say, is history.' The pride on Seamus's face was hard to miss, and Mary felt another rush of love for her husband.

'You met only six months ago?' Beth said.

'When you know, you know,' Seamus answered good-naturedly.

'And where are you from, Mary?' Kathleen asked, offering another slice of cake to Seamus, who gratefully accepted it.

'I'm from Dublin.' Mary felt a bead of sweat trickle down her back. She never liked talking about her personal life. They'd only been here twenty minutes, but it felt double that time. And the two girls kept glaring at her. Was she imagining that? No. They were definitely glaring. She couldn't for the life of her work out what she had done to offend them.

'And do your parents still live there? I'm sure your family will miss you now that you've relocated to Cork,' Kathleen continued.

'My parents are both dead,' Mary replied, doing her best to keep her voice even.

An awkward silence followed this. 'I'm very sorry,' Ellen said, reaching over to pat Mary's hand. 'I'm sure that must be difficult for you. I miss my parents too; God rest their souls.'

Joanne's face softened at this. But the other girl, Beth, was still glowering in Mary's direction.

'I miss my ma. It was tough not having her by my side for our wedding,' Mary replied. 'And my da, of course.'

'I miss my dad too,' Joanne replied defiantly, as if she was daring Mary to challenge her on this.

Mary saw Beth put her arm around her friend's shoulder, and as Joanne leaned into her, she began to understand why the girls were being so frosty.

'When we move into the cottage, I want you to know that you are welcome to visit any time you like,' Mary said, offering what she hoped was an olive branch.

'That's kind of you,' Ellen replied.

Joanne smiled her thanks too. Perhaps a softening there. But the friend, Beth, threw another loaded look.

'How do you think you'll manage as a keeper's wife?' Kathleen asked.

Mary held her hands up, 'Jaypers, I have no idea what to expect! I suspect my work in the factory won't be that relevant to this new role.' She glanced at Kathleen and Ellen through her lashes to see how they reacted to her admission that she was a factory girl. Did she see a slight sniff from Kathleen? Maybe, and there was definitely a sideways glance towards Ellen. Mary sat up straight and lifted her chin, refusing to be cowed down by these women. 'I've been on the factory floor ever since I left school at thirteen. I made some good friends there. And I'll miss them all terribly. Salt of the earth, all of them.'

Another silence fell between them. Mary couldn't imagine living in the cottage next door to Kathleen Kenefick, who made her feel so unworthy.

'There's a very nice garden out the back of the cottage, that I think you'll enjoy,' Kathleen said.

'We've got drills of potatoes, and a decent vegetable garden, with cabbages, carrots and parsnips. Oh and spring onions and lettuces too,' Ellen said. 'You need to watch out for the caterpillars though. And the pigeons.'

'Why?' Mary asked.

'They'll ruin your crop!' Ellen replied.

'You'll have to make a pit for the winter of course,' Kathleen said.

Mary's head reeled at the thought of why she might need a pit. She glanced at Seamus for support, but he was scoffing his second slice of cake and didn't seem to be paying attention.

'I'm afraid I don't know much about gardens,' Mary admitted.

Kathleen and Ellen exchanged another look, before Ellen went on to explain. 'You'll have to preserve your potato crop for the winter. So you dig out a pit, line it with straw, then put a layer of potatoes in, with a layer of soil over that, and so on and so forth for a few times. You'll get the hang of it quickly enough.'

Mary had had enough. Feeling their eyes judging her, watching her every move was so tiresome. She'd thought she was to be a keeper's wife, not a farmer. 'I need to take some air, so please excuse me for a moment. Don't get up, Seamus. You stay here. I'll be back in a jiffy.'

She walked to the front door and stepped onto the pavement, leaning against the gable wall of the cottage. A sea breeze fanned her face, and Mary closed her eyes as the cool air comforted her.

'Afternoon, Mary,' a voice called out. She opened her eyes in a start. Across the street stood a middle-aged man wearing a trilby hat.

'How do you know my name?' Mary asked, feeling a little startled.

He didn't respond, only smiled. Mary's head swam as she tried to work out who the man was and how he knew

85

her. With one last nod, he walked up the hill towards the Bayview Hotel.

'My mam wants to know if you are unwell?' Beth asked from the front door.

'I'm fine. By any chance do you know who that boyo is?' Mary pointed to the retreating back.

'No idea. Doesn't look local. Why?'

'He called me by my name, and I can't understand how he knows it,' Mary replied.

Beth snorted, then said, 'Maybe your reputation precedes you.'

That was the final straw for Mary, whose nerves were already shot from the afternoon she was having. She'd had enough mouth off this young girl. And as she'd dealt with far worse in the factory, she wasn't scared.

'What is your problem? You've been making snide comments since I arrived, and I cannot work out what I've done!'

'Well . . . you're making my friend and her family homeless,' Beth said meekly, all bravado disappearing now that she'd been called out. Her cheeks flamed red.

'How do you work that out?' Mary was dumbfounded.

'You are moving into Joanne's house. Her dad has died and now they have nowhere to go except to their creepy uncle's house, who wants a free housekeeper and farm workers. Or maybe worse.'

This was all news to Mary. 'Start from the beginning, Beth. Tell me everything.'

Beth finished her tale of sorrow in one garbled breathless recount.

'And I'm sorry for being so mean to you,' she finished. 'I'm not normally like that. But I'm so scared for Joanne.'

'It's grand. I understand,' Mary said. 'Friendships are important, and Joanne is lucky to have you.'

'I wanted to tell you that you are so pretty too. I love that red lipstick you are wearing. I think we could be great friends because I love lipstick too.'

Mary opened her small pillbox handbag and pulled out a Revlon lipstick, pressing it into Beth's hands. 'I have two of them in this shade, so this is yours now. And I'd very much like to be your friend too. I'll need a few on my side to help me settle in and ensure I don't say or do something silly or unbefitting a keeper's wife.'

'You'd do best to do the opposite to me, so. I'm afraid I might be a bad influence,' Beth said breathlessly.

Suddenly Seamus appeared, pulling out a packet of Sweet Afton. 'Are you coming back in? Mrs Kenefick will send out a search party soon.'

'Tell your mam I'll be back directly,' Mary said to Beth. 'I want to have a quick word with Seamus.'

Once Beth had hurried off inside, she quickly filled Seamus in on Ellen's predicament.

'That's a tough spot to be in. But it's par for the course. And she's had almost six weeks to find somewhere else to live.' Seamus passed a lit cigarette to Mary, who took a deep drag.

'I know. But still. It's not easy for them. The thing is, I've been thinking that I'll be in the cottage alone when you leave next Friday for the island, which seems silly. How about the Craig family stay where they are for a

87

little longer? I don't mind sharing. And it will be company for me while you're away.'

'I'm not sure about that,' Seamus said pensively. 'We've just got married. I don't want to start our life together with a house full of strangers.'

'I want you all to myself too, Seamus. But you will be gone for three weeks, until the eighth of June. What if we gave them that long at least to stay? It could take the pressure off if they have a little more time to find somewhere new to live.'

Seamus whistled, 'Wow-wee, you have the biggest heart I've ever come across,' he paused, looking nearly convinced. 'And you're sure you wouldn't mind house-sharing?'

'Look, I've shared a flat with five factory girls for years. There were three of us in that front bedroom, if you remember! I'll be grand as long as I can move into our own bedroom.'

'Well, from what Kathleen has shared, there are three bedrooms in each cottage. I'm sure the Craigs can manage in two,' Seamus said, blowing a perfect O of smoke into the air.

'Does that mean you will agree to it?' Mary asked.

'I can't say no to you. But, this is a temporary solution,' he warned. 'When I get back from my first rota, they'll have to go. I want to walk into my new home, and carry my bride over the threshold, without an audience watching us.'

'Deal!' Mary said, jumping into her husband's strong arms. He spun her around and kissed her firmly on her lips. She had never loved him more.

'Come on. Let's tell them the good news,' Seamus said, and the two of them walked back into the parlour holding hands. Four pairs of eyes looked up at them in question.

'I'm sorry for disappearing,' Mary began, but Kathleen held her hand up.

'It's me who owes you an apology. It must have felt intimidating, with us all asking so many questions. We were not being nosy, just curious to learn a little more about you. And don't worry about the potatoes, I'll help you with all of that,' Kathleen said, her brows knitted together in worry.

Mary exhaled deeply. She hadn't been expecting an apology, but it was most welcome. 'Thank you, Mrs Kenefick. As it happens, I wanted to discuss something with my husband that we'd like to put to you, Mrs Craig.' Mary turned to face Ellen. 'As you know, Seamus will leave for the island on Friday.'

Ellen paled and quickly jumped in, 'The commissioner said we could stay in the cottage until then. You can't ask us to leave yet,' Ellen said, her eyes wide and dark pools on her white face. She turned to Kathleen, panicked, 'I haven't found anywhere else yet.'

Mary quickly jumped in, 'We know that – I'm quite comfortable in the hotel until then. I promise we are not looking to throw you out. The opposite, in fact.' Mary took a deep breath as she looked around the parlour. 'What if you didn't move out? What if you stay put until Seamus returns from his rota? I don't need the whole cottage to myself. There are three bedrooms. I thought if I could have one for Seamus and me, maybe you could share with Joanne or Ger?'

The room silenced. Nobody spoke as Ellen looked at Kathleen, Joanne and then back to Mary again.

'Why would you do that?' Ellen asked, her voice sharp with suspicion.

'Let's just say I know a little about being pushed out with nowhere safe to go. And I hope that it might help to have an extra three weeks to get yourself sorted,' Mary said.

Seamus looked at her, questioning. Mary flushed, realizing she had said too much. She needed to clarify. 'After my parents died, I was on my own. And the kindness of some friends who took me in has always stayed with me.'

'You'll never be on your own ever again, my love,' Seamus said, kissing her cheek softly. She moved closer to him. He would never know how much he had become her safe harbour.

'I'm touched by the generosity,' Ellen said in little more than a whisper.

'My wife has a big heart. It was all her idea. And as I intend to follow my father's advice on marriage, I shall always say yes to my wife!' Seamus joked, with evident pride in every muscle and line on his face.

Joanne's face brightened for the first time in weeks.

'What do you think? Will the commissioner allow it?' Ellen asked Kathleen.

They all turned to look at Kathleen now. She stood up and looked out the bay window towards the black lighthouse tower that loomed in the distance. Then she turned back to the room and said, 'I think it is a perfect – albeit temporary – solution. And a generous one at that.

I'll telephone the commissioner personally to ensure he understands it is the right thing for everyone. I'll tell him that Ellen will stay on to help Mrs Mythen to settle in, in an advisory role. There'll be no overcrowding, the house has room for you all.'

An audible sigh of relief came from both Ellen and Mary.

'Beth, get the sherry, please. I want to raise a glass to Mr and Mrs Mythen, our new assistant keeper and his kind wife.'

'Thank you, Mrs Kenefick,' Mary said, flushed as everyone's eyes watched her. And she felt a new emotion trickle in: *hope*, that this might work out here.

Kathleen walked towards her and clasped Mary's hands between her own. 'I'm so pleased that we are going to be neighbours. But I hope that we can be good friends too. So there will be no more "Mrs Kenefick". I insist that you call me Kathleen.'

Beth ran over and threw her arms around Mary, hugging her close. 'And I know we are going to be *best* friends! Come on over, Jojo, join in too!'

As Mary returned the girl's embrace, her eyes moved to the window and the now empty road outside. She recalled the stranger who'd greeted her and felt a shiver run down her spine. She couldn't put her finger on what, but there was something about him that made her uneasy.

ELEVEN

Mollie

Monday, 10 July 2023

Cork University Hospital, Cork

Mollie, her dad and Aunt Jane sat on either side of Beth's hospital bed while she slept. Hearing how ragged and laboured her breathing was made Mollie's heart constrict in sympathy. A grave-faced doctor told them that Nana Beth had pneumonia, with inflammation in both lungs. Mollie felt groggy and fatigued, with a tension headache that wouldn't budge, despite the Nurofen a kind nurse had given her.

As Mollie watched her grandmother's chest rise and fall, she replayed the last conversation they'd shared – with Nana Beth confessing her vulnerability about dying, and her worry about heaven and hell. Her grandmother had led a good life. At least as far as Mollie understood, anyway.

Did the letter she received earlier that week, talking about family secrets, have anything to do with her grandmother's agitation? Was there some truth to it after all?

'When we went for our walk, Nana admitted to me that she was worried about dying. She spoke about having to face her sins,' Mollie shared in a low voice.

Aunt Jane tapped her chin thoughtfully. 'That's a little odd,' she said slowly. 'Mam did the same before she died, too.'

Mollie had met her great-grandmother Kathleen a handful of times. But that was a long time ago. Mollie had been only thirteen when she died. However, the word in the family street was that Kathleen was a devout woman. Pillar of the community. Maybe it was a religious thing, worrying about hell, that Mollie didn't understand.

'Whatever sins Mom thinks she has to repent for, Granny Kathleen certainly had none!' her dad said. 'Everyone loved her. I remember when she died, her funeral was so packed they had to put speakers out in the streets for those who couldn't fit into the church.'

Aunt Jane nodded. 'I still get people coming up to me saying that Mam helped them somehow. Little acts of kindness that she never spoke about publicly. Only last week I bumped into a woman who said Mam had been in the room when she was born. She assisted the midwife, Ellen Craig, in the delivery. And then when she realized that the woman had very little food in her larder presses, she went around the neighbours and filled her shelves with food for her. Times were hard back then. People complain about being broke, but they don't know the half of it.'

Mollie tried to picture life for her nana back then. But the picture felt grainy as it was so hard to equate that life with the one she knew of her grandmother, living in Camden.

'Wasn't Ellen Craig Granny Kathleen's best friend?' her dad asked.

'She was. And most families in the area knew and loved Ellen Craig too. She was the midwife, and not many children in the fifties were brought into the world, in Ballycotton at least, without the helping hands of Ellen. Myself included,' Aunt Jane added. 'But I often thought that family had a curse hanging over them.' She quickly made the sign of the cross on her chest.

'How so?' Mollie asked.

'Well first of all, Peter, Ellen's husband, died young. And Ger, their son, wasn't much older than his father was when he died himself. His widow is over in Spain, last I heard. Dervla, Ger's daughter, is a Garda – she's up at the farm now, on her own with a baby. No sight nor sound of the baby's father. Some families have it tougher than others, I suppose.'

Should she tell Aunt Jane about the letter, Mollie pondered? She decided to ask some open questions and then play it by ear.

'Did Granny Kathleen ever say what she felt guilty about when she spoke about dying?'

'You'd have to ask your nana Beth that. Those two were as thick as thieves. She moved in with our mam for

94

a few months before she died. And I'll always be grateful that she did. It helped to have my big sister here, sharing the load.'

Mollie watched a shadow pass over her dad's face. She knew this topic was a difficult one for him. While he was still grieving the loss of his father, her nana Beth had decided to move to Ireland to help take care of her mother, leaving him on his own with his grief.

'Mom never really left Ireland, did she?' her dad said flatly, looking at Beth. 'Maybe that's where she went to in her head, when she cut herself off from Dad and me.' His jaw clenched as he thought about those painful moments.

They never knew when Nana Beth would shut down, removing herself from the world, locked in her mind. Mollie remembered one morning when she was perhaps twelve or thirteen. One minute Nana Beth was kneading dough and the next she left the kitchen, bread unmade, and retreated to her bedroom, where she remained for nine days. They also never know how long her bouts of depression would remain. She refused therapy, but her doctor had managed to get her to at least take some medication, which had helped over the years.

Aunt Jane broke the heavy silence that now hung between them all, recalling warmly, 'Mam and Dad would light up as bright as the beacon over on the island as soon as Beth walked in the door to visit. They understood that her life was in Camden, but they loved it when she returned home to them. Beth always said she couldn't stay away from Ballycotton, no matter how hard she might try.'

Could Nana Beth's pull to Ireland have something to do with a secret she was harbouring? A shared secret with her mother, perhaps? Mollie *had* to find a window into her nana's past; everything was feeling too much like a coincidence to her.

Interrupting Mollie's thoughts, a nurse popped her head round the door and reminded them that only two were allowed in at any one time. They agreed to start a rota, taking turns to sit with her, with Mollie staying on now, while her dad and aunt went home.

The room was quiet with the others gone. Mollie walked over to the bed and gently brushed a lock of her nana's hair away from her forehead.

'You've got to fight this, Nana,' she whispered. 'We need you.'

As she turned to move back to her chair, her foot caught on something. She looked down and saw her grandmother's black handbag topple over. Aunt Jane must have brought it in the ambulance. A pack of Fisherman's Friend lozenges fell out, and a Rimmel lipstick. Mollie bent down and scooped them up, placing them back into the bag – and there, sitting inside the handbag, was a long white envelope. Mollie picked it up, her heart hammering fast as she took in the typewriter font.

Surely not? With a shaking hand, Mollie pulled out the contents. A single sheet of folded A4 paper, from the envelope, with a black-and-white photograph of a large group.

You can't keep this secret buried any longer.
You have to tell the truth.

Mollie peered in closer at the image. It showed what looked like a family group, in front of a terraced cottage with a thatched roof. In the centre were four women, side by side. She recognized Nana Beth and Granny Kathleen immediately, but didn't know the other two women beside them. Crouched in front of the women were four children dressed in school uniforms. Three of them looked to be about ten or eleven. And the last around fifteen or sixteen. She turned the photograph over, and written in tiny script was *Powers Terrace, 1951*.

'Oh Nana, what are you hiding?' Mollie said, reaching over to clasp her grandmother's hand, as unease rippled its way through her.

TWELVE

Beth

Beth didn't plan to compromise herself or her relationship with Ted. But when she sat in the audience for the circus with her mother and siblings and saw Christian move effortlessly through the air on his trapeze, she knew she had to see him again. On her own. And when she did, she had to feel his lips on hers.

Beth had been looking forward to the circus for days. And it didn't disappoint. Calliope music filled the air. Exotic animals moved through the large red-striped big top. Lion tamers faced man-eating beasts. Children squealed, and adults gasped at their daring. Monkeys and clowns made everyone laugh till their bellies hurt as they performed tricks. But as each act wowed the audience, Beth waited impatiently for one person.

When Christian and his fellow trapeze artists walked into the main ring, wearing dazzling costumes in gold-and-white, Beth's heart began to race. He scanned the audience before he climbed the rope ladder to the trapeze. And his eyes locked with Beth, making her face flush. He bowed in her direction, and it took every shred of self-control to hide her elation from her mother.

He was not wrong when he boasted that she should wait for the main performance. It felt like Beth held her breath for the entire time Christian defied the laws of gravity and soared through the air without a safety net. She knew she would never see anything as thrilling in her life again.

Once the show was over, they moved outside to the smaller tents. Her mammy gave them each a couple of pennies to play games of chance. Beth's younger brother John won a stuffed animal by beating the coconut shy and then they all went for a ride on the Ferris wheel. Ballycotton had never felt so exciting. As her mammy pointed out the lighthouse, telling them to wave at their father and Ted, Beth pushed down a flash of shame. Her father would be horrified if he knew what his daughter was thinking. As for how heartbroken Ted would be – well that made her stomach clench again, in what had become an ongoing battle between her conscience and her heart.

The smell of popcorn, candy floss and hotdogs made their stomachs grumble and the children begged their mother for another treat. She surprised them by acquiescing with little pressure and they sat side by side on a bale of straw and licked their fingers once they'd finished their juicy hotdogs.

A few moments later, Joanne and Ger moved towards them, their eyes excitedly bright.

'It's good to see Ger so happy,' her mammy said to Joanne.

'First time he's smiled in days,' Joanne agreed. 'Mam didn't feel up to it, but she could see Ger needed a brief break from home. So I brought him.'

'It's been a hard time for you all,' her mammy said. 'And you've been a credit to your mother. Helping her out. You are a good girl, Joanne.'

Beth decided this was too good an opportunity to miss. She saw a chance to escape her mother's watchful eyes, using Joanne as an excuse. 'Can I go for a walk with Jojo? To let her have a little break? I'm sure Ger would love to play with John and Katie.'

'Oh, that would be lovely. Please?' Joanne implored.

'Yes, but meet me back here in an hour,' Kathleen instructed.

Each clutching the other's hand, the girls promised not to be late and then ran off into the crowds of people. A clown on a unicycle whizzed by them and they passed a man eating fire.

'It is the greatest show on earth,' Joanne whispered, turning in a full circle to take it all in.

'Look!' Beth said, spotting a woman wrapped from her neck down to her waist with a snake.

They ran over and watched as the woman charmed her snakes and her audience. Beth was lost in the wonder of it all, when she heard a voice whisper her name. She felt breath on the back of her neck, making her shiver delightfully. *Christian.*

She turned around slowly.

He'd changed from his gold-and-white costume to tight jeans and a white T-shirt, which clung to his abs.

'You were incredible up there,' Beth said.

He inclined his head, accepting the compliment.

Joanne nudged Beth's side.

'This is my best friend, Joanne,' Beth said, remembering her manners.

Christian picked up Joanne's hand and kissed it, making the young girl blush bright red.

'Did you enjoy the show too?' Christian asked.

'I've never seen anything like it before,' Joanne said. 'Your act took my breath away.'

One of the circus staff walked by, a camera hung over his neck.

'Take one of me and the ladies,' Christian called out to him. And his friend duly obliged, with Beth beaming with delight beside him. Christian told them both, 'I'll get a copy for you.'

'You were so daring, Christian. And your costumes were beautiful. The gold so ornate,' Beth said breathlessly, once the photograph was taken.

Christian looked at them both for a moment, then said, 'Come with me.'

He weaved his way through the crowds, and they half ran, half walked to keep up with him. Soon they were in a small tent behind the big top, filled with rails of costumes.

'This is where we keep all the costumes. We have every colour, every gem, and every size. Why don't you both try one on? See what it feels like to be a circus artist,' Christian said.

The girls looked at each other and giggled.

His eyes looked them up and down, and then he pulled two costumes from the rails, passing one to each. 'You can get changed behind that curtain. No one will see.'

'We can't take our clothes off in public!' Joanne exclaimed, looking around her, her forehead creased in a frown, but Beth was enthralled.

'Why not? We all must try new things to feel alive. You might like it,' Christian urged.

Joanne pulled her friend's arm. 'Come on; we should go, Beth.'

Beth shrugged her away and held up the costume Christian had picked out for her. It had a plush red velvet bustier with a short gold tutu frill at its end. She longed to feel it on her skin. She'd never owned anything as beautiful as this in her life.

'What harm can it do?' Beth whispered to Joanne as she made her way towards the curtain. She closed her ears to the sounds of Joanne's protestations, feeling exhilarated by her daring. With a racing heart, Beth pulled her clothes off and then shimmied her way into the costume. She realized it fit like a glove as she reached behind her to pull the zip up. She looked down at herself, not recognizing her breasts that swelled from the top of the bustier. She was no longer the young girl who teetered on the brink of adulthood. At that moment, Beth felt like a woman.

102

Wishing she had high-heeled sandals, she stood on her tippy toes and moved from behind the curtain. She placed one hand above her head and the other on her waist, just as she'd seen the circus performers do earlier, and posed. Christian whistled in appreciation, but Joanne was frowning at Beth's provocative stance.

'What do you think?' Beth asked, fluttering her eyelashes in what she hoped was a flattering way.

'You look like Gina Lollobrigida,' Christian said.

Joanne said nothing, her eyes moving from each of them and back again. 'I don't think your mother would be happy to see you in that. You are as good as naked,' she finished with a hiss.

'Don't be such a stick in the mud,' Beth said. 'Go on, put on yours, Jojo. It feels so good! You'll look so beautiful in it.'

Joanne shook her head vehemently. 'I'm leaving. And if you have any sense, you'll get dressed and follow me.'

'We have loads of time before we have to be back to meet Mammy,' Beth replied. 'I'm staying.'

'So much for doing something together,' Joanne said, giving her one last look of anger and hurt, before she left.

Beth's head told her that she should do as Joanne asked and follow her. That she wasn't being a good friend nor girlfriend in this moment. She should find her mother and siblings, walk home to their cottage and leave her dreams in this small tent.

But Christian moved closer to her, and her heart regained control. She knew she wanted to feel his breath on her neck again.

'I can't stay long . . .' she said breathlessly.

103

'Then we better not waste any time *ma chérie . . .*' Christian replied, running a finger down her cheek, to the nape of her neck.

Beth felt her breath quicken. Whatever he wanted, she would give gladly.

THIRTEEN

Kathleen

Sunday, 13 May 1951

Ballycotton, Cork

Kathleen watched the children spin around on their carnival ride, laughing as she caught sight of their faces alight with joy while they sped by.

'That looks like good fun,' a voice remarked.

Kathleen felt a flutter of nerves jump into her stomach as she recognized the face from the pier. It was Charles Davis, who had just walked up beside her. What was it about this man that unnerved her so? She'd been unable to get him off her mind, so she'd called up to the Bayview Hotel yesterday for morning coffee, hoping she might see him, despite not even being entirely sure that's where he was staying. But when he was nowhere to be found, her own disappointment at this had confused her. So much so that it made her tell Beth an unnecessary lie when she'd commented on her hairstyle. Why hadn't she just said she had been at the hotel instead of stating an untruth about visiting Maureen Doyle?

'Oh, hello there, Mr Davis,' Kathleen responded, composing herself as she greeted him. 'The children are indeed having the time of their lives. But alas, I think it might be a bit too much fun for me. The speed of the Ferris wheel is my limit.'

'The same goes for me. But a little adventure is good for us all.' He took a step back and examined her closely. 'The excitement of the circus suits you. You look like a twenty-year-old woman, standing there with the gentle breeze whipping through your hair; your cheeks flushed the colour of a pink rose.'

Kathleen looked away in confusion. It had been a long time since anyone had paid her such a flattering compliment. There was a time when Patrick would tell her every day that she was beautiful. But that was a long time ago. Kathleen held a hand up to her face, unsure how to respond. 'I think you may need glasses, Mr Davis. It's been nearly two decades since I was twenty.'

'Age is but a number. But I apologize. I did not mean to offend. I forget myself and have been too forward with you.'

'I'm unused to flattery, Mr Davis; it surprised me, that's all. But I'll accept your gracious comment with thanks.'

'I'd prefer it if you called me Charles. I've never cared for formalities.'

'Then you must call me Kathleen.'

Her heart sped up at her daring. Because she was Mrs Kenefick to most around here, except for close friends and family. But there appeared to be magic in the air at the circus, which made her feel reckless and young again.

'Did you enjoy the circus acts earlier?' Charles asked.

'They were wonderful. I've been before, but to a smaller show. This is unlike anything we've had in Ballycotton before. My eldest daughter is off exploring with her best friend, Joanne. They are desperate for their independence.'

'I remember what that was like. Oh to be young again.'

They smiled in recognition of that truth, the sounds of excited chatter drifting toward them with the return of John, Katie, and Ger.

'Here are my younger two and my friend Ellen's son.'

'Your friend is here too?' Charles asked, looking around him.

'No. Mrs Craig is recently widowed and did not feel up to the crowds,' Kathleen explained.

'I heard that there had been a tragic loss in the village, but I did not know it was someone so close to you. Such a sad time for everyone, I am so sorry.'

Before she could answer, the children surrounded Kathleen, jumping up and down, eyes aglow with happiness, 'Can we go on again?' John asked.

'Are your heads not dizzy from all that spinning?' Kathleen said, laughing along with them. It was hard not to be infected by their evident excitement. 'Have you spent all your pennies?'

They nodded remorsefully.

Charles stepped closer to the children and leaned down conspiratorially, 'No circus trip should ever finish without a sugary treat. How about some cotton candy – with your mother's permission?'

This suggestion made all the children so frenzied that Kathleen knew she could not refuse the offer.

'That's very generous of you. But I'm happy to pay for it,' Kathleen said, feeling a prickle of unease ripple down her, accepting the generosity of a stranger.

'Please allow me this indulgence,' Charles said. 'It's been a long time since I got to spoil little ones. You would make an old man happy.'

Kathleen studied him, trying to decipher his age. No more than fifty, so not old, she decided.

The children soon had spun sugar in their hands, and they found a spot to enjoy their treat, where a trio of clowns were performing.

'I wish you would have let me buy you something too,' Charles said.

'Ah, it's very kind of you. But I don't need anything right now.'

'But that makes no difference. A woman should be spoiled and cherished, as I'm sure your husband does for you when he's not on the lighthouse.'

Kathleen turned her back to him, afraid Charles might see a betrayal on her face. An ache had squeezed Kathleen's heart for every occasion she had brought the children to fairs or events without their father.

Patrick should be here, with her, spoiling them all. But he was on Ballycotton Island, miles away. Was he even thinking of them? Did he miss Kathleen? Did he ache to have her lie beside him at night?

She shook her head at her fancifulness.

'You look sad,' Charles remarked, watching her thoughtfully.

Kathleen rolled her shoulders back, and smiled brightly. 'It's impossible to be sad in such a fun place.'

And with perfect timing, two clowns squirted water in the children's general direction, making them squeal as they tried to protect their candy floss. The clowns somersaulted and cartwheeled in front of their audience, ducking and diving as they continued to shoot water at each other. One of the clowns then picked up a steel water pail and ran towards them, grinning mischievously before throwing the contents directly at Kathleen, Charles and the children. They all squealed in fear and merriment, but the pail was only filled with multicoloured tissue confetti, which rained down over them all, tickling their faces.

Kathleen spun in a circle, laughing joyfully in the unexpected colourful shower.

Charles reached over and pulled a yellow strand from her hair. 'You have as pretty a laugh as you have a smile.'

Kathleen felt her heart quicken. This was the third compliment that Charles had given her in less than an hour. There was no doubt that this man was now actively flattering her. She could see interest in his eyes and could not deny how alive it made her feel. But she could not respond to his words. She was a married woman. Her husband, the respected and revered principal keeper. This was crossing a line.

Kathleen took a step back from Charles. And she could see understanding in his face, as he placed his arms behind his back. They watched the rest of the clowns' impromptu show in silence.

'Those clowns! It's been a while since I laughed like that,' Kathleen said, when the clowns took their final bow.

'I suspect you've had a sad time supporting your friend through her recent loss,' Charles said, his face softening with sympathy. 'Just know that I'm a good listener. If you would like, you could share with me your burdens.'

Kathleen had longed for Patrick's counsel these past few weeks, and his silence from the island, save for a couple of short letters, had cut her deeply. She glanced at Charles's kind eyes, and felt a warm glow. There was something so comforting about the man. Was it the soft Texan drawl, with echoes of an Irish accent, almost forgotten? No, it was definitely his eyes, which twinkled with mischief and warmth. It was odd, but Kathleen felt as if she'd known him for decades rather than a few days.

The children were now playfully throwing confetti at each other, a few feet from them. Kathleen lowered her voice, 'I find myself in a difficult position. Ellen and her family must leave their keeper's cottage, so the new keeper and his wife can move in. The new keeper's wife has kindly said they can stay for three more weeks, but after that, they have nowhere to go. I want to help them. I *need* to. I cannot stand by and watch them lose everything. But I am unsure as to what I can do.'

Kathleen sighed, closing her eyes for a moment. 'There are no properties available to rent in Ballycotton at present. So, it feels likely that Ellen will have to leave the village. Which will break the children's hearts. I've accompanied Ellen to Cork city to view a number of options that are available. All within her price range. But that is about all I can say in their favour. One was above a butcher's, and the smell . . .' Kathleen held her hand over her nose, just thinking about it. 'Another was so cramped, and they would all have to share a bedroom.

'I wish . . .' Here she paused as she tried to formulate all she wanted for the Craigs and, if she were honest, for herself too, into one sentence.

'What do you wish?' Charles asked, moving closer to her.

'I wish my husband were here to offer me advice.' She bit her lip as she decided whether to tell Charles about a plan she'd been forming over the past twenty-four hours. His gentle smile of encouragement made her open up to him. 'The thing is, we have some savings. My parents gave me a dowry, which is untouched. A fisherman's cottage is for sale on the Chapel Road. It is smaller than their current cottage in Powers Terrace, with no garden, and it's in need of repair. I don't have enough to pay for the cottage outright, but maybe Ellen could borrow the balance from the bank.'

Charles's eyes widened in surprise. 'That's very generous. I'm sure Ellen would be so grateful. Or do you think she would not accept your offer?'

Kathleen frowned. 'I would hope she would accept in the same spirit the offer would be made. But that is not my problem. The problem is that I am not sure my husband would allow me to do this for Ellen.'

111

'You need his permission? I thought you said the money was yours originally,' Charles asked, raising his eyebrows in surprise.

'What is mine became his when we were married. So yes, I do need his permission.'

Kathleen knew that she could borrow a boat, and row herself out to the island to see Patrick. She'd not done it before, but occasionally one of the wives or girlfriends had made impromptu visits to their menfolk. Kathleen worried though, that if she did that and Patrick refused her request to give money to Ellen, where would that leave them all? A thought snaked its way around her mind. *Don't ask him.* But theirs was not a marriage where they had secrets from each other.

Kathleen's cheeks flamed as she felt Charles's eyes search hers. Would she tell Patrick about her friendship with Charles? No. So there were some secrets she *was* willing to keep, then.

'Hmmm . . . you know, I may be able to . . .' Charles began to speak, then closed his mouth, leaving the sentence unfinished. 'Forget I spoke.'

Kathleen touched his arm, 'Please, finish what you were about to say.'

A shadow passed over his face. 'I like you, Kathleen. Which is why I am conflicted.'

'About what, Charles?' Kathleen's heart began to beat faster as she watched her new friend struggle with his thoughts.

'As you know, my home has been in Texas for a long time now. There, I work for an oil company – one of the world's biggest. It's an exciting time. Even more so, because we have just leased a new piece of land and have struck oil. Our investors are about to come across a windfall.

'Your generosity in helping your friend has deeply moved me. And I would like to help if I can. We closed off investors just before I arrived for my sabbatical, but if I can persuade them to accept one more investment from you, maybe we can find a way for you to get that money for your friend *and* replace your savings. All before your husband even knows what you've done.'

Kathleen's eyes widened in shock at the suggestion. 'I cannot believe you would do that for me,' she said quietly. But then, she thought about the kindness that this man had shown to her children, to her, in the short time she'd known him. She should not be surprised that he would once again offer the hand of kindness to her now that he'd heard about Ellen's circumstances. 'I am truly grateful for your offer.'

Charles frowned, his brow furrowed as he thought, 'Don't thank me yet, it could be tricky. I'd have to call in several favours. But I'm owed them. I could make it work.' His eyes narrowed, and he leaned in, lowering his voice, 'I do not mean to be indelicate, but how much money do you have available to invest?'

'Three hundred pounds. The property I would like to buy for Ellen is on the market for £575,' Kathleen said in a shaky voice.

'A considerable sum. And I can see why you are worried about this. But if you invest, I am confident that your return could be as much as one thousand pounds.'

Kathleen exhaled deeply. If this were true she could

buy the cottage for her friend outright and still leave her savings untouched. Without Patrick even knowing she was doing it. 'I don't know what to say.'

'Good things do happen to good people, you know. It would be my greatest pleasure to make this happen for you.' Then he reached down and touched her hand for the briefest moment, sending an electric shiver down Kathleen's back.

FOURTEEN

Mollie

Tuesday, 11 July 2023

Ballycotton, Cork

Mollie had been awake since 6 a.m.; her body clock had not yet adjusted to either vacation or Irish time, her mind running over and over her worries. After a cup of coffee, she began to pace around the kitchen, picking up a tea towel to dry the already dry dishes that sat on a rack. She wiped the clean countertops. Then plumped the cushions on the sofa, rearranging them twice, before putting them back the haphazard way they were initially. Finally, her phone beeped with a message from her dad. Results from the cultures taken from Nana Beth now pinpointed the cause of her infection. A change was being made in the antibiotics. She was still asleep, which the nurses assured them was normal.

Nothing from Nolan, though. He had been quiet, with no calls or text messages since she'd asked him for space. She was grateful that he was doing as she requested. But why, then, did it hurt?

Mollie picked up the local newspaper and flicked through it, stopping when she came to a piece about the Ballycotton Sea Adventures, which offered tours to the island.

An hour later, wrapped up in a warm fleece, Mollie made her way down the steep incline from the little rental cottage to the pier to find the boat, ready to board the first tour of the day. It had been an impulse booking, but now as the sun peeped its way through white wispy clouds and the wind tickled her face, she knew it had been a great decision. Just sitting around, waiting for news on Nana, was doing her no good.

Mollie made her way towards the end of the pier and found their guide, who was handing out lifejackets to the gathered group awaiting. There were ten passengers in total, but she was the only one on her own. The others in their group were from one extended American family, happily chatting about what they might expect on tour.

Their guide, a grey-haired man with a bright smile and twinkling eyes, addressed them once they were on board their boat, *Yassy*. 'Welcome aboard,' he shouted over the churn of the engine. 'I'm Eddie, your tour guide for the day. I'm retired, but I was a lighthouse keeper, stationed here for three years in the 1960s.'

As the early morning whipped around her, Mollie felt excited at the connection that might exist between Eddie and her family. She raised her hand, and said, 'My great-grandfather was principal keeper here in the early fifties. Patrick Kenefick. Did you ever meet him?'

Eddie weaved his way through the passengers towards Mollie and shook her hand enthusiastically, telling the rest of the group, 'Well now, everyone, this here is keeper royalty – the Kenefick family!' Then he turned back to Mollie and said, 'My father and your great-grandfather were friends. They were stationed together in Fastnet at one point. I remember your grandmother too! Beth, isn't it? How is she?'

Mollie wasn't sure how to answer this. Would they think she was frivolous, out on a day trip, while her grandmother was so ill? How could she explain that she needed a distraction because her every instinct was to be in the hospital by her nana's side? And in a way, choosing to do this tour somehow made her feel closer to her nana. Lighthouses had been woven into her family DNA for generations. Aware that Eddie was waiting for a reply, she settled on a non-committal, 'Nana is doing okay. I'll let her know I've met you when I see her later today.'

The put-put-put of the engine as it roared its way to life filled the air around them and their captain took the boat out of the harbour. It was a beautiful sunny day, with clear skies and calm waters. Eddie pointed out the Smiths Reef, where the SS *Sirius* ran aground in 1847, a pivotal historical moment that led to the Ballycotton

Lighthouse being built. It was a fifteen-minute journey, with spectacular views of the black lighthouse with each passing moment. When the winding path leading to the tower and the keeper's cottage on top of the island came into view, Mollie felt the strangest sensation. It was as if she could feel her ancestors' presence, those keepers and their wives who had walked up craggy rocks on lighthouses around Ireland. Mollie felt a connection to her past so acute it made her breathless.

Once they docked at the small landing pier on the island, they began their trek up the steep grassy incline towards the lighthouse. Eddie ensured that there were many stops along the way to enjoy the views as he shared some history and gave everyone a breather.

'This is the elbow,' Eddie said at the halfway point of their climb. 'Take a minute to imagine how arduous it was for the keepers, who had to carry their loads from the boat up to the top.'

Mollie shivered once again as she imagined her great-grandfather taking a moment to rest in this very spot. She looked out to the blue sea, watching four gulls swoop and swerve overhead, landing on the green grass side by side. Eddie pointed out Mine Head, Old Head of Kinsale and the Gale mountains. Excitement rippled through the group when they spotted several wild goats that still lived on the island, precariously nibbling grass on narrow rocks. They continued their trek upwards and came to the cottages, which once housed not just the keepers but also their families. Eddie explained that before the turn of the century, families had all lived here together, with the children rowing to Ballycotton to go to school every day.

Until a mighty storm destroyed their accommodation beyond repair.

A light breeze kissed her cheeks, and Mollie felt like she was on vacation for the first time since she'd left the TV studios. She took a quick selfie of herself to send to her producer, Lucia. Then sent a second text, asking her to let her know if any further letters arrived similar to the one she and her nana had received. She became aware of eyes watching her. Two women in the group were looking in her direction as they whispered, with their heads bent low. Self-consciously, Mollie smoothed down her hair. Had she been recognized? It would surprise her if so; generally, nobody had a clue who she was in Ireland.

'Excuse me, could I have a selfie with you?' one of the women finally called over in an American accent, holding her phone up. 'We're from Portland. I love watching you and Donnie every morning. Never miss the show.'

'Of course,' Mollie replied, putting on a bright smile.

'We thought it was you. What are the odds?' The woman clapped her hands in delight.

A second woman joined them and said, 'Although you look very different here to the glamorous person we see on our screens daily.' Her face was solemn with disappointment.

'The wonders of a hair and make-up stylist,' Mollie said, shrugging. This wasn't the first time she'd been told this. It never failed to shock her how people could be insulting while they begged for a selfie or autograph.

'It must be lovely to have a beauty squad at your beck and call. Is Donnie as nice as he seems?' the first woman asked.

'Even nicer,' Mollie confirmed, then dutifully posed for the selfie, which in turn made the rest of the family pull out their phones so they could get in on the action too. Before she knew it, Mollie was squished in the centre of the large group, wishing she'd worn a little make-up.

Their tour guide, Eddie, watched everything unfold with amusement, and then he asked for a photograph, too, declaring that he'd never had a celebrity on his tour before.

'Sorry,' Mollie whispered to Eddie as the group began to move upwards again, feeling self-conscious from the unexpected attention. But the kind man waved aside her apologies.

They followed the group into the lighthouse. Mollie marvelled at the granite steps inside the entryway, at the oak handrail that curled its way upwards, a stark contrast to the fossilized shell of the ceiling. She slowly climbed the steps to the observation deck, not because she was tired but because she wanted to take in every moment. She savoured the smell of the ocean and glorious panoramic views as she went.

At the top, Mollie's breath was taken away as she looked out towards the pier at Ballycotton, trying to imagine how hard it must have been for both the keepers and their families: being so close, and yet so far from each other. She couldn't help but wonder if her dad and Nana Beth's sometimes strained relationship had something to do with her grandmother's upbringing. She didn't have a loving father at home much. Had that left its mark?'

Her phone beeped. Ducking away from the others on the tour and swiping it open, Mollie saw she'd received a text message from Lucia with an image attached.

Lucia: *As it happens, I've found post for you that matches the description you gave me.*

Mollie clicked on the image; sure enough, it was the same style and typewriter font as the other two letters. Mollie pinched the screen to zoom in, and saw an Irish postmark again. She typed a response to Lucia.

Mollie: *Can you open it and photograph the message inside, please?*

Then she pinged a follow-up message.

Mollie: *I think I have a stalker.*

Mollie stared at her phone, waiting for the returning message. And when she opened the image Lucia sent, she cursed softly.

She needs to tell the truth.

Who needs to tell the truth? Mollie thought frantically. *Nana Beth?* She pulled out the photograph she'd taken from her grandmother's handbag yesterday and looked again at the faces she recognised of her family – Kathleen and Nana Beth. What were they hiding?

FIFTEEN

Mollie

Wednesday, 12 July 2023

Ballycotton, Cork

Mollie awoke as the warmth of the sun hit her face. She opened her eyes, squinting as bright early morning sunlight flooded her small bedroom. Glancing at her watch, she saw it was almost 10 a.m. She'd slept in. Her neck was stiff, and her back ached the way it did when she'd had a fitful night's sleep.

Mollie looked over to the empty side of the comfortable double bed, the pillows plump and untouched. If Nolan were here, she'd have woken up feeling the weight of his arm and leg draped across her. He was a wriggler and cuddler. Mollie had to suffice with wrapping her arms around herself, feeling more alone than ever before. She missed his calm presence. His strength and practical nature. It had been days now since they'd spoken.

As if she'd conjured him up by merely thinking about him, her phone buzzed, with Nolan on a video call. She propped herself up on her pillows, wiped the sleep from her eyes, and felt her heart quicken as Nolan's face emerged on the screen. His chestnut hair was messy, and his stubble was peppered with grey. Even after all this time, he could make her stomach flip. He had always been so damn sexy.

'Hello,' she said, feeling shy.

'Hello back,' he replied in his soft Boston accent.

'It's so early for you!' Mollie said, doing the mental math and working out that it was 5 a.m. at home.

'I've got an early start today.'

'I'm glad you have! I wanted to talk to you . . . it's been strange not seeing you.'

He smiled sadly, then asked, 'How are you? And how's Beth doing?' His brown eyes were filled with concern as they searched hers.

'I'm good,' Mollie answered truthfully. With all the distractions of her grandmother and the letters, she hadn't thought about IVF or babies for days. And that was a relief. 'But I'm afraid Nana Beth is in hospital, she collapsed shortly after we arrived.'

Nolan cursed under his breath then said, 'Thank goodness you went!'

'I know. But she's holding her own. When I visited yesterday, she slept through. But the doctors reassure us that sleep is the best medicine for her right now. She's responding well to the antibiotics too.' Mollie peered closely at Nolan's face. 'How are you? Are you eating properly?'

'Ben and Jerry are taking good care of me,' he joked, then added: 'I'm eating. Promise. But I have to tell ya, I'm happy to see *you* looking so rested.'

'I just woke up, and it's ten in the morning here. Honestly, I haven't slept that long in forever. It must be the sea air.'

They looked at each other in silence for a moment which seemed to stretch across the thousands of miles between them.

'Nolan . . .'

'Mollie . . .'

They both said simultaneously.

'You go first,' Nolan said, grinning.

'Okay. I was going to tell you that I miss you,' Mollie blurted out, which wasn't what she had thought she would say.

Relief flooded Nolan's face. 'Oh, sweetheart. I'm so glad to hear that. I miss you too.'

'I know. And I feel awful that I've put you through all this.'

'It's not on you. There are two of us in this relationship,' Nolan said graciously.

Another silence sat between them, but this one fitted more easily and pulled them closer together.

'Guess what I've been thinking about?' A small smile played on Nolan's lips.

Mollie smiled back, 'What?'

'Bagel Sundays.'

Bagel Sundays. 'Wow, we've not done one of those in a while,' Mollie said, her mind flooding with dozens of memories. For years, bagel Sundays were sacred for them both. They both worked long hours, six days a week. Sundays were the only day when it was just for the two of them. No alarms were set.

Nolan would go out to get the newspapers when they awoke while Mollie made bagels and coffee for a mini picnic. Then they'd return to their bedroom and spend hours reading the papers and supplements. At some point, they'd move towards each other, the news forgotten as they reconnected, making love. Then they'd lie in each other's arms, talking, sharing, and loving each other.

Mollie's body trembled with regret and longing. How had they ever let those precious days go?

'Sundays used to be my favourite day of the week,' Nolan said, his voice now almost a whisper.

'Mine too.'

'Why did we stop them?'

'You know why,' Mollie said as another reel from their memory archive played through her mind. The one where their spare time became filled with ovulation charts, failed pregnancy tests and needles, jabbing, jabbing, jabbing, until every part of them was bruised and battered.

'I wish . . .' Nolan said.

And even though he didn't finish the sentence, Mollie said, 'I know, me too.'

They both smiled, and suddenly, the last of the distance between them disappeared, and they were back in sync again – Mollie and Nolan. Nolan and Mollie. United.

'There's been some bizarre things going on here if you have time to listen?' Mollie asked, crossing her fingers that he did.

'I've always got time for you.'

So Mollie told Nolan about the letters and the photograph. To his credit, he let Mollie tell the story without interruption.

'What do you think we should do next?' Mollie asked.

'Do what you do best, Mollie. You were a journalist – and a damn good one at that – long before you became a TV anchor. If Beth can't talk right now, then find someone who will.'

Mollie felt a familiar tingle in her fingertips that she always got when she felt a story was in her grasp. 'My instinct is to find out who everyone is in the photograph. I'm not even sure they are alive, though I mean, the photograph was taken over seventy years ago.'

'Could you check archival newspaper headlines to see if anything jumps out from that period?' Nolan suggested.

'That's a good idea. I'm spending a lot of time sitting by Nana's bedside while she sleeps anyhow, so I might as well bring my iPad and do some research.'

'Now you're talking,' Nolan said with approval. 'Take back control. You've got this.'

SIXTEEN

Mollie

Wednesday, 12 July 2023

Cork University Hospital, Cork

'The word is out that you're in Ballycotton.' Jane didn't beat around the bush as Mollie walked into her nana's small hospital room later that afternoon. She was there to take over from Jane for a few hours. 'My Facebook is lit up with messages,' Aunt Jane continued. 'The Ballycotton Sea Adventures page posted a photograph of you, and it's gone viral! Over fifty shares already, like!'

'I'm not sure I'd call that viral, Aunt Jane,' Mollie replied, smiling. She gave her great-aunt a quick hug, then leaned down to kiss her grandmother's forehead. Beth was still deathly pale. She was on a ventilator to help her breathe, and was receiving antibiotics through an intravenous line. She looked frailer than Mollie had ever seen her. 'Any change?'

Aunt Jane shook her head sadly. 'She's still sleeping. The nurses say that she's doing well. That we have to wait and hope the antibiotics do their job.

'Anyway, look at this,' Aunt Jane went on, handing her phone to Mollie, before standing up to stretch her back.

American TV celebrity Mollie Kenefick, descendant of Ballycotton Lighthouse principal keeper Patrick Kenefick, joins the Ballycotton Lighthouse tour.

A photograph of a beaming tour guide Eddie beside Mollie was posted underneath the text. Mollie felt a moment of thanks that she'd made the decision years ago to use the family name of Kenefick as her work pseudonym. Nana Beth had been the one to suggest it, in fact. She hoped she was making all the Keneficks proud, those alive and those gone. Then Mollie felt her stomach lurch as a thought snuck up on her: maybe her nana might not get to see this photograph.

Come on, Nana, you need to get better. I need you. We all do.

'See, there's over a hundred comments, gurl. That's viral as far as Ballycotton goes!' Jane said, interrupting her thoughts.

Mollie found it hard to be excited by the article, her mind so filled with worry for her grandmother, and also, by the anonymous letters. How had life gotten so complicated, so fast?

'Before you head home, Aunt Jane, I need to talk to you about something.' Mollie took a deep breath, then said, 'I've been receiving anonymous letters, which talk about a family secret. I thought it was some kind of hoax, or something aimed directly at me, but while I was at the hospital with Nana yesterday, I found a similar one in her handbag.'

Mollie went on to give her the details of each one. Jane's eyes widened in shock as she listened.

'The letters were all posted in Portlaoise,' Mollie said, pointing to the postmark on the envelopes she had.

Aunt Jane grabbed her reading glasses that sat on the bedside locker and examined the envelope closely. 'That's the central sorting office postmark, gurl. These letters could be posted from anywhere in the country. And there's nothing special about these envelopes either. You can buy them in any supermarket or stationery shop.'

'Oh,' Mollie said, feeling a little deflated that no clues were immediately visible. She pulled out the photograph. 'This photo, taken in 1951, was with Nana's letter. Do you know who's in this picture with Nana Beth and Granny Kathleen?'

'That's your great-aunt Katie and your great-uncle John there,' Jane said, pointing to two of the children in the front row. Aunt Jane pointed to a slight older woman with mousy brown hair tied in a bun. 'And that's Ellen Craig. Those have to be her two children – the little boy is Ger and the older girl in the school uniform has to be Joanne.' Her eyes squinted as she peered closer at the photograph. 'But I don't know who that young woman with dark hair is.'

129

'She looks very glamorous,' Mollie said, taking in the perfect red pout and pinned curls.

'It looks like the photo was taken in front of Powers Terrace, the keepers' cottages. So I'm guessing the mystery woman must be one of the keepers' wives. But 1951 is before my time. And the photograph was with the letter?'

'I can only assume so. It was in the envelope,' Mollie answered.

'What a hateful thing to do, it makes my skin crawl, thinking about someone sending letters like this. To what end?' Aunt Jane asked, her forehead wrinkled in a frown.

'At first I thought it was just a crank. I get a lot of strange fan mail, some from people with too much time on their hands, trying to upset me. Others with tales of woe, begging for money. I've even had a couple from people swearing they have compromising footage of me. I've learned to ignore it all. But now I'm not so sure. Seeing Nana also had a letter really threw me.'

They stood in silence, looking at the letter. Mollie wasn't sure what the next step should be for them. With Nana Beth incommunicado at the moment, they couldn't even ask her, the one person who might have some answers.

'Maybe we should call the Gardaí,' Aunt Jane said hesitantly.

Mollie held her hands up, panic rushing through her at that suggestion. 'Before we call the Gardaí, we need to consider that Nana might be hiding something for a reason. We might risk getting her into trouble if we get the Gardaí involved. Which brings us back to my point:

we need to know what this secret is before we make any big decisions.'

Mollie watched her aunt grapple with this. She walked a few steps to the small hospital window and looked outside.

'You know that Mam had dementia in her latter years,' her aunt said. 'As the disease progressed, she became more and more agitated. So she moved in with me and your late uncle Francis. Mam was confused and tearful most evenings. There were days that she didn't recognize me. Believing me to be a stranger in her home. Others when she thought that I was Ellen, from the keeper days. Rarely, but wonderfully when it happened, she knew it was me.'

Mollie moved closer to her aunt and put a comforting hand on the small of her back.

'Our doctor recommended that we go along with her delusions. The changes in her brain were creating a distorted reality and to try and persuade her she was wrong was too upsetting for her. So, I'd pretend I was Ellen. And she would quieten, calm down, holding my hand as she recalled moments from her life as a lighthouse keeper's wife.

'Mam also used to call out for Beth continuously. Most evenings, she'd ask me to get her, saying she needed to talk to her. But she'd never share with me about what. Her face would cloud up, her forehead rippled in a deep frown, and her eyes filled with tears. That's why I was so relieved when your nana returned home to Ireland for a few months, to help me care for Mam. Because when Mam saw Beth, her face lit up with joy and relief too.

She needed Beth in a way that she didn't seem to need me.'

Aunt Jane's voice trembled as she shared this, locking eyes with Mollie for the briefest moment.

'While I'll always be grateful for Beth's help back then, it was difficult at times too. Beth and Mam were so close. Not easy to feel like the third wheel, gurl. Your grandmother and I are close now. But back then, we were almost strangers. Beth had left Ireland before I was born, so we didn't really know each other.' Aunt Jane's voice now had a hard edge. 'I overheard them once, and I've never been able to let it go. Maybe it's time to get it all out in the open. If there's secrets in this family, I'll not add to them.'

The sound of Beth groaning in her sleep startled them both and they paused for a moment, watching her until she quietened.

'A few months before Mam died, I overheard her say to Beth that she was going to tell Dad what they'd done. Poor Mam spent most of her last years believing that Dad was still alive. Another gift from dementia. I remember Beth saying to Mam that they'd made a vow never to tell . . .' Aunt Jane paused here, her eyes moving from Mollie's to her sister's. 'I walked in and demanded to know what they were talking about. Beth tried to push me out of the door. I wouldn't let her though, and went to Mam's side, telling her that she could tell me whatever it was that was upsetting her. Mam had no peace, she was driving herself crazy with the burden she carried and I wanted to help.' Aunt Jane frowned as she watched her sister lying on the hospital bed. 'Beth told me that I was making things worse. But Mam grabbed my hands, a smile lighting up her face.'

'What did she say?' Mollie asked in a shocked whisper.

'Mam thought I was her friend Ellen again. So I played along. Again. And she said that out of everyone, I should be the one to understand that a wife shouldn't keep secrets from her husband. And that if Peter were still alive, I'd have confided in him about what we did.'

Aunt Jane took a deep breath, closing her eyes for a moment. 'I ignored Beth, who was physically trying to pull me from the room at that point. I literally had to shake her off me. And then I asked Mam what did she want to tell my father, and she said – I'll never forget it . . .' She faltered, her voice thick with emotion. She picked up the letters and photograph, looked at them, then clasped them to her chest.

'What did she say?' Mollie demanded, the hairs on the back of her neck rising in fear. Somehow she knew that, whatever her aunt said, it would be life-changing for them all.

Jane looked at Mollie and answered with a shaky voice, 'Mam said that she needed to confide in Dad what they had all done, while he was on the lighthouse. She said . . . she said that they had killed a man.'

SEVENTEEN

It's quiet. The night is at peace, still and calm.

I sit at the small table, then feed a sheet of paper into the green Imperial 66 typewriter in front of me. It's time to begin my next message. But first, I take a moment to reassess and think.

My gut has been telling me all along that Beth is the key to all of this. When I sent a letter to Mollie too, I hoped to give Beth an extra nudge to finally tell the truth. But I never expected her to get sick. I can only pray that Beth recovers soon. I don't like to think of her in that hospital. At least she has her family around her. This almost undoes me. I push my fingernails into my palms, and I'm okay again.

I pick up my phone and scroll until I find the Ballycotton Sea Adventures post, sharing their delight at having a celebrity in their midst. And I wonder what it must feel like, to be known by so many, receiving adoration from strangers every day. Such a different life to the one I live.

Then I remember the day I took the tour to Ballycotton Lighthouse myself, a few years ago. I posed for a photograph in the exact same spot as Mollie. And somehow, standing there, with the majestic lighthouse tower behind me, I felt hope shimmer its way through me. As if the lighthouse was going to help me, guide me to unveiling the secrecy, once and for all.

I tremble, as a wave of sadness rushes me. And I take a deep breath.

I tell myself that Mollie and her father being in Ireland is good. They might force Beth to tell her family about what really happened in 1951.

I begin to type.

Welcome to Ireland . . .

EIGHTEEN

Kathleen

Wednesday, 16 May 1951

Ballycotton, Cork

Kathleen awoke before the sun had risen. The past couple of days had been a whirlwind. Charles confirmed that he could invest her money, as promised. She'd signed the paperwork yesterday, and handed him her savings. A bank strike the previous year had meant that Patrick had withdrawn their money and hid it at home in a small metal safe. It had felt like a betrayal of Patrick, lifting the loose floorboard and secreting the money in her small brown leather handbag, but she told herself she would tell him when he came home. And she was sure he would understand the reason for her actions.

As Kathleen got dressed, she heard the back door creak shut. Looking out the bedroom window, she saw

Beth whizz off down the street on her bike. There was no sign of Joanne with her, which seemed unusual. Where was her child going to at this early hour? And without her best friend and partner in crime? Unease rippled through her.

Kathleen busied herself with the morning's chores. She cleaned out the Aga stove and then went out to the back garden to get coal from the bunker, making a mental note to order more from the coalman. They were running low. Their unexpected heatwave had disappeared and now the weather was unseasonably cold. Once the fire was set and lit, she prepared the porridge and hung the children's uniforms in front of the stove to warm them through. Patrick would say she spoiled the children. But they were only young for such a short time. Look at Beth, so independent now. Kathleen felt a pang of loss for the little girl who once snuggled on her lap.

She noticed that John's shirt collar looked frayed. She put on her reading glasses and grabbed her sewing kit, unpicking the collar, then turning it inside out, before sewing it back on again.

Once she'd awoken Katie and John and got them ready for school, she was going on an adventure with Ellen. Her stomach danced nervously as she thought about the surprise she'd planned for her friend.

'You look tired,' Kathleen said in sympathy when she saw the dark circles under Ellen's eyes. They were walking slowly, in step with each other, linking arms.

'Not sleeping much,' Ellen admitted. 'My mind is tormented. Do we stay in Ballycotton, close to loved ones at Benny's farm? The children would have a large family

137

home, it's a future for Ger, who would one day inherit the land. And they could continue their education at the same school.'

'But at what cost?' Kathleen asked.

Ellen bit her lip and shrugged. Both of them knew it was unlikely that Ellen could control Benny. Kathleen worried that Ellen and her children would be little more than servants if she said yes to that man.

'What's our alternative, though? There's no news on the job in Glanmire. So I've applied for a job in a sweet factory on McCurtain Street. But if I get it, we'll have to move to Cork city.' Ellen shuddered, before she continued, 'I went back yesterday to view more options.'

'Anything decent?'

'One was a boarding house on Parnell Place that offered bed and breakfast. Three brass beds, all in one room, with a basin and a chamber pot in the corner.' Ellen shuddered, showing clearly what she thought about that option. 'And I went back to that bedsit we viewed above the butcher's. The smell of raw meat was so overpowering that it made me gag. But I suppose we'd get used to it.'

Kathleen felt a rush of gratitude for her own privileged situation. She knew that she would never be without a home, with family on both sides to turn to for support and shelter. But Kathleen also knew that she was in the minority. Thousands were leaving Ireland every year, emigrating to England to escape poverty and in hope of improving their dire circumstances. She half expected Ellen to suggest a similar move for her family.

Kathleen itched to tell Ellen about the fisherman's cottage. She had to purse her lips tight to stop herself blabbing it there and then. But she wanted to show it to her before she told her the plan. She steered them towards Chapel Road, passing the statuesque village church, pausing in front of one of the neighbouring fishermen's cottages.

'Whatever I decide, it has to be in the children's best interests,' Ellen said. 'I don't want them to have the childhood I had.'

Kathleen looked at her in surprise. Ellen rarely spoke about her early years.

'Let's just say that I have few happy memories from then. We were destitute. And I thought I'd put that difficult past behind me, but I'm scared it's about to become a reality again.' Ellen looked away, but not before Kathleen saw her face crumple.

'I won't let that happen,' Kathleen said, then pulled Ellen to a stop. She pointed to the cottage to their right. 'Speaking of which, this cottage has been vacant since Paudie O'Connor died at sea last year. God rest his soul.'

The two women blessed themselves with the sign of the cross, as was the way when talking about the deceased, before Kathleen continued.

'Paudie was a bachelor, and I discovered the cottage was bequeathed to a nephew who lived in Dublin.' She turned to look at her friend as she said this. 'And it's for sale, for £575. Diarmuid Kearney is handling the sale and he's given me the key so that we can look around it.'

Ellen sighed, irritation flashing over her face. 'I can't afford this, as well you know.'

Kathleen ignored her and strode towards the front door, placing the key in the lock.

'The roof needs re-thatching,' she continued as she walked in. 'But Diarmuid reckons minor repairs could be handled yourself, just to get you through the first year. Patrick and Ted can help with that. And a good wash, sand down and lick of paint, sure this front door would look brand new,' Kathleen remarked. 'You can't beat a half door, Ellen. Keep the children in and the animals out, as the saying goes!' But Kathleen's attempt at humour fell flat, with Ellen barely acknowledging her words. Instead she was staring at the property, mouth slightly ajar.

The air inside smelled of dampness and decay, and spider webs draped from the ceiling to every corner. But despite the neglect, Kathleen hoped Ellen could see the cottage's charm. The kitchen was small, with a deep hearth fire located against one wall, that extended to the ceiling. A large Belfast sink sat atop a kitchen unit. Flagstone floors were covered in thick dust but looked in relatively good condition, with only a few cracks running across them.

'Sunshine yellow. That's what you should paint here. We'll put all our kids to work; what do you say?' Kathleen said, which finally made Ellen laugh, and lose her frown, if only for a moment or two.

The second room downstairs was a front parlour, where they found a bird's nest burrowed into an old armchair.

'This is the parlour, your good room. But I thought it could be your bedroom. Let the kids have upstairs; you might even get some peace at night. If you put a single bed in here, there's room for a small wardrobe and even a

140

dressing table,' Kathleen said, using her arms to measure the room.

'You make it sound so simple,' Ellen said. She followed Kathleen up the small, winding stairs.

'Watch your step,' Kathleen replied, choosing to dodge her friend's comment. 'There's a wonky board that will need to be nailed down again. Ted could do that for you. He's very accommodating,' Kathleen said.

'He wants to keep his potential mother-in-law happy. I'd say he'd say yes to anything you request!' Ellen replied, a wry grin lifting her lips.

'Don't go buying a hat just yet,' Kathleen said cryptically over her shoulder. She'd confide in Ellen about her worries over Beth's love life soon enough. For now, this was the priority.

There were two bedrooms upstairs, both of which had beautiful views of the bay.

'Maybe I should take this room myself,' Ellen said, as she looked around the largest of the two, taking in the stunning blue sea, which rippled calmly in the distance.

'Now you're talking! You are so right. Give Joanne downstairs. She'll move out in a year or two, anyhow. A lovely girl like her will be snapped up and married in no time. Then you can make her room a parlour again.'

Ellen laughed out loud now, turning to her friend, 'You are a marvel. You spin such a wonderful tale; I half believe you that it's possible. But I'm afraid I could only afford the £75 part of the asking price. That leaves me £500 short.'

Kathleen shrugged, smiling mysteriously. 'Leave that to one side. Would you like to live here? If money wasn't an issue?'

'Of course! Being in the village, close to everything, would be a dream. I could pick up some work in the Bayview Hotel; perhaps, along with my midwifery and Peter's pension when it comes through, we could manage.'

Then, with the crashing realization that this was a pipe dream, Ellen's shoulders slumped. She turned her back on the view and started to make her way downstairs.

'I'm going to give you the money to buy this,' Kathleen called out, stopping Ellen as she was halfway down the stairs. Ellen whipped around, her eyes round with astonishment.

Kathleen's face was flushed, and her eyes glistened with emotion. 'I have so much to tell you. Let us sit out on the front step.'

They moved downstairs and sat on the cold concrete, side by side as Kathleen told her friend about her investment into the Texas oil fund.

'This all sounds too good to be true. It's as if you are describing a movie,' Ellen stuttered.

'I know. It is quite incredible. But all true. Charles thinks he will have a return for us within the next two weeks. His projections suggest I should have enough to buy this cottage for you outright and replace my savings. All before Patrick comes back from the lighthouse, so he doesn't even need to know!'

Ellen started to shake, her body trembling as she digested the news. Clasping her friend's hand tightly, she could not find words at first. Eventually, she managed to muster the strength to speak coherently. 'I will never forget what you are doing for my family. And I will spend the rest of my days trying to find ways to repay you.'

Then she frowned. 'What about Patrick? If he finds out about this, I can't even begin to think what he'd say. I cannot be the cause of any discontent in your marriage.'

'He won't,' Kathleen insisted, cutting her off. She still hadn't decided if she should tell Patrick about it, once he returned home. Part of her knew that it was too big to keep from him. Unforgivable even. But also, Kathleen couldn't help but admit to herself, that she enjoyed taking charge of the situation. She had found a solution to her friend's issue all by herself. 'Now, let's lock up and get home. We still have to work out where you will stay until the sale of this goes through. But I have an idea that might work.'

Ellen looked at her friend in wonder. 'What else have you up your sleeve?'

'We need to ask Diarmuid Kearney to put it to the owner that you could rent the cottage just until the sale goes through. You can put an offer in, stating you'll buy in cash within the month. But in the meantime, he'll get four weeks' rent. It's a win-win for everyone.'

Kathleen felt a stab of satisfaction when she took in Ellen's mouth, forming a perfect O of astonishment. It was nice to surprise people every now and then. She locked the front door, placing the key in her handbag. Then, arm in arm, they began to make their way back home.

The sun had come out while they were inside. Ellen looked up to it, and said, 'It's like a message from the gods that my luck is now changing. Or a sign from Peter even. We always planned to save up so that one day we'd have enough to buy a small cottage for our retirement, but we never managed to save very much – there was always something more pressing to spend our money on . . .' Her voice broke: 'I . . . I suppose I believed that Peter would grow old beside me.'

'Fate has another future in store for your family. I know it's not the one you would choose, but that doesn't mean you cannot be happy again,' Kathleen insisted kindly.

They heard the sound of a tractor approaching, so the two women moved close to the road's edge to allow it to pass. But the vehicle braked, pulling up beside them. Benny Craig leered down at them both, his eyes roaming every inch of their bodies. Kathleen pulled her shawl tighter around her dress as he climbed down and moved in close.

'Where are you both off to in the middle of the day? Well for you, nothing to do.' Benny's eyes lingered over them, making Kathleen's skin prickle and crawl.

'None of your business,' Ellen replied, lifting her chin in defiance. But her face had paled and Kathleen felt her body shake beside her.

'It is my business. Because no woman of mine will be allowed to gallivant around the place. Not when there's work to be done,' Benny said.

'Well thank goodness that I am not your woman,' Ellen said defiantly.

'Oh, you will be soon enough. I hear you are out of Powers Terrace at the end of the week. I'll be expecting you and yours by the weekend.'

'Well, that's where you are wrong!' Kathleen said, moving closer, stepping in front of her friend. She felt her temper quicken and wanted desperately to take the smug smile off Benny Craig's face. 'Ellen and her family have already secured a new home.'

Benny's eyes narrowed, and he looked over Ellen's shoulder to Paudie O'Connor's vacant cottage just a short way up the road. 'You don't have the money to buy that.'

'Are you so sure about that?' Kathleen said, with a smirk. Then she turned to Ellen. 'You don't need to listen to one more word from this man. Let's be on our way.' And with that she motioned for Ellen to follow her as she moved past Benny.

But Benny was too quick for them and blocked them. He grabbed Ellen's shoulders between his rough hands as he leaned close to her. His breath stank of stale whiskey and something rotten lurked between his broken yellow teeth.

'Mark my words, I'll enjoy whipping the spirit out of you.' Then Benny pulled Ellen in close, thrusting his groin into her thigh, laughing out loud when she gasped in response.

'Get off me,' Ellen said, her voice shaking as she spoke. His eyes darkened, and he responded by squeezing her shoulders so tightly that Ellen cried out in pain as his fingernails dug into her skin.

Kathleen moved fast, grabbing Benny's arm. She roared at him to let Ellen go, but he shook Kathleen off as easily as he would a fly.

Then a man's voice called out from behind Kathleen. They all turned to see who it was. Standing a few feet behind them was Charles Davis. His pristine grey suit and trilby hat starkly contrasted with Benny's muddy overalls and work boots.

145

'Are you okay?' he called to Kathleen as he strode over.

She shook her head, never so grateful to see someone arrive.

'We just want to be on our way,' Kathleen said.

'It's clear that the ladies wish to pass you, sir,' Charles said, moving forward.

Benny looked so shocked by Charles's intervention that he took a step back, his face angry, allowing Ellen to scuttle past and fall into Kathleen's arms.

'It's okay, I've got you,' Kathleen said, shooting a look of fury at Benny.

'Come back here. I'm not done with you yet,' Benny shouted over to Ellen.

'I suggest we keep walking. Let's go to the hotel for a warm drink,' Charles said, offering an arm to both Ellen and Kathleen.

Kathleen clung to him as they made their way towards the Bayview. A few choice curse words drifted back to them from Benny, who was unimpressed by the turn of events.

'What a charmer,' Charles remarked drolly.

'Unfortunately, he is my brother-in-law. He has decided that, as my husband is dead, it is his duty to marry me.' Ellen shuddered, the thought of this getting no easier to bear today than it was when first touted by Benny.

'And I trust you are not amenable to that suggestion?'

Ellen shook her head mournfully.

They made their way towards the residents' lounge in the hotel. Charles directed Ellen and Kathleen to a quiet table near the back of the room then went to place an order for their drinks.

'Thank goodness for Mr Davis,' Kathleen said, nodding at the man's retreating back.

'His arrival was most welcome. I have to admit, I was scared,' Ellen said, her hands shaking still.

'It was horrible. That Benny Craig is far too familiar with you,' Kathleen said. 'I cannot imagine what he would be like if you lived with him.'

'Sweet tea on its way. But in the meantime, I took the liberty of getting these,' Charles said, handing each of them a sherry.

'Thank you. Not just for this, but also for your help with Kathleen's investment,' Ellen said, once she'd taken a sip.

Charles's eyebrows raised. 'So Kathleen told you of her plan.'

'She wanted to give me hope that my luck would change soon.'

'I can understand that. But, ladies, you must keep this transaction between ourselves. I do not want anyone else to know about this opportunity. Walls have ears. And I could be in trouble with my bosses if they knew I'd leaked news of the oil find to anyone . . .' He looked around the room as if expecting someone to be listening.

'I won't say a word to a soul,' Ellen promised.

'Nor I,' Kathleen agreed. 'Have you heard back from your colleagues in Texas yet? When do you expect to have news on my investment?'

Charles took a sip of his drink as he considered this question. 'I do have an update for you. News of the new oilfield will be formally announced over the next ten days or so. We should see an immediate reaction on the stock

147

exchange. The time to sell your shares would be within a few hours of the announcement. I promise you I will watch and advise you when you need to make your move to sell.' He inched closer to them. 'I've fallen in love with Ballycotton. And if all goes as I hope it does, I plan to sell my shares and retire. I should like to find a cottage of my own and spend my last days here.' His eyes locked with Kathleen's as he spoke.

'I'd like that very much too,' Kathleen said. Then she felt her cheeks flush pink when she saw the expression on Ellen's face as she watched her.

Ellen drained the last of her sherry and said, 'Should we make our way home now?'

Kathleen nodded her agreement. 'But only after we visit Diarmuid Kearney.'

They all stood up. As they left the hotel, Charles waved to them both and wished them luck. Together, they returned to Main Street and the small auctioneer's in the village centre to make their offer for the cottage.

NINETEEN

Mary

Saturday, 19 May 1951

Ballycotton, Cork

Mary swallowed down another wave of emotion. Since she'd said goodbye to Seamus the evening before on the pier, she'd been fighting back tears she promised him she would not shed. Mary had watched his boat speed away towards the island and the black lighthouse, knowing that she had to toughen up. For at least the next three years, this would be her life. Three weeks without Seamus, then one glorious week with him. She vowed to make that one week each month the very best. She would dedicate her life to making her husband happy.

They'd moved into the keeper's cottage on Powers Terrace on Thursday. Mary and Seamus now occupied the main bedroom upstairs. Ellen shared with Joanne, and Ger was in the small box room.

Their first night in their new home should have been a milestone moment in their marriage. But it had felt peculiar knowing the Craig family was on the other side of a thin dividing wall. They'd held back giggles as Seamus pulled her nightdress over her head.

'Ssh, they'll hear,' Mary had whispered. But as her husband's touch moved over her body, all thoughts of anyone else but Seamus left her. She flushed now, thinking about their passionate love-making. They craved each other, and Mary could not see that waning ever. Three weeks seemed intolerable to wait until she fell into his arms again.

Now, a little after 7 a.m., Mary stood in her new kitchen, which didn't feel like hers, wondering if she should start breakfast for the Craig family. Her stomach grumbled, which was her answer. A noise startled her from behind, and Ellen walked in, dressed for the day.

They looked at each other shyly, Ellen it seemed, unsure how to navigate this new living arrangement too.

'Seamus got off okay yesterday? You went straight to your bedroom when you got back,' Ellen said.

Mary nodded as she felt tears rush into her eyes and cursed herself for weakness. She would guess that Ellen never cried when her husband left each month. And then she felt a stab of shame, as this thought was followed by the fact that Ellen no longer had a husband.

Mary noticed Ellen look towards the kettle on the Aga stove. *Jaypers, she should have started breakfast.* The two women both moved towards the kettle, reaching it together. In unison, they said, 'I'll make the tea.'

Ellen snapped her hand back and backed away from the Aga, 'Excuse me.'

Mary shook her head and replied quickly, 'No. I'm sorry. You should do it.'

They stood looking at the kettle momentarily as if concrete had secured their feet to the ground, neither making a move. Then the ludicrous moment made Mary giggle, which made Ellen join in until they clung to each other's arms as their bodies shook with mirth.

'How about I make the tea, and you can make the porridge,' Mary suggested.

Ten minutes later, as they both sat down with their tea, Ellen said, 'This is your home now, Mary. If you do not treat it as such, then this kindness of yours will not work.'

Mary acknowledged the truth of the words with a nod. 'But equally, you must still treat it as your home too. For the same reasons.'

They clinked teacups to seal the deal.

'You'll miss Seamus. Which is totally normal, for us keepers' wives.' Ellen bit her lip, then finished, 'It reminds me of how Peter and I were when we got married.'

'I can't imagine how difficult this is for you,' Mary said, reaching out to touch Ellen's shoulder gently.

Ellen clasped the younger woman's hand under her own for a moment. 'I hope you never find out the pain for yourself. It still feels so surreal. I'm not sure I'll ever get used to him not being here.' Then Ellen smiled brightly, 'But it's a joy to me, seeing you and Seamus together. Proper sweethearts you are.'

'I love him so much,' Mary whispered, feeling another wave of emotion rush over her.

'And he loves you too. I always say that the time goes slowly at first, but once you reach the halfway mark, it will speed up double time. I promise you. Try not to think about it too much. Find something to focus on while he's gone.'

Mary nodded, looking around her new home. She'd like to do quite a few things to make it feel more like hers. 'I like it here, in Ballycotton. Everyone is so friendly and welcoming. But I wish our first placement meant we could live together rather than apart like this.'

'That will come – plenty of lighthouses allow the keepers' wives to live beside their men. When we were newlyweds, we spent several years at Hook Lighthouse. And as I watched Peter do his job, I learned to be a keeper myself.' She shook her head sadly, muttering, 'I could do that job in my sleep.'

'It should be you taking over Peter's job, not my Seamus,' Mary acknowledged a little sheepishly. 'You're very capable.'

'Could and should are two very different things. Women have been keepers unofficially for hundreds of years here in Ireland. We have a bit of catching up to do, with how other countries operate. Did you know that in America, the first woman lighthouse keeper was appointed in the 1700s.'

'I didn't!' Mary said. 'One day, there will be women lighthouse keepers in Ireland, too! I think I should like to try my hand at it, if I were allowed.'

'I hope I'm here to see it,' Ellen said, and they both clinked their cups for a second time to that thought. Then Ellen added, with a little wink, 'You might be glad to get this station out of the way before children come along.

Better to be stationed *with* your husband when you have small ones. Peter was great with my two. He always kept me company on my night feeds, when he'd be up anyhow, on light watch.'

Mary beamed as she imagined cradling a baby in her arms. Starting a family with Seamus made her want to weep with joy. They would give everything to their children that her parents had not been able to provide her with.

'Have the wives ever surprised their husbands on the island? You know, taken one of the boats over to the lighthouse?' Mary asked tentatively. 'I could bring a picnic maybe . . .'

Ellen laughed, shaking her head as if Mary had suggested armed robbery. 'As if! No, the island is for the men. The wives stay here. Well, in the main. There are always exceptions!'

'But what if you need to talk to your husband? If there is an emergency?'

'Then you use the semaphore flags. Tradition is that the wives and children congregate on the pier every Sunday afternoon for a weekly flag chat with the keepers. You'll be there this Sunday. It will be nice for Kathleen to have the company.'

Ellen did not have to mention that she no longer needed to go to the pier herself. It hung in a cloud of grief between them.

'Will you teach me how to use the flags?' Mary asked. 'I wasn't a quick learner in school. I'm not sure I'll be much use at it. If it wouldn't be too upsetting for you, that is.'

'It would be my pleasure to teach you. And you'll pick it up soon enough,' Ellen said kindly. 'And if you need anything else, just ask.'

Sounds of the children getting up floated down the stairs. Ger came rushing into the kitchen, followed by Joanne. They stopped at the door when they saw Mary sitting at the table. It was as if they'd forgotten she would be there. They each said a whispered hello as Ellen told them to sit for breakfast. She ladled porridge into bowls and passed them to each. Silence fell into the kitchen again. Mary felt like an intruder, and awkwardness had returned despite the earlier breakthrough with Ellen. Mary wanted to escape, so she stood up from the table.

'I think I'll take a walk,' she announced suddenly. 'Enjoy your breakfast children. And I'll see you later, Ellen.'

She grabbed her woollen coat and then escaped from Powers Terrace.

Walking down the road, she met Beth cycling, jumping off her bike, her face glistening with sweat.

'What time is it?' Beth asked, looking around her furtively.

'Just after seven thirty. Are you in a rush?'

'I'm in so much trouble if I get caught!' Beth said. 'I snuck off earlier for a . . .' She paused and didn't finish the sentence. But judging by the blush on her cheeks, Mary guessed it was a romantic dalliance she was returning from. 'It's easier to be home before Mam gets up, that's all. She was asking too many questions yesterday.'

'It seems quiet in there. You might get away with it yet,' Mary said, amused by the girl's predicament. She remembered what it felt like to be that age, with adventure around every corner.

'I should be used to being in trouble. I'm always in bother for something or other,' Beth replied, grinning.

'Was it worth it? Wherever you were this morning?'

Mary's answer was the smile that lit up the girl's face.

'Good luck!' she called after Beth's retreating back.

Mary continued walking through the village. Ellen had also mentioned to her that some wives sent semaphore messages from the grounds of the Bayview Hotel, which offered a perfect vantage point to and from the island. As she was passing, she decided to check the location out. If Seamus looked in this direction, seeing her tiny silhouette standing on the edge of the cliff would be a pleasant surprise. Mary began plotting what her first flag message might be. It could only be one, she thought. Her first lesson would be learning to say, I Love You. It felt pretty romantic the more she thought about it. Absence *would* make their hearts grow fonder.

'Hello, Mary,' a voice called out as she walked onto the driveway to the Bayview Hotel.

She stopped, swivelling around in surprise. It was the same man from outside Powers Terrace the previous week. And now she was sure it was also the same man who'd been watching her on the day they'd checked into the hotel.

'Good morning, Mr . . .' she replied, deciding it was time to find out who he was.

'Mr Davis. Charles Davis.'

155

'How do you know my name? I don't believe we have met before,' Mary said. She didn't like the way he looked at her so knowingly. Unease trickled its way down her back. She took a closer look at him, and his smile slipped. Something about his eyes, as they narrowed, watching her, triggered a memory. She'd met him before; she was sure of it. But for the life of her, she could not work out where.

'You'd be surprised by how much I know about you, Mary. Or rather, about who you used to be. This version of you, the respectful lighthouse keeper's wife, is one I need to become more acquainted with.'

A shiver ran down Mary's spine that chilled her to the bone. He knew her from before. And he was playing games with her. She lifted her chin defiantly and said, as firmly as possible, 'I don't care for your tone, Mr Davis.'

He held his hands up in mock surrender. 'I wish only to be friends. That's all.'

Mary had met enough liars in her life to recognize one in front of her. He wanted something from her, but *what*? 'Just spit it out. What do you want?'

He moved closer to her, his eyes dancing with amusement. 'I have a question for you. Have you told your husband about who you are? Or rather, who your *father* was?'

Something about his tone, about the way his lip curled as he spoke, about the way his eyes darted to her face gave Mary a sudden flash of clarity. She knew where she'd seen this man before.

In Mountjoy Prison.

PART TWO

Friends are like lighthouses, with the sources of light coming from their hearts

Tom Baker

TWENTY

Mollie

Thursday, 13 July 2023

Cork University Hospital, Cork

Mollie put down her iPad when she heard the rustle of bedclothes beside her. Her stomach flipped when she saw Beth's eyes open, wide with confusion as she looked around the small hospital room.

'It's okay, Nana, I'm here, you're safe,' Mollie said softly, reaching out to clasp her grandmother's hand.

Nana Beth closed her eyes again and Mollie thought she'd gone back to sleep, but then she opened them and smiled at Mollie.

'You look pretty.' Beth's voice was little more than a raspy whisper. 'You've caught the sun.'

Mollie had to lean in close to hear her. She kissed her

nana's forehead. She felt a pang in her chest, her heart aching with bittersweet joy that Beth was finally awake. For days, she'd slept through every visitor who'd sat with her, and Mollie had assumed that today's visit would be like all the others.

'Dad left half an hour ago. He's been by your side pretty much every day since you came in,' Mollie told her.

'He's a good boy. Always has been.' Beth shifted in her bed. 'What time is it?'

'Two o'clock. How do you feel?'

'Tired,' Nana Beth said. 'Sleepy. Thirsty.'

Mollie poured a fresh glass of water and held it to her grandmother's mouth so she could take a sip.

'Tell me about your day,' Nana Beth said, as she sank back into the soft white pillows.

'Well, I went for a long walk this morning before I came here. I started off at the Ballycotton cliff walk. Gosh, it's breathtaking.'

'Describe it to me,' Nana Beth asked, closing her eyes again.

Mollie reached over to hold her nana's hand, taking a moment to find the right words to give justice to Ballycotton. 'The Atlantic Ocean roared today, spraying my face with salt, as waves crashed onto the Ballycotton cliff edge.' Mollie licked her lips and could still taste it. 'Dark craggy rock peeped out from the black waters, with grasses and gorse. And of course, keeping a watchful eye on everyone was the majestic black lighthouse.'

A glimmer of a smile played on her grandmother's mouth as Mollie spoke. As she was clearly enjoying listening, Mollie continued.

'Remember how we used to look for dolphins when I was a child? I looked for them today, but couldn't spot any.'

'They are hiding in Ireland's Atlantis,' Nana Beth whispered.

Mollie looked at her in surprise. 'Atlantis?'

'There used to be another village. But it's under water now.'

As a kid, Mollie had been told about the erosion that submerged the original Ballycotton village hundreds of years ago. She'd forgotten it until now.

'I often wonder . . . if all the souls lost to the sea . . . now live in that ghost town,' Nana Beth said brokenly. Her face changed, her eyes darkened and her lip trembled.

Mollie felt a shiver run down her spine and decided to move on from any further talk about ghosts.

Nana Beth began to cough, so Mollie gave her another drink.

'Try not to talk, Nana. I'll do the talking for us, okay? Now where was I? I ended up at Powers Terrace. I've not been there in years. It was nice to see your childhood home. It looks great. The owners have painted it recently.'

'Happy memories there,' Nana Beth whispered.

She opened her eyes again, and looked at Mollie. 'We didn't have much, but we had each other. A tight-knit group in those terraced houses. Looking out for each other. We shared a garden across the road. I spent hours on the green, skipping, playing tag and chase with the Craig children.'

Mollie loved seeing her grandmother's obvious joy at this memory. And she knew that this was the perfect time to ask her nana more about the secret. But she worried that, if she did, she might upset her.

'What is it?' Nana Beth asked.

'You don't miss much,' Mollie replied with a smile.

'Ah, your face has always been an open book. What's on your mind?'

Mollie reached into her crossbody handbag and pulled out the photograph she'd found with Beth's letter.

'I found this and the letter in your handbag. It fell out. I wasn't snooping, I promise,' Mollie said. 'This photograph was taken in front of Powers Terrace, wasn't it?' She handed it to her nana.

If Nana Beth was surprised to see Mollie with the photograph, she didn't show it. Just nodded in response.

'Who is this, Nana?' Mollie asked, pointing to the mysterious dark-haired young woman. Her heart began to race at the thought that finally she might have some answers.

'Mary Mythen. She became a very dear friend to me.' Nana Beth smiled wistfully. She pointed to the glass of water and Mollie lifted it to her lips once again. 'I remember the day they arrived in Ballycotton, Seamus and Mary . . . How happy they looked.' She paused for a beat. 'The way Mary looked at her husband, and the way he looked back at her – they adored each other.'

'Is Mary alive still?' Mollie asked.

'Yes. I went to see her in Wexford last week. She's almost ninety-four years old. It was good to see her.'

'How is she?'

'Ready to die.' She gave a weary smile. 'Seamus went years before Mary did. She wants to go to him.' Beth looked down to her wedding ring wistfully. 'We all ended up widows in the end. Our husbands going before us. I often think of that: lousy luck or payback.'

A stray tear escaped from Nana Beth's grey eyes. Mollie plucked a tissue from a box that sat on the bedside locker and dabbed the tear away from Beth's cheek. 'I'm sorry, Nana. I didn't want to upset you.'

Her grandmother closed her eyes, and her breathing slowed down. She'd fallen asleep again. So Mollie sat back, returning the photograph to her bag. It was frustrating. She had so many questions to ask, but for now she had to leave them.

Mollie picked up her phone and tapped the screen saver to look at a photograph of Nolan and herself, laughing as they posed on a night out, cocktails in hand. She felt an ache of loss and regret.

And then Nana Beth began to move on the pillow, tossing her head back and forth. She mumbled words that didn't make any sense. Mollie leaned in close again, trying to decipher what she was saying, but it was gibberish, spoken in stupor.

Mollie whispered words of comfort to her grandmother. It was so strange to see her looking this frail and vulnerable. And she obviously had demons from her past that tormented her. Mollie's mind raced with Granny Kathleen's dementia and how she'd spoken about killing a man. She shuddered, then shook her head as if to throw the thought away. That was nonsense. Whatever her grandmother had done, it couldn't be that.

She gently stroked her nana's hand until she quietened once again.

TWENTY-ONE

Mollie

Friday, 14 July 2023

Ballycotton, Cork

A burnt-orange sun flooded the kitchen windows. Mollie had spent several frustrating hours on her iPad, researching events and headlines, trying to uncover anything that might have happened in Cork in 1951. While she didn't come up with any firm clues, her journalistic juices were flowing and she couldn't wait to continue delving into her nana's past.

'You look less stressed than I've seen you for weeks,' her dad said, smiling at his daughter as she filled the water in the Nespresso coffee machine.

'I'm just so relieved Nana's improving. It felt so good to hear her voice again, if only for a short time when she awoke. Do you think it's a good sign?' Mollie asked her dad hopefully.

'I do. I thought her colour was better yesterday too.'

Mollie exhaled deeply, feeling lighter than she had done in days.

'I have a meeting with her doctor today, and hopefully the update will be positive. I want to see you smiling again; there's been too many frowns recently for my liking,' her dad said softly. The sound of the Nespresso machine whirring into life filled the kitchen. 'What are you planning today? I'm heading to the hospital shortly.'

Mollie opened her notebook and turned it around to show her dad the family trees she'd compiled of the people in the photograph. 'It's sad, really. From what I've gathered from Aunt Jane and Nana Beth, the only people alive are Nana Beth, this girl here, who is Ellen's daughter, Joanne, and Mary Mythen – but she's quite frail. I'm not sure she'll be much help to me. I've been scouring the internet, looking into any headlines or stories that might be linked to whatever the big secret is!'

Her dad raised an eyebrow as Mollie sipped her coffee and peeled a banana. Mollie had filled him in on all the developments with the anonymous letters, the previous evening. 'And have you had any luck?'

'Well, I looked online for death records in 1951 in the Ballycotton area. Surprisingly complicated! You have to have a name to search effectively on the digital platforms. I thought I might visit the graveyard. Go old school and see if I can see any headstones for the right time period.'

Before her dad could reply, Aunt Jane walked in through the back door, a full brown paper bag clasped in her arms. She wore a flowing maxi dress in bright rainbow colours. 'Hello all – lovely soft day out there.'

'You look great,' Mollie said, complimenting her.

'Thank you, gurl! And I have soda bread for you, baked fresh this morning. Not by me, I hasten to add. With a cut of cheese and the tomatoes I gave you yesterday from the garden, that's lunch sorted.'

'Sounds delicious. You don't have to keep coming by with food for us though. You have enough on, what with visits back and forth to the hospital.' Mollie stuffed the last of her banana into her mouth to stave off hunger pangs in the meantime. Never mind losing pounds while on her vacation – she'd return to the TV studios another stone up if she wasn't careful. Her great-aunt was a feeder and kept tempting her with gorgeous food that was hard to say no to. 'I'm hoping you can help me fill in some gaps in my family history. I've been drawing family trees for the Kenneficks and Craigs. By any chance do you remember how Ellen Craig died?'

Aunt Jane stopped momentarily, her nose wrinkling up as she pondered the question. 'Gosh, that's a long time ago – 1975 or 1976, it must have been, because I'd started seeing Francis. I remember him coming to the funeral with me. Terrible to say it, but it was a great night afterwards. We drank and danced it out in the Pier Bar until the wee hours. Nothing like a good funeral to pull everyone together.'

Mollie and her dad exchanged a smile. Their aunt was renowned for being a party animal, always the life and soul whenever there was one, dancing and singing until she was the last person standing.

'Ellen must have been quite young then?' Mollie asked.

'She was, yes. Early sixties. It was a stroke, God bless her. Her daughter Joanne found her and called an ambulance as I recall, but Ellen didn't last more than a few hours in Cork General Hospital. Mam was devastated. Rarely a day passed that they didn't see or speak to each other. Of course by this stage, Mam and Dad had moved back to Ballycotton. They bought a house, knowing they wanted to spend their retirement here.' She paused again, before adding, 'That's right, it's coming back to me now. Dad would have been stationed in Galley Head at the time, working month on, month off.'

Mollie felt a pang of sympathy for her great-grandmother. She must have missed her best friend, when she died. And also a little envy of their friendship too. 'I've been thinking that I should pay a visit to the Craigs. Either to see Joanne, or Dervla, Ger's daughter? Maybe they will hold a key to help unlock this secret of Nana's.'

'You can't just go barging into someone's house gurl.' Aunt Jane looked horrified at the idea. 'We need to keep this quiet, not tell people willy-nilly.' Two spots of red danced on her cheeks now. 'And Joanne isn't even up on the farm anymore. She moved into a retirement home, last I heard.'

Mollie looked at her dad for support and he didn't let her down.

'Mollie knows how to be discreet. Plus we need to find out who knows what. What if Ellen told her kids about this big secret before she died, and they in turn told the grandkids? Dervla might have answers for all of us,' he answered.

Aunt Jane frowned, drumming her fingers on the countertop. 'You don't think . . . ? No, it's absurd to think the letters are coming from one of the Keneficks' oldest family friends.'

'Well, someone is sending the letters. And the only way to work out why is to find out what the secret is,' Mollie insisted. She felt her eyes fill up with unexpected tears. This trip to Ireland had been unplanned but, now that she was here, Mollie was convinced that it was for a reason: to protect her beloved grandmother – from the person sending the letters, and to the secret they alluded to. 'I'm going to visit Dervla Craig, no matter what you say.' Then before they could come up with any more reasons why she shouldn't go, Mollie grabbed her car keys and ran out the door.

The farm was only a few miles from the cottage, so it didn't take Mollie long to get there. She drove between two old pillars, with a shock of green moss growing on their tops like a cap. Two heavy red iron gates lay open. The driveway, a laneway with loose gravel, took her to a large two-storey farmhouse. Haybarns and outbuildings stood to the left, all with matching pillar-box-red roofs.

It was as if time had stood still here. Hedgerows and stone walls framed a patchwork of earthen fields. The sound of a tractor in the distance echoed into the car.

She made her way to the front door, which was painted a rich emerald-green. Mollie rapped the large brass knocker, and then she heard the sound of footsteps.

Mollie took a step backwards, stumbling, as the sound of a baby's cry echoed towards her. Then a pale woman, roughly her own age, with dark circles under her eyes came to the door.

'Hello?' It was a question rather than a greeting.

Mollie gathered herself and flashed her best hallmark smile. 'Hi! I don't think we've ever met but I'm Beth Kenefick's granddaughter, Mollie. I'm on vacation here from Maine. And I just thought I'd stop by and say hello. My grandmother, Beth, and her mother Kathleen and your grandmother were all great friends.'

There was a polite smile of acknowledgement from the woman as the sound of her baby's crying increased in volume. 'Sorry, I'm about to feed my baby. He's hungry – with little patience, as you can no doubt hear for yourself.'

Mollie felt a stab of embarrassment. Her great-aunt had been right; it was unfair to just call unannounced. 'I'm sorry. I shouldn't have just landed on your doorstep. I can come back at a more convenient time.'

A smile broke over the woman's face. 'If you're happy to chat while I feed Kian, you're very welcome. I'm Dervla, by the way.'

Mollie followed Dervla into a bright, cream-painted hallway with black-and-white flagstone tiles on the floor, then into a large open-plan kitchen and family room.

'This is lovely,' Mollie said. 'What a gorgeous space.'

'I gutted it after I moved in. This part we're standing in is an extension.'

Mollie could see the pride on Dervla's face as she picked up her baby from his crib. He immediately stopped crying as she nestled him close to her. She thought of Nolan, and the many times she'd witnessed him be a baby whisperer to his nieces and nephews, whom he adored. He instinctively knew how to rock a baby, while Mollie always felt awkward and unsure. She took a seat opposite Dervla on a comfortable L-shaped sofa.

'He's a mama's boy,' Mollie remarked, seeing the baby look up adoringly to his mother.

'He is. A little pet and no bother at all. Until bedtime. I'm currently at war with him, trying to get him to sleep through the night. I don't normally look so tired. You caught me not quite looking my best.'

Mollie uttered reassurances to the contrary.

Dervla picked up a prepared bottle from a bowl of hot water, tested the temperature on her wrist, and then began to feed Kian, who reached up two chubby hands to clasp the bottle tightly.

'You make that look easy,' Mollie said.

'I learned pretty fast. But you should have seen me the first week. I was all fingers and thumbs. And terrified. I was alone and never wished my mother was around more than in that moment. She lives in Spain. She relocated there, after my dad died,' Dervla said.

Her honesty touched Mollie, and she felt a rush of warmth towards her. She couldn't help but wonder where the baby's dad fitted into the equation.

Dervla's face softened as she looked down at her baby. Her tiredness seemed to disappear, and in its place came contentment. Mollie felt her own heart swell at the sight of mother and child. And she placed a hand on her stomach for a moment, imagining another world where the IVF had worked and right now, she was pregnant. Her body slumped as she fell back into the soft cushions.

Mollie exhaled deeply, unable to hide from the truth that she still only felt stark relief. But there was no time to process this. Not here.

'You said my grandmother Ellen knew your grandmother?' Dervla asked once Kian was settled into his feeding routine.

'Yes. My grandmother, Nana Beth, is in hospital at the moment. And I thought it would be a nice surprise for her if I put together a scrapbook of her life. And as Kathleen and your grandmother Ellen were such good friends, I wondered if you had any photographs we could get a copy of?' Mollie didn't want to mention the letters yet; if Dervla had never heard of any old family secret, she didn't want to scare her – and if there was any chance it *was* Dervla sending the letters, it would be better not to mention them yet.

'Oh, that's a lovely idea! I bet Beth will love that. I'm sorry to hear she's been unwell. I'd love to be the kind of person who scrapbooked. I'm afraid I'm rather unorganized.'

Mollie felt like a fraud. Like Dervla, she hadn't scrapbooked in her life either.

'The thing is, all of Ellen's photo albums are with my aunt Joanne – she was Ellen's eldest kid. She's in a retirement home in Glebe now.'

Mollie was sure she noticed Dervla's jaw tense as she mentioned Joanne. She stored that away in her brain.

'She's sharp as a tack still. Her legs aren't what they used to be – she's run several marathons over the years

– but her brain is years younger than she is.' There was no doubt now – Dervla pulled a face, throwing her eyes upwards. 'Aunt Joanne keeps all of us on our toes.'

'You don't get on?' Mollie asked.

Dervla laughed. 'Am I that obvious? I'd never be a poker player, would I? She's my aunt, and for that, I'll always give her respect. But she's a . . . difficult woman. Always has been. I'm her only family around here, which means it's up to me to visit. I do it for my grandmother and father's sake more than anything else.'

Mollie took a beat to digest all of this. 'Families, eh?'

'Tell me about it.'

Mollie knew this was as good a segue as she was likely to get. She took a deep breath and dived in. 'They're always full of secrets too. It's like pulling teeth to get Nana Beth to open up about what she and the other lighthouse keepers' wives got up to when they were all stationed here in Ballycotton in the early fifties.'

Mollie watched Dervla carefully. But the woman didn't flinch or move a muscle in response to Mollie's words.

'Funnily enough, that time is all Joanne talks about when I visit her. About her father – Peter – in particular. And what it was like to be the daughter of a lighthouse keeper. She had a lot of pride in him. I sometimes think the only time she was happy was when he was alive. He died when she and my dad Ger were so young.'

Mollie felt a wave of sadness. How awful to have been so changed following her father's death at such a young age. She couldn't imagine life without her own dad. He'd always been there for her, from her childhood to now.

Mollie's mind raced as she tried to work out how to

bring up the subject of secrets. In the end, she figured an open and honest approach was probably the best bet.

'This might sound strange, Dervla, but Nana Beth mentioned some secret she shared with your grandmother Ellen. And Nana Beth's mother Kathleen. Have you ever . . . heard anyone mention it? Your aunt or anyone else in the family?'

Dervla looked blankly at her as she rubbed little Kian's back, winding him following his bottle. 'Gosh, not to my knowledge. But sure, all best friends have a few skeletons in their closet, don't they? Goes with the territory. If my pals spilled the beans on what we got up to back in the day, I'd be in trouble.'

Mollie laughed along with Dervla at her joke, but inside she felt only sadness. Whatever skeletons were lurking in her family's closet might have the power to hurt her grandmother. And that thought terrified her.

'Would it be okay to visit your aunt Joanne?' Mollie asked. 'I'd love to see those photo albums of hers.'

'Oh God, yes, please do! It would be more than okay. I've been feeling awful that I've not gotten in to see her this week.' She frowned as she admitted, 'I couldn't face her while this sleep deprived. I need the full of my health to listen to her disapproval of my life choices.'

Mollie bristled on Dervla's behalf. She hated people who passed judgement on others.

'From where I'm sitting, your life choices look pretty decent to me.' Mollie smiled warmly. 'I'll leave you and Kian in peace – if you could give me the address of the nursing home, that would be great.'

With the Eircode stored in her phone, Mollie said her goodbyes. It was time to see what Joanne had to say.

TWENTY-TWO

Mollie

Friday, 14 July 2023

Oaklodge Retirement Home, Glebe, Cork

The twenty-minute journey to Oaklodge Retirement Home passed in a flash. Mollie thought over her meeting with Dervla as she drove; she liked her. And she couldn't imagine her being behind the letters.

'Not a bad place to end your days,' Mollie said quietly to herself as she turned into the driveway of the retirement home. The imposing horseshoe building sat nestled in a patchwork of green fields.

She parked up and then made her way to the glass atrium entranceway.

Mollie noted the receptionist's name badge before she spoke. 'Hello, Sandra. I'm a family friend of Joanne

173

Craig. Her mother and my grandmother were childhood friends, and I hoped to visit her.'

'Oh, how lovely. Joanne hasn't had anyone in to see her for a couple of weeks. She was grumbling about that earlier. This will cheer her up,' Sandra replied. 'One moment, and I'll just find out where she is.' Sandra walked through the double doors into the main building, telling her to take a seat. Mollie scanned the area, where two rooms with glass doors sat on the left of the reception, each with a sign overhead: Library and Television Room.

A few minutes later, Sandra returned, beaming, and Mollie felt a frisson of excitement as she followed Sandra down the corridor. This woman was a tangible link to her grandmother's past – her best friend back then.

Joanne's room was painted a bright lemon, and the early afternoon sunlight streamed in through a large window, dancing around the room. A large flat-screen television was playing a quiz show, and Joanne sat in a comfortable wing-backed chair, watching them curiously as they entered. She was thin and bird-like, her face gaunt and lined.

'Joanne, this is the family friend I mentioned. I'll leave you to have your visit together,' Sandra said, her voice rising slightly as she spoke.

'I'm old, but I'm not deaf, you silly girl,' Joanne replied acidly.

'Good luck,' Sandra whispered ominously to Mollie as she turned her back on Joanne and left the room.

She squared her shoulders and moved forward, too, wondering what gems Joanne might fire her way. 'I'm

Mollie. Albie's daughter. Beth's granddaughter. Lovely to meet you.' She held her hand out, but Joanne ignored it. She looked her up and down.

'You look like *her*,' Joanne said. The emphasis on 'her', almost spat out, wasn't lost on Mollie. God, this woman was blunt.

'Granny Kathleen or Nana Beth?' Mollie asked.

'Both, but more Beth. And I daresay you are as full of yourself as Beth always was. You being a celebrity and all that.'

There it was – that biting charm Dervla had hinted at. And as Dervla said, Joanne was sharp. It seemed she knew exactly who Mollie was and what she did for a living. But Mollie didn't mind. She found the woman entertaining.

'Nana Beth always told me I was allowed a couple of notions. I've tried to keep them to a minimum, though,' Mollie added, standing her ground.

'Well, if anyone knew about notions, your grandmother did,' Joanne replied, her mouth curling in a sneer.

'And you would know all about her, you being such *good* friends and all that,' Mollie decided to throw back her own grenade.

To Mollie's surprise, Joanne started to laugh. 'Sit down. You're making the place look messy standing there like a big eejit.'

Mollie pulled up a seat and sat opposite Joanne. 'It's nice here.' She pointed to a row of framed photographs on the mantelpiece above an electric stove, with flames flickering in its centre. 'Is that you as a kid with your parents?'

Joanne's face softened, and tears glistened in her milky

175

grey eyes. 'Yes. That's the last photograph we had taken as a family before Dad died.'

Mollie searched the photograph for clues to the family. Ellen sat in a high-backed wooden chair, with her husband standing behind it, a hand on Ellen's shoulder. He looked serious, but you could see the warmth in his eyes. Joanne and her younger brother Ger kneeled in front of their mother. Despite all four of them trying to look sombre, Mollie could see the twinkle of laughter in each of their eyes. Dervla looked like her grandad Peter, she noted. They had the same eyes and mouth.

'I understand how precious this photograph must be for you. I know my dad gets great comfort from looking at photographs of his father.'

'He was too good a man for Beth,' Joanne replied.

Mollie sucked in a gasp of air. 'That's a little harsh!'

'The truth hurts. But I say it like it is. If you don't want to hear my thoughts, you know where the door is.' She waited for a beat, but when Mollie made no move to leave, she continued, 'Beth never thought of anyone but herself. Facts are facts.'

Mollie grimaced.

'I'm sorry you feel like that. But that is not the Nana Beth that I know and love. She has always been kind to me, and for the record, I've never heard her say a bad word about you.'

Joanne shrugged, unabashed by Mollie's words. 'So what do you want? Why this visit out of the blue?'

Mollie pointed to the photographs, then used the same line as she had with Dervla. 'We hoped you might have some pictures of Granny Kathleen or Beth from years ago. I'm putting together a scrapbook of memories for Nana. She's in hospital at the moment, recovering from pneumonia. I'm particularly interested in the years my great-granddad Patrick was a lighthouse keeper in Ballycotton and you all lived in Powers Terrace.'

Silence filled the room. And it wasn't the comfortable kind.

'Are you sure Beth wants to be reminded of that time?' Joanne asked. 'Because I'm not sure she does.'

Mollie swallowed hard. 'What happened back then that was so bad she'd want to forget?'

Joanne looked at her sharply, then closed her eyes momentarily as if pondering what to say next. 'Let's just say that it wasn't all fun and games. Times were hard. For some of us more than others.'

'Can you tell me more? I'd like to hear.'

'Money was tight for most,' Joanne answered. 'And we were the lucky ones, with fathers working for the lighthouse commissioners and earning a decent wage. But the world was still living under the chokehold of the Second World War. Rationing. Food shortages. With the cost of living increasing every week.'

Mollie had never thought about that side of living back then. She'd romanticized life on the lighthouse for her ancestors, thinking of them saving lives, diverting danger for ships and boats. Once again, she realized how lucky she was. She'd grown up in a family where money was never an object. And now was independently wealthy.

'But we could bear it all . . . until Dad died.' A tear escaped Joanne's eye and trailed down her weathered cheek.

Mollie reached out to clasp her hand, but Joanne snatched it away, unwilling to accept any warmth or comfort. Instead, she pulled a tissue from the cuff of her green cardigan and blew her nose noisily.

'Have a look in that sideboard behind you. There are a couple of photo albums in one of the drawers that belonged to my mother. You might find a few pictures that are of interest to you.'

Mollie swivelled around in her chair and began looking through the dark oak wooden drawers one by one. She found two large albums. They were chocolate brown and cream, worn around the edges, with the wear and tear of time. Mollie passed them to Joanne, who began to flip her way through each page. Mollie was mesmerized by her facial expressions: one moment, Joanne would be sneering at a photograph, then breaking into a smile for the next. Her face truly was an open book.

'Here's one you might like – your great-aunt Katie's first Holy Communion, in 1948.' Joanne carefully took a snap from the page and handed it to Mollie.

She recognized the location immediately; it was Ballycotton Pier. Beth's younger sister, Katie, wore a white communion dress with a shoulder-length veil and shiny patent shoes. Standing on either side of her were Kathleen, Beth and John.

'The dress was knitted. One of the lighthouse keepers used to knit communion dresses to while away the time on the island. The intricacy was incredible.'

'I've never seen this before,' Mollie said, her eyes wide in wonder. 'How small Katie looks.'

'She was a sweet kid,' Joanne said.

Mollie looked up in surprise, wondering if the woman was being sarcastic. But no, she seemed genuine.

'I remember that day so clearly.' Joanne shut her eyes again, as if lost in memory. 'Kathleen had baked for days before the communion, and we had the most glorious meal after the service. We brought Katie to the pier to dance for Patrick. He stood on the island with his telescope, waiting to catch his first glimpse of her.'

Mollie felt a lump grow in her throat, picturing the scene. She could only imagine how her great-grandfather must have felt, knowing he was missing such a big family occasion – and how Kathleen might have felt, experiencing it without him.

'Katie was shy. At first, she wouldn't dance for her dad, but then my mammy started to sing – Mammy was always singing back then. "Boogie Woogie Bugle Boy" – she loved the Andrews Sisters. Beth and I grabbed Katie's hands and twirled her around. And then Kathleen grabbed John and Ger. And on that pier, we danced for Daddy, Patrick, and Ted too.' Joanne's voice was thick with emotion.

This was another glimpse into the lives of Mollie's ancestors. 'I've never heard this story before. Thank you for sharing it,' Mollie said gratefully. 'My great-aunt Katie was a lovely woman and always very kind to me when I came over for vacations as a kid. I'll treasure this new memory of her.' She saw an opportunity to move the conversation nearer to her objective, so took it. 'It's sad that the keepers missed so many big moments, right?' Mollie sighed. 'It must have been tough for my great-grandfather Patrick.'

'When Daddy died, one of Patrick's closest friends, I'm not sure it bothered him in the slightest.'

179

Mollie frowned. 'Sometimes we hide how we truly feel. Not everyone is as open as you are with your feelings, Joanne.' Her voice had an edge of irritation now. 'I get the feeling that you didn't care very much for my family.'

Joanne shrugged, but she didn't deny it.

'After your dad died, you must have been a great support for your mam,' Mollie said, trying another tactic.

'I'd like to think so,' Joanne replied. 'She was the best mother any girl or woman could ever ask for. Her whole life was devoted to us kids. We'll never be able to repay her for all she did for us.'

Mollie could not work out Joanne at all. She was such a contradiction. There was no hiding the love she had for her parents – or conversely, the resentment she had towards Beth and the Keneficks.

Joanne returned her attention to the photo albums, flicking through the pages one by one. She paused, and her face crumpled for a fraction of a second, as she stared at a photograph, but then she quickly flicked the page with a shaking hand, before Mollie could see what she was looking at. Joanne continued moving through the album and then paused again, pulling out another photograph and handing it to Mollie.

In this one, a young man stood between two girls, his arm loosely woven around their two backs. The girls – her nana Beth and she guessed Joanne, both wore summer cotton dresses with flat court shoes. Their hair was pinned back with soft waves reaching their shoulders. The young man was in a white shirt, open-necked, with sleeves rolled up to his elbows and a pair of grey slacks with braces. His smile was broad and open; both he and Beth were smiling for the camera. But Joanne wasn't looking at the camera. She was looking up adoringly at him.

'I was about sixteen there, Beth a year older – it was only a short time after Ted took the position as assistant keeper at Ballycotton. We spent much of our spare time hanging around the village.' She paused. 'It wasn't long after that, that he started to court Beth.'

'He looks so handsome,' Mollie murmured, running her finger across the photo.

'I think every woman in Ballycotton was in love with him,' Joanne said softly.

You were in love with him too, Mollie realized suddenly. And that would explain why she held on to resentment toward her grandmother – unrequited love.

'One more photograph for you,' Joanne said, with a sly smile now lifting the corners of her mouth. 'That's your nana Beth with her good friend Christian. They became very close during the summer of '51.'

Mollie peered down at the last image. In this one, a young and fresh-faced Beth and Joanne stood either side of a young man with movie-star looks. His hair was slicked back, and he wore a shirt and tight trousers. They were in front of a striped circus big top.

'When the circus came to Ballycotton, it was quite the spectacle. The whole village went to see the show sometime over the week it was here. And we all held our breath as the trapeze artists flew through the air. Of course, Beth was luckier than most of us. She had several *private* showings with Christian. Set many a tongue wagging. Your great-granny Kathleen was rather dismayed with it all.'

Joanne could barely contain her glee at this nugget of gossip.

'Can I take these with me?' Mollie asked. 'I can make copies and get the originals back to you.'

Joanne nodded. 'Keep them. I don't have any need for them anymore.'

'Thank you,' Mollie said, standing up. 'I'll tell Nana that I saw you today looking so well.'

'Don't bother. I'm sure she won't care any more than I do.'

Biting back a retort, Mollie left.

'What a horrible woman,' Mollie whispered to herself as soon as the door closed shut behind them.

'Did you have a nice visit?' Sandra the receptionist asked, looking up from her desk as Mollie approached her.

'Joanne is quite the ticket, isn't she?' Mollie replied as diplomatically as she could.

Sandra giggled as she nodded. 'She keeps us all on our toes, that's for sure. But she's all bark, no bite. I think she's lonely. I'm not sure life has been kind to her.'

Mollie thought that perhaps Sandra had something there and felt a pang of sympathy for the woman. Maybe she had good reason to be so caustic. Mollie said goodbye to Sandra, but as she turned to leave, a staff member walked out of the Library. The swinging doors revealed a resident sitting at a table, using a typewriter.

Mollie's body tingled with excitement.

She'd come to ask Joanne about the past, to see if she could dig into the secret. Was it possible that Joanne was behind the letters after all?

TWENTY-THREE

Beth

Monday, 21 May 1951

Ballycotton, West Cork

As Beth swept the flagstones in the kitchen, her mind was filled with Christian. She had been sneaking back and forth between her cottage and the circus to spend time with him. The way Christian made her feel when he touched her sent shivers down her body. When he whispered '*Je t'aime*' or '*ma chérie*' into her ear, she was putty in his hands.

She was playing with fire. Sooner or later, someone would get hurt. Last night she was tormented by dreams of breaking Ted's heart. She had never meant this to happen, to go this far. A harmless flirtation had now become her everything. But she was powerless to stay away. Beth spent her days daydreaming about Christian. And her nights longing to feel his touch.

She itched to tell Joanne, who had for many years been her go-to confidante, but since she'd left her in the costume tent at the circus, Joanne had refused all efforts Beth had made to talk to her. It was clear she disapproved of Beth's friendship with Christian. What would she think if she'd seen what Beth had done since then in the arms of the charming Frenchman?

Beth wished the circus had never come to town to throw her into this turmoil. Her mind flitted from how she felt about Ted to Christian and back again. She'd had passionate embraces with Ted, but he'd always pulled back, not allowing either of them to get carried away. But Christian showed no such restraint. When his hands followed the curves of her body, she didn't want them to stop.

She washed her hands and face, then re-pinned her hair.

'I've emptied the Aga stove, re-lit it, prepared the stew for dinner, swept the floor and made all the beds,' Beth called out to her mother, who was upstairs. 'I'm going for a walk.' Then without waiting for a response, she ran out the front door. She hadn't planned where she might go, only that she needed to escape. Her growing sense of unease about the situation she'd placed herself in with Ted and Christian was making her ill. She couldn't eat, her sleep was fitful. What started out as fun had become extremely complicated.

'Hello,' Mary called out as she passed. Her new

neighbour was kneeling by the flower beds along the small driveway to her cottage.

'Hi Mary. Gardening?'

'Yes, I'm planting some wildflower seeds. They will look pretty in the summer. I love flowers, don't you?'

Beth had never really given them any thought. 'I suppose.'

'Would you like to come in for a cold drink? I need a little break,' Mary said, standing up and wiping her hands on the apron she wore over her clothes.

A chat with Mary was tempting. Although she'd only known her for a short time, Beth trusted her. Could she help her make sense of the muddle her life had become? She looked towards the Craig cottage front door, frowning. Or the Mythen cottage as it was now, she supposed. It had been a second home to her for years. But with a new rift between her and Joanne, she felt awkward about going in.

'Is anyone else in there?'

Mary shook her head. 'Both the kids are at school. And Ellen has gone to visit a mother-to-be. The cottage is all mine. For now, at least.'

Beth had been in this cottage hundreds of times, but it felt different today. The changes were small, but she could see that Mary had already made her mark on her new home. Pops of colour jumped out, making the once old-fashioned space seem hip and vibrant. New red-and-white gingham curtains framed the kitchen window. A multicoloured vase had a bunch of bright yellow flowers in the centre of the table. Which now boasted a cherry-red tablecloth on its wooden surface. Beth also noted tea, coffee and sugar canisters on the kitchen countertop, each in a bright red.

'It looks amazing here,' Beth enthused, spinning around to take it all in. 'I've just given our kitchen a top-to-bottom clean, and it's so drab in comparison. I wonder if I can persuade Mam to change our curtains.' She ran a hand over the checked fabric.

'I love bright things. They cheer me up. My mother always said that the smallest tweaks could make any house a home,' Mary said, looking around her in satisfaction. 'I might paint the kitchen cupboards a sea-green to give them a new lease of life next. What do you think?'

'That would be so lovely,' Beth said, envisioning it in her mind's eye.

'The things is, I've been worrying about whether I can make drastic changes to the cottage. The curtains and accessories can all come down whenever we leave for our next post. But paint . . .' Mary shrugged.

'If you've done it, and it looks great, they won't ask you to change it back. I say go for it,' Beth replied.

Mary snorted laughter at this. 'I like that! Now, what would you like to drink? Milk, water or perhaps a treat? I have red lemonade!'

'Oh yes please!' Beth asked, licking her lips in anticipation. She only occasionally had that treat with Ted when he returned from the island. Had she thrown all that away with Ted now? The thought made her head thump.

Mary pulled two glasses from the kitchen cupboard, took a bottle of pop from the fridge and flipped the top open with a bottle opener.

'Isn't that sound just scrumptious?' Mary said as the echo of fizz filled the air.

'Yes, scrumptious,' Beth said, taking note of the word. She loved how it sounded when she rolled it off her tongue.

Beth and Mary took a sip of their drinks, and both sighed happily in satisfaction. Beth watched the other woman from under her lashes and felt a stab of envy as she took in her effortless style. Mary wore a pair of high-waisted red trousers with a patterned shirt tied in a knot at her tiny waist. Beth looked down at her navy skirt and blouse, which she had thought looked chic this morning, and now felt old-fashioned and boring.

'Let's get to know each other a little more. Tell me something that no one else knows, and then I'll do the same with you. That way we can be firm friends forever,' Mary declared.

'You first,' Beth said, feeling a little shy, but also hopeful. While Mary was three years older than her, Beth felt closer in age to her than she did to Joanne. The rift between the once best friends had deepened and Beth wasn't sure how to make it right again.

'Well, this morning, I went down to the pier and sent Seamus a message on the flags. I've been practising daily for hours with the help of Ellen. And I had rehearsed a message ready for him.'

Beth smiled encouragingly at Mary. The twinkle in Mary's eye told her that there was a twist in her tale.

'Well, the problem was that Seamus didn't read it. It was Ted who saw it, your beau!'

Beth grinned, picturing the scene. 'What did you say to him?'

'I said I love you, and wait until I get you home!' Mary began to giggle. 'He sent me a message back, kindly saying that he would pass the message on to Seamus.'

'Too funny. Imagine if it had been my dad! New rule, Mary. You have to determine who is at the end of the semaphore flags before you begin!' Beth said, laughing too now.

'I'll be the talk of the island,' Mary said, shrugging and clearly not overly worried. 'Now it's your turn.'

Beth looked at Mary, trying to decide what she would share about her life. She could tell her that she had swiped some of her mam's make-up earlier. But without planning to, she opened up in a way she had not intended.

'I've been seeing one of the circus artists. Romantically.'

Mary's lips formed a perfect 'O' of surprise. 'Now that is a delicious secret that I was not expecting. Tell me more, Beth.'

'You won't tell anyone else?'

'That's what a secret is. Yours is quite safe with me.'

Beth felt a ripple of excitement rush through her. She had been dying to talk about Christian with someone, and now was her chance. 'He's French. And has the most glorious eyes that pierce my soul. His name is Christian. And I can't seem to keep away from him.'

Mary watched her. 'He sounds divine. And how does he feel about you?'

'He says he loves me.' Beth's smile turned to a frown as she asked, 'Mary, can you love two people at once?'

Mary considered this, taking another delicate sip of her drink. 'I would say that only you can truly answer that. I can't imagine loving anyone else while loving Seamus. But that's me. What about Ted – do you love him too?'

Beth nodded, feeling her excitement slip away. 'That's just it – I think Ted is just about the most perfect man there is. I have so much fun with him. And I know he loves me with all his heart. He treats me like a princess. He's funny, he makes me laugh.'

'Your face lights up when you talk about him,' Mary said.

Beth leaned in. 'I have another secret. I know that Ted is planning to propose. He's asked my father for permission. Who, of course, was delighted to give it. His only ambition for me is to marry a keeper.' She rolled her eyes dramatically.

Mary listened attentively, without interruption or condemnation. Beth liked that about her. Joanne would not have been able to keep her opinion to herself – and she would have been so cross with Beth.

'Jaypers, you are in a pickle. Do you want to marry Ted?' Mary asked gently.

Beth bit her lip. 'I don't want to get married. Not yet, at least. And I especially don't want to be a keeper's wife. I want to travel. To see the world.'

'Have you told Ted how you feel?'

'The last time I saw Ted, I feigned a headache when he brought up the subject of our future. And I've not seen him for weeks now, because like my father, his last shore leave was cancelled, to cover for poor Peter. May he rest

189

in peace. So while Ted's been working around the clock, I've been . . .' Beth couldn't finish the sentence, she was so ashamed. She hid her face in her hands. She was not proud of her actions. She peeked out between her fingers to check Mary's reaction.

Mary's eyes narrowed as she took this in. 'Is Christian another headache, I wonder?'

Beth dropped her hands, her face scrunched in confusion. 'I don't understand.'

'You know that you can't keep pretending you have a headache to avoid a proposal from Ted. So, having this fling with Christian – that's a form of self-sabotage. Christian becomes your headache.'

Beth looked at Mary in wonder, her wise insight making her doubt everything she thought to be true. A rush of bewilderment hit her, making her breathless. Her feelings for Ted and Christian all felt muddled together into one big mess. 'But is Christian still a headache if I'm falling for him?'

'Hmmm . . . that's a different story. Say Christian was to ask you to go with him, to run away with the circus, would you go?'

'I don't know,' Beth answered; then, to her surprise, felt tears spring to her eyes. 'I do know that I don't want to end my relationship with Ted.'

'But Beth, you must know that you will have to choose between them.'

Beth knew she was right. But she didn't like hearing it. 'Being a grown-up is not fun.'

Mary sighed, 'That I know for sure. Look, you have some time before Ted comes home. Spend it wisely. Speak with Christian and try to work out what it is between you. Is it just a flirtation, or something that could lead to marriage?'

Beth had not thought about Christian in those terms before. When they were together, they rarely talked; it was all physical. The truth was, she knew very little about who he was – and he'd never asked her about her life either.

Beth tried to imagine bringing Christian home to meet her parents, but she could not picture him in her family's life. He was from a different world. But wasn't that what she wanted and yearned for? Beth felt confusion tug at her heart.

'How did you know that Seamus was right for you?'

'There are so many reasons. But the most important one was that I could not picture spending the rest of my life without him by my side,' Mary answered. 'I knew it was him, only him, from the first time we met.'

'I can't imagine Ted not being in my life!' Beth cried. Her hands began to shake.

'And Christian?'

Beth's stomach plummeted. She did not have an answer to that. 'I don't know. You're right – I need to work that out.'

'Good luck,' Mary said, hugging Beth tight before she left. 'Trust your heart. And your head. In my experience, both are equally important. One more thing, Beth.'

Beth looked up at her, watching Mary as she took a moment to speak.

'Are you being careful? When you are with Christian?'

Beth felt her cheeks flame at the question.

'I don't want to embarrass you, Beth. But if you don't want to get married, it's probably best that you don't get yourself in the family way . . .'

'I haven't . . . at least . . . not that . . . not yet . . .' Beth stammered. 'Thank you. This has been really helpful. I've decided to see Christian now, maybe it will help me understand how I truly feel.'

Then with a quick wave goodbye, she snuck around the back of her cottage and took her bicycle. As she jumped on, she heard her mam call her name, but she pumped the pedals harder. Her mam would have to wait. Her stomach flipped with every turn of her pedals. Mary's words flew around her mind. She had been careful, so far. But she wasn't sure she had the willpower to continue that way.

When she arrived at Murphy's field, a dozen people were picking up litter, getting everything ready for the evening's performance. Several called out hello to her as she passed by. Beth had become known to them over the past few days.

She found Christian in the big top, practising on the high ropes with his sister Delphine. Beth sat on the benches and watched him move back and forth, the muscles on his arms rippling with exertion.

Even though she'd watched him rehearse and perform several times, the sense of wonder and awe never left. When he finished, he ran over to her, a broad smile lighting up his face. Delphine watched the two of them from a distance. Beth waved over to her, and the woman nodded hello in response. While Delphine had always been friendly when they ran into each other, Beth couldn't shake the feeling that she did not approve of her.

'Hello, *ma chérie*. This is a nice surprise.' He kissed her swiftly.

'Hello Christian. I liked that last move. A triple somersault?'

'*Mais oui!* I've been working on that for some time. Can you come to the show this evening? And you must come to our last show on Friday.'

'I'll try. But my father returns on Friday from the lighthouse, so I'm not sure I'll be able to get here. And we have to be careful, in front of him. He works with Ted . . .'

Christian's face clouded. 'I do not like to think of you and another man, *ma chérie*.'

Beth had never lied about her relationship with Ted. She'd been upfront from the beginning. Another flash of shame made her stomach flip. She could not say the same about Ted. How had she ended up in such a mess?

'When does the circus leave?' Beth asked, taking hold of his hand.

Christian looked out the big top, 'Saturday. Then we move on to Limerick.' He turned back towards her, and mischief danced in his eyes as he asked, 'Will you miss me?'

'Of course,' Beth replied. 'Will you miss me?'

'Everyday, *ma chérie*,' he said, leaning in closer to trail his thumb down her cheek.

Yet you have not asked me to go with you, Beth thought. Would he say goodbye without even a backward glance?

'Will I ever see you again?'

'With all my heart, I hope so,' Christian replied.

'Hey!' a man's voice called out gruffly. 'If you have time for canoodling, you have time for more training. Get back to it.'

Christian grunted a response, then turned back to Beth. 'That is the ringmaster. And it's best not to upset the boss. Promise me you will come back tonight?'

'I promise,' Beth said.

With one last lingering kiss, she left the big top. As she approached the entrance, she saw the curtain shimmer and shift. Then she saw a flash of blue fabric flutter as someone scurried away. Someone had been watching them. She quickened her speed and ran out into the field.

Darting between two cages, too far ahead to catch, was Joanne.

TWENTY-FOUR

Mary

Tuesday, 22 May 1951

Ballycotton, Cork

As Mary laid the table, Ellen prepared dinner, washing the dirt off new potatoes. Nat King Cole crooned out 'Mona Lisa' on their wireless, and both women hummed along.

'It's good to see you smiling,' Mary said. Most nights she heard Ellen cry in her bedroom, grieving for Peter. But she'd noticed a change in the older woman over the past few days. She seemed lighter somehow, like a weight had been lifted from her shoulders.

Ellen wiped her hands on her house coat, then turned to Mary. 'I think my fortune is about to change. You must be fed up with having us all under your feet and no doubt you can't wait to start your married life together in peace.'

Mary quickly reassured Ellen, 'Please don't feel pressured. I've loved having you all here this past week. You've made my time without Seamus pass by so quickly.'

Mary didn't add that she found it a comfort to have Ellen in the house, especially once she'd realized who the man at the hotel was. Since then, she'd been careful to avoid the Bayview, staying close to home. Her every instinct told her that she should avoid him at all costs.

'And you've helped us all enormously too. You are so good with the children. They love being with you. Listening to your music has helped lift the dark cloud that has followed us,' Ellen replied.

'Thank you,' Mary said, feeling touched by the sincerity in Ellen's words.

'I bet you cannot wait to see Seamus. Two more weeks to go.'

'I'm counting down the hours,' Mary admitted, feeling a rush of joy at the thought.

'Many locals gather to welcome the keeper back for the changeover, once the new keeper has swapped places with them. It's quite something. Kathleen and I have formed a little tradition. We always walk down together to the pier . . .' Ellen paused, her smile dropping, 'I mean to say, we used to do that. Now it will be you and Kathleen who will go to the pier to wait for the relief boat to get in. Then you'll all walk up home together. The keepers always wear their full uniform, and as they march up Main Street, neighbours and friends call out to welcome them back. It's a lovely occasion. Sorry, I'm babbling on.'

Mary felt a rush of sympathy for Ellen, knowing what it must have cost her to be so strong these past few weeks. Her ache of loss so acute, but Ellen had held that to one side to take care of her children. 'It must be so hard for you. So many parts of the keeper's life that you feel you are no longer part of.'

Ellen acknowledged this with a sad smile. 'I was so proud of Peter. Proud to wait for him and greet him. Proud to walk by his side as we returned home. Proud to spend the day cooking and baking all his favourite foods.' She exhaled, then finished, 'But we must adapt to our new life.'

The subject of special meals for the returning keepers made Mary look at Ellen nervously. Would the Craigs find a new home by the end of Seamus's rota? She had hoped to host a welcome-home supper for Seamus too. And would like to spend time with him on their own. Her mind then returned to another worry. Should she tell Seamus about being recognized by the man staying at the hotel? On one hand, it would be a blessed relief to have her secret out in the open with her husband. She hated lying to him. But on the other hand, she worried that learning about her family's history might colour Seamus's feelings for her.

'One potato or two?' Ellen asked, adding them into a saucepan of water to boil.

'One,' Mary said. She decided to ignore the issue of her past for now and let her mind go back to how she might broach the subject of the Craigs moving out. Ellen had mentioned that she was working on a solution, but had been quite vague. But as Mary had promised her husband it would be just the two of them when he returned, she couldn't put it off any further. 'I wondered—'

Ellen put her hand up, interrupting her. 'When are we going? I'm sorry. I didn't want to say anything until I had everything firmed up. But I'm hopeful that we will be ready to leave here long before Seamus arrives home.'

Mary felt her shoulders slump with relief. She tried to keep the joy at this news from her voice. Mary could never have put the Craigs out on the street, so finding out that the problem was resolving itself was most welcome. 'Where will you go?'

'I'm still finalizing the details, but I expect news on a possible new home later today. Whatever happens, this house will be yours and yours alone, as we promised, when Seamus comes home.'

Her new friend's consideration touched Mary. 'Thank you. That means a great deal. And honestly, as I said earlier, please don't feel under any pressure from me.' An unpleasant thought struck her, so she quickly asked, 'I hope you are not re-considering your brother-in-law's offer?'

'Never!' Ellen said quickly. She lowered her voice, looking to the door to ensure nobody was in earshot. 'I want to tell you about my plans, but I am sworn to secrecy . . . can I trust you to say nothing?'

'Of course,' Mary said, feeling a rush of excitement. This would be her second confidante in as many days. Who knew that a small village could hold so many secrets?

198

'There's an investor in Ballycotton. He's an oil tycoon from Texas. And he has befriended Kathleen. As a favour to her and me, he allowed her to invest her savings into an oil company he works with. They are about to announce a new oil find that will double the share prices. Kathleen plans on giving me the profit from the investment, so I can buy a cottage for sale in the village.' Ellen was breathless as she told her friend the news. 'I can scarcely believe it.'

A prickle of unease ran over Mary's skin. Her mother always said that if something looked too good to be true, it most likely was. 'That does sound exciting. Who is this oil tycoon? I don't think I've ever met one of those before.'

'His name is Charles Davis. He's a guest at the Bayview Hotel. Such a gentleman. From Cork originally, but he made a successful life in Texas, America.'

Mary felt her stomach clench. The room began to spin around her. She begged silently that it wasn't the same man. 'I . . . think I may have seen him when I was staying at the hotel. Grey hair, wears a trilby?'

'Yes, that's him! He's hard to miss. Very different from most men you see around Ballycotton. I think he looks like Cary Grant! He rescued Kathleen and I the other day when Benny accosted us on Main Street.'

Mary's heart raced as she listened to Ellen continue to tell her about the incident. Her mind whirled with panicked questions. 'Did Kathleen give him much money?' she asked, interrupting Ellen's story.

'All her savings, bless her. And I shall repay every penny one day, even if I have to keep working until my dying breath.'

199

All hope left Mary at this news. While she didn't know what this Charles Davis was up to, she did know, without a doubt, that his promises would be false. Ellen and Kathleen would never see that money again – unless she could do something to help them get it back.

Running to the hall, she grabbed her coat. 'Sorry, Ellen, I'll be back soon. I've just remembered I have an errand to run.'

TWENTY-FIVE

Mary

Tuesday, 22 May 1951

Ballycotton, Cork

Mary practically ran the quarter mile to the Bayview Hotel. She sped into the reception, scanning the seating areas. And in the corner, reading a newspaper, was Charles Davis. Every inch of him insulted her, from the casual lean of his arm onto the back of the chair, his leg crossed, to his hat sitting on the table in front of him. Without planning what she might say, she marched up to him.

He didn't look up but continued reading his paper as he said amicably, 'Yes?'

'I know who you are,' Mary hissed.

Charles was unfazed. 'I wondered how long it would take you to remember.'

As Mary watched the man before her, a rush of memories overcame her, of a difficult day three years ago that she had desperately tried to forget.

It had been a cold morning, with frost in the air, so her breath looked like puffs of smoke when Mary visited her da, George Martin, in Mountjoy Prison. Cigarette smoke, body odour, and stale food filled the air, making her want to gag. And the sound of prison guards shouting, as inmates cheered or screamed, deafened her. It was chaotic and terrifying, an assault on her senses. But Mary knew that she had to do this. See it through.

She had not seen her da since he had been arrested for the murder of a young nurse who had startled him when he was burgling her home. He swore he hadn't meant to fire the shot that killed the woman, but that mattered not.

Mary and her ma had spent years being terrorized at the hands of George Martin. He was a monster to them, and after his arrest, they ignored all his requests to visit him in jail. Then, shortly after he was convicted of murder and sentenced to death, her ma had a heart attack. While headlines appeared in every newspaper in Ireland, blasting George Martin's name out in bold, Mary had held her ma's hand in the hospital, willing her to recover. But her wishes and will were not enough. Her ma died – with a literal broken and shamed heart.

After her mother's funeral, Mary had found herself homeless at the young age of eighteen. If it wasn't for the kindness of a friend of her ma's from the factory, Mary would have been out on the streets.

Mary had done her best to put her da from her mind, refusing to think about him. If anyone brought his name up, she walked away. But no matter how hard she tried, someone would ask, are you related to George Martin? In the end, she moved away from Dublin's inner city to Cabra. She switched to her ma's maiden name, and found work on another factory floor – Bachelors. Mary wiped her da from her family history. But late at night, in the darkness of her bedroom, as she listened to the soft snores of her housemates, Mary found it hard to sleep and thought about the things she wanted to say to him.

Three months before his execution date, she applied for a visitor's pass and went to Mountjoy Prison. When her da shuffled in, wearing his grey prison uniform, she gasped in shock. He'd shrunk since the last time they'd seen each other. But it was his eyes that she'd never forget. They were as dead as her mother, who lay in a cold grave in Glasnevin.

'I didn't think I would see you again,' he said. His face was gaunt, and new lines marked his forehead and upper lip.

Mary's rehearsed speech went out of her mind. And she sat across from him, mute. She felt eyes watching her from the left and turned to see an inmate at the neighbouring table. Unlike her da, he seemed full of health, his greying dark hair combed back in a perfect quiff. He looked dapper and, in stark contrast to her father, appeared to be flourishing rather than dying in prison. He nodded a hello in her direction.

'Who's that?' Mary asked her father, averting her eyes from the man.

'My cellmate. Robert. In for fraud. But he plays a good hand of sevens.'

The thought of her father playing cards, having fun with his cellmate, while her ma was cold in the ground, infuriated Mary. Rage filled her body, making it tremble and shake. She hissed at him, speaking slowly so that he heard every word, 'I despise you. You have the blood of that nurse you murdered on your hands, but you also have my mother's. You might as well have stuck a knife into her, because there is no doubt that you killed Ma too.'

She waited for a reaction and felt a crash of disappointment when none came. He simply stared at her, making no comment to the words she'd uttered. What had she hoped to gain by visiting him? She stood up and said in a stronger voice than she knew she possessed, 'This is the last time you will ever see me.'

She waited a moment, wondering would her father try to change her mind, stop her, or say one kind thing to her before she left. But he remained true to his cold, cruel self. And it wasn't him who raised a hand to stop her. It was her father's cellmate.

'That's not a nice way to speak to your father, Mary. He talks about you at every opportunity. He keeps your photograph hanging over the sink.'

Mary faltered at this news. Part of her longed to turn around, to look at her da one more time. See if perhaps he cared about her after all. But then she thought of her ma, and she replied, 'You are mistaken, sir – I have no father.' Then she walked out of the prison.

'Still pretending you're an orphan?' Charles Davis said, bringing Mary back to the present, in the Bayview Hotel.

'You were called Robert back then,' Mary said in wonder. Charles inclined his head in acknowledgement.

None of that mattered. Mary pushed her da from her mind. Right now, she had to get to the bottom of whatever scam Davis was running.

'You've taken money from my friend.'

Charles Davis folded his newspaper carefully, placed it on the table and looked up for the first time. 'And?'

'And? And you cannot do that. You cannot con money from Kathleen and expect to get away with it. The Keneficks are good and decent people.'

Charles shrugged.

This incensed Mary, and she shouted, 'You have to give it back to them.'

He nodded to the seat beside him, hissing, 'You are making a scene.'

Mary looked around her. Nobody was paying them any attention. Even so, she took a seat.

'That's better,' Charles said with approval.

'I said you have to give the money back to Kathleen,' Mary repeated.

He didn't look remotely fazed by Mary's request.

She tried again, 'You need to make an excuse. Tell them that their investment was not accepted. If you leave Ballycotton, we can all pretend it didn't happen.'

'I'm afraid that won't be possible,' Charles said forlornly.

'You have to make it possible. Or—'

'Or what?' His voice had dropped, low and menacing, and he grabbed her wrist and pinched it between his hands.

205

Mary pulled her wrist from him and lifted her chin defiantly. She'd grown up in inner city Dublin and had faced down bigger gangsters than this man in her time. 'Or I will tell them who and what you are!'

Charles leaned back in his chair and laughed. The sound of that laughter shocked Mary more than his earlier flash of anger.

'Kathleen Kenefick has taken her family's savings without permission from her husband. She won't thank you for telling the whole village her business. Especially when I reluctantly admit that she's been having an affair with me.'

Mary's stomach dropped at this news. 'You wouldn't dare.'

'Oh, I would. It will be particularly shocking for everyone to hear how she plans to run away to Texas with me.'

'No one will believe that!' Mary exploded.

'Maybe not. But how does the saying go? There's no smoke without fire. The village will be agog, and plenty of people will enjoy thinking that the respectable keeper's wife isn't so perfect after all.'

The conversation was going very differently to how Mary had envisioned. She had thought it would be straightforward to threaten him and persuade him to leave. But she was out of her depth. She realized that she did not know this man. Or what he was capable of.

'Poor Patrick, over on the island, working hard. And he has no clue about his wife's secrets. Tut-tut. Secrets between a husband and his wife are never good, are they?'

The way he looked at her as he spoke made the hair on the back of Mary's neck rise.

'Listen to me, Mary. If you tell your friends who I am, I shall return the favour for you.'

'What do you mean?' Mary asked. She heard her voice tremble and hated the satisfaction that came over Charles's face when he heard it too.

'Does your husband know who your father was? That George Martin hanged for murder?' He cackled when he saw the truth on Mary's face. 'He doesn't, does he? I knew it.' As he considered this, Charles drummed his fingers on the table before him. 'I'll warrant your new friends also do not know that they are living alongside the daughter of a murderer. Quite the scandal that would cause.'

Mary wanted to shout at him to do his worst. That she did not care. That her past did not define her.

But doubt and fear made her mute again.

'Are you sure your husband could overlook such a dark past? Or the fact that you kept it a secret from him?'

Mary opened her mouth, but the words would not come.

'All you have to do is look the other way. But if you choose to mess with my business, I will destroy you and Kathleen. That is not a threat, Mary. That is a promise.'

TWENTY-SIX

Beth

Wednesday, 23 May 1951

Ballycotton, Cork

Beth arrived at the entrance to the circus and surveyed the tents and trailers scattered like confetti in the green grass. She could not fathom that this eclectic group of artists and performers would all be gone in a couple of days' time.

The air was still, and a faint breeze tickled the dewy grass at her feet. The trailers were darkened as the artists rested and the animals slept. This was Beth's favourite time of the day, before the sun had risen. Yesterday was gone, and today was a fresh beginning, a chance to let the past go.

She walked towards the backyard, behind the big top, where the smaller tents sat. Christian would be waiting for her in the dressing room, where the costumes were kept. It had become their spot.

Everything about the lives of the circus entertainers was glamorous. She'd seen the show on three occasions, and the same adrenaline rushed through her body each time the performers stood side by side to take their final bow. She loved it all, from the limber contortionists to the feather-head-dressed women who did tricks on horses and elephants, from the high jinks of the clowns to the death-defying flying through the air of Christian and his trapeze team.

Beth felt wide awake, on high alert, though she ought to be tired. She'd tossed and turned all night, thinking about her future. She still moved back and forth between her love for Ted and infatuation for Christian. Time was ticking on, and Beth knew she had to make her mind up. What did she want? Or rather, *who* did she want?

'Will you be joining us when we leave on Saturday?' a voice called out as she passed a brightly coloured wagon.

It was Delphine, Christian's sister, leaning against the wagon, holding a pack of cigarettes in her hand. She wore a purple robe, with her dark hair falling in waves down her back. She looked glamorous and exotic, making Beth feel like a gauche child in her pedal pushers and blouse. Delphine was regarding Beth with interest.

Had Christian mentioned to Delphine that he'd like Beth to join them? Beth's heart raced at the thought.

'I think it must be such incredible fun to travel the world with the circus,' Beth replied, looking around her in wonder. 'To wake up to this, in a new destination every couple of weeks . . .'

'I love it. But it's the only life I've ever known, so I am accustomed to it,' Delphine replied. 'The stress of circus life is not for everyone, though. Long days. Punishing routines on your body. And the pay is not great.'

Beth was a little taken aback by Delphine's searing and forthright reply.

'I warrant all jobs become tiresome after a while,' Beth said.

'That's for sure.' Delphine watched her momentarily, then she lit a cigarette, inhaled intensely and blew out a perfect ring. 'Do you love Christian?'

'Maybe.' Beth was still working on that question.

Delphine raised her eyebrows in surprise. 'I thought you had something about you. More sense than the others to fall for my brother's charms.'

Now she had Beth's complete attention. 'What others?'

Delphine moved closer, a combination of tobacco and spicy perfume filling the air. 'Christian likes women. You've heard the saying about sailors having a girl in every port? Well, that works for trapeze artists too.'

Beth felt like she had been punched. She had not been naive enough to think that Christian had never had love affairs – she had a boyfriend after all, so she could hardly talk – but Delphine's statement shocked her all the same.

'I'm not trying to upset you, Beth. I like you. And maybe you *are* the one for Christian, and he's ready to settle down.' While the words were slightly encouraging, Delphine's face was clouded with doubt.

'But you don't think so,' Beth stated.

Delphine took another drag of her cigarette. 'I've seen a lot of girls like you, scattered in towns all over Europe,

210

with broken hearts and dreams when he waves goodbye to them.' She inclined her head. 'Although to be fair, he seems more taken with you than I've seen him with anyone else for some time.'

Beth swallowed down a rush of emotion. She could hear and see the sincerity in Delphine's words. 'I appreciate your warning. Thank you. But you're right in thinking that I'm unlike the other girls you mentioned. I've enjoyed my time with Christian, but I've always known it would end. I am not expecting anything from him that he does not wish to give.'

Delphine shrugged, then walked on, heading back towards her wagon.

Beth moved on to the dressing room tent with conflicting emotions. Did she care what Christian had done in the past? Probably not. His actions now were what mattered.

'*Bonjour, chérie.*'

His voice, as always, sent all logical thought from her mind. '*Bonjour*, Christian.'

He kissed her, and her body moulded into his.

'Tomorrow is our last day, before my father returns on Friday,' Beth said breathlessly.

'I cannot think of that. Must you torment me?' Christian replied, pouting.

'It will feel strange not to see the brightly coloured wagons in this field. Or hear the sound of a lion's roar or elephant's trumpeting.'

Christian took her hand. He turned two buckets upside down, and they sat on the makeshift seats, facing each other.

'I hope you will miss more than that!' he said. Then his eyes softened. 'I've liked my stay in Cork. I find myself wondering what life would be like in a place like Ballycotton.'

Once again, Beth could not imagine Christian sitting down to a Sunday roast with her family.

'And I wonder what life would be like travelling the world as you do, seeing new places and people every week.'

'The grass is always greener, no?' Christian reached over to caress her cheek. His dark eyes pierced her as he said, 'If I asked you to come away with me, what would you say?'

Beth swallowed. 'I don't know. Ask me, and let's find out.'

Christian took a steadying breath. He watched her in wonder and then said, '*Ma chérie*, would you like to come with me? I cannot offer you much, but you will always have a roof over your head, food in your belly, and love in your heart.' He placed his hand over her heart, which was now hammering in her chest.

This was Beth's chance to escape Ballycotton. To have a life filled with adventure and colour every day. To wake up to a new dawn with hope and excitement.

'At the end of June, we will leave Ireland, and our tour will go to France, then Italy. *Ma chérie*, I cannot wait to show you the beauty of the French countryside.'

Beth closed her eyes as Christian spoke. She imagined them walking through the cobbled streets of Paris as the sun set on another romantic day. It sounded idyllic.

'Of course, everyone must pay their way in the circus.

You could work in the admissions booth, selling tickets. I will organize it. Well, *chérie*? Will I tell the ringmaster we have a new member in our circus?'

Beth didn't want to think about the mundanity of work. She only wanted to think about Christian. Her body ached in a way she'd never felt before. She wanted to feel Christian's weight on top of her. She wanted to experience every part of him and her, together.

'If I go with you . . . where would I sleep?' she asked, her body shivering. She knew she was standing on the brink of an abyss, about to fall in so deep that she might never get out again. But she was powerless to stop.

Christian locked eyes with her, and his lips brushed hers. He whispered, 'I have my own wagon.'

Beth met his eyes. 'Take me there, please . . .'

TWENTY-SEVEN

Kathleen

Wednesday, 23 May 1951

Ballycotton, Cork

Kathleen sat in front of her dressing table, looking at her reflection as she brushed her long dark hair. She automatically began to coil it into a low bun at the nape of her neck. She'd worn her hair like this every day since she became Mrs Kenefick.

Then she opened her hands, and her hair fell into soft waves down her back. She moved her head from side to side and watched her hair swish. She felt young again. If she ignored the fine lines around her eyes and mouth, she wasn't much different now from the young girl she had once been.

Maybe it was time for a change, she thought – and the image of Charles Davis's face flitted through her mind. Her cheeks flamed scarlet as she imagined his hand touching her lower back, sending shivers down her spine. She thought about how his eyes searched hers as she spoke. The way his voice caressed her as he said her name.

At thirty-seven years of age, Kathleen Kenefick had a schoolgirl crush.

On Friday, her husband would return from the lighthouse. She would wash and starch his shirts, prepare his favourite food, rub oil into his left shoulder, which gave him trouble, and pretend that all was well in their marriage.

That she had not been tempted by a Texas oil tycoon.

That she had not spent days longing to feel another man's lips on hers.

Friday.

Time was running out.

Kathleen had not acted on her crush.

Yet.

She decided to take a walk to the Bayview Hotel. She told herself that it was because she hoped for an update on her investment. Charles had mentioned that the oil company would release their statement to the stock market around now. And, of course, she was desperate to finalize this transaction so that Ellen could buy her new home.

But Kathleen knew she was lying to herself. She had to go today because this was her last chance to act on her fantasy. When Patrick returned, the bubble would burst.

215

She smoothed down her chambray blue dress, pinched her cheeks to add colour, then slicked on a thin layer of pink lipstick, generally reserved for mass on Sundays or special occasions.

As she passed the children's bedroom, she peeked her head in to rouse John and Katie. 'It's time for school, you two.'

She knocked on Beth's door, which swung open to an empty room. Her bed was neatly made, with her nightdress folded on the end of her bedspread, just as she'd been taught to do. But Kathleen frowned. She hadn't spoken properly to Beth since she'd told her about Ted's plan to propose. Had she been so wrapped up in her own head and thoughts of Charles that she had been neglecting her eldest daughter? Beth had always been a worry for her. Maybe Patrick was right and the sooner she married Ted and settled down, the better for them all.

Kathleen hurried downstairs and stoked the embers of the Aga stove. She added two lumps of turf to bring it back to life. Then she filled the kettle and began preparing the oats. Thirty minutes later, the children had eaten a creamy bowl of porridge, and Kathleen was shooing them out the door with their school bags slung over their shoulders.

She gave John a bundle of kindling to carry, to help get the fire going in the old school when they got there, and handed Katie their billycans and sandwiches for later.

'Bye, Mam,' they both said cheerily and began walking up the road.

Kathleen followed them to the end of the small driveway and looked up and down the road, hoping to see the familiar sight of her daughter pedalling on her black bike, moving like the wind. But the road was empty. She turned around when she heard the Craigs' front door swing open. Joanne and Ger walked out, followed by Ellen.

'Morning!' Ellen called out, smiling brightly.

Kathleen's heart jumped with delight at seeing her friend so happy. She knew it was a sin to feel pride in doing a good deed, but she couldn't help feeling a satisfied buzz that she was playing a part in changing Ellen's life for the better.

Ger ran up the road to catch up with John and Katie. But Joanne hung back, kicking her shoes on the footpath. Her shoulders were slumped, and she looked like the weight of the world was on her.

'Have a good day in school,' Ellen said, reassuringly touching her daughter's shoulder.

She was clearly struggling very much with the loss of her father.

'Why don't you call us after school today? Spend some time with Beth. I know she'd love to see you,' Kathleen suggested.

Joanne looked up at her. 'Oh, Beth hasn't got time for me anymore.' Her voice was sharp. 'She's far too wrapped up in her new friend.'

'What friend?' Kathleen asked, feeling a bristle of unease run over her.

'Christian. The trapeze artist. They're inseparable.' This information, ironically enough, elicited a smile from the girl. She left, grinning as she skipped off after the children.

Kathleen stood looking after her, mouth agape. Beth was spending time with one of the circus performers? This was news to her. Was that where she'd been disappearing to every day?

'I swear, if that girl tells me she's running away with the circus, I'll throttle her,' Kathleen muttered.

Ellen laughed, 'Don't worry. I'm sure Joanne is exaggerating. She's a bit down in the dumps with everything going on. There must be a full moon on the way. Mary's just the same. I haven't gotten more than two words from her since yesterday.'

'That is strange, all right. Your new housemate is quite the chatterbox.'

'I think we might have overstayed our welcome. I hope Diarmuid has news on the fisherman's cottage today. If not . . .' Ellen left the thought unfinished. Then looked Kathleen up and down, as though only just noticing her appearance. 'You look nice. Are you going anywhere special?'

Kathleen blushed as she felt her friend's eyes shrewdly take in her best dress and cascading hair. 'No. I just felt like a change. Patrick likes my hair like this, so I thought why not, as he's home on Friday.' How easily the lie tripped out of her mouth, she thought in dismay.

'Oh.' Doubt filled Ellen's face. Then she asked, 'Will you be seeing Charles Davis later today?'

Kathleen flashed her a look of annoyance. She didn't care for her friend's inquisition or tone. Ellen could obviously see straight through her. But she immediately felt contrite when she saw hurt on Ellen's face. Kathleen wasn't angry with her friend, she was angry with herself, because she knew that she was behaving in a way most unlike her. She forced a smile and said evenly, 'I might call into the hotel to enquire about my investment.'

'In that case, I'll keep you company,' Ellen said.

Kathleen put her hand up quickly. 'No need. I'll go on my own.'

Ellen nodded, as if she'd expected this. 'Be careful, Kathleen.'

'With what?' Kathleen asked, daring her friend to say out loud what she obviously suspected. 'I can assure you that I always act with caution.'

Ellen looked at her. She opened her mouth to speak, but left the words unsaid. Kathleen turned back into her cottage, and closed the door. Wrestling with her conscience, she walked to the dresser in the kitchen and twisted her hair into a bun once more, feeling more and more foolish with each bobby pin she inserted.

TWENTY-EIGHT

Mollie

Friday, 14 July 2023

Cork University Hospital, Cork

'You look so much better than you did yesterday.'

Mollie was perched on the edge of her grandmother's hospital bed. Nana Beth was sitting upright against a fluffy white pillow, a slight smile on her lips.

'I'm still alive, at least,' Nana Beth replied. 'The doctor said I might get home next week.' Her voice was stronger, the thin rasp had almost gone. While she still had an IV drip in her arm, she was off the ventilator.

'That's the best news ever! We've been so worried,' Mollie said with a smile.

Nana Beth frowned. 'Not the holiday you expected. Coming in here every day to see me.'

'Where else would I be?' Mollie replied. 'By the way, I visited an old friend of yours today.'

Mollie waited for a beat for her grandmother to respond. Nothing.

'I went to the Craig farm and saw Ellen's granddaughter Dervla and her new baby, Kian.'

Beth's eyes narrowed as she digested this news. 'I've not been up to the Craig farm in a long time. How was your visit?'

'Pleasant. Dervla's nice. But she looks exhausted.'

'Babies will do that to you, all right. Especially when you're raising one alone, as I hear young Dervla is.' Nana Beth regarded Mollie again, tapping her chin thoughtfully as she did, 'I might be off base here, but in case I'm not, I wouldn't mention the baby to your aunt Jane. She'll be asking when you'll have your own.'

Mollie fidgeted in her seat. 'She'll have to join the queue. A lot of people are waiting for an answer to that question.'

'I don't know what's bothering you, but I've watched you over the past year and can see that something has changed with you and Nolan. Maybe you don't want children. Or maybe you are having difficulties conceiving. Either way, it's not my business. Or Jane's.'

As usual, her grandmother missed very little. 'Thank you, Nana. Can I tell you something?'

Nana Beth nodded encouragingly.

'I was in awe of Dervla as she nursed little Kian. She made it look easy.' She hesitated. 'But no matter how hard I tried, I just couldn't imagine myself doing the same one day.'

Her grandmother nodded slowly. 'Mollie, I made the mistake of ignoring what I wanted when I was a young girl. Trust me when I tell you there is always a price for that.'

This conversation was moving in directions that Mollie had not envisioned. Afraid her grandmother would close up again, she asked quickly, 'What mistakes did you make, Nana?'

'We're talking about you, Mollie, not me. Do you want children?'

Mollie was so used to hiding her true feelings that she almost shrugged. But maybe it was time that she was more honest with herself and those she loved too. 'Every day, when I popped the foil in my contraceptive pill pack, I wondered when my maternal instinct, my need for a child, would kick in. But it didn't. When Nolan suggested we start trying, I stopped taking the pill and thought, okay, let's see what happens. Watching him with his nieces and nephews, I could see what a great dad he'd make.'

'Hmm. So are you saying you don't want children right now, or ever?' Beth asked, pushing for clarification.

Mollie dodged the question. 'When we didn't get pregnant naturally, I would have been happy to leave it. But when I turned thirty-five, Nolan suggested we go to see a fertility specialist, and before I knew it, a plan was hatched, money handed over, and I was jabbing myself with hormones every day.'

Nana Beth inhaled deeply, her eyes sympathetic.

'When the last IVF didn't take, you know what I felt, Nana?' Mollie put her hands over her face. 'I was relieved.'

222

They let this confession sit between them. Nana's hand touched hers, bringing her back to the room. Her hand was ice cold, but she withdrew it before Mollie could encase it between her own.

Beth asked gently, 'Does Nolan know that's how you feel?'

Mollie shook her head. 'I don't really want to talk about Nolan . . .'

'Well, I won't repeat what you've told me. Your old nana can keep a secret.'

The irony of this statement made Mollie giggle, which sparked laughter from Beth, too.

Wiping tears from her eyes, Mollie said, 'Oh, I needed that release.'

'Me too, love. Me too.'

The term of endearment, rarely given by her grandmother, made Mollie tear up again. She laid her head on her lap. Nana Beth stroked her hair softly, and beneath her canopy of love, Mollie felt safe.

'I don't want to be a mother,' she admitted breathlessly.

Mollie felt lighter. Just saying it out loud was an emotional release.

Her grandmother didn't offer any platitudes. She just continued stroking her hair, offering silent support. Mollie clasped her hand tightly.

'Thank you for understanding.'

A few moments later, when Mollie had wiped her eyes and sat up, her nana changed the subject. 'Did you see Joanne too when you were at the farm?'

'No. She lives in a retirement home now. In fact, I visited her there.'

This got a reaction. Nana Beth's thin eyebrows raised, and a faint colour flamed her cheeks. Mollie waited for her to ask about the meeting, but her jaw set, and she refused to take the bait.

'She gave me some photographs that you might like to see.'

When Mollie showed her the photograph of Katie's first Holy Communion, Nana Beth's face lit up. 'I can't remember what I did yesterday, but I remember that day so clearly.' Then she glanced at the other two images, the one of her and Joanne with Ted, and the other with Christian. 'Goodness, I look so young.'

'You were gorgeous,' Mollie said.

'Don't know about that. But I can see I was pretty.' She gave a small smile. 'Joanne and I had a lot of fun together back then.'

Mollie couldn't help but wonder what happened to change their friendship. She took in the way Joanne looked at Ted again. 'It's interesting, these images of Joanne. It's like two different people. The one with Ted, she looks happy. The one with Christian, she's almost scowling.'

Nana Beth looked at each photograph again, nodding slowly. 'A lot happened in between those photographs.'

'Was Joanne . . . in love with him?' Mollie asked, pointing at Ted.

'Yes. I believe she was.'

Mollie had been right, then. 'So she was jealous of you. Is that why she looks so cross in the photo with Christian?'

'No. That was more to do with her broken heart. Her

father had died, and her family were about to be evicted from their cottage in Powers Terrace. And then there was her uncle, Benny Craig . . . Oh, he was an awful man. He . . .' She paused for a moment '. . . was inappropriate with Joanne. She was deeply uncomfortable in his company.'

Mollie's heart raced. She still couldn't work out if this made Joanne more likely to have written the letters or not. Her head spun with it all.

Beth was staring at Christian now, a look of wonder on her face.

'Joanne hinted that you and he . . . ?' A faint blush tinged Mollie's cheeks as she questioned her grandmother.

'She's always loved gossiping with people about that. But yes, I was . . . involved with Christian.'

'A trapeze artist. Wow, Nana, you never fail to surprise me.' Mollie felt a little in awe. 'What else are you hiding?'

'I think my life started off with a bang. But it got pretty mundane as it went on.' Beth tapped the photographs with her finger, 'I'm surprised Joanne kept these.'

'Nana . . .' Mollie paused, trying to phrase the next thing she said as delicately as possible. 'I know you and Joanne used to be good friends but . . . um . . . I get the feeling that she isn't a big fan of yours anymore?'

'She's hated me for years; that's no secret,' Nana Beth replied mildly.

Mollie swallowed, steeling herself for the next question. 'You know I found that letter you received. Well the thing is, I've had some letters too, all talking about family secrets. I think . . . or rather I wonder, could Joanne have sent them?'

225

Nana Beth's eyes widened in shock. 'Tell me about these letters you've received.'

Mollie filled her grandmother in on all that had happened while she was so ill. 'So you can see why I'm anxious to find out who is behind it all.'

'I'm so sorry that you have found yourself messed up in this,' Nana Beth said, tears filling her eyes.

'Don't worry about me. It's you we are all concerned about.' And as Mollie saw her grandmother's face pale, she cursed herself for bringing the letters up at all. 'We don't have to talk about this now. Close your eyes. Rest. It will all be okay, I'll make sure of it.'

Nana Beth closed her eyes, and Mollie sat by her side silently. She thought her nana had drifted off to sleep, but a few moments later, she opened her eyes and said in a weak voice, 'Joanne is capable of betrayal. I've experienced that first-hand. But this doesn't strike me as her style. If Joanne had something to say, she's never been behind the door about coming forward.'

'But there could be lots of reasons? For spite, or perhaps to cause trouble for you and your family. Maybe she's after money.'

'She doesn't need money. The Craig family sold a wedge of farmland a few years back – that new development located just outside Ballycotton used to be their land. Besides, Joanne loved her mother more than anyone else.' Beth paused, and a faint line of sweat formed on her forehead. She swallowed then continued, her voice growing weaker with each word. 'I don't think she'd ever do anything that might . . . besmirch her name. And Ellen . . . she is mixed up in all this.'

Mollie chewed her lip in frustration. 'In what, Nana? Please tell me.'

Just as Nana Beth was about to respond, a nurse walked in and frowned as she took in her pale face.

'I think Beth needs to rest. We don't want to overtire her, do we?' The nurse began rearranging the pillows, so that Beth was now lying down once more.

'I'm sorry,' Mollie said, her stomach somersaulting as the nurse checked Nana Beth's vitals and then changed her IV bag. She'd pushed her grandmother too far with all her questions.

'Close your eyes again. I'll sit here until you fall asleep.'

TWENTY-NINE

Mollie

Friday, 14 July 2023

Ballycotton, Cork

When Mollie returned to the cottage, she found her dad staring at a white envelope on the kitchen table, his face creased with worry lines. 'Someone put this through the letterbox.'

Mollie picked it up with a racing heart; her name was in the same typewriter font as the previous letters.

'They know I'm here,' Mollie said. She looked around her, feeling vulnerable and exposed. And judging by the look on her dad's face, his feelings echoed hers.

'You've been in the local paper and all over the social media.' He reached a hand to stop her ripping open the letter. 'Use a knife. That envelope could be evidence.' He handed a small butter knife to Mollie.

She slipped its blade under the sealed flap and gently opened the envelope, pulling a single sheet from it. Her dad peered over her shoulder as she unfolded the page, revealing the words inside.

Welcome to Ireland, Mollie. As a reporter, you must seek the truth. Are you willing to do that?

Mollie wasn't even aware she had been holding her breath until her dad touched her arm, concern written all over his face. She exhaled deeply and held on to the island for support.

'That's it. We're going to the guards,' he said firmly. 'What does this person expect you to do? Write a tell-all exposé on your grandmother? This person is nothing more than a damn coward hiding behind a keyboard.' Her dad squared his shoulders and held his two hands in fists by his side. He was ready to go to battle for his daughter.

Mollie gave him a weak smile of thanks, grateful that he was here by her side. Then a thought crossed her mind. 'Dervla Craig is a Garda. And she's also Ellen's granddaughter. Why don't I ask her for advice? That wouldn't be reporting it to the authorities. Not officially at least.'

Her dad murmured his approval at that suggestion. A rap on the front door made them both jump, then laugh self-consciously at how shaky they were.

To Mollie's surprise, Dervla stood on the doorstep, carrying baby Kian in a sling. There were no smiles on her face this time. She looked thunderous as she walked into their cottage.

'When you called earlier, you asked me about family secrets. Then lo and behold, a few hours later, the post comes. And I receive this! What the hell is going on, Mollie?' She slapped a white envelope onto the island.

'Damn it,' Mollie said, holding up her letter. 'I'm so sorry, Dervla. There's something I need to tell you. I've also received letters – three of them.'

Shock replaced the anger on Dervla's face as she took this in. Then, she opened the envelope and showed Mollie and her dad the letter.

> **It's time to unbury the truth about what the keepers' wives covered up in 1951.**

'I better put the kettle on,' her dad muttered, walking over to the sink to fill it. As he began preparing tea, Mollie filled in Dervla on all they had been dealing with to date, showing her the letters and photographs she had.

'And you have no idea what the secret is or who's sending the letters?'

'We're trying to piece it all together as best we can. Nana has been so ill, it's been difficult to get answers from her. That's the real reason I called to see you. I'm sorry for the subterfuge.'

Dervla waved aside her apology.

Mollie took a deep breath, 'One more thing. We've recently found out that before my great-grandmother died, she had dementia, and she . . . she spoke about killing someone. My aunt Jane always thought it must be nonsense, but between the letters now and that photograph . . .'

Dervla's eyes widened in shock. 'You're putting two and two together and making eight. I can't believe that my grandmother was involved with killing anyone. She was a midwife. She brought life into the world, not took it, for goodness' sake.'

Her dad placed mugs with milk and sugar on the table, along with a plate of biscuits. They all sipped their drinks in silence for a moment.

'Are Beth and my aunt Joanne the only ones in that photograph still alive?' Dervla asked, stroking her baby's head softly as he slept against her chest.

'Well, Mary Mythen is still alive. In fact, Nana Beth saw her last week, before she arrived in Ballycotton. She's quite frail, from what I've been told. I'm not sure she can help us. So I've been researching online, looking for clues in newspaper archives. I've come up blank.'

'Maybe I can help you with that. If we can work out who died in 1951, then it might help us work out what we are up against,' Dervla said.

Mollie offered her a tentative smile. 'It will be good to have your help. It's been a little overwhelming.'

'It will be nice to have something to do that doesn't involve bottles or nappies,' Dervla answered, 'I'll take a look into Mary Mythen, see if I can track down her family.'

Baby Kian began to move, opening his eyes and looking up at his mama. 'Sshhh . . .' Dervla soothed, and like magic, he closed his eyes, falling back into slumber again. 'He'll be awake looking for his bottle soon enough, so I better get home. I need to think about all of this. Let's keep in touch. And not go jumping to any mad conclusions. I'm sure there'll be a simple explanation.'

Once they'd swapped contact details, Dervla got up to leave. 'One more thing, are you one hundred per cent sure that, other than you both, and your aunt Jane, there isn't anyone else in your family who knows about the secret?'

'My mother, of course. But nobody else. Of course, we only found out about this when the letters arrived, so I can't say for definite,' her dad said.

But as they waved goodbye to Dervla, Mollie couldn't help but wonder if that was true. With Kathleen's dementia, who was to say what she might have said to the wrong person. She may have broken her vow more than once.

THIRTY

Where are you off to now, Mollie?

I pull my hoodie up, tightening the toggles so that it stays in place. Then I follow you, ensuring I keep a few steps behind.

Mollie stops, pausing at the cliff's edge, and takes her phone out, snapping shots of the Atlantic. She turns her back to the ocean and pouts for a selfie. Can she be taking my letters seriously?

Should I show myself? Confront Mollie now? Tell her what I want? But look what happened the last time I tried to speak to someone about this. No, I decide. It's too risky.

The letters will work. I know they will.

Mollie turns around again and peers down over the dark craggy rocks into the waters behind. She looks around her, and her eyes drift over in my direction. I move behind a navy HiAce van, my heart racing as I take cover.

When I peek again, Mollie has continued walking towards the village.

I wait. Then, once again, I follow.

THIRTY-ONE

Mollie

Saturday, 15 July 2023

Ballycotton, Cork

Mollie couldn't shake the feeling that someone was following her. She picked up her pace as she made her way through Ballycotton village. Was she imagining a danger that didn't exist? Despite it being a bright day, she shivered in the warm sun.

Her dad had dropped her on the outskirts of the village, which was busy with summer tourists, before he made his way to see Nana Beth. Cars were parked along the side of the narrow Main Street, which meant that passing vehicles could only move in single file. Three kids passed her by, licking impossibly tall whipped ice-cream cones, and Mollie felt reassured by the presence of strangers. Safety in numbers. For now at least.

She glanced at her phone, following the Google Maps directions. Five minutes to go until she reached the graveyard.

Mollie had no clue what to expect when she got there. It was like looking for a needle in a haystack – when you didn't know what the needle looked like.

The Star of the Sea Roman Catholic Church appeared on a steep hill. It was a freestanding gable-fronted four-bay building, and like most buildings in Ballycotton, it had a stunning view of the bay. A steeple tower jutted upwards into the blue sky overhead. Mollie's research told her it was built in 1901.

Mollie made her way through the wrought iron gate, glancing backwards at the sound of gravel crunching behind her. But again, there was no one there. She began to regret telling her father not to come with her.

She made her way to the rear of the church where hundreds of headstones jutted out of the green grass. Taking a deep breath, Mollie moved through them, pausing to look at each for a moment, her eyes searching for a death dated 1951.

Some graves only had marker stones at the head or foot of the grave, with the name and date of the person buried. Others had more decorative headstones, with inscriptions and carvings. A few had sculptures, like crosses or obelisks, angels and weeping women. Fresh flowers sat atop a newer grave.

Mollie had trouble reading some of the headstones; age and time had faded the letters, and moulds, algae and lichens obscured the inscriptions. Each time she came to a grave that showed a death in 1951, she photographed it. The names of the deceased meant nothing to her. But she would look them up when she returned to her laptop later.

When Mollie came to the Kenefick plot, she felt a rush of emotion that she had not expected. Underneath her great-grandfather's name, an inscription said, *He stood his watch faithfully*. And below that, was her great-grandmother's name.

'What secrets did you take to the grave, Granny Kathleen?' she whispered. A sea breeze moved through the graveyard, and Mollie jolted when she heard a noise beside her. She laughed out loud in relief when she saw that it was only a flowerpot overturned in the wind on a nearby grave.

Mollie continued moving up and down the rows through the graveyard, zig-zagging her way through uneven ground. Finally, she came to another name she recognized. The Craig family.

There was an ornate granite headstone, which looked like a new addition. Joanne must have erected this headstone, Mollie surmised. She felt another pang of sympathy for the woman, remembering Joanne's face softening when she spoke about her parents. Once again, Mollie acknowledged that Joanne may be more complicated than first glance might suggest. Mollie snapped a photograph, then moved on to the grave alongside it. She stopped in surprise when she saw that it was a second Craig grave, with four people buried in it. One name jumped out.

Benny Craig, died 27 May 1951, aged 48

Joanne's uncle. Nana Beth had said what a horrible man he was. And he'd died in 1951, the year the photograph was taken. Mollie felt a rush of fear and excitement. She couldn't wait to discuss it with Dervla, who she was meeting shortly for lunch.

Ten minutes later, she was buckled up in the passenger seat of Dervla's Land Rover. 'It's such a nice day and you've spent so much of your holiday in the hospital, so I thought a picnic on the beach would be nice. There's a little takeaway van called Trawler Boyz that I think you'll enjoy!'

'No Kian?' Mollie asked, noting the empty car seat behind them.

'He's with his dad.'

Within twenty minutes, they were seated on two folding chairs, sitting side by side eating golden crispy scampi and fat chips laced with salt and vinegar. It was, as Dervla promised, the tastiest meal she'd had in a long time.

'Benny Craig died in 1951,' Mollie said, trying to keep her voice nonchalant.

Dervla raised her eyebrows. 'And you think our grannies killed him?' she asked with a shaky laugh. They made a face as they looked at each other uncertainly. 'Let's finish our meal before we discuss our grandmothers' murderess potential.'

A group of children ran towards the sea, throwing

themselves into the water, and squealing with delight as the waves lapped them.

'I've been looking forward to a few hours to myself. But hearing those children play, all I can do is think about my baby.' Dervla rolled her eyes.

'What's it like? Being a mother?'

Dervla let out a short laugh. 'Nothing you can be prepared for! Exhausting. All-consuming. Terrifying. Exhilarating. Wondrous. There aren't enough words to describe it. The best thing I've ever done in my life – it's so hard to share how it feels. Every bit of my love is now squished into his little body.'

'When do you have to go back to work?'

'I've got another six months off. I saved up all my holidays and am taking an extra month unpaid. I can't imagine leaving Kian with anyone else yet. But I can't also imagine not working. I love my job and I'm itching to get back to it.'

'What exactly do you do for the Gardaí?'

'I work with a Community Policing Team in Cork city, which suits me perfectly. A short commute, but far enough that I'm not on the doorstep of where I'm policing.'

'What does it involve?' Mollie asked.

'Typical Gardaí duties. But I also support community crime prevention programmes. We're essentially supporting communities, reassuring them, helping reduce the fear of crime. I like it. Hours are okay, typically eight-hour shifts, which will work better for Kian.'

She sighed. 'Some of the things I see every day in work scare the life out of me when I think about a future world that Kian will have to navigate.'

'Well, he's lucky to have you on his side,' Mollie said.

They shared a smile. They had quickly established the kind of easy comradeship that Mollie knew was rare, and she was grateful for it.

'You ever thought about having kids?' Dervla asked. Then she slapped her leg, cursing softly under her breath. 'Don't answer that – I should know better than to ask such a stupid question. I spent years dodging similar ones. My only excuse is the baby brain. It's a real thing. Gave me a momentary lapse of judgement.'

Mollie laughed, surprised not to be offended by Dervla's question, which usually sent her skin bristling. 'You're okay!' she reassured her quickly. 'As it happens, my husband and I have just finished another round of IVF. No joy.'

'I'm sorry,' Dervla said softly. 'That must be tough.'

'It's not fun, that's for sure. I'm in awe, watching you with Kian. You make it look so easy.'

Dervla laughed. 'That couldn't be further from the truth. The first time I bathed Kian, he slipped through my hands, and I swear, I thought I'd drowned him. I cried for a solid two hours after that. If there's a mistake to be made, I've made it. You learn on the job with parenthood. Anyone who tells you that it's easy is lying.'

You never know what is going on behind closed doors, Mollie thought. Her admiration for Dervla continued to grow every time they met. 'Do you miss your life from before?'

Dervla shook her head. 'Not for one second. I'm where I'm meant to be. I know I'm not doing things the traditional way. Having a baby on my own. But while it wasn't planned, it feels right.'

Mollie could see that. Motherhood suited Dervla. 'Is it too personal of me to ask about the dad?'

Dervla glanced over and smiled. 'I asked you a personal question, so you can do the same. His dad is a Garda too. Kevin. We were only casually dating. Nothing serious. But then I got pregnant. I'm forty, so honestly, I thought I'd missed the boat when it came to having a family. I'd made peace with it.'

Mollie's breath quickened as she asked, 'You always wanted kids?'

'I did. I used to assume I'd meet someone and fall in love, do the whole marriage and two point two kids and a fluffy Labrador. But life doesn't work like that. I've yet to meet the right guy. And I suppose I may never meet him.'

'Kevin isn't the right guy then?'

'Nah. We don't love each other. It was fun for a while. We worked together on several projects and flirting turned into a few nights of fun, which was lovely. But it fizzled out as quickly as it burned. And when I found out I was pregnant, I knew I had no interest in marrying someone just to conform to some societal expectation. So I told him I wanted to have the baby and that he could be as involved or uninvolved as he liked. Once he got over the shock, he decided he wanted to be part of it all. We're still navigating how that looks, but I'm happy he's there for Kian.'

Mollie felt so much respect for Dervla. There was no bull with her; she was a straight talker who was refreshingly honest. And she found herself opening up in return. Perhaps her conversation with Nana had opened a door for her. 'It's a little different for me. I . . . felt relieved when I learned I wasn't pregnant.'

Mollie waited for a gasp of shock, but none came. Dervla simply replied, 'Then it's probably just as well the IVF didn't work.'

'Yeah, probably.'

They finished their lunch, continuing to get to know each other, chatting about their lives in Ireland and America. And with each passing moment, Mollie felt her smile get bigger. She'd not had as much fun talking with another woman for years.

THIRTY-TWO

Mollie

Saturday, 15 July 2023

Ballycotton, Cork

It had been a long day, but when Mollie arrived back at
Peony Cottage, with a bright sky that promised a pretty
sunset, she felt hopeful. The fresh air and sunshine had
been a tonic, and after lunch she had picked up the car
from her dad and visited Nana Beth. Worryingly, she was
back on her ventilator again and slept through the visit,
but the nurse reassured her that it was precautionary,
rather than anything she needed to fret about.

As Mollie parked up, the strangest sensation overtook
her, and she shivered involuntarily. Like earlier, on her
walk to the graveyard, she had the most peculiar sense
that someone was watching her. She scanned the area, but
she couldn't see anyone in the vicinity.

She remembered her grandmother's story about the submerged old village under the water. 'Maybe there are ghosts here,' Mollie whispered, feeling foolish at the thought.

Leaning against the car, she pressed Nolan's number on impulse. He answered her call immediately, pulling off his hard hat, he wiped the sweat from his face with the back of his hand as he greeted her. 'One second, I'll go outside; it'll be quieter.'

Mollie felt a tug on her heart. Recognition of love and need for this man. 'I miss you!' she cried out when he appeared on screen again.

The answering smile on his face made her heart dissolve into a puddle of emotion.

'And I you. Gosh, you look so beautiful.'

'Thank you! A little windswept, I think. Look how beautiful this view is . . .' Mollie turned the camera around to take in the blue sky reaching down to kiss the green leafy garden beside the whitewashed cottage.

'You look like an Irish colleen of no more than twenty. You've even got freckles on your face!'

'I'll give you one hour to stop complimenting me like that.' Mollie touched her husband's face on the screen, tracing his cheek and wishing she could crawl into the image and fall into his arms. They looked at each other for a moment, matching grins on their faces.

Then Nolan's smile slipped. 'Have there been any more letters?' he asked. 'I've not been able to stop thinking about it all. I don't like it, Mol.'

'I must admit it's getting a bit freaky Friday here, Nolan. Have you time to listen?' Mollie looked around her again, making sure she was still alone.

'Always time for you.'

Mollie told him about the latest discoveries and her day with Dervla, watching the shock and surprise on his face at each stage of the update. 'I don't like the sound of any of this, Mollie. I've been thinking . . .' He paused, his brows knitted together. 'What if I flew over to Ballycotton? I'm supposed to be on vacation anyhow. Then I could be there, in person, to support you.'

Mollie felt a flood of emotions rush her. Her initial excitement that she might get to see Nolan was followed swiftly by worry that seeing him would mean she had to discuss their future – with or without children.

'It would be amazing to have you here, to help me muddle through it all, but I don't want to be selfish. After all, we agreed last week that . . .' She couldn't finish the sentence.

They fell back to an uneasy silence. Nolan's jaw tightened and Mollie could see she'd hurt him again. She seemed to be doing that a lot lately. 'I'm sorry, Nolan,' she whispered.

'You're right. I get it. Listen, try not to worry in the meantime about all this stuff with your grandmother. It will all be okay, Mollie. You'll see.'

And at that moment, Mollie almost believed him.

After they'd said their goodbyes and hung up, she turned back towards the roadside – and saw a flash of movement in the corner of her eye. A person wearing a black jacket with the hood up ran out of sight from the end of the driveway. Her muscles stiffened as she heard the sound of tyres spinning on the road as a car sped off.

And while she couldn't prove it, somehow Mollie knew that whoever was behind the wheel had been the one watching her. She felt her body shudder involuntarily.

She walked into the cottage, locking the door behind her. Her dad called out hello from the stove, where he was putting something in the oven.

'Dad, I think I'm being watched,' she said, a little sheepishly. 'At the graveyard, then at the cliff's edge. And just now, I saw someone run off and drive away – in a black hoodie, pulled down low, so I've no idea if it was a man or a woman. I can't help but think it's related to the letters.'

'Moving fast or slow . . . ?' her dad asked quickly, heading to the window to look outside.

'Does it matter?' Mollie replied.

'It could. Surely, it's not Joanne scurrying into a car?' He turned back to her.

Mollie shrugged. 'Dervla told me earlier that she takes Pilates daily. She's a sprightly woman for her age.'

'I don't want you going anywhere alone until we get this sorted,' her dad said, his forehead wrinkled in a frown.

'Dad, I'm not thirteen. I can take care of myself.'

Mollie's phone began to ring. It was Dervla. 'Hey. While you visited your nana, I tracked down Mary Mythen's son – a guy called Jim. I gave him a call.'

'One sec, I'm gonna put you on loudspeaker, so Dad can hear.'

They both leaned in close to listen.

'Mary isn't up to any phone calls or visits. She's in hospice care now. It's not an option to chat to her. Jim said his parents had a happy life together. Mary became a keeper herself in the seventies and, after Seamus died, she took over from him in Hook Lighthouse. But wait till you hear this. As soon as I asked Jim if his parents had ever mentioned any family secrets, he got really defensive. Angry almost. Said he was disappointed that Beth had spoken about his grandfather. And that his grandfather's actions didn't define his family's history. Then he hung up on me!'

Mollie and her dad exchanged shocked glances. 'This is getting more and more twisted. Who was he talking about? Mary or Seamus's father?'

'That I can answer. It's all on public record. I've managed to find out that Mary grew up in Dublin, an only child. Her father – a guy called George Martin – was convicted of murder in 1948 and sentenced to death. He spent his last days on this earth in Mountjoy Prison in Dublin and was among the last people in Ireland to be executed by hanging.'

Mollie felt a tension headache begin to nag her. There was so much to take in. 'Who did he murder?' Mollie asked, her skin prickling with fear.

'A nurse who disturbed him while he was burgling her house. There was a list of petty crimes he'd been involved in for years before that. I found newspaper cuttings about the trial. I can't imagine Mary had a nice childhood.'

Mollie felt a wave of sympathy for the woman. What a family legacy to live with.

'Oh, but I'm not finished yet,' Dervla said. 'Half an hour after he'd hung up on me, Jim called back. Guess who just received a letter?'

'No!' Mollie and her dad said at once.

'Yep. Similar thing, asking him if he was ready to share his mother's secret.'

Mollie shook her head in disbelief.

'I calmed Jim down. Explained that we had both received letters too. He's agreed to stay in touch if he thinks of anything else that might be useful.'

'He could be double-bluffing us. Pretending he got a letter so we don't suspect him,' her dad said.

'I thought of that. But remember, Jim thinks the secret relates to his grandfather, George Martin. He's either a very good liar, or the letters are not coming from him,' Dervla said.

Mollie slumped into a chair by the table. Exhaustion from her long day was setting in.

'Is it time to talk to the Gardaí yet?' her dad asked.

'I am the Gardaí,' Dervla reminded him.

'I know. But you're involved. I think it's time we formally reported the letters.'

'I still think we need to wait. Let whoever is doing this show their hand, and then we can make a call on next steps. Try not to worry. I've got this. I'm going to visit my aunt Joanne as soon as I can, to see if she can shed any light on things. The time for dancing around the secret is gone. We have to ask difficult questions,' Dervla said gently. 'But you need to remember this: my grandmother's dead. Mary doesn't have much more than a few days left. But Beth is alive.' She paused. 'Do you understand what that means?'

There was a further pause, and before anyone spoke, Dervla continued: 'If there *is* evidence of a crime, she's the only one left to be questioned.' She hesitated again. 'And the only one who will have to face charges for it.'

THIRTY-THREE

Kathleen

Wednesday, 23 May 1951

Ballycotton, Cork

Kathleen and Mary were helping Ellen pack the family possessions up all afternoon. The front parlour was now filled with crates and boxes stacked with everything they owned. Framed photographs, candlesticks, the good Ainsley crockery set that had been a wedding gift.

It was earlier that morning when Diarmuid Kearney finally gave Ellen the news that she had desperately been praying for. Paudie O'Connor's nephew had accepted her offer to purchase the cottage, agreeing that she would rent initially until the sale went through. When Ellen called around to tell Kathleen, their earlier misunderstanding was instantly forgotten, as the two women clung to each other in relief.

'You okay?' Kathleen asked Ellen, seeing her face swell with emotion as she looked down into the boxes.

'The crockery. We never used it. We said we'd save it for a best that never came.' Ellen sighed.

'There's a lesson there,' Kathleen said. 'When it comes time for our children to marry, we'll insist that they never save anything.'

'Every day should be a day for Sunday best,' Mary whispered.

And the three women shared a sad smile.

Ellen wiped her hands on her apron and looked around the room with satisfaction. 'That's everything but our clothes and toiletries. I'm ready to leave Powers Terrace as soon as Diarmuid can give me the keys.'

Kathleen felt a lump catch in her throat. She'd been so busy trying to find Ellen a new place to live that she'd not taken a moment to think about how much she'd miss having her friend next door. They caught each other's eye and Kathleen reached for her hand.

Mary began rubbing the coffee table with a cloth.

'I think it's clean,' Ellen said kindly, nudging Kathleen and nodding in Mary's direction.

'What? Oh yes. Right,' Mary replied, putting down the cloth.

'I'm going to run down to Diarmuid's office, see if the contracts have arrived yet. I'll be back shortly,' Ellen said.

'Fingers crossed,' Mary said distractedly as she picked up her cloth and began polishing the table again.

'I'll go with you,' Kathleen said, her eyes on Mary. Mary had seemed so lively and talkative at first, but these last couple of days she had retreated into herself and clearly had a lot on her mind. Kathleen wondered if she was worried about her husband's return – but they had seemed smitten with each other when Seamus was here. Kathleen frowned; she hated seeing anybody upset. She moved closer to Mary and leaned in to say softly, 'I'm a good listener, if you need to talk.'

But this offer seemed to make matters worse, judging by the speed at which Mary was scrubbing the table.

As Kathleen and Ellen reached Main Street, Beth whizzed past on her bike.

'Beth! I need to talk to you,' Kathleen called out, but her daughter only acknowledged this with a distracted wave.

'Everyone is acting very strange today. I think you're right – there must be a full moon!' Kathleen said to Ellen, who laughed along with her.

'The deeds are on their way from Mr O'Connor's solicitor in Dublin and should be ready this evening, Mrs Craig,' said Diarmuid Kearney at the auctioneer's. 'I can see that time is of the essence, so why don't you call back in the morning to sign contracts, pay your deposit and a month's rent and then I can give you the key?'

'That suits me perfectly,' Ellen replied.

'We'll need a few days to give the place a good top-to-bottom clean, to make it habitable, before you move in,' Kathleen said.

'Do you think Peter would be happy with this news?' Ellen asked suddenly, her face crumpled in doubt.

'Of course he would,' Kathleen said firmly. 'He would want you and the children to settle down here. He loved Ballycotton, it was his childhood home, after all. You should be proud of yourself, Ellen. I'm not sure I could have handled the same situation, with as much grace as you've shown. Now why don't we go home. The children will be home from school any minute. You've got lots to share with them.'

As they left the auctioneer's, they heard the sound of a bell, and the Cork City Fire Brigade truck trundled past in a cloud of smoke. Kathleen and Ellen stared after it in surprise, and Kathleen felt a prickle of unease. In the distance, a cloud of dark, dense smoke curled into the blue sky.

'There must be a fire; it looks close enough,' Ellen said.

Maureen Doyle came out of the corner shop, her little baby in her arms. She moved towards them. 'I heard that it's one of the cottages on Chapel Road gone up in flames.'

Before Kathleen could speak, Ellen picked up her skirt and ran towards Chapel Road. Kathleen had no choice but to run after her, her chest and head pounding with every step she took. All the while thinking that God would not be so cruel as to dangle hope in front of Ellen, only to take it away.

Panting and out of breath, Kathleen and Ellen came to a standstill where a crowd had gathered, blocking the road twenty feet from the burning building.

The firefighters had released their hoses and were dousing the flames on a burning thatched roof.

Kathleen blinked through the black smoke that stung her eyes and made them weep.

The cottage in flames was Paudie O'Connor's.

She felt Ellen sag beside her, falling to her knees.

Thank God she didn't sign the contract yet, Kathleen thought, as she leaned down to comfort Ellen.

'It's a desperate sight to see, isn't it?' a voice said from behind them.

Kathleen whipped around to face Benny, who was chewing a blade of straw in the corner of his mouth.

'That's the problem with those old thatched cottages. One flick of a lit cigarette and the whole place will go up like a light. Pity that.'

'You did this!' Ellen cried out, jumping back to her feet.

'That's a terrible accusation. Some would say it's slander.' Then he pulled out a pack of John Player, tapped the box and placed a cigarette into his mouth, lighting it with a match.

'How could you?' Ellen stammered, her body shaking as anger overtook her.

Kathleen moved closer to her friend, and placed a protective arm around her.

Benny took a long drag from his cigarette, then blew the smoke directly into Ellen and Kathleen's faces, making their eyes smart and tear up. 'Why are you getting so upset?'

'You know why. This was to be our home. It was all arranged.' Tears were falling down Ellen's face.

Benny smiled, enjoying her distress. Then he grabbed her wrist, holding it so tight he left indents on her pale skin. 'Not any more, it's not. I'd say it's time you started being nicer to me. Because you and your children are about to find yourselves on the streets, unless . . .'

'Get your hands off her, you wicked man,' Kathleen shouted, pushing down on Benny's hand to remove it from Ellen.

'It will be over your dead body before I move into your house,' Ellen spat.

'Fighting words. But you'll come begging soon enough. Of that, I'm certain.' Then he flicked his half-smoked cigarette to the ground and added as he moved to leave, 'Put that out, will you? You can't be too careful.'

As he swaggered away, whistling tunelessly, Ellen collapsed into Kathleen's arms. 'That's it then. I have nowhere to go.'

THIRTY-FOUR

Mary

Wednesday, 23 May 1951

Ballycotton, Cork

Moments after Ellen and Kathleen left, the front door of Mary's cottage flew open, and Beth Kenefick rushed into the kitchen.

Mary took in the tangled mess of Beth's hair, noting how her face was flushed. 'Are you okay?'

'Delphine says that Christian has a girl in every port and that he can't be trusted, but he asked me to run away with him when the circus leaves on Saturday!' Beth exclaimed in one quick and tumbled explanation.

Mary's eyes widened. 'And are you going to leave with Christian?'

Beth looked up, her eyes pools of emotion. 'Mammy and Daddy would never forgive me. And how can I do that to Ted? He's planning to propose to me on his next shore leave. What will I do, Mary?' Beth reached over to grab Mary's hand. 'Whatever you say I should do, I will.'

Mary doubted that very much. The girl had a will of iron and would clearly follow her heart's desire. 'You know that I can't tell you that. If you love Ted, you should stay. If you love Christian, then you should consider going. But whatever you do, you must be honest with everyone. If you leave, walk with your head held high; don't run away in the darkness of the night.'

'That's easy for you to say!' Beth said. 'My parents will lock me up and throw away the key if I dare to be honest with them.'

'They might surprise you,' Mary said. 'Listen to me, Beth. Running away is never the answer. I tried that. But the past has a way of catching up with you, no matter how many miles you put between you and it.'

Then to Mary's horror, tears welled up deep inside her and coursed down her cheeks.

'What's wrong?' Beth asked, her face turning from surprise to worry.

'I'm fine. Ignore me.' Mary wiped her eyes, feeling foolish for letting herself get emotional in front of Beth; she was supposed to be the adult, the strong one. 'Sleep on this, Beth. This is huge, and making a rash decision will change your life forever. Do you want to work and live in a circus? Every day, every night, day in, day out? What will you do for money? Will Christian support you financially? Is he proposing marriage? Or will you live together without a ring?'

Beth shrugged, doubt filling her eyes.

Mary thought about Kathleen and the betrayal she would feel if Beth went through with this. 'Promise me that you won't leave without talking to me again.'

But before Beth could make that assurance, the door flew open once more. This time it was Ellen who ran in, with Kathleen racing behind her.

Ellen's eyes were red and angry. Her face was covered in a layer of grey soot, leaving two white trails where she'd been crying, but now she clenched her fists by her side. 'I'm going to kill him. So help me God, I will put a knife in his heart and watch him bleed.'

Mary couldn't respond at first, such was her shock at Ellen's words. But she could see that Ellen was at the end of her tether. She tried to coax Ellen to sit down. But Ellen was so pent up she couldn't be persuaded. She continued to pace the room, making no sense as she spoke of murder.

'What is it? What happened?' Beth asked.

'He put a light to Paudie O'Connor's cottage. It's burned down to the ground,' Ellen cried out.

Mary and Beth joined Kathleen, standing in front of the half-crazed Ellen.

'Who did such a horrific thing?' Mary asked.

'Benny Craig. He stood beside me and all but admitted it.'

Mary felt Beth's hand reach for her own, and she clasped it gratefully. She was shocked by Ellen's news and more so by the idea of arson.

Kathleen groaned, sinking to a seat at the table, 'It's my fault. I should never have told Benny you planned to move in there. I just wanted to wipe the smug smile off his face.'

Ellen shook her head. 'He would have found out from someone else. And done the same. He's an evil man.' Her body shook, and she cried out, 'I can't do it! I can't move into his farm. I will swing for him before I do that.'

'You won't have to,' Kathleen said, pulling her friend into her arms and holding her tight. 'Once the children are home from school and settled, I'll go to see Charles. And I'll make sure he understands the urgency of the situation. With any luck, there will be news today, and my shares can be sold. Benny Craig may have burned down the cottage. But there are other properties, Ellen. We'll use my money to buy somewhere else. We'll go to Sergeant Cody and report the crime. Benny won't get away with it. I won't let him.'

Beth looked at her mother in confusion.

'I'll tell you later,' Kathleen replied. Then she turned to Mary, 'If we need some extra time, can Ellen and the children stay on for another few weeks?'

Mary nodded absently. It went without saying that she'd never see the family out on the streets or in a boarding house in the city. Seamus would understand that. But she had more pressing worries. These women were now placing their trust in a scoundrel and a con-man. Mary knew that they would never see Kathleen's investment again.

She had fretted and worried about this knowledge for days, but she knew that she could no longer hold on to her secret. Because if she did, she would never be able to look at herself in the mirror again.

'We need to talk about your shares, Kathleen,' Mary said.

'What shares, Mammy?' Beth asked, her face scrunched up in confusion.

Kathleen paled. 'I'll explain it all later in more detail. But I've invested money into an oil company, which was going to help pay for the fisherman's cottage.'

'I don't understand,' Beth said, biting her lip.

'What do you need to tell us?' Ellen asked, turning to Mary.

Mary tried to speak, but her throat was tight. She walked over to the table and took a long drink of her water. Then she cleared her throat. 'You'd better take a seat, ladies. I have something I need to tell you.'

THIRTY-FIVE

Kathleen

Wednesday, 23 May 1951

Ballycotton, Cork

The room was silent, save for the tick, tick, tick of the clock on the mantelpiece. Kathleen shivered as a damning thought popped into her head.

Time was up.

But for whom?

'There's no easy way to say this. So I'll just get straight to the point.' Mary's voice trembled, and she rocked back and forth in her seat. 'I'm afraid Charles Davis is not who he says he is.'

Of all the things Kathleen had thought that Mary might come out with, hearing Charles's name shook her to the core.

'What do you mean by that?' Kathleen snapped.

Mary winced at her tone. 'When I first saw Davis at the Bayview Hotel, his face seemed familiar. I was sure I'd seen him before but I couldn't place him.'

'He has one of those faces . . . the kind people often mistake for . . . for someone they know,' Kathleen countered, fear making her stammer.

Mary shook her head. 'It was only when he approached me on the second occasion, that it came to me how I knew him.'

She paused, and they all waited for what felt like an intolerable time for Mary to continue.

'Well, spit it out, girl,' Kathleen demanded.

Beth looked at her in shock, and Kathleen knew her tone was too abrasive. She tried to swallow her fear, to take back control of the situation.

'There is something about my father that I never share with people,' Mary admitted, two spots of red appearing on her cheeks. She covered her face in her hands for a moment. Then in a whisper, said, 'Three years ago he was executed for murder.'

'Murder?' Beth repeated, her eyes large and round in her face.

Mary nodded tearfully. 'The things he put my ma and me through, and more importantly, the life he took, I can never forgive or condone.'

All worries for herself disappeared as Kathleen saw pain etched onto every line on Mary's face. Goodness knew what she'd been through in her young life.

Ellen reached out to touch Mary's hand. 'To carry this on your shoulders . . . I'm so sorry.'

'Does Seamus know about your father?' Kathleen asked gently, as her mind tried to understand what Mary's father might have to do with Charles.

'No.' Mary paused for a moment, a flush creeping up her cheek. 'I have not kept this part of me from him without thought. But I've learned that it's better to keep who I am to myself. People assume like father, like daughter.'

'What a burden to have to hide,' Kathleen added, her heart wrenching in sympathy for Mary. She thought of her own parents and the idyllic childhood they'd given her; she felt nothing but pride that she was their daughter.

Mary wiped a tear with the back of her hand. 'Shortly after Da was arrested, my ma died. I decided that I wanted to see Da one more time. I wanted to draw a line under it all, I suppose.' She breathed deeply before adding, 'While I was at Mountjoy Prison, I met Da's cellmate.'

The blood in Kathleen's veins ran ice cold. 'Don't say it. Please . . .'

Ellen gasped. Beth looked at each of them in shock and confusion.

'I'm so sorry. But that man was Charles Davis.'

'Our Charles?' Ellen said weakly.

'Yes. He went by the name of Robert then, but I am certain it's the same person.'

Kathleen felt her chest tighten. *Charles with his American drawl, his impeccable manners, how he made her feel when he complimented her . . .* Then her head swam as the lies, the subterfuge, the sheer horror of the situation she'd allowed herself to fall into rushed at her. She felt her body sway as the floor rose to meet her.

'She's going to faint!' Ellen said as Beth cried out, 'Mammy!'

Kathleen held on to the table to steady herself and closed her eyes as the women around her fussed.

'I'm fine,' she said a few moments later, batting them away with her hand. She turned to Mary, 'Are you absolutely certain?'

'Yes,' Mary said firmly. 'He recognized me before I did him. But by that time, you'd already invested your money.'

Kathleen's heart raced so fast she wondered if she was having a heart attack. Pools of sweat formed under her arms.

'I confronted him. Insisted he return your money. Charles told me that if I told you about his true identity, he would tell everyone who my da was. Including Seamus. That he would blacken my name, expose me as a liar.'

'But we don't care what your father did,' Beth cried out. 'That's not your fault!'

'Thank you,' Mary said, 'that's kind of you to say. But that's not how most people feel. After Da was arrested, my ma and I were shunned by most of our neighbours and friends. But I'm not so worried about myself. Charles also said . . .' She glanced at Kathleen. 'He said that if I told anybody who he was, he would tell Patrick and the whole village that you and he were having an affair.'

Kathleen's life flashed before her eyes. Sitting on her mother's knee as a young child at Hook Lighthouse. Walking down the aisle to Patrick on her father's arm.

Loving Patrick, rearing children with him, living their lives with honesty and integrity.

Until now.

Kathleen had ruined it all. How easily she'd allowed all common sense to leave her. Her vanity and her need for flattery would cost her everything. Shame filled every part of her, making her stomach flip and turn and she ran outside the back door, retching into the long grass.

When her stomach was empty, she staggered back inside. Ellen wet a towel and handed it to her.

Beth moved closer to her as she cleaned her face. 'Mammy, it's not true, is it? Are you and Charles having an affair?'

'Of course not!' Kathleen fanned her cheeks, which she knew were now flaming red. She felt the women's eyes on her, filled with doubt. 'On my children's lives, I am not lying. I have never been intimate with any man but my husband.'

Physically at least this was true. But emotionally, Kathleen knew she had betrayed her husband. There was no mistake about that.

Relief filled Beth's eyes, and she moved into Kathleen's arms, hugging her tight.

'But I have done wrong.' Kathleen's body trembled with every word. 'I took our savings and gave them to a conman, behind your father's back.'

'I'm so sorry,' Mary said, sniffing back tears.

'It's not your fault.' Beth was frowning. 'Or Mammy's! It's that horrible man!'

Ellen whispered, 'So Kathleen's money . . .'

'Is gone?' Beth finished tremulously.

'I would say yes.' Mary swallowed. 'Charles Davis is many things, but an oil tycoon is not one of them.'

'A conman,' Kathleen said flatly, retaking a seat at the table. 'What a foolish woman I've been.'

'Oh, Mammy, what will Dad say?'

Kathleen had to make this right. She could never let Patrick know that she'd lost their savings because she'd allowed herself to be flattered by a stranger. 'I'll go to see Charles, and I'll tell him that he must do the right thing and return my entire investment.'

'You'll be wasting your time,' Mary said. 'If he's not gone already, he'll be gone by the time the keepers return from the island. He won't want to be here then, for fear of retribution.'

'So we let him leave here with the money?' Ellen asked incredulously. 'That's it – he gets away with it? All because you wanted to help me. And look where it's landed you.'

'This is on my shoulders, not yours. I've been so stupid. I should have just given you my savings. But no, I was greedy, trying to double it.' Kathleen shook her head. 'I trusted someone I'd only known for a few days. I deserve all I'm going to get from Patrick.'

'Mammy! You are not stupid. You are lovely and kind,' Beth protested, again throwing her arms around her mother's shoulders.

Kathleen swivelled her body around and sobbed into her daughter's chest. It was the first time in her life that her child was giving comfort to her, not the other way around.

Mary stood up, scraping her chair behind her. 'We have to try to get the money back. We can't let Davis get away with this. And we can't let Benny bloody Craig get away with burning down your home either. These men are taking us women for fools. No more tears, ladies. Ellen, make some tea. Beth, I baked a fruit cake yesterday – take it out of the larder and cut four thick slices. We need sugar for the shock. Then we're going to make a plan.'

Kathleen sat up straight and wiped her face, hope trickling back to her. Was Mary right? Was there a way to fight back?

THIRTY-SIX

Beth

Thursday, 24 May 1951

Ballycotton, Cork

It was early morning once again, not quite 5 a.m., but this time Beth was not on her way to see Christian. She was in a small wooden rowboat called *Brave*, painted bright yellow. The boat belonged to a neighbour, and she planned on having it back in the harbour before they even knew it was missing. Beth had a couple of hours before she had to be home, so that their plan could be put into place, to retrieve their money. But first of all, she had to see Ted.

As Beth moved the oars back and forth, steering the boat towards Ballycotton Island, adrenaline rushed through her body. While it was dry, an easterly wind whipped across her face, and it took all her strength to stay on course to the lighthouse. The short trip was about a nautical mile long. Within twenty minutes, she had arrived at the small jetty that sat at the bottom of the island, beneath the towering black lighthouse.

As with most adventures in Beth's life, she'd not thought the trip through. What if her father were on watch and had spotted her? He could be waiting for her. She'd have to think on her feet if that were the case. But luck was on her side. Because it was Ted's voice she heard calling out her name when she jumped out of the small boat and tied the rope to the pier.

'Beth! What are you doing here?' Ted was racing towards her. 'I thought my eyes were deceiving me as I stood on watch!'

'I wanted to say good morning,' Beth said.

Ted threw back his head and laughed out loud, the sound echoing through the air along with the seagull's caw. 'Well, what a sight for tired eyes you are! Your father is asleep. I'm not sure he'd approve of your surprise visit! And Seamus will be relieving me of my watch at six o'clock.'

Beth glanced upwards to the lighthouse, at the paraffin burner light shining out across the ocean. Her heart raced as her mind tried to find words to say to Ted. She had to be brave and lay everything out between them – see if love was enough for them. Could they find a way to be together, where they both got what their hearts desired?

'I've missed you,' Ted said gently.

He moved closer, looking over his shoulder up the path, to make sure nobody was watching, then leaned in to kiss Beth. He pulled her in tight to him, and as the wind picked up speed, Beth felt her body respond to his touch. She moved her hands up around his shoulders, feeling his muscles flex, hard, toned, strong.

Ted groaned, pulling back, once again looking up to the lighthouse, doubt flickering in his eyes.

'Stop thinking about my father. Concentrate on me,' Beth said.

She wanted more from Ted than she ever had before, as the moment swept her away from all thoughts of anything but now. She didn't want to talk about Christian or being a keeper's wife; her only thought was of Ted and how he made her feel. She could see matching desire in his eyes as he pushed her against the grey rock. The stone bit into her back, but she welcomed the pain. It made her feel alive and free and when she pulled his face down to hers, there was only the two of them, as one.

And as they made love for the first time, the sun's golden hues rose into the sky, dipping over the vast Atlantic Ocean.

'I've wanted to do that for a long time,' Ted said afterwards, his voice filled with emotion.

'Me too,' Beth replied.

'I want you to know that I plan to . . . that is . . .' Ted began.

Beth placed her finger on his lips. 'I know.'

He kissed her again and Beth wished it could be like this, just the two of them, every day. But then she glanced up at the lighthouse, a towering reminder of her future if she chose Ted.

'I love you, Ted. But I'm not ready to be a keeper's wife. Not yet, anyhow. I want to travel. I want to see what's on the other side of that big ocean.' She waved out to the blue sea.

Disappointment clouded his face. He couldn't hide the pain her words caused him.

'I'm sorry,' Beth said, reaching up to caress his cheek.

He took her hand and kissed it as he asked softly, 'Where do you want to go?'

'I want to ski in the Swiss Alps or dive in the Great Barrier Reef. Drink coffee in Paris, Amsterdam, London . . .'

'That's a lot of travel, Beth,' Ted said.

'There's a lot of world out there, Ted,' Beth replied.

Soft grey rain began to drizzle down. And waves began to make themselves known, crashing to the ragged shoreline.

'I need to think about what you've said. And we need to talk about all of this. Whatever happens, we'll work it out. Together. Because I can't lose you, Beth. I love you.' He paused and looked out to the waves crashing into the rocks. 'But not now, Beth. There's a storm coming and if you don't go back now, you'll have to stay here on the island. And I'm not sure I fancy answering your father about what we've been up to during your visit.'

Beth smiled, reaching up to kiss Ted again. Her heart swelled with love for him. He wasn't saying no to her. He was listening to what she wanted, and he was happy to discuss it further.

'I love you,' she shouted to him as she jumped back into the small rowboat.

'I love you too. I'll be watching until you reach the harbour. And Beth . . .'

She turned back to look at him.

'That was amazing. The best good morning I've ever had. I'll see you next week when I return.'

With her cheeks aching from smiling, Beth began to row back to Ballycotton. She knew, without glancing back, that Ted's eyes never left her. The wind was in her favour this time and helped her, pushing her closer to home. Beth knew that it was Ted who she loved. Whatever she'd shared with Christian disappeared as soon as Ted kissed her. Beth would tell Christian that she could not go with him. And next week, when Ted returned on shore leave, they would talk.

Beth also knew that she had to decide whether she should tell Ted about her short dalliance with Christian. He deserved to know the truth. But what if he couldn't forgive her? Beth would seek Mary's counsel. She'd help her decide what was best.

Fifteen minutes later, soaked through to her skin, she tied the boat back to where she had taken it. And then with one last wave in the direction of Ted, she ran back to Powers Terrace and snuck in the back door – where Kathleen was waiting for her.

'Were you at the circus?' Kathleen asked wearily.

'No. I was at the lighthouse. With Ted.'

Beth saw a range of emotions fly across her mother's face. Relief, worry, understanding.

'You'll catch your death in those wet clothes. Get dressed.'

* * *

An hour later, Kathleen called up the stairs to Beth, letting her know John and Katie had left for school.

Beth came hurtling down the stairs, two at a time, pulling a red knitted jumper on over her capri pants and T-shirt.

Kathleen's face creased in a frown. 'I don't like you being involved in this.'

'I'm not a child anymore. I want to help,' Beth insisted.

There was a tap at the front door, and Kathleen opened it to Ellen and Mary. Each wore a matching grave face.

'Did you manage to sleep?' Kathleen asked them.

They shook their heads, which was unsurprising.

'I had the weirdest of dreams,' Ellen said. 'I awoke in the early hours, in a pool of sweat, following a nightmare in which I'd been running away from Charles Davis, hiding in a cottage that went up in flames, courtesy of Benny Craig.'

Beth barely listened. She longed to get Mary on her own, so that she could tell her about her tryst with Ted. But it would have to wait until after they'd dealt with Charles Davis.

'Joanne knows something is up. She didn't want to go to school.' Ellen shook her head. 'I had to practically push her up the road.'

'She says little but hears everything, that one,' Kathleen said. 'But it's best she remains out of this today. She's still a child.'

Beth felt a stab of guilt. She'd not seen Joanne in a few days, and the last time they spoke, it had been a strained conversation, each disappointed in the other. Joanne didn't approve of Beth's relationship with Christian, and

Beth didn't approve of Joanne's conditional terms for their friendship.

She thought of Ted, over on the lighthouse, going about his duties, maybe thinking about her, just as she was him. Her heart panged with love for him. And she knew with a burst of welcome clarity that he was her future. Ted had not said no, to her need to travel. He accepted that she had to see the beautiful colours of the world for herself. Equally, she would have to understand if Ted wished to stay here, to continue his work as a keeper. They had much to discuss. *We'll work it out. Together.* That's what Ted had said. She clung to that.

But first things first. Beth had to help her mother and Ellen. There was no way she could even consider leaving Ballycotton before this problem was resolved. She returned her attention to the situation in hand.

She picked up the pot of tea that Kathleen had already brewed, and poured four mugs and then added milk and sugar into each.

'Let's go over the plan one more time,' Mary said.

THIRTY-SEVEN

Mollie

Sunday, 16 July 2023

Ballycotton, Cork

The sound of an incoming text awoke Mollie. Sleepily she reached for her phone and tapped the screen to read it.

> **Lucia:** *Sorry to interrupt your vacation, Mollie, but there's a piece about you and Nolan doing the rounds online. I would have kept it from you, but it's personal. I think you'd prefer to see it.*

Mollie felt her stomach plummet. This was all she needed. She and Nolan were in a precarious place as it was, and Mollie didn't want anything to jeopardize that. She silently prayed that whatever the story was, it couldn't hurt her or her husband.

Mollie: *Can you send me the link? And thank you, you did the right thing in letting me know.*

Lucia: *Remember, it's clickbait. And not worth getting upset about. Read it, then delete it and put it out of your mind. Here's the link.*

Mollie moved her finger to the link and pressed. A web page opened to a glaring headline.

Mollie Kenefick's Marriage Crisis

Underneath the damning headline was a photograph of Mollie and Nolan talking animatedly. Nolan was frowning as Mollie gesticulated wildly with her hands. They didn't look very happy in the shot, that was for sure.

Mollie zoomed in as she realized when and where the snap was taken. They were standing outside Dr Laslo's fertility clinic. Mollie braced herself and read the article.

A family friend confirmed that popular TV broadcaster Mollie Kenefick and her husband Nolan, a property developer from Portland, Maine, are having crisis talks about the state of their marriage. Mollie fled their townhouse to her ancestral home in Ballycotton, Cork, earlier this month. Friends of the *Breakfast with Donnie* star have said that Mollie and Nolan's marriage has hit a rough patch following her decision to put her career first over having a baby. Her distraught husband has begged Mollie to fulfil her promise to start a family. Mollie and Nolan are wearing their wedding rings, but friends have said they fear the worst for this couple.

Mollie's hand shook as she re-read the article a second time. She looked down and saw that it had already received over two thousand likes and had been shared 975 times on social media.

Damn it.

She quickly texted Lucia back.

Mollie: *Can you find out who this 'family friend' is?*

Lucia: *I'll make a call. But I'll be honest, Mollie: they probably won't give up their source. Somebody recognized you, took the shot, and sent it in to make a few bucks. And the journalist made the story up. That's all.*

Mollie: *Okay. But try, just in case. And if anything else turns up, will you send it to me too? Thank you x*

Mollie sat up cross-legged and texted Nolan.

Mollie: *I'm sorry to start the day on a bad note, but there's a story about us online. Lucia just sent it to me.*

Nolan: *Do I need coffee before I read it?*

Mollie: *Probably. I'm sorry. I hope it doesn't upset you too much.*

Five minutes passed as he read the article, then another text came in.

Nolan: *I'd like to know who this family friend is.*

Mollie: *Lucia thinks it's just an opportunist looking for a few bucks. That's all.*

Nolan: . . .

But whatever Nolan wanted to say, he decided against it and no message came through.

She knew he had to be smarting about the 'Distraught husband' comment. The article felt like such a personal attack. And there were so few people who knew about their IVF. She also knew that Nolan must be confused too. About her reaction to their last appointment and her decision to come to Ireland rather than go home to talk it through with him. He deserved better than this.

Mollie would have to find the courage to open up to Nolan. Tell him how she really felt. If he couldn't accept her decision, where would that leave them?

An hour later, Nolan finally sent another text.

Nolan: *I suppose it could be a wild stab in the dark, and they happened to hit close to the target. But hey, at least it's a good photo of us. We look hot when we 'argue'.*

Mollie smiled, as she knew Nolan had intended her to, by making light of the situation. But unfortunately, both of them knew that it wasn't just the friends quoted in the article who feared the worst for the couple.

She did too.

THIRTY-EIGHT

Beth

Monday, 17 July 2023

Ballycotton, Cork

Monday morning brought good news. Beth was well enough to come home. Her doctor recommended bed rest, but her lungs were now strong again. By midday, Beth was back in Peony Cottage. She allowed Albie, Mollie and Jane to fuss over her, with minimal complaining. And for a few hours, the Kenefick family were at peace, all thoughts of secrets forgotten.

Until she received a phone call from Wexford. In the small hours of the night, Mary had gotten her wish, and joined her beloved Seamus.

'Can I do anything for you?' Mollie asked, concern etched on her face.

'Actually yes,' Beth replied. Then she whispered a request to her granddaughter.

While Beth mourned the loss of her dear friend, she knew that Mary was ready to go. She'd reached the grand age of ninety-four, seen her children grow up and have families of their own. And she'd lived a good life, making her ma proud, as she'd always hoped she would.

Beth moved outside. A bench had been carved around the gnarly roots of the weeping willow tree, and she took a seat there. She had successfully avoided thinking about the events of that summer's day for years, until the letters had dredged it all up again. Occasionally, it would consume her, and she'd retreat into herself, lost in horror. She'd learned that she was powerless to do anything but ride out the storm that raged within her. But now, with Mary gone, the storm threatened to return. She couldn't let it. Her son and granddaughter needed her to be strong this time. To stay with them, to help them fight whatever it was that threatened them.

'I thought you might be hungry,' Albie said, arriving with a tray. He'd prepared tea and sandwiches and placed them on the table before her. They sat side by side, and Beth was surprised by the grumble in her stomach. Her appetite was returning after a week of little food, and she enjoyed her impromptu picnic.

As she nibbled on a ham sandwich, Albie's eyes watched her, full of reproach and confusion. She owed him an explanation.

'Are you strong enough to talk about what happened in 1951? You have to tell us your secrets so we can understand,' Albie said.

Pain passed over Beth's face. 'I know, son. Now that Mary is gone, I am the last one standing. So who am I protecting? Myself? It's time I told the Gardaí what we did. And I'll face the consequences. Earlier, I asked Mollie to call Joanne and Dervla Craig for me. They're coming over here shortly.'

'She told me. But you don't have to do this today. I'm worried you're not well enough yet,' Albie said, his brow knitted in worry.

Beth's heart filled with love for her son. The years fluttered away like the leaves that moved on the willows around her. He was her little boy again. Looking at her with the same frown he wore in childhood whenever Beth found herself lost in a dark place.

'You always found a way to bring me back,' Beth whispered.

'From where?' Albie asked, confused by her words.

'From in here,' Beth said, pointing to her head. 'I know it must have been difficult when I withdrew from you and your father. I'm heart sorry for that.'

Albie nodded, lost in memory. 'You'd go quiet for days, remaining in your bedroom, sleeping all the time.'

'I never knew when . . .' she paused, searching for the right word, but knowing only one was accurate, '. . . my depression would find me. Life would be great, but then it was as if my entire energy reserve drained from my body. I was left an empty shell, and all I could do was sleep through it.'

'Oh Mom, I wish you would have shared this with me before. Why did you never say?'

'When I think about who I was before and who I

became after . . . night and day . . .' Beth paused, leaving the sentence between them.

'I'm sorry,' Albie said. 'I think perhaps I should have been more understanding. I spent years thinking about this from my perspective, not yours.'

'You have nothing to apologize for. You've been a good son. And as I said, it was always you who brought me back again. I'd hear your voice, feel your touch. And that filled me up again, so I could keep going.'

Albie's eyes filled with tears, and he reached over to clasp her hand.

'I know I don't say this enough, but you need to know that I always loved you, even in those moments where I couldn't show you that love,' Beth said.

The breath caught in Albie's throat as he held on to a sob. 'I love you too, Mom.'

They held each other's gaze, and a thousand misunderstandings and hurt feelings faded to nothing.

'Watching you with Mollie, your relationship with her, makes me proud. You're a good man. Like your father was.'

'Thank you,' Albie said, his voice still choked with emotion.

They looked up when the sound of a car approached the front of the house.

'It's Joanne Craig.'

'Send her over here to me, son. I'd like to talk to her alone first of all.'

Albie leaned down and kissed his mother's forehead. And it was almost Beth's undoing. She breathed deeply, trying to regain her composure as Albie spoke to Joanne and pointed her in Beth's direction.

When she'd heard Joanne was in a retirement home, Beth assumed age had caught up with her. But the woman moved with the ease of someone decades younger. Only when she got closer could Beth see her lined face, telling tales on her true age.

'You look well,' Beth said.

Joanne looked her up and down and replied, 'I can't say the same for you. I wouldn't have recognized you; you've gone so haggard.'

'Why do you hate me so much?' Beth lifted her chin. 'What did I ever do to you?'

Two blotches stained Joanne's cheeks as she returned Beth's gaze unflinchingly. 'That's the thing that's so aggravating about you, Beth. You sailed through life, unaware of the devastation you left in your wake.'

Beth shook her head, feeling anger begin to bubble its way up inside her. She was done apologizing for simply existing. 'You are going to have to do better than that.'

'All right. Do you want the truth? I loved Ted. From the moment I met him, he was all I could think about. But you never once considered that, did you? As far as you were concerned, once you decided he was yours, that was it. Nobody else was allowed a look in.'

Beth felt irritation nip her. 'Surely Ted had a part to play too? He chose me. If he had wanted you, he could have had you, and I would never have stood in your way!'

Joanne sat down beside Beth on the bench, and the air between them sparked with anger.

A robin redbreast flew towards them and took a moment's rest on a nearby willow branch before continuing its journey down the garden.

'You should have told me how you felt back then,' Beth said, her voice filled with disappointment.

'What would have been the point of that? You would have laughed at how silly I was.'

'Is that what you think of me? That I'd have been so callous?' It was many lifetimes ago, but Beth hadn't been a bad person.

Not until *that* day at least.

Joanne rammed her walking stick hard onto the ground. 'Callous. Now there's a word. That's *exactly* what you were. And the cruellest thing was watching you treat Ted like dirt.'

This was getting too much for Beth. 'I loved Ted. Be careful, Joanne.'

Joanne snorted, then laughed, a bitter shrill sound without any mirth. 'Well, God help all those you don't love, is all I'm saying. Because you didn't show much love to Ted when you were cavorting with the trapeze artist.'

Christian. Over seventy years later, that part of her life felt like a dream. She had not thought of him until she saw that photograph. And yet, Joanne was still biting about it all. Why was that?

Joanne shifted on the seat beside her, then changed the subject abruptly. 'Why have you asked me here today?

After all these years, I can't imagine that you want to play catch-up.'

Beth looked her old friend full in the face. Her bones ached with fatigue. She was weary of it all. 'I don't want to fight with you, Jojo. You were my closest friend once. Can we call a truce? Because I've been keeping a secret for over seventy years. It's time to break that silence. And as this affects your mam, you have to be here.'

THIRTY-NINE

Mary

Thursday, 24 May 1951

Ballycotton, Cork

'I gave Charles Davis the note, then he ruffled my hair and smiled like an indulgent uncle,' Beth said with irritation, when Mary joined her outside the hotel. 'I'd love to wipe the smug look off his face.'

Mary nodded. 'So would I. If all goes to plan, we'll do just that. Right, it's almost nine thirty. He should be leaving soon to meet your mam. You know what to do. Go on in.'

While Beth went back into the hotel, Mary found a place behind a hedge to keep out of sight. She waited, checking her watch for the umpteenth time. Within five minutes, right on time, Charles sauntered past Mary, on his way to meet Kathleen, as her note requested. The skies overhead were grey, and a soft, misty rain had begun to fall. But this didn't bother Charles. He whistled as he walked, as if he didn't have a care in the world. He looked dapper in a brown two-piece suit under a red-and-brown windowpane checked overcoat. And, of course, the look was completed with his signature trilby hat.

Once Charles was safely on his way, Mary entered the hotel and scanned the reception area. A middle-aged couple were deep in conversation with Dáithí, the hotel's manager. A slick of sweat glistened on his forehead.

Beth appeared, and as she passed by, she whispered, 'Room 119,' before making her way outside to keep watch.

Mary exhaled a breath of relief.

Beth had done her part, noting the number of Charles's key when he handed it in to reception.

When they first met, Mary had thought Beth's head was full of clouds and dreams. But the girl was no fool. And she was proving herself older than her years today.

Mary felt conspicuous standing in the lobby as if her very presence there was a red alert that she was about to commit a crime. The couple in the queue in front of her seemed to be disputing their bill. Every second delayed felt like an hour. Mary looked at her watch again. Five minutes had passed since Charles left. He would be with Kathleen at the meeting point in another ten minutes. Her eyes searched the cubbyhole of keys behind the mahogany reception, each with a little brass label showing the room number. Third row, fourth from the left, she located the key to Room 119.

Finally, the couple moved away. Dáithí threw his eyes upwards as he beckoned Mary to the reception.

'Good morning, Mrs Mythen. How lovely to see you again,' Dáithí said. 'Sorry to keep you waiting. That was . . . complicated. How can I help you?'

Mary flashed her brightest smile, then said, 'I'm so sorry, but I've mislaid my gloves. I've looked everywhere, and they are nowhere to be seen. It struck me that I last wore them when we were guests at the Bayview. I wonder if perhaps they were handed in?'

'It would be my pleasure to check for you. Can you describe them?' Dáithí asked.

Mary stumbled momentarily, kicking herself that she'd not rehearsed an answer to this logical question. 'Red leather, with three buttons at each cuff.'

'They sound delightful. One moment,' Dáithí said, retreating into the room behind reception.

Mary knew she didn't have a second to waste. She did a quick three-sixty, relieved to note that nobody was behind her. Then she pulled a handkerchief from her pocket and dropped it to the floor behind the reception. As it fluttered to the ground, she reached for the key, then scooped to pick up the handkerchief, using it to conceal her loot. Mary felt rather proud of that move. Then she quickly stepped back to the other side of reception, with seconds to spare before Dáithí returned.

'Alas, no luck, Mrs Mythen.' He shook his head sorrowfully. 'I have an umbrella, a deck of cards and a pen. But no gloves.'

'I could do with a new pen,' Mary joked, which made Dáithí smile. 'That's okay. I appreciate you trying.'

'Tell you what, I'll ask the head of housekeeping when she finishes her shift if she's seen them. Perhaps she can help us.'

'Please don't go to any trouble,' Mary replied, flashing her brightest smile.

Then she turned to leave, moving slowly. She sat in one of the lounge chairs and leaned down to fasten her shoe, smiling at Dáithí as his eyes rested on her ankles. *Look away,* she thought to herself, willing him to be distracted so she could make her way to the entrance to the guest bedrooms.

Luck was on her side. The couple returned for a further round of discussions about their bill, and Mary seized the moment. She slipped between the double doors, running along the carpeted corridor until she came to room 119. She pulled the key from her handkerchief, slipped it into the lock and turned it.

FORTY

Kathleen

Thursday, 24 May 1951

Ballycotton, Cork

Kathleen looked up to the sky. The rain had stopped, but the clouds were dark and angry. The wind whipped her skirt around her legs, and she pulled her headscarf tight under her chin. The air felt heavy, and it looked like a storm was brewing.

She saw a flash of orange appear between the trees across the road to the meadow. *Ellen*. She adjusted her headscarf again, pulling the knot a little tighter. Would she have to signal for help? She hoped not. But Kathleen had no idea what to expect from Charles. So much had changed in the past twenty-four hours. The only thing she knew for sure was that she didn't know this man. Or what he was capable of.

Moments later, a figure appeared; it was Charles, walking quickly towards her.

'My dear Kathleen,' he exclaimed, taking her hand and kissing it lightly. Kathleen forced herself not to flinch. 'Your daughter is such a charming girl. Although I must admit, you hardly look old enough to be her mother.'

Kathleen forced a smile. Every part of her recoiled from being in this man's company. She trembled to think that she had ever fantasized about feeling his lips on hers.

'Where has our lovely May weather gone? It could be winter again,' Charles said as a gust of wind almost took his hat from his head.

'That's Irish weather for you,' Kathleen replied, surprised to hear how strong her voice sounded. Inside, she was like jelly, quivering. But she had a job to do. She would not let down Mary and Beth, who were taking a considerable risk now at the hotel. Nor would she let down Ellen again.

'I must admit that your note surprised me today,' Charles said.

'A nice surprise, I trust?'

'Oh yes.'

Kathleen looked at this man who had managed to turn her head so easily. She had never felt so stupid and ridiculous in her life. Seeing him now, in his red and brown check overcoat, he looked preposterous against the grey skyline. Ballycotton Lighthouse stood tall in the distance, and Kathleen bit back a sob as she thought of her husband over there. He would be working through his daily maintenance tasks – cleaning the lenses and windows, winding the clocks and replenishing the fuel. He'd be horrified if he knew what his wife was doing.

'Shall we walk a little?' Kathleen suggested.

'I don't know if the weather is suitable for a stroll. I don't like the look of those clouds. Should we return to my hotel? We can have coffee in the lounge?'

Kathleen replied, in a tremulous voice, 'I had hoped for a more private meeting. The hotel is so busy.'

Charles smiled knowingly. 'I understand. We could, of course, have coffee in my room. The concierge is discreet. No one would know. Or if you prefer, we could go to your cottage.'

'Oh no, people would talk. Besides, I would like a walk – to clear my head.'

'As you wish,' Charles moved his hand to touch her lower back, exerting a little too much pressure.

How had she thought that this was exciting? Now his touch made her shudder.

They walked side by side along the uneven, muddy track a few feet from the cliff edge as the heavens above them grumbled. Kathleen offered a prayer that the weather would hold off for a few more minutes. If Charles were to leave now, it would surely compromise Mary and Beth. Gorse bushes nipped her ankles, their coconut-like fragrance filling her nostrils.

They came to a stile on the path, and Charles climbed over it, offering his hand to assist Kathleen. When she went to step down, he reached up and placed his hands around her waist, pulling her body into his as he lowered her to the ground.

'Kathleen, you have no idea what you are doing to me,' he whispered into her ear.

She placed a hand on his chest and pushed him firmly away. Her heart thundered in her chest. 'You shouldn't say those things to me. I'm a married woman.'

'Don't be coy, Kathleen,' Charles said. And a glint hardened in his dark grey eyes. 'We both know why you asked me to join you here.'

He was so sure of himself. A bile of acid rose into the back of Kathleen's throat. Then he leaned down and kissed her as a clap of thunder reverberated around them.

FORTY-ONE

Mary

Thursday, 24 May 1951

Ballycotton, Cork

Closing the hotel room door behind her, Mary leaned against it for a moment to gather herself. Her heart was beating so fast that she thought she might faint. She noted the unmade bed and towels on the floor with dismay. Housekeeping had yet to make up the room. *Please don't come now*, she begged silently.

Mary knew she must pull herself together. She had no time to worry; she had to begin her search immediately. Running to the tallboy chest of drawers, she systematically went through each, rifling through T-shirts, shirts and undergarments, to no avail. Then she moved to a large ornate double wardrobe. She found two suits hanging side by side. She looked through the pockets, inside and out, but again found nothing.

She checked the curtains, feeling for any bulge in the lining, but to no avail. Next she moved to the bed, pulling aside the bed linen, then lifted the mattress in case he had placed the cash there. With growing despair, she kneeled on the carpeted floor and looked under the bed. There she spotted Charles's red leather suitcase. She slid it out, groaning when she noticed the lock on either side of the handle.

'The money must be in here,' she muttered. But there was no way she could risk sneaking something this size out of the hotel.

But to her surprise, the spring released when she pushed the metal latch, and the lock opened. Holding her breath, Mary opened the case, where a large manilla folder sat inside the tanned bottom, beside a pocket penknife.

'Got you!' she said, clapping her hands in delight. She flicked the folder open and found a stack of paperwork inside. Details of investments to an oil firm, with Charles's signature and that of many others. Some names she recognized from the village, including one for Dáithí, the hotel manager. Poor guy had been suckered in too. The last one was for Kathleen's investment.

But there was no sign of the cash.

She continued looking, and in a side pocket inside the lining she found a passport, and tucked inside that was a second-class ticket to Ellis Island, New York. It was dated for Sunday, 27 May. So Davis was to leave the country in three days' time. She flicked open the passport; while the photograph was of Charles Davis, the document said his name was Robert Elliot. Which was the alias? She wasn't sure it mattered.

With a sinking heart, Mary knew she was running out of options. She carefully placed the folder back into the case, then, on a whim, pulled out Kathleen's investment document. She put it in her handbag, not entirely understanding why but trusting her gut that it was the right thing to do. Then she closed the case and slid it back under the bed.

The sound of a vacuum hummed in the distance. Housekeeping was nearby. Which meant she had to leave now – without the money.

How would she break this news to the others? With a sinking heart, she picked up her bag and the room key, putting her ear to the door. Other than the sound of the vacuum, all was quiet. She opened the door an inch and peeked out. The hall was empty, so she slipped out, locking the door softly behind her.

Mary returned to the lobby unseen. Dáithí was holding up a map, giving directions to two women. With him there, she couldn't slip the key back on its hook, so she dropped it into her handbag instead. She'd have to find a way to return it at a later stage. Moving fast, she slipped out of the hotel and joined Beth outside.

'Did you get it?' Beth asked, breathless.

'The money wasn't there. He must have it with him. In that blasted overcoat of his,' Mary said. 'Has there been any sign of Ellen?'

Beth's face fell. 'Nothing. All quiet. Which means he's still with Mammy on the cliff. What do we do now?'

Mary could only think of one course of action. 'Kathleen has no choice but to report him to Sergeant Cody. And there's no time, because he's booked on a ship to America on Sunday.'

'But he said he'd tell everyone he is having an affair with my mam. If he does that . . . Well, Dad would never stay with Mammy if he thought she'd been unfaithful.'

'Then there's only one other course of action. We'll have to confront Charles. And try to get the money from him ourselves.'

FORTY-TWO

Kathleen

Thursday, 24 May 1951

Ballycotton, Cork

'I can't,' Kathleen said breathlessly, stepping back.

'Why now?' Charles asked. 'Your husband spends most of his time over on that lighthouse. He should not be surprised that a vibrant woman like you might look elsewhere for comfort.'

At the mention of Patrick, she felt a piercing shame that made her legs weak.

'I can feel you tremble in my arms. I know you want me. I've seen the way you look at me.'

The wind took up momentum, and the waves crashed into the cliff. The ocean spray hit the side of Kathleen and Charles's faces. He frowned, moving a step back from the cliff's edge. But she welcomed the icy cold. The weather was as angry as she herself felt right now. Kathleen might be trembling, but it was with rage at Charles for his deception, at her own for believing it, and to her surprise, at Patrick too.

While Charles was wrong about much, he was right that Patrick had left her on her own for too long.

Charles reached over and pulled Kathleen closer towards him. 'You're shivering.' He placed his arms around her and every part of her recoiled from his touch. She reached up to pull her headscarf off. A pre-arranged sign she'd made with Ellen that she needed her to join them. Kathleen was in over her head. With all her strength she pushed him away from her.

A flash of anger passed over his face. But his mask returned just as quick, and he smiled again as he said, 'I must insist we make our way back towards the Bayview. We are both going to get drenched through to our skins.' Charles turned back towards Ballycotton, beckoning her to follow him.

Kathleen didn't know what to do, worried that Mary and Beth were still in the hotel. But then three figures came into view a couple of hundred feet away.

'It appears we are not the only ones foolish enough to walk in such conditions,' Charles said.

Kathleen held her hand to her forehead to shield her eyes from the rain, wondering who was coming their way. Her heart leapt with hope when she saw it was Beth, Ellen and Mary. It must be a good sign; they must have found the money.

When the women reached them, if Charles was

surprised to see them, he hid it well.

'Good morning, ladies. Out for a constitutional, like Kathleen and I?'

'We were looking for you, actually,' Mary said.

Kathleen searched Beth's face, and a quick shake of her head made her heart sink.

'And what can I do for you?' Charles asked.

'You can give Kathleen back her money,' Mary replied, lifting her chin as she moved closer to him.

Charles laughed out loud, a mirthless sound that echoed into the grey day. 'I'm afraid I can't do that. Kathleen's money is now in stocks and shares of an oilfield. As she well knows.'

'I've told them everything,' Mary said. 'So you can drop the act. The only oilfield you've ever seen has been on a movie screen.'

Charles turned to Kathleen, shaking his head remorsefully. 'You know that this woman is the daughter of a convicted murderer? Who was hung for his sins. She's delusional and not to be trusted.'

'I know all of that,' Kathleen said impatiently. 'The question of her identity or family history is not pertinent. I also know how you know Mary. Her father is not the only convicted criminal around these parts.'

'You told them after all?' Charles said, half bowing to Mary. Then he turned back to Kathleen and held his hands up in surrender. 'You've got me. Now what?'

'Now you give me back my money,' Kathleen said.

'Or what?'

'Or I report you to the Gardaí. If you've managed to con me, I can only imagine how many others have been party to your schemes.'

'That's a dangerous assertion to make. All investments were legitimate. I have not coerced anyone to give me their money. Nobody will be able to blame me when the stocks . . . drop in value, shall we say? Investments are always a risk. Of course, I must admit that not all of my investors were as pretty as you, Kathleen. Or as accommodating.' He stretched this word out with relish. His eyes narrowed, and he said, 'What do you think the god-fearing neighbourhood of Ballycotton will say when they hear that their beloved principal keeper's wife has been having an affair?'

'No one will believe that!' Beth cried out.

'Really? Where there's smoke, there is always fire, I say. We've been seen in each other's company several times. And I've made sure to tell the concierge Dáithí, on several occasions, that I value his discretion. What would happen if I told him I had become good friends with you, Kathleen? I would hate anyone to hear that you'd been in my bedroom.'

'I've never been in your hotel room!' Kathleen cried out, outraged at the blatant lie.

'He said, she said. Who to believe?'

'I've had quite enough of you. Give me my money, or I promise you, I will expose you.' Kathleen stood up to her full height, her nostrils flaring and her eyes blazing. 'Then get the hell out of my village.'

'Leave – and miss all this fun? No, I'm going nowhere. In fact, I have planned my weekend already. I believe it's quite the fanfare when the principal keeper returns from the island. I'm thinking of joining the villagers to greet him. I have *much* to share with your hardworking husband.'

A ripple of thunder roared in the distance, and the rain pelted down in sheets. Kathleen's skirt was sodden and heavy. She just wanted this to be over.

Beth moved closer to her, shivering in the cold wind, and Kathleen placed an arm around her shoulder. This was doing no good. They would be better off leaving and working out their next steps at home.

But Charles was only warming up. He continued, raising his voice to be heard over the wind. 'After all, it's only fair I tell Patrick about his wife and me. Then, of course, he'll want to know that his daughter has been cavorting in the big top with a circus performer. Beth's boyfriend will also undoubtedly be interested to hear about that. Oh yes, and dear old Seamus needs to know he married a liar and the daughter of a criminal who swung for his crimes. Have I missed anything?'

The four women looked at him, their eyes wide and mouths open in shock. Kathleen noted that the cultured accent, with the southern American lilt that she'd found so charming, had now all but disappeared. She felt Beth stiffen beside her and knew that whatever lies he might be spinning, her daughter's liaison with Christian was not one of them. Fear for Beth's reputation flooded her. She had to protect her.

But the crude lies were too much for Beth. She suddenly ran at Charles. Her hands curled into fists, and she pounded on his chest, screaming in fury, 'Take it back, you take that back!'

Kathleen moved to pull Beth off Charles, but he

was too quick for her. He lifted his hand and slapped it hard across Beth's cheek, sending her flailing to the dirt track. Kathleen's stomach lurched when she saw how close her daughter was to the cliff's edge. Then dropped to her knees in horror when she saw a bloody gash on Beth's face, the gold signet ring on Charles's little finger having cut her.

'I'm okay,' Beth said, her eyes flashing angrily. Kathleen helped her up to her feet.

'Hitting young girls,' Mary spat at him. 'What a big man you are!'

Fury flashed across Charles's face, and his jaw hardened. 'If you come at me, mark my words, I'll hit back. So you best stay there, little girl,' he hissed to Beth.

'You touch my daughter again, and I'll kill you. You mark *my* words!' Kathleen responded. She reached her hand upwards to strike him, but he grabbed it, squeezing her wrist so tight she cried out in pain.

'I like this side of you, Kathleen.'

Ellen lunged at Charles from behind, half jumping on his back, screaming at him to let Kathleen go.

He released Kathleen's wrist in shock, and Kathleen curled her hand into a fist and struck his face with all her might.

Roaring in pain, Charles tried to shake Ellen off his back. But she clung to the lapels of his overcoat like a limpet. The buttons strained and popped. As Ellen fell to the ground, she took his coat with her. Mary pulled a now crying Beth into her arms.

As the rain pounded his face, Charles reached down to retrieve his coat. 'Give that back, you stupid woman!' He pulled his leg back and kicked Ellen in her abdomen. The coat slipped from her hands.

'The money must be in his coat!' Beth screamed. And she ran at him for the second time, followed seconds later by the others. They clawed at the red check fabric.

Thunder clapped again, and a lightning spear lit up the grey skies. The ground was like a mud bath, and Kathleen felt her legs threaten to slip from under her. She felt Charles's fist connect again with her shoulder and she fell onto the muddy path, a sharp stone cutting her lower back. Beth screamed, pushing Charles with all her might away from her mother, and her friends, before he could hurt them any further.

And then—

Kathleen hardly knew what she was seeing.

Charles lost his footing and fell backwards, his arms flailing as he tried to regain his balance.

He was teetering on the edge of the cliff and he tried to grab hold of Mary, who stood the closest to him. But she stepped back. And then, as the third clap of thunder filled the air, he tumbled over the edge.

The sea swallowed him whole.

PART THREE

In order for the light to shine so brightly, the darkness must also be present

Francis Bacon

FORTY-THREE

Beth

Thursday, 24 May 1951

Ballycotton, Cork

Beth wasn't sure how long they stood on the cliff's edge. Her teeth chattered, and her hands turned blue. And all the while, her mind grappled with the fact that she had killed someone.

'We need to get away.' Mary's voice sounded distant. 'We can't be seen.'

Beth could not compute what Mary was saying, and her legs refused to move. She felt her mother's hand reach for hers, and she clung to it.

'What should I do with his coat?' Ellen asked. Somehow she had managed to hold on to it during the struggle.

'Bring it with you,' Mary said. Her eyes fell to the dirt track a few metres away, where the trilby hat sat amongst the wet reeds.

'It must have fallen off during the fight,' Kathleen said. 'Should we take that too?'

'No. Leave it,' Mary commanded.

Beth realized that Mary was in charge now.

The coast road was deserted, the storm keeping all indoors.

'Beth and I will cycle home together. Kathleen and Ellen, you go ahead; we'll follow on separately.'

Beth watched her mother and Ellen half run down the road. A few moments later, Mary led Beth back to their bikes. They'd left them against the ditch at the opposite meadow.

'Can you cycle?' Mary asked gently as Beth's hands slipped on the wet handlebars.

Beth nodded, but in truth, she was moving on autopilot. She moved her legs, pushing the pedals until the bike followed Mary in front of her. If they passed anyone, she did not notice. Her head was pounding so much, she barely noticed the rain.

Somehow, Beth was back home, standing in her kitchen.

Kathleen pulled towels from the hot press, passing them. The four women stood like drowned rats, puddles forming at their feet on the flagstones beneath them.

'I . . . I . . . I . . . killed him,' Beth cried out.

'No, you didn't. He fell,' Kathleen said firmly, looking around the room for support from the other women.

'It was me who pushed him, though,' Beth said.

'As did I,' Kathleen said.

'And me,' Ellen said.

'And me. We all fought him.' Mary's voice was firm. 'He reached for me, but I stepped back. I could have saved him. So this is not on any one person. It's on us all.'

'Will we go to prison?' Beth asked, and she began to shake uncontrollably.

Her mother led her to the Aga stove and opened the door to release the heat. Then she wrapped the towel around her and rubbed her shoulders, as she used to when she bathed Beth as a child.

Beth closed her eyes and tried to focus only on her mother's comforting touch and not on the horror her mind refused to let go of.

'Nobody is going to prison,' Mary said. She paced the room, muttering, 'Think, think, think.'

Ellen sat down at the kitchen table, her face wet with tears and rain, still clutching the overcoat in her arms.

But all Beth could see, on a constant loop, was the look on Charles's face as he realized he was falling over the cliff. Could she have caught him, if she'd run towards him? She had been paralysed with shock and fear, rooted to the spot.

'Check the coat, Ellen. See if the money is there,' Mary said.

Kathleen took a sharp breath, and her hands squeezed Beth's shoulders so tight that it almost hurt.

Ellen rifled through the pockets, tears falling down her face. 'Nothing but Kathleen's note,' she whispered. 'He's dead, and we didn't even get the money.'

Mary pulled the coat from Ellen's hands and began

looking at it herself. 'Get a knife; we need to check the lining. It has to be here.'

Ellen handed her a carving knife, and Mary hacked at the material until it gave. She pulled the silk lining from the wool and reached inside.

'I don't understand,' Mary whispered when she found nothing.

The grandfather clock in the hallway began to chime.

'It's midday. In a few hours the children will be home. They can't find us like this,' Kathleen said.

'Move aside,' Mary said to Beth, not unkindly. She pushed the coat into the belly of the Aga stove. The fabric hissed and spat, and then the flames caught it and began to burn. Then she threw the note in too. 'Kathleen, do you have any whiskey? Pour four glasses. We don't have much time to get our stories straight.'

Kathleen took four tumblers from the press, then poured a good measure of Powers whiskey into each. They sat at the table, and she handed the drinks round.

Beth looked at the drink in wonder. She'd sneaked a sip of her father's whiskey when she was thirteen, and her mother had sent her to her room without any tea.

'Take a small sip,' Kathleen urged. 'It will help with the shock.'

In unison, they lifted their glasses and drank. The liquid burned the back of Beth's throat, and she spluttered. But she persevered and took a second sip. This time, she managed to do so without coughing and found the drink warmed her.

'We've probably got till tonight, perhaps the morning, before the hotel notices that Charles is missing,' Mary said.

'Are you sure we shouldn't go to the Gardaí?' Ellen asked, rubbing her hands together repeatedly.

'No!' Kathleen and Mary said together.

'It was an accident, though. It was self-defence. We can tell Sergeant Cody that he slipped and fell,' Ellen insisted.

'There'll be questions. And I'm the daughter of a convicted criminal. How do you think that will go down?' Mary's voice broke into a sob, 'I will not go to jail for this.'

'And Beth is not up to any questions from the guards,' Kathleen insisted, taking in her daughter's still trembling body. Beth wanted to protest that she was strong enough, but she couldn't find the words, and leaned in closer to her mother's embrace.

Ellen nodded her agreement. 'Okay, so what do we say when someone asks about Charles? Because they will.'

'We stick to the truth as much as we can,' Mary said. 'Kathleen, you must admit that you have had coffee with him over the past week. Platonically. When it's announced that Charles is missing, Ellen and Kathleen, you will say that you were taking a walk together and you bumped into Mr Davis, where you stopped to chat for a few moments. When it began to rain, you left and made your way home. It's important that you insist you left Mr Davis behind on the clifftop trail. People will assume he slipped and fell off the cliff edge during the storm.'

'We say we saw him? Is that wise?' Kathleen asked, confused.

'We stick to the truth as much as possible. That way, there is less chance we'll be found out in an untruth,' Mary said. 'My father never gave me much, but he passed that wisdom on whenever the Gardaí called to our house when I was a kid.'

'His hat will be found on the coastal walk, that'll confirm he was on the cliff,' Kathleen said.

'Exactly. All you need to remember is that you both left him alive and well,' Mary said.

Kathleen and Ellen locked eyes. 'Can you do that?' Kathleen asked.

Without hesitation, Ellen replied, 'Yes.'

'You were together; that's the most important thing to insist on,' Mary said.

'So we become each other's alibis,' Kathleen said, nodding in understanding. 'And you and Beth will do the same?'

'Yes,' Mary said, now turning her attention to Beth. 'We went for a cycle together, first to the hotel to enquire about my missing gloves. Then we decided to join Kathleen and Ellen on their cliff walk, but we all returned home when it began to rain.'

Beth looked at Mary in amazement. She seemed so calm and collected, while Beth was shivering like a small child. She took another sip of whiskey.

'What if someone asks about my investment?' Kathleen's hand began to shake, and whiskey spilt from her glass onto the table.

Mary reached for her handbag and pulled out the document Kathleen had signed. 'What investment?'

'How did you get that?' Kathleen asked incredulously.

'I found it in his room. I don't know why I took it. Instinct. But you need to destroy this, Kathleen. It's the only thing that links you to him.'

'But it's also proof that he stole Mam's money!' Beth said, looking at each of them in horror.

'That money is gone. You've got to accept that,' Mary said. 'No judge would believe that Kathleen did not intend to kill Charles if they knew he had swindled her out of money. That gives you motive.'

Beth felt something warm trickle its way down her cheek. She reached to wipe it and saw a dark ruby-red stain on her fingertips.

'Oh, pet,' Kathleen said, seeing the blood.

'Let me.' Mary walked over to the sink, wet a hand towel, and wrung it out. She placed it gently against the cut on Beth's face and applied pressure, leaning down to kiss Beth's head. 'You've been so brave today.'

Beth reached up and clasped Mary's hand. She didn't feel brave. She had never been so scared in her entire life.

The girl who planned to escape Ballycotton, to travel the world to exciting new places, was gone now.

Everything changed the moment Charles Davis fell into that abyss. Because he had pulled her with him, and she was still falling now.

FORTY-FOUR

Kathleen

Friday, 25 May 1951

Ballycotton, Cork

Kathleen stood with Beth, Ellen and Mary on the pier at Ballycotton, waiting for the relief boat to return from the island with Patrick. The skies overhead darkened, and a rush of wind whipped across each of the women's faces.

Beth's cut was weeping again, but the girl didn't seem to notice. Kathleen pressed her handkerchief against the wound, red blood staining the white cotton.

Katie, John and Ger skipped rope behind them, with Joanne standing alone, watching them, her lips pursed tight. Kathleen made herself smile in the girl's direction, but Joanne didn't return the gesture.

'Whist,' Ellen called out to the children. 'The handover is happening.' Kathleen saw her friend wince and clasp her side in pain. She glanced at Beth and wished she could wave a wand that could send her daughter over to Joanne, to giggle and gossip about their lives. A year older than Joanne, their age gap had never seemed to bother them. Until recently, when it began to stretch between them so taut, it could snap and break at any moment. And now, while Beth might still look young, her innocence was gone. Tarnished forever after the events of the previous day.

'There it is,' Mary said, as the dark clouds parted to reveal the lighthouse beacon as it flickered across the Irish Sea towards them.

Beth began counting the beats between each flash of light, a childhood habit.

Kathleen wanted to cry to the heavens that she knew she had let her daughter down; she felt it with every part of her. It was as if they were caught in a storm, spinning them around relentlessly. She wished time could slow down, so she could manage to put everything right.

But she had to push that aside for now.

Kathleen placed the bloodied handkerchief in her pocket. 'If anyone finds out, we'll hang for what we've done. Make a solemn vow, here and now, that we will never speak of what happened yesterday. Not to each other, nor to another living soul.'

Nobody spoke, and a seagull's caw echoed around them.

'I never thought I'd have a marriage with so many secrets and lies,' Mary said. She looked close to tears. But none of them had the luxury of those. Not now.

'We had no choice,' Kathleen replied as she placed her hand in front of her. 'What's done is done. Now, let's swear our silence and put a smile on our faces. The principal keeper is coming home.'

Beth made a strangled sob, then placed her hand atop her mother's and said, 'I swear.'

'I swear,' Mary said, adding her hand on top of Beth and Kathleen's.

Ellen looked to each of the women as she placed her icy-cold hand on top of theirs, and whispered the final, 'I swear.'

As the relief boat inched its way to the pier, the children raced ahead of the women as they all moved to greet the keepers' arrival.

'Wave to your father,' Ellen instructed Katie and John, who jumped up and down enthusiastically, signalling their hellos to the shadows of men barely visible on the boat. 'Come on, love,' she shouted to Joanne, who was shuffling slowly behind them on her own.

The four women waved until their arms ached. But their hearts were not in it. The ritual of welcoming her husband home that had once been so important to Kathleen somehow seemed trivial now.

Kathleen wiped her hands on the side of her skirt, flinching as another stab of pain seared through her. Charles Davis might be gone, but the bruises he'd left would last for some time. They'd patched themselves up yesterday to hide evidence of their fight, but she would have to be careful undressing in front of Patrick so he did not see them. And they'd fabricated a story about Beth falling, to account for the cut on her face.

And then Patrick was off the boat, looking handsome in his uniform. Kathleen started when she noticed that he'd grown a beard, which she'd never seen on him before. While it suited him, the change in his appearance confused her too. What had Patrick been dealing with this past month as he came to terms with the death of his dear friend Peter? Guilt stopped Kathleen from running towards him as she normally would. She hung back and, when he approached her, she offered him her cheek to kiss. Then he flung his arms around John and Katie, who were excitedly telling him their news. He embraced Beth, then turned back to Kathleen again and pulled her into his arms to hold her close.

Another ache hit Kathleen, but it was the familiar pang of love this time. She felt Patrick's eyes search hers, taking her in, and she flushed in the intensity. Echoes of their early married life, where every touch and look was a promise of love, rushed Kathleen.

Kathleen glanced over to Ellen, Joanne and Ger, whose faces were all masked with sorrow. It wasn't hard to imagine what they must be thinking. Their loss and loneliness, as they must surely be remembering the many times that they had welcomed Peter home. But that would never happen again. Kathleen swallowed back a sob. If she began to cry now, she wasn't sure she could stop.

Beth continued to be a worry. She had said so little since the cliff. Her eyes darted from side to side as if she expected someone to grab her again.

Then Patrick walked over to Ellen and the children. He wore his formal uniform – a navy suit, a white shirt and navy tie, a white peaked hat with navy trim and gold brocade. And he reached up to take his hat off as Patrick addressed his neighbour.

'Peter was one of the best lighthouse keepers I've ever had the privilege to work with.'

'Thank you,' Ellen said, tears filling her eyes.

Patrick reached for his long duffel bag and opened it, pulling out a long rod made from bamboo with goat's whiskers as feathers at its end. 'This was Peter's fishing rod. We thought Ger might like it.' He handed it to the young boy, who accepted it tearfully. 'Your dad was the best fisherman we had. Thanks to Peter, we had pollack for supper – as much as we could eat.'

Ger clutched the rod like a trophy.

'Your dad liked to sketch, as you know. And I've brought his artist pad with some drawings that I thought you might like,' Patrick added, handing it to Joanne.

Joanne let out a strangled sob. Ellen's body shook as a new wave of grief overcame her.

So much had happened to this family since Peter's death. Kathleen knew that Ellen had pushed her sorrow and grief deep inside her, as she looked for a place for them to live and dealt with Benny and his demands. But now her grief was back and ready to topple her over.

'On behalf of the Ballycotton lighthouse keepers, we want you to have this.' Patrick handed an oil wick lantern to Ellen last of all. 'It's one of our original lanterns, and we hope that when you light it, you remember Peter, who always kept a good light.'

If Kathleen had not steadied Ellen, she would have fallen.

'Peter was my dear friend. I've thought of little else but him and you these past few weeks. And I am so sorry I wasn't here to help you in person.'

'Thank you, Patrick. Your wife has proven herself to be the best of friends to me. I couldn't have survived without her kindness. Or Mary's and Beth's.'

'As it should be,' Patrick said. 'The keepers' wives always look out for each other.'

An image of the four women fighting and clawing Charles Davis flashed into Kathleen's mind. Patrick would never know how true that statement was.

Then it was time to begin their walk back to Powers Terrace. Patrick and Kathleen led the procession, with John and Katie proudly carrying their dad's duffle bag between them. Beth walked beside Mary, her head hung low.

Ellen, Joanne and Ger hung back a little, leaving some distance between them and the Keneficks. Villagers stopped on Main Street and greeted Patrick as he passed them by.

'Welcome home!'

'Pint in the Pier Bar waiting for you when you're ready for it.'

'Good to see you; you brought the sunshine!'

But when their eyes reached the Craig family, they bowed their heads low in sympathy.

When they reached Powers Terrace, Patrick said, 'It's good to be home.'

Kathleen paused when she saw Ellen move to Joanne, who had started to cry. 'Where will we go from here,

Mammy? We don't have a home,' Joanne said, her bottom lip wobbling.

Ger looked down at his fishing rod and the tears that had been threatening began to fall. Ellen looked down at her lantern. 'If only this would shine a light on what I should do next.'

It broke Kathleen's heart to see her friend so lost. 'You'll find your way. You're strong. But first things first – why don't you come into ours for a cup of tea?'

FORTY-FIVE

Beth

Friday, 25 May 1951

Ballycotton, Cork

Beth lay in her bed, as still as a statue, listening to the sounds of her family and the Craigs below. John and Katie were chatting happily with their dad, and he answered their incessant questions with good humour. Beth envied them for their innocence.

She wiped fresh tears away from her cheeks and then dug her nails into the palms of her hands.

There was a knock on the door, and when Beth looked up, Joanne stood in the doorway, awkward and silent. Beth didn't have the energy for her changing moods. If Joanne wanted to remain mute, that suited her fine.

'We're all going to the circus,' Joanne said. 'Are you coming?'

Beth had forgotten that tonight was the last show. Tomorrow, Murphy's field would be empty, with nothing but track marks and sawdust left behind.

Beth tried to muster up the enthusiasm. But the truth was, she didn't care. She couldn't reconcile the foolish girl she had been a few days ago with the woman she now was.

'Can you give a letter to Christian for me please?' She opened her bedside locker, and pulled out the pretty stationery set that she'd received for Christmas the previous year. What should she say? In the end, she kept it short and to the point.

> *I cannot go with you.*
> *Beth*

'What's wrong, Beth? Are you in love with Christian? Is that it?' Joanne asked, as she accepted the sealed envelope.

'No, I don't love Christian. It's over.'

Joanne's nose scrunched up, clearly not understanding what was wrong with her friend. 'Mary and Mam are hiding something. They keep whispering and when I walk into the room, they go quiet.'

Beth understood that Mary and Ellen must be as fearful as she was. Living on their nerves as they waited for Sergeant Cody to come knocking on their door. Beth reached up and touched her neck, thinking of Mary's father, who had been hung for murder. Would that be

319

her too? Beth's body began to shake, and she pulled her bedspread up to her chin.

'I saw Mam crying earlier today. I think Mary has told her we have to leave. I don't know what to do. I have to help, but I don't know how.'

Beth wanted to offer sympathy. But words of support froze in her mind, as the now-expected gripping fear that had overtaken her since yesterday returned.

Beth felt Joanne's eyes watching her as she shivered under her bedclothes.

'What happened to your face?' Joanne asked, catching sight of the cut on Beth's cheek.

'I fell.'

'That's weird. Your mam said yesterday that you hit it on the door.'

'I hit it on the door, then I fell,' Beth replied. 'I'm tired, Joanne. Why don't you go skip rope or something? I'll talk to you tomorrow.'

Beth saw hurt fly across Joanne's face. She was sorry that she'd caused her pain, but she couldn't do anything about it now. She no longer had it in her.

Beth rolled over and shut her eyes.

The next morning, there was a gentle knock, and Kathleen peeped her head around the bedroom door.

'Oh, you are awake. That's good.' She moved in and sat on the edge of Beth's bed. 'Your dad is worried about you. Will you come down to have breakfast with him?'

Beth shook her head. How could she face him and pretend that all was okay?

'You barely said a word to him yesterday evening.'

'Tell him I'm sick. It's not a lie. I do feel ill.'

Kathleen frowned. She placed a cool hand on Beth's forehead. 'You don't have a temperature.' She lowered her voice. 'Is your face sore? That was a hard blow you took.'

Beth's cheek stung still, but she shook her head. She welcomed the pain; it was a distraction from the endless torment in her mind.

'He'll get suspicious if you continue to hide up here.'

Beth didn't know what to say. She felt broken. It was as if her body was now in pieces. And she'd never be able to glue herself back together.

'I'll come down tomorrow,' Beth said, but she wasn't sure she believed that.

'Do you want to talk about what happened?' Kathleen asked gently.

'No!' Beth cried out quickly. That was the last thing she wanted. 'I'm trying to forget it, Mammy. I can't get it out of my head. I think I'm losing my mind.' She pulled at her hair, and to her surprise she saw a clump of brown strands come away in her clutched hand.

'Don't do that, love. Please.' Kathleen smoothed Beth's hair with her hand, back and forth, back and forth, in gentle strokes.

'Listen,' Kathleen began, 'why don't you tell me about what happened with you and your friend at the circus?'

This was unexpected. She'd seen her mother's face when Charles threw the accusation about her and Christian. She'd almost forgotten that part until now.

'I'm not cross. You can tell me,' Kathleen said.

And Beth could see sympathy in her mother's eyes, with no reproach or recrimination.

'Were you in love with him?' Kathleen asked.

Beth shrugged her shoulders. 'I thought I might be, for a while. The circus is leaving this morning, so it doesn't matter.'

'Do you want to say goodbye to him?' Kathleen said kindly. 'I'll take you, if you want to go.'

Beth buried her face in the pillow. 'He asked me to leave with him. He said I could work in the ticket booth.'

Kathleen clutched her chest as if she was having a heart attack. 'Run away with the circus?' Her voice had risen several octaves, 'And what did you say?'

'I'm not going with him,' Beth said flatly. It was impossible to ignore the relief that flooded her mother's face.

'I'm glad you said no. I would have been devastated if you'd gone.' Her mother's voice trembled as she spoke. 'Does that mean that you still love Ted?'

'I can't think about him right now.' Beth turned her back on her mother and closed her eyes, willing sleep to save her from her living horror.

She awoke a few hours later, feeling eyes on her. Her father hovered in the doorway, watching.

'Not like you to hide away in your bedroom,' he said. 'Dinner is almost ready. Your mother has gone all out. We've got roast chicken with all the trimmings.'

At the mention of food, Beth's stomach flipped and turned. She held a hand to her mouth.

'You've gone green,' Patrick said, alarm on his face. 'Stay where you are. I'll get one of the lads to drop you a bowl of soup later.' He turned to leave, but then paused and looked back at Beth. 'There's nothing wrong, is there? Your mother is . . .' He took a moment to think of the right word, 'jittery.'

She forced a smile. 'A stomach bug, that's all.'

'I know that this has been a difficult month for you all. Dealing with Peter's death. I'm sorry I've not been here. And I know Ted has been fretting for you too. You're all he talks about over on that rock, you know. He loves you.'

'I know, Dad. Thank you, but I'm so tired. We'll chat later,' Beth said. Then she forced a yawn and closed her eyes until she heard her bedroom door close once more.

FORTY-SIX

Kathleen

Saturday, 26 May 1951

Ballycotton, Cork

That evening, with Beth asleep in her bedroom and Katie and John playing outside, Kathleen was alone with Patrick. He sat in his favourite chair, and Kathleen was busying herself preparing the supper.

Patrick surprised her by pulling her into his lap as she passed him.

'Leave the food for a moment and give your husband a cuddle,' he said, almost shyly.

It took a beat, but she relaxed into him as he wrapped two strong arms around her. He smelled of paraffin oil and the sea, and Kathleen breathed him in as she laid her head on his shoulder. She closed her mind to Charles

Davis and the horror he'd left in his wake and instead focused only on the comforting embrace of her husband.

They stayed like that until the kettle whistled its readiness.

'I needed that,' Patrick said, almost gruffly.

Kathleen couldn't speak; she was filled with such emotion. 'Me too. It's been a tough couple of weeks.'

'Aye. I can only imagine.' Patrick looked into her eyes. 'Losing Peter, it made me think. Reassess things.'

Kathleen's heart began to beat so fast, she was sure he could hear it. 'Like what?'

He took Kathleen's face between his hands. They were calloused and felt rough to her skin, but she welcomed the touch like a lost friend. 'I've been careless with you. With our relationship. And I realized that if I'd died that night, instead of Peter, I would have left you unsure of my love for you. When I accepted the promotion to principal keeper, it was a proud day for me. And I've put everything into that role, making it my sole focus. That shames me now. You need to know, Kathleen, that I love you as much today as I did when you agreed to be my bride.'

Tears filled Kathleen's eyes as her heart filled with joy at Patrick's words. 'If you've been careless, then so have I. And your words have reminded me of how much I love and need you too, Patrick.'

She leaned in and kissed his lips, gently at first, then as they used to when they first courted each other.

'Tell me what's been going on,' Patrick said when they pulled apart. 'I want to hear everything I've missed.'

Kathleen winced inwardly; there was so much she could never share with him.

Instead, she spoke about Peter's funeral. And Benny Craig's proposal, followed by his threats about the fisherman's cottage Ellen had hoped to rent, and that was now burned down.

'And you think it was Benny who did that?'

'He admitted as much,' Kathleen said.

'The bastard. He always was a contrary fecker, but I didn't think he'd go that far. Has Ellen reported her suspicions to Sergeant Cody?'

'Not yet.'

'I'll call up to see the sergeant. And I'll also pay a visit to Benny next week. It's time someone put him straight.'

Kathleen looked at him in surprise. She hadn't expected Patrick to get involved in any way.

'I owe Peter that much,' he said. 'We put in a lot of hours by each other's side on that lighthouse. And if it were me in the ground, I know he'd look out for you all.'

Then, to her shock, Patrick started to cry.

Kathleen had only seen her husband show this level of emotion once, and that was when his mammy died ten years ago.

She leaned in again and embraced him, 'Hush now, it's okay.'

'He was like my brother.'

'I know. And Ellen is like my sister.'

'I've written to the Ballast Board, applying for a pension for Ellen and the children. Hopefully, they'll grant the application immediately.'

'How much will that be?' Kathleen asked, feeling a trickle of hope that help was coming for Ellen.

'Pensions are £6 per annum for the widows and £3 per child until sixteen. So Joanne won't be eligible. But Ellen should be entitled to £9 at least. Better than nowt.'

'It will be most welcome for them,' Kathleen agreed.

'And I thought we'd give them a few bob too, from our savings, what do you say?' He nodded upwards towards their bedroom, and the loose floorboard.

Kathleen felt a bile of acid burn the back of her throat, and her heart began to beat so fast she felt dizzy.

'One second, I must take that kettle off the heat.'

She took her time as she tried to work out what to say. Kathleen had never felt so wicked as she did right now. She'd written her husband off, thinking he would not wish to help their friends. If she'd just waited for him to return from the island and not been so stupid as to give the money to a conman, they could have helped Ellen out now. Together.

Her stomach lurched at the predicament she was in. All from her own hands.

'You are a decent and kind man,' Kathleen eventually said. 'And yes, I agree. We must do all we can to help the Craig family.'

She knew that if there ever was a perfect time to admit that she'd lost their savings, it was now. But Kathleen had just got her husband back. Not from the island. But from wherever he'd been locked away in his mind rather than with her. She couldn't risk losing him again.

FORTY-SEVEN

Kathleen

Sunday, 27 May 1951

Ballycotton, Cork

Kathleen smiled down at her husband. He looked younger somehow as he slept. Or was it because, since Patrick had returned from the island, he'd behaved more like the man she'd married twenty years ago?

She carefully got out of bed so as not to wake him. She grabbed her quilted blue-and-pink dressing gown and slippers and left the room. Kathleen peeked into John and Katie's room, where they slept peacefully. Then, making a silent wish that Beth would have found the inner resolve to get up, she looked into her eldest daughter's bedroom.

She found Beth curled up in the foetal position in bed,

crying silently. Kathleen ran over to her and climbed into bed, wrapping her arms around her, willing Beth to give the pain she felt to her.

'My darling, it's okay, I'm here. It's okay.'

'We killed him, Mammy,' Beth whispered.

'It was an accident,' Kathleen insisted. 'We didn't set out to kill him. And he was a bad man, Beth.'

'Does that mean he deserved to die?' Beth asked.

'No. I'm not saying that. But he hurt you. Look at your face. Ellen's stomach is black-and-blue. Mary has bruises too as do I. We had to fight back.'

'It was all for nothing. We didn't even get the money back. And the Craigs are still without a home. And Ted will hate me when he finds out about Christian . . .' Another sob wracked her body.

'He won't find out,' Kathleen said firmly. 'You made a mistake – and I don't condone it for a moment, but you need to put it behind you and focus on Ted now. Be a good girlfriend. Love him.'

Beth's eyes widened as she listened to her mother. 'I thought you'd want me to tell him. To do the right thing.'

Kathleen clasped her daughter's hands between her own, 'Listen to me, Beth, trust me when I tell you this. You cannot tell Ted what happened. He won't forgive you. Promise me you'll not say anything.'

Beth nodded silently.

'Do you feel strong enough to go out today? How about I get you a basin of warm water. I'm going to walk into the village with Ellen and Mary shortly. Would you like to come? We need to check if there are any whispers about Charles Davis. It's been three days since . . .'

Beth's body stiffened at the mention of his name.

'Okay. You stay here. I'll fetch the water up for you. At least have a freshen-up. Put a new nightdress on.' Kathleen kissed her forehead. 'It's going to be okay. I promise you. We just need to get through the next couple of weeks. That's all.'

Kathleen wished it were that easy. While she urged her daughter to hide her sins, Kathleen knew that she would have no option but to confess to Patrick. For all she knew, today he could reach into their safe to retrieve the missing money. She almost retched at the thought.

Leaving a note for the family letting them know where she was going, Kathleen called into the cottage next door to collect Mary and Ellen.

They strolled along to the start of the coastal walk, noting that the trilby hat was now missing from the spot, then down to the pier and up and down Main Street. But despite meeting several neighbours and swapping pleasantries, there was no mention of a missing hotel guest. Finally, they went on to the Bayview Hotel for coffee.

'Seems quiet, doesn't it?' Mary whispered, her eyes darting around once they took a seat in the corner of the lounge and ordered a pot of tea. 'Do you think the staff know he's missing yet?'

'He was travelling on his own. Maybe nobody has noticed,' Kathleen said.

'But his ticket to America was dated for today. Which means he should have checked out by now,' Mary pointed out. 'If he doesn't show up to check out, they'll call the Gardaí, if they haven't already.'

The mention of the Gardaí was sobering, and the three women sat in tense silence.

'How are you, Kathleen?' Ellen eventually asked. 'You look . . . probably how I look too.'

'I'm in a world of trouble. Besides expecting the Gardaí to come knocking whenever I hear a noise outside, I'm worried sick about Beth. She's almost catatonic one minute, keening the next. Hasn't eaten since Thursday. Won't come out of her bedroom.'

Mary and Ellen exchanged a worried look.

Kathleen looked around her, then said quietly, 'And to add to all of that, she's worried that Ted will find out about her . . . dalliance with the circus performer.'

'Who would tell him?' Ellen asked, frowning. 'It won't come from us. Don't worry.'

'Thank you.'

'Poor Beth,' Mary said softly. 'I'll call in later today to see her. Do you think Patrick is suspicious about why she's so upset?'

'He's worried. He's tried to rouse her several times but cannot get any good from her. I've told him that she's unsure about her relationship with Ted. Worried about the forthcoming proposal – which isn't untrue. She wants to travel.'

'How did he take that?' Ellen asked.

Kathleen smiled, 'Surprisingly well. I misjudged him, thinking he'd be against her travelling. But he is willing to listen to her, to discuss the idea.' Feeling a wave of emotion, Kathleen admitted, 'I think she needs to get away from Ballycotton for a while. To regain her strength. I have been thinking about writing to my cousin in Boston.

If she spends the rest of the summer there, it might give her a chance to come to terms with everything.' She closed her eyes for a moment to compose herself, tears threatening to unravel her.

'That sounds wise to me,' Mary said. 'If questions are asked by Sergeant Cody, perhaps it's best that Beth isn't here.'

Kathleen had thought the same. 'I'll talk to Patrick about Boston again this evening. But I have another pressing problem.' She looked at her two friends. 'Patrick has returned from the lighthouse . . . changed somehow. Peter's death has hit him very hard. We are closer than we've been for a long time. But he's presented me with another issue. Patrick told me last night that he wants to give you some money, Ellen.'

Mary uttered a 'Damn' as Ellen gasped.

'I'll tell him that I can't accept the money. You can say that I'm too proud,' Ellen said.

'That won't stop him. I know my husband. He's spent weeks over on the island working out what he wants to do to help you. For all I know, he could be right now, lifting the floorboard and finding the hiding space empty. And when he realizes it's missing, I don't know what I'll do.'

'If only we'd found the blasted money in the hotel room,' Ellen murmured.

Mary threw her a wounded look. 'I searched high and low. It wasn't there.'

'I don't—' Kathleen broke off, 'Oh sweet Jesus . . .'

They all swivelled around to see Dáithí, the hotel manager, rushing out to greet Sergeant Cody, who had just entered the hotel lobby.

FORTY-EIGHT

Mary

Sunday, 27 May 1951

Ballycotton, Cork

A waitress appeared carrying a silver tray laden with a large tea pot, cream, sugar and pretty purple-and-white teacups.

She unloaded the tray, placing their hot drinks in front of each of them. Her hand shook a little as she poured the tea into Kathleen's cup.

'It's okay, let me,' Kathleen soothed. 'You're all a jitter. Are you all right?'

'I'm all over the place today for sure,' the girl said, glancing over to Sergeant Cody and her boss, who were now making their way down the corridor towards the guest bedrooms. She lowered her voice conspiratorially.

'One of our guests is missing. A lovely man – Mr Davis. Always gave me a generous tip when I served him.'

They'd expected this, but it still made Mary's blood run cold now that they faced the inevitable fallout from his disappearance.

'That's terrible news. I've had the pleasure of meeting Mr Davis a few times myself. As you said, a gentleman,' Kathleen replied.

'What do you mean, missing?' Mary asked, trying not to look too eager for news.

'Well, the thing is' – the girl whispered – 'Mr Davis was due to check out from his room today. When housekeeping called to his room, there was no sign of him. No one has seen him since Thursday. And we've all been questioned, because his room key is missing from behind reception and Dáithí specifically remembers Mr Davis handing it in.'

Mary looked down to her handbag, where she knew the missing key sat. *Why had she kept the damn thing?*

'Maybe he left in a rush,' Ellen suggested. 'It happens.'

'Oh, Mr Davis wouldn't be the type to leave without paying his bill. A pure gentleman, I told you. Plus, all his clothes were still there. And his bed had yet to be slept in.'

'That is very strange.' Mary bit her lip as her mind raced. She made a face in Kathleen's direction and hoped she understood the message.

Kathleen inclined her head in acknowledgement, then said, 'Do you know, Ellen and I saw Mr Davis on Thursday when we were walking up near the cliffs.'

The girl's eyes widened. 'Did you now? Oh, I best keep going. They don't pay me to stand around gossiping.

Enjoy your drinks.' Then she scurried off in the direction of her manager.

'Let's see how long it takes for that titbit to reach the sergeant's ears,' Kathleen said. She added cream and sugar to her tea, stirring it as she said, 'By the way, Ellen, Patrick has written to the Ballast Board to request the pension. Hopefully there'll be good news on that score soon.'

Mary watched Ellen bravely accept this information. With everything that had happened with Charles, her predicament following the fire at the fisherman's cottage had been put to one side. The sale, understandably, had fallen through. Which left Ellen back at square one. 'Look, there is no need for you all to move out when Seamus returns from the lighthouse in two weeks. That will give us all another six weeks to sort out somewhere for you to rent. Plus if Ellen isn't on the streets, Patrick is less likely to look for the money.'

Ellen's eyes filled with tears as she looked at each of them. 'I don't know what I would do without you both.'

'Nor I for you both. But that's what friends do for each other,' Kathleen said. 'No thanks are necessary.'

Ellen took a sip of her tea, looking between them nervously. 'As it happens, I have made a decision. I'm going to see Benny later today. I have a proposal of my own to put to him.'

'I don't like the sound of that,' Mary replied. She cupped her hands around the china teacup to warm them.

'He needs help around the farm. He's made that clear,' Ellen said. 'I'll tell him that our family will give him that

335

help on the proviso that the farm is left to Ger when he dies. But I'll also tell him that I won't marry him.'

Mary and Kathleen listened to Ellen open-mouthed.

'And you think that animal will keep his distance from you? Or Joanne . . .' Kathleen hissed.

Ellen clutched her chest at the mention of her daughter's name. 'I won't live under the same roof as him. But there are outhouses on the farm. We could make one of those into a cottage for ourselves.'

'I don't like this,' Mary said, waving a spoon at Ellen. 'I wouldn't trust Benny Craig as far as I could throw him. He's a dirty, good for nothing— You can't live anywhere near him.'

'I shall tell him that if he lays a finger on any of us, I will go to Sergeant Cody and report that it was him who burned down the cottage,' Ellen said.

'That'll be our word against his. We have no proof,' Kathleen said, shaking her head. 'You're being too hasty. Give it another few weeks. Let's see what else comes up in the meantime, like news of the pension.'

Ellen set her teacup down a little heavily, splashing tea onto the saucer and table. She picked up a napkin and began dabbing the wet up. 'You don't understand. It's different for you, Kathleen. You grew up without ever worrying where the next meal might come from. Right?'

Kathleen nodded, and her cheeks reddened in acknowledgement of that truth.

'I grew up living hand to mouth, without a shilling to our names. My mother spent half her life in the Cork union workhouse. I thought I'd finally changed our family's luck when I married Peter. But I can't rely on Peter anymore. It's up to me now.'

'But this cannot be the answer,' Kathleen whispered. 'If you go to that man, he'll break you. He's got a cruel streak that makes Charles Davis look tame.'

'I can take care of myself. And I have to think about the best option for the children. A family farm can give the kids a better chance at life. There's a decent living to be had there for Ger. Money for a dowry for Joanne. And a roof over their heads that can't be taken away.'

'But what about your future?' Mary asked, her eyes filling with tears. She felt so desperately sad for her friend.

'Maybe I don't deserve a future. Maybe, this will be my living penance for my part in what happened up on the cliff,' Ellen said softly.

'To hell with that!' Kathleen hissed, her eyes blazing with annoyance. 'You'll not do one moment's penance for that man. I won't let you, Mary, or Beth do it. Surely—' She stopped abruptly at the sight of Sergeant Cody making his way towards their table.

'Good afternoon, ladies,' he said, as he approached. 'May I join you?'

'Please sit down,' Kathleen stammered, her cheeks flaming.

Dáithí brought two chairs over and placed them around the table. Mary took a deep breath to compose herself. They'd planned for this moment, and it was time to make sure they didn't slip up and expose themselves.

'I'll get straight to it. I believe you saw Mr Davis on Thursday?' Sergeant Cody said as he removed his cap.

'Yes. Ellen and I were taking a walk, and we bumped into him,' Kathleen answered.

'A rough day for a walk, I would have thought?' he replied.

Kathleen smiled. 'Oh, us keepers' wives are of hardy stock. We've spent our married lives in all weather extremes by our men's side. A little rain and wind never bothered us.'

'I prefer walking in the wind,' Ellen added.

'Blows out the cobwebs, eh?' Sergeant Cody answered. 'Can you tell me what time it was that you met Mr Davis?' He pulled a small notebook and pencil from his pocket and then licked the tip.

'Between ten and ten thirty a.m.,' Kathleen answered without missing a beat. 'I'd spent the early morning baking for Patrick. I like to have his favourite dishes prepared when he returns from his shift on the island.'

Sergeant Cody smiled approvingly. 'He's a lucky man. Now, ten o'clock, you said. Can you recall exactly where you were when you bumped into Mr Davis?'

'We'd been walking for twenty minutes or so,' Kathleen replied. 'So I'd say about one mile along the cliff walk. Closer to Ballyandreen Beach than to Ballycotton village.'

'We'd passed Ballytrasna Beach for definite,' Ellen added.

'Excellent. That's most helpful. And how was Mr Davis? Did you chat for long?'

'We passed the time of day.' Ellen's voice was assured. 'Swapped the usual pleasantries about the weather. He looked in good health. And then we left him to return home.'

338

'Can you recall what he was wearing?' Sergeant Cody asked.

An image of Charles's checked overcoat burning in Kathleen's Aga stove flashed into Mary's mind.

'He was wearing an overcoat. Brown, I think. Oh, and he was wearing a hat.'

'He always wore a trilby hat,' Dáithí added. 'A man who knew how to dress.'

'A gentleman,' Kathleen agreed.

It took all of Mary's resolve not to roll her eyes. She'd scream if one more person said this man was a gentleman.

'Did you know Mr Davis well?' Sergeant Cody asked, looking at each of the women in turn.

'I met him for the first time a couple of weeks ago. He told me that he was visiting Ballycotton for its restorative powers. He'd had ill health,' Kathleen said.

'Do you know what was wrong with him?'

'I'm afraid I don't,' Kathleen said. 'We were acquaintances rather than confidantes, so I didn't feel I could ask him such a personal question.'

'Understandable. And ladies, how about you? Did you know Mr Davis well?' Sergeant Cody directed his attention to Mary and Ellen.

'Pretty much the same as Kathleen,' Ellen answered. 'I've been in his company a couple of times. But I cannot say I knew him well.'

'You both had coffee with him last week, as I recall,' Dáithí said.

Ellen didn't flinch. 'Yes, that's right. He was very kind to me. Kathleen and I bumped into him on the Chapel

Road. I was upset. So he insisted we join him for a refreshment.'

'Upset about what, can I ask?' Sergeant Cody asked.

Kathleen tutted loudly, then, allowing the irritation to punctuate her words, said, 'Surely you don't need reminding that Ellen's husband, Peter, died on the island only weeks ago. Keeping our ships and fishermen safe, on the rock?'

Sergeant Cody bowed his head, two dots of red appearing on his round cheeks. 'My apologies, Mrs Craig. Of course.'

'I didn't know Mr Davis at all,' Mary interjected, deciding to move the conversation along. 'But I saw him a few times when my husband and I were guests in the Bayview. I don't believe we passed more than a few words to each other. He was always head down, reading the newspaper.'

'Thank you, ladies. You've been most helpful. Just one more question. When you left Mr Davis near Ballytrasna Beach, did he continue towards Ballyandreen, or did he also return to Ballycotton?'

Kathleen pretended to ponder this, then said evenly, 'I'm sure he wasn't behind us. But by then the wind had really picked up. We practically ran the last mile back to the village. I have to be honest; I didn't look back. Did you, Ellen?'

Ellen shook her head too. 'No, I didn't notice either. I feel awful now. I wish I had taken a moment to look behind me.'

'Have you been in touch with his family? They must be worried sick,' Mary said, hoping her face was a picture of innocence.

'He didn't give us a next of kin when he checked in,' Dáithí said. 'We did ask. I am always most particular about that. But he said there was nobody to list on the check-in form.'

'Isn't that sad?' Kathleen said. 'Did you find anything in his room that could help you?'

'Nothing of note,' Sergeant Cody said as he scribbled in his notebook. Then he stood up. 'I won't take up another moment of your time.' He turned to leave, but paused to ask, 'When you spoke to Mr Davis, did he mention if he was meeting anyone there?'

'No. I'm afraid not,' Kathleen replied. 'But the storm was brewing, and the wind made it quite difficult to converse. It was no day to be out walking along a cliff's edge.' She placed a hand to her chest and groaned, 'Oh you don't think he fell ill while out there, do you? The poor man. You must find him.'

Ellen reached over to clasp her hand in sympathy, and Mary shook her head sadly.

'We're not ruling anything out,' the sergeant said gravely. 'We'll go straight to the cliff walk now and search the area. But I'm sure he's safe and well. No doubt he'll feel very silly when he realizes that he's made everyone worry for nothing.'

With one last sympathetic nod, the sergeant left with Dáithí trailing behind him. Mary held her breath as they walked away.

Ellen picked up her tea, but her hand shook so much that she had to place her cup back on the table.

'Do you think he bought it?' Kathleen whispered.

'I bought it, and I know the truth!' Mary said. She looked at her two friends in appreciation. 'You played a blinder, Kathleen. As did you, Ellen.'

'My stomach never stopped flipping the entire conversation,' Ellen admitted.

'Mine too,' Mary agreed. She picked up a napkin and dabbed her forehead, which glistened with sweat.

'And thank goodness Beth wasn't here. I'm not sure she would have coped with the interrogation,' Kathleen said.

'Maybe it really would be best, for her and for all of us, if she leaves for Boston sooner rather than later,' Mary stated. Then she looked down at her handbag, deciding it was time to tell the women what she had. 'When I left here on Thursday, I kept Charles's room key.'

Kathleen and Ellen gasped out loud at this.

'I couldn't have put it back without being seen, and didn't know what to do with it. So I stuffed it in my handbag.'

'You should have gotten rid of it straight away, Mary. Throw it in the ocean when we leave here,' Kathleen ordered.

'But as I still have it, I thought I might go back for another look. I must have missed something. That money *has* to be in the room.'

Mary hadn't planned on this course of action. But now that she said it aloud, it seemed like the most sensible thing to do.

'It's too risky,' Kathleen said. 'I won't allow it.'

'I'll go with you,' Ellen said.

'Are you crazy?' Kathleen gasped, turning to face Ellen. 'First, you want to talk to Benny, now you want to go back to the scene of the crime?'

'No crime has been committed in that room. Not yet, anyhow. Maybe I am crazy. But no matter what, I'm going with Mary.'

Mary turned to Kathleen, pleading with her eyes. Kathleen looked torn. Then she drained the last of her tea and stood up. 'Oh for goodness' sake. Right, if we're going to do this, we better be quick.'

FORTY-NINE

Kathleen

Sunday, 27 May 1951

Ballycotton, Cork

Kathleen had spent all of her life following the rules. As a child, she'd never complained. She did as she was told if her parents gave her an order. And when she married Patrick, she took her vow to obey seriously.

But over these past few weeks, everything had shifted. Was it the circumstances around her, or something inside? She wasn't sure.

Both reception and the corridor that led to the bedrooms were empty, so they moved quickly and entered Room 119, locking the door behind them silently. Kathleen's heart thundered so loud, it reverberated in her ears.

'I've already looked in all the usual places,' Mary said. 'We need to think outside the box. There must be a secret place where Davis kept his money in this room. Work methodically. And fast.'

Kathleen looked around her. The room had high ceilings with an intricate coved architrave. Two large sash windows overlooked the bay, framed with heavy brocade curtains in cream-and-gold. A large double bed sat on a vibrant ruby-red carpet in the middle of the room.

'Start searching. But leave everything as you find it,' Mary hissed as she pulled the suitcase out from under the bed. 'I'll start with this. Maybe I missed a hidden compartment.'

'I'll take the bed,' Kathleen said, running her hand over the bedspread.

An image of kissing Charles, falling to this bed, filled her mind. She'd wanted that. Imagined sneaking into this room with him many times. What a foolish woman she was.

'You okay?' Ellen asked her.

'I will be,' Kathleen said. She pulled the bedclothes off the bed.

Ellen called out, 'I think there's something here.'

Kathleen and Mary stopped what they were doing to watch Ellen at the double mahogany wardrobe, as she tapped the wood, feeling the grooves.

'There's a loose panel at the back of the third drawer,' Ellen said over her shoulder.

They rushed over to her, but their hopes were dashed when Ellen realized it was nothing. Kathleen returned to

345

inspecting the mattress, and Mary continued running her fingertips across the suitcase lining.

Once Kathleen had searched the bed, she asked, 'Mary, did you check the curtains?'

'Yeah. I already checked the lining, but double-check in case I missed something obvious,' Mary answered.

Kathleen used her hands to pat the curtains but came up blank too. She stood back and surveyed the sash windows, particularly the tall panels on either side.

'I'm pretty sure there used to be shutters on these windows,' she said. Then she noticed tiny paint flakes on the red carpet underneath the curtain on the left-hand side.

'Come over here,' she called out to Ellen and Mary. 'Look.' She pointed to the paint. 'It might be nothing . . .' Kathleen began tapping the painted wooden panels, one by one.

'That one moved!' Mary said. 'On the bottom right.'

Kathleen hunkered down low, and a panel wobbled when she pressured it. She used her fingernails to inch her way behind the wood. A few more specks of white paint chipped off, falling to the ground like a fresh flurry of snowflakes. 'I can't get behind it . . .' she said in frustration.

'We need a knife,' Ellen said.

Mary ran back to the bed and pulled out the suitcase. 'He has a penknife in here!'

She handed it to Kathleen, who flicked it open and ran the small blade along the panel. She gently eased it along the edge until the board popped out. Kathleen looked on in amazement. A small leather bag was sitting in the now exposed hollow of the window.

Kathleen pulled it out and slowly unzipped it, revealing a flash of purple and yellow.

'Lady Lavery never looked so beautiful,' Mary said as they looked at the tight bundle of fifty-pound notes, with their image of an Irish colleen smiling at them benevolently as she leaned on a harp.

Kathleen stifled a sob and furiously wiped her tears away. Mary put her arms around her, squeezing her tight.

'Take your money. Then I vote we get out of here fast.'

Kathleen didn't need to be asked twice. She wasn't sure that Lady Luck would continue looking out for them. She counted out three hundred pounds from the bundle, then placed the balance back in the bag, returning it to the same hiding place. Ellen quickly brushed the paint flakes away, scattering them with her fingers.

'We can only hope that they find the money, and Sergeant Cody can then make sure that all the investors are reimbursed,' Kathleen said.

'Help me remake the bed,' Mary said. And together, they quickly ensured the room was left as they'd found it.

Kathleen leaned her ear to the door. 'Seems quiet out there.'

They locked the door behind them.

'I'll throw this in the ocean on the way home,' Mary promised.

They walked quickly out of the hotel to make their way home, before they could get into any more trouble.

FIFTY

Kathleen

Friday, 1 June 1951

Ballycotton, Cork

The week passed and it was time for Patrick to return
to the island once more. Kathleen kissed him goodbye,
grateful for their renewed connection. She would miss
him, until his return in three weeks. But she would also
be grateful to have this time to herself again to deal with
the aftermath of Charles Davis's disappearance, without
the watchful eyes of her husband.

When Sergeant Cody found his trilby hat in the reeds
near Ballytrasna Beach, a search was set in motion for his
body. So far, it had not been recovered.

Gossip was rife about his real identity. Dáithí told
everyone how he had been tricked out of his savings,

and had invested in what was now discovered to be a fake company. People came forward from Ballycotton, Garryvoe and Shanagarry, all with similar tales of lost investments. Every time someone brought up Charles Davis's name in her company, Kathleen's heart skipped a beat. She felt like she'd aged a decade since that fateful moment on the cliff's edge.

News arrived yesterday that money had been discovered in Charles Davis's hotel room. Dáithí boasted to all that as he had an invested interest, he searched the room himself, one more time. This at least was a blessing. If the other investors could receive their money back, like she had, Kathleen would sleep easier. Yesterday as she brushed her hair she'd noticed a new strand of grey at her temples. And her appetite seemed to have left her too. But thankfully, at no point was Kathleen's investment discovered, thanks to Mary's quick thinking, taking the fake investment paperwork from his suitcase.

Now Kathleen must focus all her attention on her daughter. With Patrick's blessing, Kathleen had arranged for Beth to leave for Boston in a week's time. That would give the young couple seven days together. To discuss their future. If they had one, Kathleen thought. She hoped so. In her heart, she felt Ted was the right man for Beth.

Kathleen heard the sound of Ellen and Mary's voices drift in from the open window. They must be in the garden next door. She cocked her ear to listen, and smiled as she heard Ellen share tips on how to care for her vegetable patch. Ellen was due to leave Powers Terrace the following week.

Because fate had one more surprise for Ellen and her family. A good one this time.

Benny Craig was dead.

On Monday, Patrick had paid him a visit, as he'd promised. But found a corpse. He'd choked on a piece of meat, Dr Whitaker had determined, a tragic accident. And Kathleen could not find a single part of her to regret his passing – especially as Ger was to inherit his farm. She had helped Ellen plan his funeral and baked tarts to serve to his neighbours at the wake. So Ellen, Joanne and Ger would move into the farmhouse this week after all.

Kathleen glanced at the clock and noted the time. Ted would be along soon. No doubt wondering why Beth wasn't at the pier to greet him. A loud rap on the door announced his arrival.

Ted rushed by her when she opened the door, 'I need to see Beth. And don't fob me off, Kathleen. I've heard . . .' He paused for a moment, as Kathleen's stomach plummeted at the words.

'What have you heard?' Kathleen asked, her voice little more than a whisper.

'It doesn't matter . . . but I won't leave here until I speak to her,' Ted answered, his jaw clenched tight.

Ushering him into the front parlour, Kathleen ran upstairs to Beth's bedroom. 'Get dressed. Ted is here, and he won't leave until you come down to speak to him.'

'I can't, Mam,' Beth said.

'Yes, you can, girl. And you will, if I have to drag you down myself. You owe him that much. Is there any way that he could have heard something about that circus fella?'

Beth's eyes widened in shock at the suggestion. 'No. I don't think so.'

'Then what in God's name is he so angry about?' Kathleen replied as she moved to the single pine wardrobe and pulled out one of Beth's cotton print dresses. 'Thank the stars your father is gone back to the island. If he was here, there would be murder. Do you want to lose everything?'

Kathleen took a brush from the dressing table and tamed Beth's locks into submission. 'There. That's the best we can do. Your natural beauty is saving you here. Now listen to me, Beth. You cannot tell Ted about what happened with Charles Davis.'

Beth nodded mutely.

'And if he has heard gossip about Christian, you play it down. It was a harmless flirtation, nothing more,' Kathleen said.

Worryingly, Beth did not nod her agreement to this.

Kathleen led a still mute Beth downstairs and brought her into the front parlour, where a grim-faced Ted waited for her.

As he looked at Beth, his face contorted with pain. Kathleen stepped outside the room but hovered by the partially open door to watch and listen. She had to be ready to step in if Beth began to spill secrets.

'Tell me it's not true,' she heard Ted beg. 'Tell me that you have not fallen for that circus artist.'

Damn it. He had heard something. She watched Beth's face crumple with sorrow. No matter her words, Beth's shame was there for all to see.

'Why?' Ted asked with a strangled sob.

'I am so sorry.'

Ted cursed; Kathleen had never heard him do so in their company before and the profanity shocked her. 'Goddamn it, Beth, after last week on the rock! That meant something to me. It meant *everything*.'

'Me too Ted! I don't know how to explain what happened, but I'll try.' Beth's voice trembled as she spoke, and Kathleen felt a pang of pain for her daughter. 'I was a silly girl who didn't know what I wanted. But I've grown up over the past week. Everything has changed.'

'You've grown up in a week? Spare me the details,' Ted said, with fresh pain etched into his voice.

'I don't mean like that . . . I mean emotionally,' Beth continued. 'I was afraid to say what I wanted . . . but—'

'Do you love him?' Ted asked, cutting her off, his voice little more than a whisper.

'No!' Beth cried out. 'It was a schoolgirl infatuation. A childish attempt at living a different life from the one that seemed mapped out for me.'

Kathleen felt like a spy, a cruel intruder in this most painful of interactions between Ted and Beth. She was about to move away but paused when Ted asked another question.

'What was so wrong with the life you had?'

Kathleen wiped tears from her cheeks as she heard her daughter say, 'I'm the great-granddaughter, granddaughter and daughter of a lighthouse keeper. And from the moment I was old enough to understand marriage, it's been said that I would be a keeper's wife one day. Like my mam and all those who went before her.

'When I was younger, I couldn't wait for that fate. But

lately, I've been thinking about life outside of this. You know I've lived in the shadow of a lighthouse my entire life. I told you this last week.'

Kathleen clasped a hand over her mouth to stop herself crying out. Every word Beth spoke cut her. She and Patrick had put so much pressure on their daughter without realizing the pain it was causing her.

'I want to travel,' Beth went on, and her bravery made Kathleen proud. 'The thought of spending the rest of my life here, in Ireland, makes me wake up at night in a cold sweat. I want to see what's on the other side of that ocean I've lived beside forever. I want to taste food from different cultures, feel the sun on my skin on every continent, dance under the moon and stars and say I love you, in another language. Can you understand that, Ted?'

For a moment, Kathleen was expecting him to soften, to understand. She willed him to say that they could do all those things together.

But life rarely worked out like that.

'Since you told me that you wanted to travel, I've thought of nothing else,' Ted said, but his voice was hard. 'I'd decided to come with you. I was ready to leave Ireland, leave the career I adore, to be with you. To follow you to the ends of the earth. But now . . . I thought I knew you, but I don't, do I?'

Kathleen heard his footsteps as he moved towards the door, then he turned back to say, 'Go on your travels. But take your trapeze artist with you.'

He pushed past Kathleen and left the cottage without a backward glance.

'But I don't love Christian,' Beth whispered to the now empty room. 'It's you I love, Ted.'

Then she crumpled to the ground and began to sob.

Kathleen moved in and crouched down low beside her daughter. As she pulled Beth into her arms, she knew they'd made the right decision to let Beth go. If Beth was to find any peace from the horrors of the past few days, it would be away from here.

FIFTY-ONE

Beth

Monday, 17 July 2023

Ballycotton, Cork

The willow branches shifted in the afternoon breeze, and a robin sang nearby. Beth and Joanne sat beside each other, only inches apart but with a chasm between them.

It had been years since they'd been in each other's company, and decades since those weeks in May 1951 that had changed Beth's life forever.

The years slipped away, and Beth felt seventeen again, looking at her best friend Jojo for support, confused when it was not forthcoming.

'When Ted found out about Christian, and he confronted me, it was one of the worst moments of my life.'

355

Joanne made a derisory snort, then said acidly, 'You brought that on yourself.'

'Have you always been this cold? Or did life make you like that?' Beth asked. 'Nothing is ever black-and-white, Joanne. I wasn't a bad person, even if I made bad choices.'

Doubt moved across Joanne's face.

'When I met Christian, it felt like fate. I had spent years dreaming of my escape from Ireland, from my foregone future of being a keeper's wife. Christian seemed like he could be that escape. I got caught up in a madness that became impossible to explain once I stepped outside of it.'

She placed a hand on her heart. Beth could still feel the hurt she had inflicted on Ted, as though it had just happened.

'While I was busy thinking about myself, I was careless about Ted, who loved me. I didn't realize how much I loved him until it was too late.'

'So stupid.' Joanne's lip curled in annoyance, 'To risk everything for a fling . . .'

'I won't argue with you on that. When Ted decided he couldn't forgive me, I knew I only had myself to blame. And somehow, when he left me, it felt like a suitable punishment for my sins.' Beth looked out at the low sun that peeped through the tree's green leaves. 'I remember that evening, I sat looking out my bedroom window for hours, thinking he might return. But as the sun went down on the ocean, the light went from my heart too. I knew it was over.' A tear escaped her grey eyes and slipped down her cheek.

Joanne's shoulders slumped. 'I suppose I never thought about it from your perspective, really.'

Beth felt her temper quicken. That had always been Joanne's problem. She was so judgemental.

'It was you who told Ted about Christian,' Beth stated. 'But you didn't tell Ted for unselfish reasons, did you? You thought he'd fall into your arms for comfort if he hated me.'

Two spots of colour flamed on Joanne's cheeks. She crossed her arms across her chest, then uncrossed them again.

Beth could see how uncomfortable she was, and that didn't make her feel happy. Still, she was beyond caring about all of that now. She'd made her peace with that part of her history long ago.

Beth's bones ached; she'd spent too long on the cold bench. She felt every bit of her age. But she couldn't fall into her bed yet. There was more work to do. How had they come to this?

'I could have done with a friend back then,' Beth said, with a weary sigh.

'For what part, Beth? To help you cover up your love affair? Or comfort you after Ted and you split up? I couldn't. I didn't have it in me. I was dealing with my own traumas.'

'I know you had it tough back then. I'm sorry your father died. I'm sorry you lost your home. And I'm sorry I wasn't a good friend to you at times, either. But you weren't the only one dealing with . . .' Beth paused.

'Dealing with what?' Joanne asked, her eyes narrowing.

Beth wanted to avoid getting into it now. When Dervla arrived, she'd talk to them all together. Bring the past back, lay it all out. 'Nothing.' Beth sighed, running her hands through her grey hair.

'That's it. Shut down and keep your secrets. You've spent your life doing exactly that.'

'And look what it's cost me. I lost a part of myself that I've never been able to get back. And I had to run away from all I loved, and I've been running since then . . .'

'From what?' Joanne demanded.

Beth couldn't help the words that tumbled from her lips. 'From what we did!'

The air stilled. Neither of them blinked or moved.

'Mam told me, you know,' Joanne whispered. 'Before she died.'

Beth felt winded by the admission. She had been adamant to Albie and Mollie that Joanne was not behind the letters. But Joanne had known about their secret all along. Maybe Mollie's gut was right.

Rare tears filled Beth's eyes as she tried to explain, 'I was only seventeen, and my life was not supposed to start that way. I can't get away from it, Joanne. Most nights I still see Charles Davis's face. Holding in a scream as he tumbles backwards into nothing.'

Beth was surprised to feel the warmth of Joanne's hand on top of hers. And she clung to it as she felt the ghosts catch up with her again.

'For months, I can go about my life in peace. But then he catches up with me again.' Beth's eyes darted around her. 'He's waiting for me now. It's as if Charles Davis has moved from my night terrors to my waking hours. Relentless for his revenge.'

Beth slumped onto Joanne's shoulder and began to sob.

'He can't hurt you anymore, Beth. He can't hurt anyone,' Joanne held her close. And in that embrace, they became teenagers again on the brink of adulthood. Best friends once more.

'It wasn't your fault,' Joanne said. 'You were only trying to help our mothers and Mary. You can't hold on to this guilt any longer.'

Beth wiped away her tears, looking Joanne squarely in the eyes. 'If you truly believe that, you must stop tormenting everyone with those letters. Mollie has been through enough. Please, if you ever cared for me, leave it be.'

Joanne's eyes bulged wide. 'Letters? I don't understand.'

Beth could see the truth in Joanne's face. She hadn't a clue what Beth was talking about.

'Someone has been sending letters to Mollie, Dervla, Jim and me about what we did to Charles. I thought maybe you . . .' Beth shook her head. 'The letters are why I asked you all to come here today. It's time for me to confess to what I did, get it all out in the open.'

'I swear I know nothing about this.' Joanne's eyes darkened, and she said, 'I'll be by your side when you talk to everyone. You are not on your own anymore. You weren't the only one who made mistakes back then. I have my own share too . . . I think we both let each other down.'

The sound of another car pulling up interrupted Joanne.

Albie called out from inside, 'Dervla has arrived.'

Beth held on to the side of the bench to help heave herself up to a standing position. She considered telling everyone she was too tired, that she needed to go to bed.

But she knew she had to be brave, one more time. So she held out her hand to Joanne, 'It's time to go inside. Let's get this over with.'

FIFTY-TWO

Beth

Monday, 17 July 2023

Ballycotton, Cork

Albie, Mollie, Jane, Dervla and Joanne all sat around the table, watching Beth. She'd asked them all to be here, but now that they were, it was proving more difficult than she'd thought to speak about what happened that summer.

Once everyone had a drink, an uncomfortable silence filled the room as they waited for Beth to get the ball rolling.

Beth cleared her throat, then addressed the room, 'Someone has been sending letters to us all, about an event that happened many years ago. I don't know who is behind the letters. But whoever it is, they only hold the power, if the secret remains a secret. So I'm going to tell you all about what happened in 1951.'

'Are you sure you want to do this, Mom?' Albie asked.

Beth looked around the room and nodded. 'It's time.'

She looked at Jane, who grew more like her mother Kathleen every day. At Albie, who she felt closer to now than she'd done for a long time. He was his father's son in looks and temperament, which she thanked God for every day. Then at Mollie, who was her heart, and, at times, her mirror too. She saw Peter in his daughter Joanne's nose and chin and shades of Ellen in her granddaughter Dervla. The eyes, in particular.

There were echoes of her past in this room, in every single person here.

'In May 1951,' Beth began slowly, 'Mam, Ellen, Mary, and I killed someone. It was an accident, but we covered it up, swearing to each other that we would never tell.'

You could have heard a pin drop in the room; such was the silence.

'I thought the secret would go to my grave. But that's not to be.' Beth sighed as she looked around the room, eyeing each person individually. And then, all at once, the room exploded with voices, firing questions, exclaiming shock, horror and disbelief.

'Someone did tell, evidently. I'm not sure why the letters are being sent yet. I'm not sure who they're from. But perhaps we'll learn before the end of today,' Beth said.

Beth's mouth felt dry and arid. So she took a sip of her tea, which was now lukewarm, and waited for them to calm down and listen. It was Joanne, surprisingly, who took control of the room, calling for quiet so that Beth could continue.

'Nothing is ever black-and-white, and you need to understand the nuances of the situation back then,' Beth said. 'Everything changed when Ellen's husband Peter died.'

There wasn't a sound in the room as she began to speak about his death, Ellen's subsequent notice to evict Powers Terrace, and Benny's terrorizing of the family.

'When Ellen looked like she had secured a new home in the village, Benny burned the cottage to the ground. That was his way of forcing Ellen and the children to move in with him,' Beth said.

'Why did he want that so badly?' Mollie asked, chewing her bottom lip.

Joanne interrupted, 'I'll answer this, if I may. Uncle Benny was a cruel man. He wanted a housekeeper and farmhands at his beck and call, not a family.' She took a deep breath, then continued, 'He treated us with no respect. I was scared of him. The way he looked at me and Mam, it was . . . inappropriate. I believe that he would have forced himself on me if—'

'Oh my God, you killed Benny Craig!' Jane exclaimed. She turned to Dervla. 'When did he die? I bet it was in 1951!'

'He did die in 1951,' Dervla replied evenly.

'Oh for goodness' sake, we didn't kill Benny Craig,' Beth said. 'As far as I know, the only thing to kill him was his appetite for cigarettes, whiskey and greasy fry-ups.

He died of natural causes seven weeks after his younger brother Peter.'

Joanne spoke again. 'As Uncle Benny had no heirs, Ger inherited the farm. We made it a home. Ger loved working the land. He didn't know what Uncle Benny was really like. And thank goodness he never found out.'

Beth was grateful that they'd managed to keep John and Katie out of everything too. The younger kids had been blissfully unaware of what was going on around them that summer.

Mollie was frowning. 'I have to admit, Nana, I thought it might have been Benny who you killed too. If it wasn't him, who?'

'I'm getting to that. I promise, I'm not hiding any truths. I'm just trying to explain it all,' Beth said. 'Mary and Seamus were incredibly generous people. They invited the Craigs to remain in the cottage with them. And while Seamus was on the island, Mary became very close to us all. And it was Mary who realized that Mam had been conned by a man who told her he was a Texan oil tycoon.'

Another round of splutters filled the room at this bombshell. Beth went on to tell them about Charles's 'investment opportunity' and Kathleen's friendship with him as quickly and matter-of-factly as possible.

'Are you hinting that Mam and he got up to . . . shenanigans?' Jane asked, horror written over her face.

Beth shrugged. 'Truthfully, I don't know. Mam swore that it was platonic, but . . . She trusted him enough to invest her and Dad's savings in his company, believing it would return a profit that would buy the fisherman's cottage outright for Ellen.'

'The one Uncle Benny burned down?' Dervla asked in a small voice.

'Yes,' Beth answered. 'Anyhow, call it fate or dumb luck, but thankfully Mary recognized Charles Davis and knew he was a conman.'

'How?' Mollie asked.

'Mary's father was in Mountjoy Prison. And when Mary went to visit her father in jail, she met Charles there – his cellmate.'

Dervla groaned. 'Of course! That's what Mary's son, Jim, was talking about when I called him. His grandfather.'

Beth took in the shocked faces of everyone around her. She knew it was a lot to wrap their heads around. 'When Mary told us about Davis, we were dumbfounded. Mam was distraught, thinking she'd lost all our savings. Charles Davis was an evil man.' Beth's body began to tremble as she remembered his face, dark and looming at her. 'When Mam demanded her money back, he threatened to tell everyone that they were having an affair and that I was carrying on with a circus trapeze artist.'

'The bloody cheek of him, making up lies like that!' Jane said, sounding outraged.

'Well, the bit about me wasn't lies,' Beth admitted. 'I had been cheating on Ted with a Frenchman called Christian.'

'So you killed Charles Davis to keep him quiet?' Albie asked in a shaky voice.

Silence filled the room as everyone waited in terror for Beth's response.

'No, of course not. We never planned to do it. I told you already, it was an accident,' Beth said, and a sigh of relief whispered around the room.

'We didn't set out to kill him. But when he struck me' – Beth reached up and touched her cheek, which carried a faint white scar from that blow – 'it started a chain of events. Mam fought back, then Ellen and Mary. We all struggled and . . . at one point, I pushed him away from Mam, and he fell backwards, tumbling over the cliff into the sea. One minute he was there, the next he was gone forever.'

Beth was pale now. Reliving the moment was costing her dearly.

'What you are describing is self-defence,' Mollie said. 'Not murder, surely!'

'Exactly. You fought back,' Dervla agreed.

'Perhaps. Everything that happened afterwards is a bit of a blur. I was in shock. Post-traumatic stress, you'd call it now. All I know is I didn't cope well. Mam, Ellen and Mary took care of everything. I was little use to anyone, retreating inside myself as I tried to grapple with it all.'

Beth explained what happened next – the stories Kathleen had told her about breaking into Charles's hotel room and finding the money.

There was a sombre pause when she stopped.

'So Grandad Patrick never knew that Granny Kathleen almost lost their savings?' Albie asked.

Beth shook her head, 'To my knowledge, no. I left Ballycotton not long after. Ted had found out about Christian, and there was nothing left for me. And I

366

suspect Mam, Ellen and Mary were worried I might draw attention to us, give something away, because I was such a mess. It was arranged for me to go to Boston to stay with Mam's cousin.'

'At the time, I thought you left because you were upset about Christian and Ted. I didn't know any of this,' Joanne said. 'I wish I'd known. I'd like to think I would have been a better friend.'

'I made a promise to never tell. So I didn't,' Beth replied simply. Whatever they might say about her and her actions as a young girl, Beth would always hold her head up high, that she was a woman of her word.

'You were a child. To deal with all of this at such a young age . . .' Jane said, reaching over to clasp Beth's hand. 'It's no wonder you broke. And all these years, your depression, I never knew it stemmed from that.'

'I knew something was going on back then,' Joanne said. 'Mam, Kathleen and Mary were always whispering to each other. Going silent when I walked into the room.'

Beth looked at each of the people sitting around the table. Had she done the right thing, sharing this with them all? She hoped so. She looked at her watch. It was almost 5 p.m.

'Albie, please drive me to the Garda station in the village. I'm going to go in and confess it all. When the story breaks, whoever is sending the letters will know that they got what they wanted. The secret is out.'

'Nana, I don't want you to do this!' Mollie cried out, and it hurt Beth to see her so distressed. She wanted to make her life easier, not harder.

Dervla stood up. 'Don't go anywhere yet Beth. When I arrived, I noticed someone skulking a few hundred metres up the road. I didn't want to say anything at the time, because I could see there was enough drama going on without that. But I have a hunch . . . will you give me a few minutes?'

FIFTY-THREE

Mollie

Monday, 17 July 2023

Ballycotton, Cork

Dervla was gone for less than five minutes. She returned to the kitchen, half dragging someone behind her. Mollie, Albie and Jane jumped up from their seats, walking towards Dervla and the stranger.

'I found her by the entrance,' Dervla said. 'But I thought it was time she joined us. Because this is not the first time you've been hanging around outside the cottage, is it? Following Mollie.'

Dervla pulled the black hood down to reveal a woman with cropped grey hair and piercing denim-blue eyes. She was only five feet, or very little more. Wearing leggings and trainers, under the black hoodie, she looked to be

369

in her early seventies. Her mouth was drawn tight and, while she stood with her shoulders squared as if ready for a fight, Mollie could see a tell-tale shake in her body. Mollie felt a flash of recognition when she saw her, but it dissolved as fast as it had appeared. Did she know her? Or did the woman look familiar because Mollie had seen glimpses of her over the past few weeks?

'You've been following me,' Mollie stated. 'Who are you?'

'My name is Libby,' she replied.

Mollie looked around the room but saw the same enquiring look on everyone's face. Nobody knew who she was.

'Are you the person who has been sending us all letters?' Mollie asked.

Libby nodded, shifting uneasily on her feet.

Angry chatter broke out in the room. Her aunt Jane stood up, waving her hands agitatedly as she fired questions at the woman.

Then her dad stood up to join Jane, his face flushed with fury. 'You have a neck, turning up here after all you've put us through.'

Dervla held her hand up and shushed them all, nodding at Mollie to take the lead.

Mollie moved forward, 'Why?'

Libby glanced around the room, chewing her bottom lip. She reached inside her hoodie pocket and pulled out a photograph, laying it on the table before them all.

Mollie recognized the image. 'It's the same photograph you sent Nana Beth a few weeks ago. Taken outside the keepers' cottages.'

Libby pointed to each person, as she said their names softly, 'Kathleen, Ellen, Mary, Beth, Joanne, Katie, John and Ger. I've looked at this photograph hundreds of times, trying to find a clue in any of their faces.'

Dervla stepped forward, authority again in her voice, pointing to the photograph, 'A clue to what? You need to start talking or I'll have no choice but to call this in. Stalking, sending threatening letters—'

'Don't do that! Please. I just want answers.' Then to Mollie's surprise, Libby began to cry.

Mollie looked at Libby and tried to work out her connection to the photograph and the people in the kitchen. The Craigs and Keneficks, back together again. So much time had passed since they had all lived side by side in Powers Terrace. And the events of that summer had bonded them together, entwined their lives till now.

Aunt Jane passed a box of tissues to Libby, who blew her nose.

'I'm sorry,' Libby said, her tears stemmed for now. 'I didn't expect to feel so emotional, seeing you all. But it's quite overwhelming for me.'

'Who told you about Charles Davis?' Mollie's grandmother asked in a strained voice. Nana Beth looked every bit of her almost ninety years, shoulders hunched in her chair. She'd lost weight over the previous week in hospital, and her blouse and skirt hung loose on her. Mollie inched her chair closer to her and placed a protective arm around her shoulders.

Libby was silent for a moment. 'I don't know who that is. Is he here?' She looked around the table.

Mollie and Dervla exchanged a puzzled look.

'No of course not,' Albie said. 'Charles Davis died in 1951, as well you know.'

Libby looked blank-faced at them.

'Maybe she doesn't know as much as we think she does,' Dervla whispered to Mollie.

Libby was frowning. 'I really don't know a Charles Davis, sorry.'

Confused, Mollie reached down to clasp Beth's hand, her heart racing. Her grandmother looked back at her in shock. *Libby didn't know that Beth had played a part in Charles Davis's death*. Which meant that whatever the letters were about, it wasn't that. A lump formed in Mollie's throat, and it was all she could do not to burst into tears. The relief was staggering.

Nana Beth's eyes glassed over, and a tear escaped. Mollie reached up and brushed it away with her hand, whispering to her, 'It's okay. It's going to be okay.'

Then she turned back to Libby, clearing her throat to ask, 'So why did you send this photograph to Nana Beth, asking her to confess her secret?'

Libby picked up the photograph, looked at it for a moment, then placed it down again. She glanced at Beth, then back to the photograph.

'As I said in my letters, I need to know the truth.'

'About what?' Mollie asked.

'It's complicated. But that photograph is all I have to go on, and I can't go on without finding out. I'm hoping— I believe you can tell me the truth.'

'You're not making any sense,' Mollie said.

'My mother gave me the photograph. Or at least, I think she did. It was in my birth folder. All I have.'

372

Libby looked down again, avoiding eye contact with everyone. 'You see, I believe that one of the women in this photograph must be my mother.'

The room swelled with shock and confusion as everyone tried to make sense of her words.

'I was left in a basket, outside the Bessborough Mother and Baby home in the early hours of February the ninth, 1952,' Libby went on. 'I was a couple of days old. My file says I wore a long white knitted gown, with a matching cardigan and bonnet. And I had clearly been well cared for. That photograph was in the basket with a short note, asking the nuns to find me a good home.'

Aunt Jane exclaimed suddenly, 'Well, my mam isn't your mother, gurl. She can't be. She was pregnant with me when you were born. Kathleen is *not* your mother.' Then she slumped back into her chair.

Mollie's eyes turned to her grandmother, who had gone very quiet. And a thought snaked its way into her head. Could it be possible that Beth had left Ballycotton in 1951 pregnant? *Oh Nana.*

Dervla obviously had a similar thought about her own grandmother. She turned to her aunt Joanne. 'You said earlier that Uncle Benny looked at Granny Ellen inappropriately. Did he . . . I can't even say the words out loud . . . but . . . is Libby Ellen's?'

They all turned to face Joanne, whose face was ashen. But, like Nana Beth, she remained mute. Mollie had run through dozens of scenarios over the past week, but this had never entered her mind.

'I was adopted when I was six weeks old,' Libby continued. 'My parents were good people and loved me,

373

gave me a great life. I grew up on a farm, a few hours away from here in Kildare. I still live there. They're gone now, of course, and I miss them every day. Over the years, there have been so many times when I desperately wanted answers. Each time I held my children, and grandchildren, I'd ask myself if my birth mother and grandmother felt the same when they held me? Was I wanted? Was I loved? But no matter how hard I tried to find out where I came from, I failed.'

'I'm glad you had a good life at least,' Nana Beth whispered.

Mollie saw her dad's eyes watching his mother, his jaw clenched tight. She could see anger still dancing through him and she understood that. What the hell was this woman thinking of, sending letters to them? How cruel to put them through the sheer panic and fear.

'I can understand why you need to find out the truth about your birth mother,' Mollie said through gritted teeth. 'But you could have found a nicer way to do it! We've been worried sick about my grandmother, who has just come out of hospital. We didn't need to be scared to death by letters too!'

Libby's eyes darted from each of them in the room, and fresh tears started again. 'I never meant to frighten anyone. I'm so sorry. It's just I felt I had no choice. I went to visit Mary, you see. I asked her if she was my mother. My husband fancied he could see a resemblance to her. I had dark hair like her, when I was younger. He wanted to help me solve the mystery.'

Nana Beth sat up, 'When did you see Mary?'

'A few months ago. She told me that I wasn't hers, but she refused to say who my mother was and said I should forget about looking for answers. She said the keepers' wives kept their secrets for a reason. And that would never change. She was so forceful. Told me to go home and forget about the photograph.'

Nana Beth sighed, then in a shaking voice told Libby that Mary had just died.

'This must be such a sad day for you. And then me on top of it all. I really didn't mean to worry you or cause you any pain.' She took a deep breath. 'Adrian – that's my husband – well he . . . he died a month ago. He went to the doctor with a pain in his back, and within three weeks he was dead. Cancer had spread all the way through him, to his bones. One minute he was fine . . . the next . . .'

Mollie felt her grandmother's hand reach for hers. And the room fell into silence once more.

'I'm sorry for your loss,' Joanne said, the first to speak. 'That must have been such a shock for you.'

'I think I may have lost my mind.' Libby took two large gulps, then placed her face in her hands. Aunt Jane got her a glass of water. And they allowed Libby a moment to regain her composure. 'I'm not trying to make excuses for myself, I know I've gone about things all wrong. But Adrian said to me before he died that I was to find my mother. Finish what we had started together. I think he wanted to give me something to do, to take my mind off losing him. I promised him I wouldn't leave any stone unturned. I loved him. It's been difficult without him.'

'Grief makes us do things that in our normal circumstances we'd never even consider,' Joanne said.

Libby nodded gratefully for the understanding. 'You see, Mary had been adamant that I was wasting my time, even talking to you, Beth. Her words rang out in my head, over and over. "The keepers' wives kept their secrets for a reason. They will never tell."

'I've not been sleeping. One night, late, I thought, what if I send a message to Beth? I hoped you might respond . . . if you were kind of shocked into it. Then once I'd typed the first letter, I thought, well, maybe I should send one to Mollie too, and it all snowballed.'

Libby took another sip of water. Then looked around the room sheepishly. 'It seemed like a good idea at the time, but now, sitting here, I realize how crazy I must seem. And I promise you I'm not. Or at least I wasn't before Adrian died. I have a nice home. I have children, grandchildren. The only thing I don't have is answers.'

'You could have tried asking, rather than putting the heart crossways on us,' Aunt Jane insisted, tutting.

Libby's face flamed as she nodded her agreement to that sentiment.

But whatever anger Mollie felt, dissipated. It was clear that the woman was not acting rationally.

Libby went on, to further explain. 'I have tried to get answers through the authorities for years, but always came up blank. They'd tell me to go away – politely of course, but nevertheless, the same message each time – we don't know who your parents are. I tried a DNA ancestry test too, but it came back with no close matches to anyone.'

'How did you work out who was in the photo?' Albie asked. His voice was kinder now, Mollie noted.

'The lighthouse is in the background. Adrian and I did some research and it wasn't hard to work out that it was Ballycotton, as the lighthouse is so distinct, painted completely black. On a whim, my husband and I booked a tour to the lighthouse. I showed the photograph to the guide and he suggested some names, and pointed me towards the local library. I found a photograph of Mary and Seamus Mythen in an archive there, taken at Ballycotton Lighthouse.'

Mollie had to hand it to the woman; she'd been tenacious in her search for truth. Albeit a bit extreme.

'I understand that you most likely want me to leave. And why should you bother with me when I've acted so stupidly. But I'm begging you to please help me,' Libby pleaded as she looked around the room at each of them.

Then her eyes fell on Beth and she whispered shakily, 'Are you my mother?'

377

FIFTY-FOUR

Beth

Wednesday, 6 June 1951

Port of Cobh, Cork

Beth stood on the pier at Cobh port, taking in the Cunard Line passenger ship that sat in the bay. Three blood-red funnels stood proud against dark grey clouds, which were heavy with rain that had been threatening to fall all morning.

Shortly, Beth would board a tender which would take her to the ship and the start of her new adventure. She'd dreamed about this day for years. The moment when she'd get to see what lay on the other side of the Atlantic Ocean. But today, unlike in her dreams which were colourful and bright, Beth only saw grey.

'Your cousin Maeve will be waiting for you in New

York. She will accompany you from there on a train to Boston,' her mother said, for the third time that day. She reached over and smoothed down the lapel of Beth's coat.

'I remember, Mammy,' Beth replied. She could see the strain on her face. And knew that leaving Ballycotton was costing her mammy dearly.

It had been an emotional twenty-four hours as Beth had said her goodbyes to family, friends and neighbours. She'd borrowed a rowboat and went out to the island to see her father. Seamus and Lee, the other keepers on duty, had prepared a luncheon for them both. As her father kissed her goodbye, he said, 'Don't forget us. I'll be waiting here for you, keeping watch until you come back to us.'

Last night, Mary had thrown a party in her honour. As Ellen sang, Beth danced with Katie, John and Ger, promising them she'd send American candy in the post as soon as she could. Beth had tried to mend fences with Joanne. But Jojo had refused to look her in the eye as Beth tried to hug her. Finally, as Ellen began to sing 'The Banks of My Own Lovely Lee', Kathleen pulled Beth to her, and they began to waltz around the small kitchen. But by the second verse, they stopped dancing and instead clung to each other. Neither wanting to let go.

Beth swallowed back a lump, refusing to give in to tears as she remembered the tenderness of her farewells. She was loved and knew that she would cling to that as she made her way across the waters to America.

The sound of a foghorn blasted out from the bay, making her mother jump beside her. 'You are so pale.

I worry about you. Promise me you'll try to eat. You need to build your strength up. Soup, if you are feeling seasick.'

'I will, Mammy,' Beth sighed. 'I thought Ted might have called to see me last night. Did you? He must have heard that I was leaving for Boston.'

'I did. He's a man. Stubborn. Most are. And I know your heart is broken. But in time, it will mend,' Kathleen said gently.

Beth looked down to her flat stomach, and whispered, 'Mammy, what if I'm . . . carrying? What should I do?'

'Are you?' Kathleen answered, her face paling at the thought.

'I don't know. Maybe. I've not had my monthlies yet,' Beth admitted. She watched her mother work through this news.

'If you are, you write to me. And I'll come to Boston. I'll help you. It will be all right. I promise you. At least you'll be away from prying eyes at home.'

Before they could discuss this any further, a shout called out from behind them. Beth and Kathleen turned around to see a figure running towards them, waving his arm in the air.

Ted.

His face was red, sweat glistening on his forehead.

'I thought I was too late.' He bent over double to catch his breath, as he asked, 'Is it true?'

'Is what true?' Beth asked as her heart raced so fast, she thought she might faint.

'Joanne told me that you were leaving Ireland for Boston.'

'I am,' Beth replied.

'With that . . . that man from the circus,' Ted finished, his jaw clenching.

Beth recoiled in shock. She knew that Joanne had taken her father's death hard, that their friendship had fallen apart, but this was unforgivable.

'I'm on my own, Ted,' Beth stated firmly. 'I told you last week that it was over with Christian.'

Ted nodded, mute, his face wretched.

Kathleen stepped closer to them and demanded angrily, 'It was Joanne who told you about Christian last week, wasn't it?'

'Yes.'

'It's a pity you didn't believe my daughter. She may have been foolish, but she is *not* a liar,' Kathleen said firmly.

'I didn't know what to believe. I was broken-hearted.' Ted ran his hands through his hair, his face crumpling in desperation. 'I was ready to propose to you, Beth, to travel with you to wherever you wanted, only to discover you had betrayed me. I couldn't think straight.'

'I understand,' Beth said gently. She turned to her mother, and asked, 'Can you give us a few minutes on our own?'

'I'll be over there,' Kathleen said, then made her way to a nearby bench.

Ted cleared his throat. 'Joanne told me that she delivered a note on your behalf to Christian.'

'That much is true. But it was a note to say that we were over. As well Joanne Craig knows. Why she is lying about all this, goodness only knows!' Beth said.

381

Ted's face crumpled. 'I've been made a fool of.'

'I'm sorry, Ted. I truly am,' Beth repeated. 'I don't know what else to say.' She felt weary, and wasn't sure she had the strength to go through everything again. If she could go back in time, she would never have taken a bike ride to the circus that morning. But she couldn't alter the past, no matter how much she wanted to. Her life had changed since that morning, so much so, it was unrecognizable. She had to make do with what was left and carve out a future as best she could.

'I'm leaving for Boston shortly,' Beth said, gesturing towards the steamship. 'To stay with my cousin Maeve. It's time for a fresh start.'

Ted's shoulders slumped, and he emitted a groan of anguish. 'I still love you.'

Beth wiped away a tear that trickled down her cheek. 'And I love you. But can you forgive me?'

Ted paused for a moment, then nodded. 'I've already forgiven you. We've both made mistakes.'

They locked eyes.

He took a step closer, and his hand reached out to touch hers.

'Have you forgiven me enough to leave Ballycotton behind?' Beth whispered.

Ted answered without hesitation. 'I would leave everything behind me to be with you.'

'I'm not the same girl you fell in love with, Ted. This past week has been . . . difficult . . . and you need to know that I doubt I will ever want to be a keeper's wife.'

Ted reached over to touch Beth's shoulders, clasping them tightly. 'My life as a keeper is an important part of who I am. But it's not all I am. The bigger part, the more important part, is *you* and the promise of the future I know we can have together. I can't be without you, Beth.'

'What if I'm with child? Does that change anything?' Beth asked, knowing that there could be no hiding now.

As Beth watched emotion race across Ted's eyes, as he took in her words, understanding what she meant, she held her breath, waiting for his response.

'If you are, we will face that together. Always together. I love you. And if you love me too, then there is nothing we cannot face.'

Beth took a step back from Ted to look around her at the bustling port, crammed with passengers and their trunks, the multicoloured sails of the yachts that bobbed in the harbour, to the sun that was beginning to peep through the dove-grey clouds above. Colour was beginning to find its way back into her day. She caught her mother's eye, and Kathleen smiled brightly, laughing out loud as Beth threw herself into Ted's arms.

FIFTY-FIVE

Mollie

Monday, 17 July 2023

Ballycotton, Cork

Mollie held her breath. When Libby walked in, she'd seen something in her face that was so familiar, it felt like family.

But Beth replied gently, 'I'm not your mother. When I left Ballycotton in 1951, I thought – incorrectly – that I might be pregnant.' She looked over to her son. 'My husband Ted and I had only one child: Albie.' She smiled faintly at her beloved son.

Mollie exhaled deeply. Not family after all. Whatever she'd seen in Libby's face, it wasn't shared DNA.

'Which leaves either Ellen . . .' Mollie said, and then a thought struck her. She might have been a schoolgirl, but it was still possible. 'Or . . .'

They all turned to Joanne now. Her face was taut, and her hands trembled on the table in front of her. 'I was only sixteen. I didn't know what to do. Mam said it was for the best—'

'Aunt Joanne!' Dervla called out in disbelief.

Mollie heard her grandmother gasp beside her.

'Libby, it was me who put that photograph into your bassinet.' She lifted her chin and looked Libby straight in the eye. 'I'm your mother.'

Libby stared at her in disbelief. 'I never thought . . . that is . . . I think because you were in school uniform, with the smaller kids, I thought you were too young . . .'

'I'm so sorry,' Joanne said, tears now spilling from her eyes. She scraped back her chair, the sound echoing around the room, and she stood up, shakily, then moved slowly towards Libby, who stood up too. They began inching their way towards each other.

'Can you forgive me?' Joanne asked.

'There's nothing to forgive,' Libby whispered.

And as Joanne opened her arms to hug her daughter, for the first time in seventy-one years, Mollie felt a sob catch in her own throat. She couldn't take her eyes off them, and they held each other for several minutes, each unwilling to let go of the other. The sound of sobs rippled through the room until, finally, Libby and Joanne broke apart.

When the two women sat back down again, this time beside each other, Nana Beth asked Joanne softly, 'Who is Libby's father?'

Joanne faltered and ignored the question. 'We'd only just moved into the farm when I told Mam that I was pregnant. It was a shock. She was supportive and told me that she'd help me, but she also said that we couldn't have a scandal, that my life would be ruined if people found out. She made me swear not to tell anyone, until she came up with a plan.'

Libby clasped Joanne's hands between her own, the gesture of support bringing fresh tears to Joanne. She continued tearfully, 'A few days later, she gently told me that I had to hide the pregnancy and then we'd give the baby away for adoption. That it would give the baby the best chance in life. She said the nuns would find a family who desperately wanted a child and who could give that child everything that I couldn't at only sixteen. She enlisted the help of Kathleen and Mary, who were amazing.'

'Bloody hell, those keepers' wives were something else, plotting and planning,' Aunt Jane said.

Mollie couldn't deny that she had a point.

Joanne took a sip of her water, then in a stronger voice continued her story: 'I finished school. Mam was adamant that I do that. Then, once I began to show, I stayed at the farm. Hid away. Mam delivered the baby at home in her bed. She was a midwife, so that was okay. She didn't want me to have to spend weeks in one of those mother and baby homes. She had seen how hard they were for mothers. And I'll always be grateful to her that she didn't send me away to one of those, and instead risked everything to hide me with her.'

'I'm happy she did that too,' Libby said wistfully. 'That my first couple of days were in your family home, with you.'

386

'It was magical. I loved every moment taking care of you. You were such a pretty, happy baby. But two days later, Mam and Kathleen took you away. Mary stayed with me at home, because I was so distraught. It was the saddest day of my life. I loved you so much and didn't want to let you go. But I had no choice. I had to do what Mam said. She wanted me to have a chance at marriage and children, when I was older. But that never happened either ways.'

'Oh, Jojo,' Beth said, her eyes glistening in sympathy.

'This is just awful,' Mollie said. 'And nobody knew about it?'

'Ger was too young to notice. He thought I was getting fat, that's all. Kathleen asked him to stay with her for a few days when the baby came. He was delighted to spend time with his best pal John. And once Beth left for America, I had no friends to worry about me. The farm is remote, and I stayed in my bedroom if anyone visited. Mam told neighbours that I hadn't been myself since Dad died. Which wasn't a lie. The only people I could be myself around were Kathleen and Mary. They were very kind to me.' Joanne reached her hands out to Libby again, 'The dress, cardigan and hat you wore on the day you were given to the home were knitted by me and Mam. Kathleen was pregnant too, with Jane over there, so we'd all sit by the fire clicking our needles together, getting your layette ready.' Joanne brushed tears away, unbidden and unwanted. 'I'm sorry. I've hidden this part of me away for my entire adult life. It's a little overwhelming to finally share the truth out loud.'

387

'I wish I'd known,' Nana Beth said. 'I would have liked to have known.'

Joanne inclined her head in acknowledgement, but turned back to Libby again. 'I need you to know that I loved you with my entirety. I imagined every milestone moment you must be taking every day. I told myself it didn't matter that I wasn't there to witness them myself. What was important was that you had loving parents to rock you to sleep. Sing lullabies. Tie your shoelaces. Make your favourite brownies. Walk you to school. Help you with your homework. Listen to you when your first boyfriend broke your heart.'

Silence echoed around the kitchen.

'I think you were very brave to have let me go,' Libby said, grabbing more tissues for herself and Joanne.

'Did you not resent . . . the decision Ellen made for you?' Mollie couldn't help but ask.

'It was a different time back then. In the fifties, if an unmarried woman was pregnant, she was shamed and shunned. There was no way to work or be independent. She wanted me to have a life of freedom without prejudice or judgement. I know it wasn't a perfect solution. But at the time, it felt like our only option.'

'Thank goodness times have changed now,' her dad remarked sadly.

Everyone quietened again for a moment. As Mollie looked around the room, she saw mirrors of how she felt in everybody's faces. Shell-shocked and sad. She stifled a yawn as fatigue caught up with her. If she felt like this, she could only imagine how her nana felt. And Joanne too.

'Would you like a cup of tea or coffee?' she offered, turning to Libby.

'Tea would be nice. But may I use your bathroom first?' Libby asked.

Mollie showed her the way, then returned, closing the kitchen door behind her. 'I know this has been a difficult hour,' she said as she sat down. 'But listen to me, everyone. Libby does not know about Charles Davis. So before we talk about anything else, can we agree that what Nana Beth's told us stays between the people in this room? And no one else. We can't tell Libby about it. Nana Beth, Kathleen, Ellen and Mary made a vow over seventy years ago, never to tell. We have to make sure that we keep that vow. Agreed?'

And once again, a new generation swore never to tell. Nana Beth's face crumpled with relief. The keepers' wives' secret would stay buried once more.

FIFTY-SIX

Mollie

Monday, 17 July 2023

Ballycotton, Cork

When Libby returned, she turned to Joanne, taking a deep breath, then blurted out, 'I know this has been so difficult for you. But I need to ask you one more question. Can you tell me who my father is?'

Mollie exhaled slowly. She could only imagine what both women must be thinking right now. Should the rest of them offer to leave, so that they would have privacy? But she desperately wanted to hear Joanne's answer. Mollie was invested now in them both. So she turned to watch Joanne again, waiting for her to reveal the last of the secrets from that summer.

With her face stained with colour and embarrassment, Joanne said, 'No, I can't.'

Mollie's heart began to race.

'That is to say, I'm not sure,' Joanne added.

'I don't understand,' Libby said, her eyes darting around the room.

Joanne took a deep breath, then with a small shake of her head, said, 'I never thought I'd ever share this. But as we are laying everything out in the open, it's time for me to do the same.'

She looked at Beth then, two dots of pink on her cheeks. 'When I think about that time, I don't recognize myself. I can only explain my behaviour as someone on a self-destruct rampage because I was grieving.' She glanced at Libby and a flash of mutual understanding passed between the two.

'What did you do?' Nana Beth asked in a whisper.

The room was silent as everyone waited for Joanne to come clean. She swivelled to face Beth. 'You asked me to deliver Christian a letter.'

'Yes. To tell him that I did not want to be with him anymore,' Nana Beth agreed.

'Who's Christian?' Libby asked.

'A French trapeze artist, who I had been seeing that summer,' Nana Beth answered quickly, not taking her eyes off Joanne for even a second.

The air felt thick with sudden tension. A shiver ran over Mollie's body.

'I was so angry with you, Beth,' Joanne continued. 'When I called to see you, you were so dismissive of me. I asked you what was wrong, and you told me to skip rope with the younger kids.'

Beth looked down for a moment. 'I don't remember much about that conversation. I was grappling with the aftermath of what happened with Charles Davis.'

Mollie fired a warning glance at Nana Beth to stay quiet.

'Who is Charles Davis?' Libby asked, looking around the room in confusion. 'You mentioned him before.'

'He was a conman who took money from quite a few local people in Ballycotton in 1951, including Kathleen Kenefick. But he disappeared, and to this day nobody knows where he went,' Dervla said, looking around the room, daring anyone to dispute this version of events.

'Oh,' Libby said, frowning.

'I understand now that you were not yourself, but at that moment, I thought you were being callous and unfeeling,' Joanne continued. 'I wanted to prove to you, to myself, that I was as pretty as you. As desirable as you. That I wasn't just a dumb kid, only good for skipping rope.'

'Oh, jeepers,' Mollie whispered. She could see where this was heading.

'When I gave the note to Christian, he read it and took the news on the chin. If I'm honest, he didn't seem that upset.'

Beth also seemed unsurprised by this. 'His sister Delphine told me that he was a flirt with a girl in every town.'

'I felt reckless that day. So I chatted to him, made him laugh, flattered him while he was holding your note turning him down. Then I kissed him,' Joanne said.

Beth's eyes widened.

'Christian kissed me back. Then,' she paused, 'we slept together.'

Dervla's mouth dropped open so wide, it almost made Mollie emit a nervous giggle.

'So . . . Libby is Christian Banvard's daughter?' Nana Beth asked slowly, with widened eyes.

Joanne stared down, unwilling to look at Beth as she answered.

'Maybe. But there was something else . . . Oh, Beth, I was so angry with you about Christian. About the way you had treated Ted. Ted was offering you everything that I desperately craved. You so casually threw the life of a keeper's wife to one side like it was nothing. But if Ted had chosen me, I could have saved my family. Then Uncle Benny burned down the cottage we were meant to move into. Mam was beside herself, crying and pacing the floor. I *had* to do something.'

'Please don't say it . . .' Beth said, holding her crooked hands up in front of her.

'You already know that I told Ted about you and Christian. And that Friday, after he'd finished with you, he came to see me. We talked for hours. I was his shoulder to cry on. And I knew that if I could only make him love me like he had loved you, I could save my family. I could marry Ted, and we'd have a home for us all. Mam and Ger would never need to worry again. And we could tell Uncle Benny to go to hell.'

393

'Ted wouldn't . . .' Beth said, looking around her in disbelief. 'He loved me.'

'I told him I loved him. And I swore I'd never hurt him in the way that you did. He pushed me away at first. Gently, because, of course, that was his way. He said he loved you. And only you.' Joanne sat up straighter and found the courage somewhere deep inside her to continue, 'But I persisted. And . . . well . . . we slept together.'

A shocked silence filled the room. Mollie focused on her nana, who looked so vulnerable as she took in this news.

'It was only once. He wasn't interested in me, despite my best efforts. He only wanted you, Beth. I tried one more time to hold on to him, by telling him, on the morning you were leaving for America, that Christian was going with you. But I could see doubt fill his eyes. He didn't believe me . . .'

'Ted never told me he'd slept with you,' Beth said. 'He arrived at the port and we reconciled. And he promised to follow me to Boston the following month, once he'd tendered his resignation. When he joined me in Boston, we planned our future. One that involved the travel I craved.' She turned to face Joanne and said in a voice heavy with emotion, 'But at no point did he mention you, Joanne.'

Mollie's dad stood up and walked around to Nana Beth. He kneeled in front of her, clasping her hands. 'I'm sorry, Mom.'

Nana Beth leaned into her son, his gesture of support bringing a lump to Mollie's throat.

Joanne began to cry again, as she finished her story. 'Ted was a good man. It wasn't his fault, Beth. When he returned from the port that day, he came to see me. And told me that he was joining you in Boston. He apologized to me . . . to me . . .' she shook her head in wonder, 'about allowing himself to sleep with me. He chose you, Beth, as he'd always done. And when he left, my world fell apart. Because I truly did love him. I risked everything, but it wasn't enough. He didn't want me.'

'Mom and Dad had a good life together,' Mollie's dad said fiercely.

'We did, Son. And never in all the years we were together did I doubt his love. But my life was far from perfect, Joanne. We all paid a price for what happened that summer. Me, Mam, Ellen and Mary,' Beth replied.

Mollie watched Joanne, trying to understand this complicated woman. Was her acerbic tongue any wonder, now that they knew what had happened to her? Giving up her child like that had cost Joanne dearly too. And Mollie couldn't help feeling sympathy for the woman – and for the girl she once was.

'So my father could also be Libby's father?' her dad asked.

Joanne replied, 'Yes. When I found out I was pregnant, I told Mam everything. But she said we could never tell anyone about Ted's part of the story. Kathleen and Mary always believed the baby was Christian's.'

'Did Ted ever know you had a baby?' Nana Beth asked in a shaky voice.

'Of course not. When he visited Ireland, we never

spoke of that one time we slept together and what we'd done. He was always polite, but he kept his distance.'

'Another secret for the keepers' wives to hold on to,' Mollie murmured. She caught her dad's eye then, and nodded towards Nana Beth, who was so pale, it frightened her.

Her dad understood and helped Nana Beth to her feet, 'My mom is still recovering from pneumonia. We need to call a halt to this for now. She needs rest.'

'I'm sorry,' Joanne called out to Nana Beth as she walked slowly out of the room, leaning heavily on her son.

Everyone took their cue from their departure, and stood up to leave.

'Aunt Joanne, would you and Libby like to come back to the farm with me, to continue chatting?' Dervla suggested kindly. 'After all, we are family. Kian will be back from his dad's soon. He'd love a cuddle from you both.'

Both women quickly accepted.

Aunt Jane's eyes were red-rimmed, and with a hug of comfort to Mollie, she too left, claiming a headache.

Mollie walked out to the garden, taking a seat under the willow. She leaned back onto the gnarly bark and watched the little robin dance around the branches. Her body trembled and she felt a rush of emotion flood her. The tears she'd pushed back so many times today, finally fell.

Mollie wept for her grandmother and the life she'd led, carrying her secret burden and guilt with her every day. And for Joanne and Libby, who missed out on so much, because she was born in a time when unmarried pregnancy was not allowed. She couldn't even begin to understand what the implications of Libby's birth father would be for her family. But most of all, Mollie cried for herself and Nolan, and the life that they were about to say goodbye to.

FIFTY-SEVEN

Mollie

Monday, 17 July 2023

Ballycotton, Cork

The cottage was silent. Nana Beth and her father were both still in their bedrooms, and Mollie made her way towards her own. An hour had passed since everyone left. Mollie's body ached with fatigue. Yet she couldn't sleep. Her mind was restless and refused to quieten.

She moved to the bed and knocked into the locker, banging her stomach against it. And she realized that finally the tenderness from IVF needles had disappeared. She was no longer a human pin cushion, and she never wanted to be one again.

Mollie thought about every evening at the end of their working day for the previous year. Nolan gently lifting her blouse and kissing her stomach, before he'd inject her, as they'd wince in unison. Mollie would have preferred to inject herself, privately, quickly, without any fuss. But Nolan wanted to be involved. So they both pretended that this was normal behaviour.

But the truth was, none of it was normal for Mollie. As the drugs tricked her menstrual cycle and stimulated her ovaries to grow multiple egg-containing follicles to maturity, Mollie felt less and less like herself. Together, they read every piece of literature they'd been given about the IVF process. Knowledge is power, Mollie had always advocated throughout her adult life. And when warnings of mood swings were pronounced, Mollie had promised Nolan that she would never fall victim to them. She was even-tempered, had always been so.

'Our sunshine girl,' her dad had nicknamed her when she was a baby. Well, the sunshine girl was no match for IVF hormones. Her jeans no longer fit, and her mood was as unpredictable as the weather.

But somehow, here in Ballycotton, she felt glimpses of the sunshine girl peeking through again. And she wanted to continue searching for her. Mollie knew that, like her grandmother and Joanne, she had a confession of her own to make.

Taking a steadying breath, Mollie placed a video call to Nolan.

'Great timing,' Nolan said warmly when he answered. 'I was about to call you too! Fill me in on what happened today.'

So Mollie shared all the emotional revelations to Nolan, one by one.

'That's been quite the day. No wonder you're exhausted,' Nolan said sympathetically.

'I'm scared, too Nolan,' Mollie said, pulling a cushion in close to her.

'Of what?' Nolan's face was etched in fear and worry, echoing Mollie's.

'That if I tell you how I really feel, I might lose you.'

Nolan crossed his arms, 'If we've learned anything over the past few weeks, it's how damaging it is to keep secrets. Just tell me, Mollie.'

'When the IVF failed, I was relieved,' Mollie said gently. She waited for the words to sink in, her heart breaking when she saw the pain in her husband's eyes. 'I don't want to have children.'

The words sat between them, and Mollie allowed Nolan to hear them and process what they meant for them.

'Ever. Or now?' Nolan's voice was tight.

'Ever,' Mollie admitted. She had to be one hundred per cent honest with him now. He deserved that.

'Why didn't you tell me this before?'

It was a fair question. And one that Mollie had asked herself. 'Truly, I didn't know how I felt. When we first mentioned kids, it was a vague discussion that we said we would consider in the future. When we started to try, and it didn't happen, I was fine with that. But you wanted us to do IVF, so again, I went along with it.'

He sucked in a breath and swore, 'Damn it, Mollie. I didn't force you to do IVF. We made that decision together.'

'We did. Absolutely. But I was doing it for the wrong

reasons. I wanted to want kids. To make you happy.'

'And you don't want to do that anymore?' Nolan asked.

She couldn't bear to look at his brown eyes, darkened with sadness and sympathy. Mourning something that could never be.

'I love you. And your happiness is of paramount importance to me. Which is why I have to be honest with you now.' She wiped her palms onto the cushion.

'Are you sure? You changed your mind once; you might do it again?'

'I've thought about nothing else but this for a long time. I'm sure.'

'But when you feel a baby in your arms, I know you would love that child with all of your being. You are such a nurturing, caring person. You'd make an amazing mother.'

Mollie sighed. She needed Nolan to understand. 'If I had become pregnant, I would have done everything to be the best mother I could be. And I know you would be an amazing father. But the thing is, Nolan, I don't choose to be a mother. It's hard to explain, but when I see a baby, I don't feel a maternal pull or desire to have one of my own. And honestly, I like my life as it is.'

Nolan shook his head. 'You changed the goalposts. This is not what we agreed.'

'I know,' Mollie said. 'And I'm truly sorry.'

'What do you want, Mollie? Help me out here.' He pulled at his hair in desperation.

'I love you, Nolan, and want to spend the rest of my life with you. I want to curate our life on our terms. Not those dictated to us by society, which says we must have children. I want bagel Sundays every week. Have grand adventures, side by side. Travel to somewhere new every year that we've never been to before. Find a new home in a pretty New England town where we can grow old together. Take a wine tour of Napa Valley. Get matching tattoos. Go back to that all-inclusive resort where we honeymooned in Mauritius, and spend the day at the swim-up bar, drinking cocktails.'

Nolan's eyes filled with tears. 'That sounds magical. But I don't know if it's enough . . .'

'You want kids. And Nolan, I understand what this means for us. I won't hold you back, if you need to move on . . . with someone else, who can give you what I can't.' Tears streamed down Mollie's face.

'I need some time to think about this,' Nolan said.

'I understand. You can take as long as you need.'

He ended the call and Mollie sank into the pillows on the bed, rocking and keening for the pain and hurt that they both felt. Mollie knew that love alone might not be enough this time to save them.

FIFTY-EIGHT

Ellen

Sunday, 27 May 1951

Ballycotton, Cork

It was a three-mile walk to Benny's farm, but Ellen relished the opportunity to have some time to herself. She practised what she wanted to say to her brother-in-law, as the sun peeped its way through the clouds.

Kathleen hadn't wanted Ellen to come up here today. And Ellen of a month ago would have agreed with her friend, and turned back to Powers Terrace. But ever since Peter's death she'd felt an untethering. Each day, a little more of her unravelled. And today, having retrieved Kathleen's money from the hotel, she felt emboldened.

She found Benny's old grey sheepdog lying at the front door of the farmhouse, dirty and thin.

403

'Poor thing looks half starved,' she said, reaching down to ruffle its fur. She felt contempt spark its way around her body. How anyone could treat a poor defenceless animal in such a way was beyond her. If her family did move to the farm, she vowed to make the dog's life more comfortable, if nothing else.

Ellen reached up to the brass knocker and rapped the front door three times.

The door opened, and Benny stood before her in a stained vest and beige work trousers held up by a black leather belt.

'I knew you'd turn up like a bad penny.' He had a satisfied gloat on his face.

Benny walked back into the farmhouse, leaving the door open behind him. Ellen followed him in.

He moved to his stove, where a large skillet pan hissed and spat as he fried sausages, bacon and eggs. A salty, meaty aroma filled the room. Benny picked up a carving knife and cut two thick slices of bread from a white pan loaf. Then buttered them generously. He plated his food, and brought it to the table to eat. Only then did he address Ellen.

'Go on then widow woman. Plead your case. Beg me to take you and your children in.' He picked up a piece of fatty bacon in his fingers and stuffed it whole in his mouth.

Ellen gagged, looking away from him. He was the most repulsive man she'd ever been in the company of. How could he and Peter be related? It was unfathomable to her.

'I loved my husband Peter with all my heart. And I could never marry you. It would be an insult to his memory. And the life we built together.'

Benny picked up a sausage and took a bite. 'If you want to live over the brush, that's on you. But people will talk. A widow and a bachelor together in one house . . .'

'I won't live in this house either.'

'Then why are you here?' Benny said, taking a slurp of his tea.

'I have a proposal of my own for you. If you agree to renovate one of the outbuildings into a cottage for my family, I'll be your housekeeper. I'll cook and clean for you. Ger and Joanne will help out on the farm outside their schooling. You can teach Ger how to be a cattle farmer, so that one day he can take over the farm from you.'

Benny laughed out loud, his bellow echoing around the large kitchen.

'You don't get to come in here and make demands on me.'

'I'm not arguing with you, Benny. It seems to me that you are so desperate to have my family here that you broke the law, I wonder what Sergeant Cody would say if he found out you burnt down Paudie O'Connor's cottage?'

'Don't you threaten me!' Benny replied, jabbing his fat fingers at Ellen.

'Enough! The only person who has been threatening anyone is you. And that stops now. You will never lay a hand on my children or me. If you do, I will report you to the authorities. That's a promise,' Ellen said, moving forward. 'You have my terms. Take them or leave them. Yesterday I found out that I have a job with board in Glanmire. So my family and I are not as destitute as you hoped. My preference is to stay in Ballycotton, but not at any cost. If we stay, you abide by my terms.' The job offer was a bluff, but she told herself that it might come true.

Benny picked up another sausage and bit into it, the fatty juice running down his chin as he stuffed half of it into his mouth.

Ellen waited for him to answer her. Her heart raced as she tried to read Benny's face. Would he agree to her terms? And if he did, could she trust him?

Then suddenly Benny began to cough and splutter, and he held his hand to his throat. His face turned red, then purple, and sweat broke out on his brow.

Ellen moved forward to assist, but then she felt something move against her leg. She looked down to see the dog pushing its thin body against her. His eyes looked up at Ellen, and she couldn't look away.

The sound of Benny gasping for air made her look back towards her brother-in-law. He reached out his hand towards her, pleading for help. His eyes now bulged as his blocked airways stopped him from breathing.

And Ellen remained rooted to the spot, the dog nuzzling her hand as it trembled by her side.

After several horrific moments, Benny slumped forward on the table.

Ellen cried out, unable to believe what had transpired. Her heart raced and her head pounded as she took in the slumped figure of Benny Craig.

Could she still help him? Was there time to save him? To at least try?

But then she thought of her children. And knew that, this way, he could never hurt Joanne or Ger. Or another living soul.

The dog whimpered, and she leaned down to ruffle behind his ears. Then she walked over to the table and grabbed a piece of bacon and a sausage from Benny's plate. She walked out of the kitchen, closing the door behind her, with the dog at her heels.

Ellen sat down on the flagstone step, her legs trembling, and fed the meat to the dog, who ate it in two greedy bites.

'You'll never be hungry again,' she said to him. 'That's a good boy. I've got to go now, but I'll be back soon, and I'll take good care of you. I promise.'

And then she left the farmhouse and walked the three miles back to Powers Terrace. She heard the sound of children's laughter as she got close to home. The Keneficks, Craigs and Mary were all gathered in the garden across from the cottages, playing an impromptu game of rounders.

When she joined them in the garden, Kathleen and Mary came over to her.

'How did it go?' Kathleen asked, her face flushed from running.

'Did he listen?' Mary asked. 'I hope you took no guff from him.'

Ellen clasped both of their hands, and knew that this was one secret that she could not share with her fellow keepers' wives.

This one was hers and hers alone.

'I think some of what I said may have stuck in his throat a bit, but I'm glad I went and said my piece,' Ellen said. 'I left him to think about my offer. And I have a feeling it will all work out in the end.'

Then Ger called over, 'Come on, Mam, you can be on our team!'

Ellen grabbed Kathleen and Mary's hands, and they ran to join in the game.

FIFTY-NINE

Beth

Monday, 17 July 2023

Ballycotton, Cork

The sea was calm as the sun kissed it goodbye. The sun's orange glow was reflected along the bay, and tinged the sky in hues of vibrant yellow and flamboyant pink.

'I'm going to miss this view,' Mollie said, as she led Nana Beth slowly along the coastal walk.

'I don't think I've ever seen it look more beautiful,' Beth replied. 'Thank you for indulging me, by bringing me here. You're a good girl.'

Beth had fallen into a deep sleep that afternoon, which lasted until almost 9 p.m. She'd been dreaming about Ballycotton Lighthouse, and awoke, groggy and achy. She'd found Mollie curled up on her bed, half asleep.

It took her a few moments to convince Mollie to bring her out here, but in the end, her granddaughter had acquiesced.

'This is far enough,' Beth said, when they reached a bench. They took a seat side by side and looked out to Ballycotton Lighthouse. They watched the light signal flash white, and Beth counted to ten between each flash, as she used to do when she was a child.

'Does it feel weird to be here, after all that happened?' Mollie asked, leaning her head onto her nana's shoulder.

'I suppose it should. But somehow, I can separate what happened with Charles Davis from the happy moments I had along here with Mam, Dad, John and Katie.'

Beth closed her eyes and for a moment she could hear her mother, calling out to her and her younger siblings that it was time to welcome home the keepers. Oh how she missed those days, before that summer in 1951 changed everything.

'I'm a little in awe of you keepers' wives,' Mollie said. 'You were all kind of badass!'

Beth's lips twitched in a smile, 'I never thought of us like that. But today, as the secrets were all revealed, I have to admit, I was a little in awe too of all we did. I don't know how we held it together afterwards.' Beth frowned, then admitted, 'The thing is, I've always thought of myself as weak. After Davis went over the cliff, part of me did too. I've struggled to accept that I played a part in his death.'

'It was an accident,' Mollie insisted. 'You didn't want him to die, did you?'

Beth took a moment to consider this. 'No. But I *was*

angry with him. When he struck Mam, I fought back like I was possessed.'

'You were incredibly brave. Then and now, Nana Beth. I am so proud of you,' Mollie said tremulously. 'But I have to ask, are you angry with Grandad?'

Beth looked out to the lighthouse, remembering her impulsive visit to the island to see Ted, and how they'd made love against the craggy rocks. 'I wish he'd told me. I thought we had no secrets. But then again, I can't talk, can I?'

'Can you forgive him?' Mollie asked in a whisper.

'Yes,' Beth replied in an instant. 'We'd broken up when he slept with Joanne, so he didn't cheat, not really. I loved him. And he loved me right back, which wasn't easy at times. I could be difficult, you know.'

Mollie grinned. 'Oh I remember. And I'm so sorry you've had to hold on to this burden for so long, on your own. I hope you know that I am here to listen to you now, if you need to talk it through.'

Beth's heart swelled with love for her granddaughter. There had been times in her life that she'd felt sorry for herself. How tough she'd had it. But she'd got that all wrong. She'd had a wonderful life, with great loves.

'I'll remember that, Mollie. But for now, can we sit here quietly for a bit? I just want to soak up the view, before we go home to Camden.'

Mollie nodded and once more leaned her head gently on Beth's shoulder.

This was the last time Beth would see this view, other than in her mind's eye. When she returned to Camden, she would never come back to Ballycotton again. So she took

411

in every detail. The black lighthouse that parted the sun's final rays. The still waters, which looked as if they were sleeping. And Beth imagined that they were at peace with all their secrets. Like she was too. Somewhere, somehow, her mind and body had quietened for the first time in over seventy years. Amongst the chaos of the secrets and lies, Beth had found peace.

Beth closed her eyes, and whispered, 'Mary, are you with Mam and Ellen again? Side by side – friends, confidants, family. Thank you for being my safe harbour. I've always known our goodbye was not forever. I'll see you all soon.'

EPILOGUE

Mollie

Camden, Maine

Mollie pulled her woollen scarf into a tight knot around her neck as she strolled along the downtown harbour area of the seaside town of Camden. The fall air was crisp and cool, a welcome reprieve from a long week in the TV studios. And the quaint and quintessential New England town overlooking Penobscot Bay had never looked prettier.

When Nolan and she had decided to separate, Mollie moved back home to stay with her father and Nana Beth in Camden. On the days she was in the studio, she booked into a nearby hotel. Then one month ago, she passed a vintage Georgian house that overlooked the harbour,

413

with a 'For Sale' sign outside. And after viewing it, Mollie knew that she had to make it her forever home. The sale had gone through a week ago.

As she walked up the drive to her new home, she sighed in pleasure as she took in the picturesque idyll. This was her favourite time of year in Maine. A canopy of towering trees, with fall foliage of burnt-oranges, to rustic reds, framed the small harbour. Maple, hickory and elm trees, all majestic as they guarded the sailboats that bobbed up and down in the blue waters.

Her favourite room in the house was the large open-plan kitchen and family room, with floor-to-ceiling windows. This meant Mollie could enjoy her morning coffee looking out toward Rockport Lighthouse, which kept a good watch on all the residents of Camden. Like her many ancestors before her, it appeared that Mollie too needed to live close to a lighthouse.

Nana Beth would have loved it here, Mollie thought. She grabbed a bottle of rosé from the fridge and poured a glass for herself. Then raised a toast to her grandmother as a wave of emotion almost floored her. Beth had died in her sleep at the end of August, at home in Camden. The ache of loss was still fresh. It was peaceful, at least. A half-finished cup of tea sat on her bedside locker, her glasses perched on top of her current book.

Nana Beth's funeral had been more of a celebration of her life than a mournful goodbye. The church was packed with friends and neighbours. Mollie was grateful that, at this difficult time, she had been at home with her dad. Nana Beth's death hit them both hard.

On top of her grief, Mollie was also mourning the loss of her marriage. Saying goodbye to someone you loved, but knowing that love was not enough, was the kind of heartbreak that was hard to recover from.

But somewhere, over gentle walks and lengthy battles of Scrabble, her dad and she both came to terms with the events of the summer. And they took comfort knowing that, like Mary a few short months before, Nana Beth was ready to go.

There was one last show of solidarity from the keepers' wives' families for Beth too. Dervla, Kian, Joanne and Libby surprised them by coming to Camden for the service, along with Aunt Jane. Baby Kian nestled plump and content in his great-aunt Joanne's arms. There was an ease between Dervla and Joanne now that had not been there before. Dervla told Mollie that she'd asked her aunt if she would like to move back to the farmhouse, but Joanne was happy in the retirement home and elected to stay put, where she enjoyed the activities.

Her dad and Libby made the emotional decision to find out the truth of Libby's paternal parentage, so they took a DNA test, and the results had confirmed that they shared the same father. It would take a while for them both to find their feet as half-siblings. But each time they met, the two of them grew closer.

For Mollie, she felt this new family member fit perfectly. The Kenefick and Craig families had been as close as any blood relatives for years. After all, Kathleen and Ellen had been like sisters. Libby had finally connected the two families by blood.

As Mollie moved to her caramel sofa in front of the window overlooking the bay, she almost spilled her wine when she saw Nolan walking up her driveway.

She jumped up and ran to open the door, where she found him clutching a brown bag.

'Hello,' Mollie said, her heart racing in surprise to see him.

'It's a bit of a bummer, but the thing is, I can't live without you,' Nolan blurted out.

Mollie blinked, sure her mind was playing tricks on her. But he remained there, his dark eyes watching her.

'Come inside,' Mollie said, and they moved back to the kitchen.

'I keep thinking about that life you painted for me a few months ago,' Nolan said, as he passed the brown bag to her.

Hardly believing this moment to be true, Mollie opened the bag up, then laughed out loud when she spotted the logo of Mister Bagels from Congress Street staring at her.

'My favourites. For our bagel Sundays.'

'There's more. Keep looking.'

She pulled out an envelope, opened it and found a voucher for a place called L'Encrerie.

'That's a tattoo parlour in Paris. Two items from your curated life of dreams in one, with that,' Nolan said, looking a little smug.

Mollie started to laugh again, her heart exploding with joy. 'We always said we wanted to go to Paris.'

'I want to do all the things on your list. *With you, Mollie.*'

'What about children though? I'm not going to change my mind.'

'I know that. And I'd never try to make you. The thing is, if the choice is you or someone else with children, I choose you every single time.'

Mollie locked eyes with him. She was grateful for so much in her life. Her career. Her home. Her friends, old and new. Her family and their many secrets, that somehow had helped her to accept not only who they were, but also who she was too. And most of all, she was grateful that it seemed that love was enough, after all.

'I choose you too,' Mollie said, and then Nolan pulled her into his arms and kissed her.

AUTHOR'S NOTE

When my sister-in-law Evelyn and Adrienne suggested a short weekend break in Ballycotton, little did I know that it would inspire a novel! We booked a tour with the Ballycotton Sea Adventurers to visit the Ballycotton Lighthouse. I've always been fascinated by the tall, majestic towers dotted around rugged coastlines. I think it's because they are beacons of hope and safety – preventing disasters at sea and saving countless lives.

Our tour guide for the trip was a lovely, friendly woman called Annemarie, who quickly entertained us with fascinating facts about the iconic – and rare – black Ballycotton Lighthouse and its history in the area. The journey from the pier to the island is a short fifteen-minute spin and offers 360-degree panoramic views of the bay, as far as Kinsale Head. As we walked up the steep, mossy path towards the lighthouse, Annemarie shared anecdotes about the keepers and their families who lived in this small maritime community. We learned that the Keepers and their families initially lived on the island in small cottages. The children were rowed over to the village every day to attend school. Then, in 1899, the families were relocated to cottages in Ballycotton village, where they became an integral part of the community. The last Keeper left the island in 1992, and the light is now monitored from the Irish Lights Headquarters. The only residents are the goats, who we all cheered for when we spotted them precariously nibbling grass on the edge of a rock.

As Annemarie continued sharing stories of the lighthouse's history, I couldn't help but reflect on the heroic keepers who lived on the island in isolation. Each keeping a good watch. And I also thought of their families, who lived across the bay in the village. Annemarie shared a story about a keeper who had to miss his young daughter's First Holy Communion, as he was on duty. He stood on the island's highest point with his binoculars, waiting for a first glance of his little girl, who danced for him on Spanish Point in her pretty white dress. This made me think about the many sacrifices the families had to make back then. And how the wives must have supported each other as their menfolk worked on the island. What strength and loyalty they must have possessed, to their keepers, but also to each other.

And that's when my imagination took flight, and a story began to take root.

By the time we returned on *Yassy* to Ballycotton Pier, a scene had come to me almost fully formed, becoming the opening prologue of *The Lighthouse Secret*. Four women vowing to keep a secret about a crime they committed

419

while their husbands were stationed on Ballycotton Lighthouse.

Several secrets and mysteries run through this story. Inspiration for unravelling the secret with Beth's family in the present day, came from my great aunt Margaret, who died several years ago. She had dementia, and towards the end, she spoke about a secret that greatly distressed her. My mother, sister, niece and I all tried to offer her comfort, but she died without revealing her secret. And that's as it should be. But what if she had told us? Would there have been repercussions for our family? When you are cursed with a writer's brain, as I am, it's impossible not to think of the *What-ifs*. Aunty Margaret, if you can see this from up above, I hope you approve of my wild flight of fancy.

Aside from the many mysteries in *The Lighthouse Secret*, one of the themes running through the 1950s and the present-day chapters is the societal pressure placed on women to get married and start a family. I wanted to explore this subject because I've always believed there is no right or wrong way to live our lives. My hope is that in the same way a lighthouse beams its light to show us a safe path, Mollie and Beth's story might spotlight that there is more than one path to living a fulfilled life. Putting your own feelings first does not make you selfish. It makes you strong and brave.

If you are as interested in lighthouses as I am, here are books that I greatly enjoyed over the years: *The Great Lighthouses of Ireland* by David Hare, *The Lightkeeper* by Gerald Butler, *Ireland's Guiding Lights* by Dennis Horgan, Gerald Butler, Tim McCarthy, *The Lamplighters* by Emma Stonex, *The Lighthouse Keeper's Daughter* by Hazel Gaynor, *The Light Between Oceans* by M L Stedman, *To the Lighthouse* by Virginia Woolf.

I'll end by sharing that my aim for this story was to explore the sisterhood and friendship of women, celebrating their resourcefulness, determination, strength, and bravery. Especially when they face their greatest adversities. I hope that through Mollie, Beth, Kathleen, Ellen and Mary's stories, I've managed to demonstrate all of that.

Thank you all for reading,
Carmel

ACKNOWLEDGEMENTS

Sincere thanks to:

Our home is my haven, and it's my favourite place because that's where Roger, Amelia, Nate and George Bailey are. I don't care how cheesy it sounds, but I feel so blessed to be loved by these four. And yes, I'm including my dog. He never leaves my side and keeps my feet warm while I write. Luckiest gal alive!

My agent, Rowan Lawton, and I have been on quite an adventure over the past seven years, and I'm grateful for her guidance and friendship. And when I say to her, I've got this great idea for a novel, she *always* listens, and is as excited to read my words, as I am to write them. I cannot wait to see where the next seven years take us. I would also like to thank Eleanor Lawlor and the entire team at The Soho Agency, ILA, Abigail Koons at Park & Fine Literary and Media and Rich Green.

My publisher, Lynne Drew, for her editorial advice and support as I took the early draft of this story to where it is today. Every time she asked me to dig deeper, she was right, and I'm so proud of how my keepers' wives evolved. There are so many others in HarperCollins UK and Ireland who have worked on and supported this book, too, including Morgan Springett, Lucy Stewart, Kimberley Young, Kate Elton, Lucy Upton, Susanna Peden, Sarah Bance, Francisca Fabriczki, Holly MacDonald, Fleur Clarke, Emily Merrill, Sophie Waeland, Abbie Salter, Patricia McVeigh, Tony Purdue.

To Eddie Fitzgerald, a retired Lighthouse Keeper. Thank you for chatting with me, answering my questions, and sharing stories about your time as a Keeper at Ballycotton Lighthouse. Your kindness and eloquence are greatly appreciated. And I loved hearing your anecdotes about the Keepers and their families, which were fascinating and amusing!

To Jen and David Elderkin, my on-the-ground research team when they visited Camden, Maine, last year. I work hard to research every aspect of my character's lives and the locations in which the story is set. Jen and David took video footage of several areas in Camden that Mollie lives in. Even finding me a jogging trail that Mollie uses, in one of the opening scenes. Thank you both sincerely.

Hazel Gaynor and Catherine Ryan Howard – I often say how important it is for an author to find their tribe, as it's a solitary profession. Because on those days when things are going well, you need people who will always be happy for you, no matter their circumstances. But also, just as importantly, you need people who will pick you up on the days when it all sucks. No question, Hazel and Catherine are my biggest cheerleaders. Everyone needs a Lady G and CRH in their lives. But I'm pretty jammy because I have the best support from the writing community, too, both here in Ireland and in the UK – Caroline Grace-Cassidy, Alex Brown, Claudia Carroll, Vanessa O'Loughlin, Sheila O'Flanagan, Patricia Scanlan, Ciara Geraghty, Cathy Bramley, Milly Johnson, Katie Fforde, Debbie Johnson and so many more, thank you.

To all the branches of the O'Grady and Harrington family tree, thank you for another spin around the sun, filled with laughter, mischief, and much love. Tina, Michael, Fiona, Michael, Amy, Louis, Shelley, Anthony, Sheryl, John, Matilda, Eva, Evelyn, Adrienne, George, Evelyn, Seamus, Paddy, Leah, as I always say, *All that matters is Family*. Special shout-out to my first reader, my mum Tina.

To my friends, too many to mention, who are always in my corner, I appreciate every single one of you.

To the book retailers, media, bloggers, reviewers, libraries, book clubs and festivals whose passion for putting books into readers' laps helps authors, including me, every day.

And last but not least, to my readers. Thank you for choosing to read my books. There are moments when writing can feel overwhelming. And on particularly bad days, I question myself and my life choices! But somehow, just as I need it the most, a reader gets in touch and shares their love for one of my books and how my words have impacted their lives, and this time, it's me who is uplifted by *their* words, and I'm once again ready to keep going. Please know how much I appreciate your support.

Thank you,
Carmel

READING GROUP QUESTIONS

1. Of the four Keepers' wives, Kathleen, Ellen, Mary and Beth, which character did you relate to the most? Why?

2. There are two mysteries in this novel – one in the past and one in the present. Did you guess what the crime was in 1951? And did you guess who was writing the anonymous letters in the present day?

3. Did any of the events in the novel, leading up to the unravelling of the mysteries in the past and present, take you by surprise? Did you see the twists coming?

4. One of the themes in the novel explores the family and societal pressure on women to get married and have children. Beth and Mollie, generations apart, both experience this pressure. Did you relate to either narrative?

5. As always with Carmel's novels, the settings are a huge part of the story. Did you fall in love with

Ballycotton and Maine? Would you like to visit there one day?

6. Lighthouses have fascinated people for hundreds of years. Have you been to see Ballycotton Lighthouse or any other lighthouse around the world?

7. Have you read any other books that are set on Lighthouses?

8. The sisterhood between the Keepers' Wives develops throughout the summer of 1951, as events unfold for each of them. And they are forced to do things that they never thought they were capable of. Did you understand why they behaved as they did?

9. Beth says in 2023, that each of the Keepers' wives ended up a widow at a young age. And that was perhaps payback for their sins. Do you agree with her? Or do you think that those who came to an untimely end, deserved it?

10. The bond between Mollie and her grandmother Beth, was evident in the story. Did you have a similar bond with your grandparents?

11. Did you enjoy walking in the shoes of the four keepers' wives in the historical part of this novel? Was the past brought to life through Beth, Kathleen, Mary and Ellen's story?

12. How did you feel about the ending for each of the characters? Were you surprised? Would you change the ending for any of them?